Relationship Goals

"A pitch-perfect rom-com from start to finish, *Relationship Goals* is funny, unique, and utterly charming. Balancing heat, heart, and humor effortlessly in this score of a soccer romance, it's a fantastic edition to the sports romance lineup. Kelley is a breath of fresh air in the best possible way." —*USA Today* bestselling author Grace Reilly

"A delightfully unhinged and refreshing romance for fans of *Ted Lasso* and *How to Lose a Guy in 10 Days*. *Relationship Goals* had me laughing and swooning from start to finish! Sparkling, hilarious, and fun."

—Stephanie Archer, author of *Behind the Net*

Relationship Goals

BRITTANY KELLEY

Berkley Romance
New York

BERKLEY ROMANCE
Published by Berkley
An imprint of Penguin Random House LLC
1745 Broadway, New York, NY 10019
penguinrandomhouse.com

Copyright © 2025 by Brittany Kelley

Interior art: Soccer icons © Iconic Bestiary / Shutterstock
Book design by Alison Cnockaert

Library of Congress Cataloging-in-Publication Data

Names: Kelley, Brittany, author.
Title: Relationship goals / Brittany Kelley.
Description: First edition. | New York: Berkley Romance, 2025.
Identifiers: LCCN 2024050111 (print) | LCCN 2024050112 (ebook) |
ISBN 9780593819081 (trade paperback) | ISBN 9780593819098 (ebook)
Subjects: LCGFT: Romance fiction. | Sports fiction. | Novels.
Classification: LCC PS3611.E4363 R45 2025 (print) |
LCC PS3611.E4363 (ebook) | DDC 813/.6—dc23/eng/20241223
LC record available at https://lccn.loc.gov/2024050111
LC ebook record available at https://lccn.loc.gov/2024050112

First Edition: July 2025

Printed in the United States of America
1st Printing

The authorized representative in the EU for product safety and compliance is
Penguin Random House Ireland, Morrison Chambers, 32 Nassau Street,
Dublin D02 YH68, Ireland, https://eu-contact.penguin.ie.

*For the man who willingly signed up for a
lifetime of Gollum impressions*

Relationship Goals

CHAPTER ONE

Abigail

MY LEG JANGLES nonstop on the floor, and I twist the leather purse strap in my hands, even though Jean's giving me that look, the one that plainly says *Get your shit together*. I can't help it, though. This meeting with the owners of the LA Aces is so far out of my wheelhouse it may as well be in the Mariana Trench.

Is that what it's called? I frown.

"What are you thinking about?" Jean asks. I can read her exasperation in the way her brows try to furrow but don't quite make it there, thanks to her overenthusiasm for Botox injections.

"Underwater topography," I blurt. "Is it called topography if it's underwater?" I tilt my head and study the sunlight cascading through the floor-to-ceiling windows.

Ah, yes, there's the good old ADHD showing up right on time.

"Suuuure," she sighs. "Listen, these men we're meeting with—" She pauses, her eyes narrowing on me, likely making sure she has my scattered attention. "They're businessmen. Sharks, you get me? Aaaand"—she draws out the word—"they know Richard Grace *personally*. You need to make a good impression. You know how men talk."

I close one eye, then the other, finally squinting at her.

I know all this. *She* knows I know all this. Jean's as nervous as I am. Her anxiety shouldn't offend me. She wants me at my best. That's a good thing.

We both want me to nail this project. Richard Grace is *the* director in Hollywood to work with, and the fact I've snagged a role in his film is everything I've ever wanted. Sure, the press is going wild with rumors that my ditzy personality and less-than-stellar acting chops won't be enough for a part of this caliber—but *he* believes in me. Enough that he set up this meeting with the LA Aces owners so I could bring "the proper knowledge and gravitas" to his upcoming film about the International Football Federation's corruption scandal.

I can do this. Probably. Most likely.

I inhale deeply, letting oxygen flood my body, trying to calm my nerves. Not that breath work has ever really helped still the constant electric hum of energy that rattles through me every waking moment. People call it a superpower, but they don't seem to understand that sometimes all I want is peace and quiet in my own skull.

If I pull it off, this could be my big break. It could finally mean a role that's more than just the quirky best friend or the manic pixie love interest. I mean, a film about team owners and league officials taking bribes from cities who want to host the international soccer finals? *All* the top brass were guilty of things like racketeering and fraud, even blackmail. That spells a character I can really sink my teeth into, and Grace sending me out to research with the Aces . . . it means more than just shutting up the press.

I am going to take this moment, this opportunity, and I'm sure as hell going to make the most of it.

My nose scrunches up.

Jean's Italian leather heels tap lightly on the tasteful gray-veined marble floors.

A bird winging past the huge floor-to-ceiling windows catches my attention for a moment, and it arcs over the emerald-green practice field below.

My smile disappears, replaced by pursed lips I'm 99 percent sure will result in new lines guaranteed to be featured in before and after pictures on social media down the road.

Richard Grace is known to be as exacting and demanding as they come, and being cast in this film could change everything for me. It's already generating Oscar buzz, and it won't even come out for another couple of years.

Fear surges through me. What if the press is right? What if I can't pull it off—

"Abigail," Jean says, and her snappish tone tells me it's not the first time she's said my name.

"That's me." I make myself look away from the blue sun-soaked sky out the window and turn on my smile.

"Tell me you're taking this seriously," Jean pleads quietly. Her forehead spasms for a split second as she attempts to cinch her brows in seriousness. "Tell me you're not going to go all over the top in there. Tell me you're not going to start rambling about underwater topography."

"I am a businesswoman," I tell her, all stoic seriousness. "You know I'm ready for this. Just look at me. I'm business personified." My heel taps the floor as I shake my leg. "You'll find my headshot in the dictionary under *businesswoman*."

My agent barely clamps down another sigh, giving me a frayed smile instead.

"After what happened last year, we need this to go well, hon. Okay?"

What, you don't want me to blurt out that I think this project's terrible writing is going to annoy fans everywhere, like when I ruined everything? The question swims at the back of my head, but I swallow it before I can make an ass of myself.

This time, at least.

I know all too well the incident from last year Jean's referring to—

the one that had me sacked from an up-and-coming teen drama series. The one that had me labeled as ungrateful and difficult to work with, and had me killed off in the season finale, a fate that being the side-kick to a vampire mermaid couldn't even save me from.

I squeeze my eyes shut, trying to block out the embarrassing memory that tends to replay itself in situations like this, which are rare these days, and nearly every night as I fall asleep.

For an *entire* year.

As if my presleep shame ritual remembrance isn't enough, no one else is going to let it go, either. I thought my career was over.

Finished.

Until I nailed the audition for Richard Grace and wound up here.

I blow out a slow breath, a rush of air that barely steadies me.

Jean's irritation doesn't bother me. Hell, I can't blame her for worrying. I've certainly proved to be a cannon so loose I might as well fall right off the pirate ship I'm strapped to in a riotous explosion of wood splinters and smoke.

She's one of the best in the business and helps me keep my shit together, which is more than I can say for myself. I'm the queen of random interviews, the princess of paparazzi weirdness, and if it weren't for Jean, I'm positive my acting career would be even more of a joke.

For some reason, though, Jean believes in me. She always has, ever since I came to LA as a teenager fresh out of school with high hopes and stars in my eyes. My parents were semi-supportive, though they still constantly ask if I have a backup plan, ask if I've thought about going back to school, if I'm sure this is right for me.

Jean *knows* it's right for me.

That means something.

I smooth my dress, ignoring the fact that my palms are sweating.

This is phase one in my plan to reinvent myself after the red carpet fiasco: impressing these guys and the celeb gossip sites. I have to demand respect to get it. Be so good they can't ignore me.

What phase two looks like? I have no idea.

One step at a time.

I twist the buckle on the front of my off-brand leather tote, a present from my mom several Christmases ago, delivered with the message that it would be a great bag to carry a laptop in, and did I know my old high school was looking for a theater teacher?

She means well . . . but it still hurts.

My fingers work the buckle back and forth, back and forth, until Jean rests her hand on my wrist, silently telling me to stop. I flash her another smile, this time grateful for the physical reminder. Taking a deep breath, then another, I exhale slowly.

"They're ready for you, Ms. Hunt," a pretty blond woman says, opening the door. She's the embodiment of LA—immaculate, toned, and tanned—a Sunset Boulevard demigoddess.

Jean and I stand, finally leaving the sunny waiting area we've been relegated to while the owners presumably readied themselves for us.

Here we go.

"Just Ms. Hunt," the woman says to Jean sweetly.

"You okay with that, Abigail?" Jean asks, too professional to throw a fit in front of the secretary.

Am I okay with that?

I specifically asked Jean to come with me. She's become a deft hand at blocking the foot I keep trying to shove in my mouth.

I swallow hard and channel my inner business baddie.

"Of course." I nod brusquely but then soften it by grinning at her, and like most people, she smiles right back.

Worst comes to worst, I'll just charm their pants off.

I step into the conference room and immediately regret that thought.

Two older men stand as I walk in the room, holding out their hands.

No pants off. Pants on. Pants very much on.

I very much do not want to envision anyone in this room sans pants.

"Charles Treadwick," one introduces himself. "So nice to meet you. This is John Pugilisi. We own the Aces."

"Hello, hi," I say, shaking their hands and smiling as big as I can.

"Ms. Hunt, thank you so much for coming today," John says. A soft crop of snow-white hair sits atop his head, and if I hadn't researched him already, I'd think him a kindly old grandpa. He's not, though. Not even *close*. John's renowned as a killer in the business world, and I'd be an idiot to let his looks deceive me. "We're thrilled to have you here with us. Dick told us you'd be in and out of here for the next few weeks?"

It takes me a few seconds to realize that *Dick* is Richard Grace, and I'm so busy digesting the nickname that I don't have time to falter at the extended timeline.

A few weeks?

I assumed it would be a couple of interviews at most. This is *fantastic*.

"Oh, no, *thank you*," I tell him, beaming. "I couldn't pass up the opportunity to get to see the inner workings of the LA Aces. Thank you so much for meeting with me."

The gray-haired man, Charles, nods, slightly surprised. "Are you a soccer fan? Dick didn't mention that."

"Absolutely." My smile grows as I try to cover up the lie. Shit. Why did I lie about that? "I'm a casual fan more than anything, but what's not to like?"

Backtrack, backtrack, backtrack.

"Casual fans still buy tickets." John laughs, but his expression is eagle-eyed, and I just *know* he can smell the lie. "For instance, my granddaughter loved you in that vampire mermaid show. I could be called a casual fan of your work there, too. Definitely tuned in more than I care to admit!"

This gets a laugh from Charles, and I force one out, too.

I shouldn't read into it. For a while there, *Blood Sirens* was the crown jewel in the teen melodrama lineup. He probably isn't making a jab at me with everything that went down after my disastrous last premiere red carpet.

My throat tightens, my pulse hammering in my neck.

"I'm glad to hear she enjoyed it." I listen to myself say the words, and there's a weird, fuzzy quality to them, like I'm watching myself from afar.

"Of course, sweetheart," John says, adjusting the cuffs of his shirt.

The word *sweetheart* snaps me out of the momentary panic. I blink, trying to reorient myself in my body, in the moment. The only people allowed to call me *sweetheart* are my parents, but I stop myself from blurting that out at the very last minute.

"Who's your favorite player?" Charles asks, raising an eyebrow at John.

Goddammit. He knows! He *knows* I don't know much about soccer at all.

My carefully constructed Academy Award dreams are about to plumb the depths of the Mariana Trench.

"You couldn't possibly ask me to play favorites," I say slowly, batting my eyelashes. "Besides, it's not one player that matters, it's the whole team, right?"

John's mouth quirks in a smile, and I swallow a relieved sigh.

I had a theater teacher who used to say that every day. *It's the whole cast that makes the play, people!*

We used to finish the sentence with her, and a real smile curves my lips at the memory.

"What do you know about the IFF scandal?" Charles asks, steepling his fingers, watching me carefully, a cat playing with a mouse.

My nerves increase, and I clear my throat again.

"Just what I've researched since speaking with Mr. Grace about the film." I shrug a shoulder. "It's not great, is it?" That's true, at least.

"It's a real black mark on the sport," John says slowly, also steepling his fingers. "But the thing about shining light onto the dark parts of any business is that it usually inspires change."

I blink.

I didn't take him for an idealist. Not sure I do now, either, despite that little comment.

"That's why you're allowing me here? You want the film to inspire change?" I try to keep the questions as neutral as possible.

John snorts, wrinkles creasing around his eyes. "Sports films have a trickle-down effect. Doesn't matter to me how bad Dick's movie makes IFF look. It'll sell tickets, and that I care about."

Can't say I love that answer, but it's not entirely surprising.

"Kinda like how your little TV program made my granddaughter absolutely wild about mermaid tails for a while," John adds. "She was torn up when it was canceled. Show really went downhill after they killed your character off." He gives me a long look, and it's calculating, like he's waiting to see how I react.

Unease makes me shift in my chair.

"Publicity is good for business." I tuck a strand of hair behind my ear. "I know that as well as anyone. It's just too bad the publicity I got took such a toll on my character's health." I wink at him, which I regret immediately, icked out at myself.

Charles laughs, too, then spears me with a slightly apologetic glance. "You do have *quite* the reputation with the press."

"I have a tendency to say what I think," I manage, making myself laugh along with him. "I'd like to believe I've learned from my, ah, mistakes."

There. That's about as much as I would like to address the damned *Blood Sirens* scandal. My heart's pounding, my stomach in knots, and a cold sweat's broken out on my palms. It still hurts to think about, that the rest of the cast thought I was throwing them under the bus, the way I gave the press just enough ammunition to do a hit job on the show and my career.

"Honesty. We like that about you," John tells me, and there's real warmth in his eyes when I force my gaze back at him. "Of all the actresses Dick ran past us, you were one of the few we wanted to come on board and study the organization."

I try not to react. He asked these guys for casting input? They know *their* industry, sure, but they seem to be the least likely people on Earth to have a say in Grace's decisions.

"We thought you'd be the most fun," Charles agrees, interrupting the flow of my thoughts.

That catches me by surprise, and I let out a laugh to hide my discouragement. They thought I would be the most *fun*?

That doesn't sit right with me. I'm not sure much of this conversation is sitting right with me, if any.

"Good to know." I swallow past the tightness in my throat. "A few weeks, you said? Well, we will definitely have the chance to have fun, and I look forward to learning everything I can."

A chair creaks as John leans farther forward.

"Sure. Dick said to give you the opportunity to sit in on meetings, practices, games, whatever you wanted access to—within reason—for the role." Charles folds his hands in front of him.

"And having a celebrity at our games never hurts," John adds.

My heart's beating faster now, as the reality of what they're saying sinks in. Regardless of why these two thought I'd be good in the role of the badass whistle-blowing woman, or why they wanted me here, I am here, for a few weeks, to research my role.

My role. *Mine.*

Four weeks, six at most, to soak it all up, so I can give this role my absolute best. I inhale slowly through my nose. A few weeks of research here with the Aces. Going to meetings, games, practices.

"We'll work with your schedule, of course." John peers at me with concern at my silence. "We know you're busy working, but we're going to pair you up with Michelle Oxford, our new director of operations. You'll have to sign an NDA for all things considered proprietary, and our lawyers will get that over to you today."

He shrugs a shoulder as he mentions the NDA, but I barely clock it. Of course they'd have me sign an NDA. That makes sense.

"What else is happening today?" I tilt my head. "Do I get to sit in on anything?"

"Today?" He squints at me, as if surprised by my go-get-'em attitude. "Today we're just giving you the lay of the land. We have a tour planned—"

The conference door opposite me bursts open, and one of the most striking men I've ever seen stalks through, his clear blue eyes locked on me. He's handsome, but not in the easy Hollywood way most men around here are—his nose is slightly too large and there's a bump where it looks like it broke and was never set right. His jaw is almost aggressively strong, as are the thick slashes of dark eyebrows above those memorable light blue eyes.

He's visually arresting.

Powerful.

My eyebrows rise, and when he smiles at me, slow and wicked, I swear to god, my heartbeat quickens. Now my palms are sweaty for an entirely different reason. I start to fan myself, but drop my hand halfway up.

It hangs limply at my side. Right. This isn't awkward at all.

"Luke Wolfe," my mouth says.

I recognize him—he's probably the only player on the team I would. He's famous. Famous for being an utter asshole, but at least I know who he is.

John and Charles wear matching expressions of surprise.

I stand up, smiling at Luke, and extend my hand.

He stares at it, grunts, then addresses Charles. "What the fuck's she doing here?"

"She's here to learn more about soccer and the team," Charles says. "Remember?"

"I remember." Luke Wolfe doesn't take my hand, and all too aware of it, I set it on my hip just to give the poor abandoned appendage something to do.

"And you remember what we discussed yesterday?" John asks him sharply.

"What did you discuss?" I ask, a thin smile stretching across my face. I don't mind confrontation—I'll stand up for myself—but I do not like this power struggle playing out in front of me.

"None of your business," Luke tells me.

I blink but recover quickly.

"Luke—" John starts.

I snort, interrupting whatever he was about to say. "Well, you certainly live up to your reputation," I tell Luke cheerily. "Good for you. On brand. You'll have to give me some pointers. I'm always looking for ways to strengthen my image."

His icy blue eyes scan me from head to toe, and I just grin at him.

"For starters, don't trust a word out of these fuckers' mouths," he finally answers.

Charles barks a laugh, but Luke scowls at him. "You told me you needed to see me?"

"That's right," John tells him, and there's a pointed quality to it, like Luke is being stupid. "We thought it would be best if you could show her around the facility, since you're one of our star players." The last sentence drips with acid, and the vitriol takes me by surprise.

John really doesn't like Luke Wolfe. As for Luke Wolfe, he's staring at me like watching me squirm would make his day.

I might like to see silver linings when they're actually just gray, but I'm not an idiot. Luke might not like the idea of giving me a tour, but there's nothing he can do about it. I'll just kill him with kindness.

"What a great idea," I gush, fluttering my eyelashes. All three men give me a look, and I get the impression I've slightly overplayed my hand. What else is new? "Mr. Wolfe, I'd love to get a tour."

He says something under his breath, and it takes me a full second to realize he's grunted his first name at me.

"Luke," I repeat.

He doesn't even move, just keeps staring at me.

Do I have something in my teeth? My hair? My nose wrinkles.

"Come on, then, I don't have all day," he barks.

I laugh because, man, it's been a minute since someone has been so freaking rude to my face. Not the snide, typical LA passive-aggressive shit—I get that a lot—but straight-up rude?

It's . . . weirdly refreshing.

"We'll send a packet of franchise information over, along with the NDA and a list of potential meetings for you to attend as well as our practice and home game schedule. We also had a package of merchandise prepped for you."

"That would be great," I gush. *Manifesting!* That Academy Award is going to look so good on my mantel. I wonder if I can get one of the big fashion houses to dress me for the awards ceremony. Yes. I can do this!

Probably.

John Pugilisi folds his fingers on top of the glossy conference table. "We will have plenty of time to get down to the nitty-gritty details." He says it slowly, like he's talking to a favorite granddaughter. I can't decide if it's charming or patronizing. "You just go with Luke and enjoy the introduction to the football club today. We'll ease you in." To Luke he says, "Take her to meet Michelle when you're done."

Luke grunts.

"Thank you so much," I say, offering my hand for another round of handshakes, and the two owners oblige me.

Hell fucking yeah.

I have a close call with the urge to fist-pump but manage to restrain myself . . . barely.

Luke gestures impatiently for me to follow him, and I do, almost forgetting to snatch my handbag off the chair.

"Thanks so much for taking the time—" I turn to say as we walk out the door, and it shuts in my face.

Luke doesn't look surprised, just disgruntled. That's probably his usual expression, though. RAF. Resting ass face.

"You got something you want to say to me?" he asks, challenge in every syllable.

I don't think he'll appreciate my observation about his RAF, so I blurt the first thing that comes to mind instead.

"You're very tall," I tell him. I almost say something about how muscular he is, too, but that feels like outright creeper behavior, so I don't.

"That's right. Good observation skills," he says acidly. "Come on."

Silent, I follow him down the plush carpeted hallway. I don't like silence. Nope.

I pull my phone from my handbag, because if Jean were here, she would at least be able to act as my personal verbal human shield. A message lights up the screen.

> **JEAN:** I'm heading out. The owners came out to shake my hand and said you were going on a tour. I trust you to stay out of trouble. -Jean
>
> **JEAN:** Please stay out of trouble. -Jean

I can't help snorting in amusement. Despite my misgivings and the weird vibe from . . . well, everyone, at least Jean thinks I will be fine on my own. Jean, who always worries I won't be able to figure out who's texting me unless she signs her name.

Luke's long legs have taken him far ahead of me, and I double-time it, my heels sinking awkwardly in the carpet as I try to catch up. The tight pencil skirt doesn't help matters, and I have the distinct impression that I look absolutely absurd.

I start to say something to fill the silence. The moment I open my mouth, Luke turns and silences me with a look that practically drips with derision.

My jaw snaps shut automatically.

Inhaling through my nose, I fight the need to talk.

This is why my parents put me in theater when I was four—*put that talkativeness to good use*, they always said.

And then my mouth opens again, and the first thing on my mind pops out.

"You have the worst reputation," I say out loud. "That's how I remembered who you were."

Oh god. Why did I have to say *that*?

Luke frowns at me from over his shoulder. "Do you ever think about what you're going to say?"

It comes out milder than any reproach I expected, but I wince all the same.

"Not often," I admit. "Definitely keeps things interesting."

He grunts, the only sign he's heard me.

I should apologize, but I don't. Instead, I watch his backside as he leads the way. Muscles ripple under the thin fabric of his shirt, and my eyes widen in appreciation.

Creeper McCreeperson, that's me.

"What are you looking at?" he asks, glancing back at me again.

"Just trying to catch up." My voice comes out a little hoarse. "Are you always this rude?"

"Yes," he says, one thick eyebrow raised. "I don't give a shit what you think, or anyone else. I'm here to play soccer, not be a fucking tour guide."

"At least you're equal opportunity about the lack of shits you have to give." I laugh in spite of myself. "I can't imagine why they wouldn't hire you to do both. You're such a *charming* tour guide." He's too easy to bait. It shouldn't be so much fun to do so.

He stops in his tracks and turns, bearing down on me, all intimidating size and cold blue eyes.

I bat my eyelashes at him, unable to resist poking at the so-called Wolf of LA soccer. If he can say whatever he wants to me, then I'll say whatever I want right back.

Kind of refreshing, actually.

"I see why they call you the Wolf," I manage. "Do you like being the villain, too? You must know they call you that. 'The bad boy of soccer.'" I do air quotes.

He barks a laugh, and it surprises us both, the sound echoing off the narrow walls.

"You really do always say what you think, huh?"

"I'm a little infamous for that, actually." I grimace, unable to hide it.

"I don't like being the villain," he finally answers, raising one strong eyebrow.

God, his face is really interesting, different and appealing and manly.

"I don't trust people. Neither should you. Especially not those motherfuckers." He jerks his chin toward the way we just came.

"Who?" Confusion wrinkles my brow.

"The owners. Pugilisi and Treadwick."

"Oh." Huh. "Thanks for the advice," I say, nodding like I'm considering it. I'm not. Refusing to trust anyone? That sounds lonely as hell.

As for the owners . . . It just affirms my own vibes about them.

The Wolf squints at me as if my response has surprised him. "That doesn't bother you?"

"That you don't trust people or that you're telling me not to? Should it?" I honestly don't understand this guy. Is he trying to upset me?

My nose crinkles, and I stare into those light blue eyes, at a loss.

"I think most people are fucking assholes," Luke says, and it's my turn to laugh.

"You know, *you* have a bit of a reputation for saying whatever you're thinking, too."

"Nah. I usually don't say much at all." He turns back around, and I have to do an impression of an Olympic speed walker just to keep up. Damn it, this tight skirt was a real choice.

"Well, I heard a rumor *you* said enough that they threatened you with suspension from the league," I say too sweetly.

This time when he stops, it's not just intimidating, it's menacing. Angry.

I grin at him.

What can I say? Maybe I do love getting a reaction. I am an actor, after all.

CHAPTER TWO

Luke

"YOU READ UP on the team," I say gruffly.

"I didn't have to read up on the team to know who you are," she responds slowly.

Dammit.

Abigail Hunt already knows who I am. She knows I'm a total asshole, and I don't quite know how I'm going to convince anyone otherwise. I agreed to what the owners put me up to, starting with this goddamned tour, for the exact reason she just said.

To avoid being suspended from the team. I'd gotten one too many cards last season, mouthed off to one too many refs, gotten a reputation for being a fucking diva with the coaches. Being the bad boy of soccer hasn't earned me many fans inside the organization.

My molars grind, and I stare at her mismatched eyes, trying to figure out what to say to her.

I could tell her none of it's true. I could tell her it's all true.

The thing is, the truth is somewhere in the middle. Gray, like truth usually is.

I'm not a diva. I just don't put up with shit from people. I say it like it is.

People don't like that.

More than anything, though, I want to finally get fucking traded to Seattle, where I can be close to my family. The owners know all too well how badly I want to get back home, to be close to my sick mom, and they're gleeful at finally having something to hold over my head. They forced my hand.

Said they'd take me off the protected roster of players and approve the trade to Seattle, as long as I did something for them.

Pretend to be her *boyfriend*. Sell our fake romance to the press, to the paparazzi, and watch ticket sales to our games soar.

Fuck them.

Charles and John seem to think that Abigail Hunt is the answer to all their prayers. Apparently, me—the bad boy of soccer—dating her, the wholesome girl next door turned actress with her own built-in fan base, will translate to massive crowd turnout.

Everyone loves a tabloid romance, they said, dollar signs in their eyes. Fucking owners.

"You underestimated me." She interrupts my thoughts, tilting her head and giving me the same grin that was plastered all over every conceivable surface in town just a few years ago. There's no mermaid tail in sight, but it's unmistakable. I haven't seen it much since, though I can't remember what happened to whatever show she was on.

Too bad.

It's a good smile.

I grunt, unwilling to let her know it has any effect on me whatsoever.

"Don't act like it's the first time," I say, turning around.

She laughs again, and the sound is surprisingly genuine and completely out of place in the back halls of this fucking football club.

"All right, Abigail—"

"Yes, oh big bad Wolfe?" she asks in that same singsong voice, and I bite back a surprised laugh of my own.

No one fucking talks to me like that.

"You're stuck with me for your grand tour. I'm a shitty tour guide, so I'll make it quick." I stick my hands in my pockets, then immediately take them out. "Ask questions—I probably won't answer them."

"Wow. I have to say, I love the honesty."

"I'm an unrepentant asshole; I'm not honest." That's the truest thing I've said to her since the moment I saw her in the conference room.

And everything from this moment forward will be a fucking lie. Can't say I didn't warn her.

Maybe fake dating the stunning woman standing in front of me, smiling at me like she sees right through my bullshit, won't be as horrible as I thought.

Maybe it will be worse.

Fuck it.

"Do you want to go to dinner with me?" I blurt out the question, narrowing my eyes.

She'll say no. It can't be that easy to ask out a semi-famous actress.

"Tonight?" I add.

She's busy, there's no way she isn't busy already, and I can tell John and Charles that I tried and was shot down—

"Is that . . . part of the tour?" Her eyebrows are sky-high, her strange, mismatched eyes, one hazel and one green, full of mischief and delight.

"Fuck no," I say, jamming my hands in my pockets. *Say no, say no—*

"Then yes." Her grin is so infectious I almost smile back before I remember the reason I'm a fucking liar. I need to remember I'm not doing this for her; I'm doing this for me.

For my career.

Not for her grin.

"Yes," I repeat, slightly stunned and more pissed off than ever.

"Yep," she agrees, still smiling that Hollywood smile.

I frown at her. "Fine."

She lets out another laugh, like I'm the most hilarious man in the world.

Abigail Hunt said yes. I'm going to dinner with Abigail Hunt. John and Charles are about to get their way again.

Fuck me.

"I don't think I've ever seen someone so disgruntled after I agreed to go on a date with them."

I grunt, finally tearing my gaze away from her pretty face and turning.

"Let's get this over with." Fuck.

"So we can get ready for dinner?" she asks, and I wince.

When I glance back at her, though, she seems thoroughly amused by my bad attitude, and it pisses me off even more.

"Hey, Wolfe." Our keeper, one of the few other players I can stand on the team, comes around the corner.

I clear my throat.

"Gold," I reply, jerking my chin up at him. He runs a hand through his tousled blond hair, grinning in that unselfconscious way he has.

"Want to grab dinner after practice—" His eyes cut to where Abigail stands next to me, and the perfect white smile he's known for, brand deals galore to his name, grows even wider.

"Is that Abigail Hunt?" he asks, awe clear in his voice.

"Hi," Abigail says, holding out a hand and beaming up at him.

"The one and only Tristan Gold," he responds, winking.

Winking!

He's so fucking personable that if I didn't like him, he would make me sick. But the way he's looking at her, like he'd like to eat her up, makes me want to punch him in the face. It sure would help his orthodontist earn his keep.

"I'm taking her to dinner tonight," I find myself growling at him.

Gold's lips twist to the side, one eyebrow quirking up in surprise. "What? *You?*"

"Don't act so fucking surprised."

"We could all go. Make it a team thing." He elbows me in the ribs. "It would be good for you to go out with all of us instead of taking out your delightful personality on just me. Spread the love, if you will."

Abigail laughs as if Gold's said the funniest thing in the world.

I'd never thought I'd want to be funny until this moment.

"It's not a team thing." I force the words out.

"It's a date," Abigail says smoothly, her lovely eyes flitting from Gold's face to mine. "He feels so terrible about how we got off on the wrong foot that he wants to make it up to me."

I pinch the bridge of my nose. Yeah. That, or taking her out is the only way I can get myself off this team and back home.

"He's a good guy." Gold addresses Abigail, who's still smiling sunnily at both of us, apparently completely unbothered by how pissed I am. "Unfriendly, mean, and downright rude, but don't let that stand in your way."

"Shut up," I tell him, but Gold just chuckles.

"I mean it. Don't let any of that distract you. He's a nice dude under all that." He flicks a finger, pointing at the space between us. "*If* you can get under it. Luke's probably my best friend on the team. If you break his heart, I'll be obligated to be pissed at you."

I squint at him, waiting for the punch line he surely is about to deliver. He doesn't, though, just lets that pronouncement hang between us all.

When nothing else comes, I clear my throat, running a finger around my collar.

"Good to know," Abigail says, taking all of this unasked-for information in perfect stride.

"Nice to meet you, Abigail," he says, pulling his blond hair up into a stupid man bun. "Good luck at dinner. Yell for us if you need help."

I roll my eyes, and Gold strolls down the hall toward management offices like he doesn't have a care in the world.

"Locker room is down there." I jerk my head at the way Gold went. "We got out of practice not too long ago, so you might see some of the guys still hanging around."

Abigail grins at me, arching one perfectly groomed eyebrow. "Do I get a locker room tour?"

I squint at her, unable to tell if she's joking or not.

"I can tell you what it looks like: a locker room. It smells like sweaty feet and a bunch of wasted potential."

She laughs at that, even though I didn't really mean it to be funny.

"We're not going to the locker room," I tell her.

No fucking way am I taking her in there so all the guys can stare at her like Gold did. A protective need surges in me, taking me by surprise.

Nah. I'm not subjecting her to that.

"It's your tour," she says casually. "I'm just along for the ride."

Ride. And just like that, with that little four-letter word, I'm thinking about what she'd feel like on top of me, what she would look like. I clamp down on the thought, a muscle in my jaw twitching.

"Rehab and medical offices," I say shortly, pointing down the hall in the opposite direction.

I want this over with. I stride away, practically jogging.

"Field is through here," I call out over my shoulder, but there's no answer. I glance behind me, only to swear under my breath.

Abigail's surrounded by my teammates, barely visible as they tower over her. Her laugh rings out above the low thrum of their voices, and an unpleasant, vicious feeling grips me.

"I loved *Blood Sirens*," Logan, the youngest player on the team, is telling her loudly. The kid has one volume, and it's loud.

Blood Sirens. Right. That's the mermaid show that was blowing up a year or so ago. She was everywhere.

"That episode where they kill you off, that was one of the worst things I've ever seen on TV," Marino adds, giving her his patented heartbreaker stare. "The show was shit without you, too. What you said in that interview? You were right about it. The writing was a mess."

Her smile falters, and that strange protective urge surges in me again as her lower lip trembles.

"Hey, back off!" I shout, jogging back to the crowd that's assembled around her. She's so tiny that she's almost lost from view among the athletes swarming.

"Can you bring Serena to one of our games?" Logan adds, a hopeful puppy dog look on his face. "You know, the actress who plays Serena the Blood Siren?"

Abigail's face falls completely at that, spurring me into action.

Glaring, I shove Rodriguez and Marino out of the way. "Give her some fucking space, you assholes."

"Jesu Christo, Wolfe," Marino says in his thickly accented English, rubbing his hip like I've hurt him.

"Go fucking cry about it," I snarl. "I'm surprised you're not rolling around on the floor."

Marino affects a wounded expression, and disgust ripples through me. Not at him, though, at myself.

I shouldn't care. It's true. Marino is the biggest drama queen on the team. Tap him on the shoulder and he's down, trying to get the refs to call a foul. Every damned game.

Guy's as much of an actor as the woman standing in front of us.

Doesn't matter, though. I'm *the* asshole. My entire reputation on and off the field is built on that.

It's who I am.

And it makes other players think twice before they fuck with me.

"What the hell, Wolfe?" Rodriguez asks. "We just wanted to meet the beautiful Abigail Hunt."

"I don't mind," Abigail says, and I realize she's signing things for them.

I rip the white stretchy cloth out of her hands, fury firmly holding me in its grip.

"Do you make anyone else sign your fucking briefs?"

"Hey, if he wants to wear my name on his ass, that's his business." Abigail gently extricates the briefs from me, handing them back to Rodriguez with a grin. Her fingertips brush across my knuckles, and the surprise contact takes me aback enough that momentarily I lose track of what I was saying.

"I will tattoo it on there for you," he says sincerely, a shit-eating smile on his face. He grabs her hand, pressing a kiss to her knuckles, and my vision goes red.

"Show some respect," I say. I might not care about Abigail, no more than anyone else, at least, but this behavior is low. "What would your grandmother think of this, Rodriguez?"

Rodriguez manages to look slightly chagrined. "I didn't think you cared about my grandmother, Wolfe," he tells me. "I didn't think you *cared*."

I pause, then bark out a reply. "I don't, but I sure as shit know she wouldn't want you handing your fucking briefs to a woman to sign."

"Sorry, Wolfe," Rodriguez murmurs, and there's something like hero worship in his eyes.

Probably aimed at Abigail.

"Don't apologize to me." I nod at Abigail.

"Sorry, miss," he tells her.

Abigail shoots me an amused look, but there's blatant relief in it, too.

It makes me feel like maybe, just fucking maybe, I did something right.

The remaining players crowded around her mutter, casting me dark looks, but they also listen, giving her some space. Marino gives me one last withering stare before finally leaving her in peace.

I turn back to her, unsure of what to say.

"I'm sorry," I try, the words sticking in my throat. I don't say that a lot. Feels fucking weird.

"There's nothing to apologize for." She shrugs. "It's my job. Comes with the territory."

I give her a long look. "Signing that jackass's underwear is not part of your job."

She crosses her arms over her chest, and her smile—that brilliant, sunny smile—finally melts off her face. "So, what, I'm supposed to say no? And then he goes and sells that story to the press? I can just see it now: 'Diva Hunt Refuses to Play Nice with Soccer Team.'"

I grunt. "You thought of that just now? That fake headline?"

"Oh, that's the kind of thing that's on repeat in my head twenty-four seven. Gotta keep one step ahead." Her smile has a brittle quality to it now, her eyes glinting with some emotion I can't name.

I don't know what to say to that. Seems completely at odds with how . . . sweet she is. How innocent she seems.

After my dad left, though, I felt the same way. Her comment takes me right back to that very moment. Like if I could just be perfect, be good enough on and off the field, he would come back.

I inhale slowly, swallowing the memory, shoving it back down where it belongs.

I gave up on anything vaguely resembling perfection a long time ago.

"I'll show you the field. Let's go." My voice is gruffer than I mean it to be, but it doesn't have anything to do with her.

Not this time, at least.

I finish up the tour as fast as possible, letting her walk the field, trying not to ogle her lovely long legs or act like that fucking asshole Marino. I should've asked her to take off her stupid shoes. I sigh, pinching the bridge of my nose, but the thought of one of the guys seeing her bare feet sits wrong with me for some reason. Her heels sink into the turf, and I keep waiting for her to fall, or complain, or do something annoying—to give me a reason not to like her.

Anything so I don't have to feel as guilty about lying to her.

But she only carefully takes off her heels, holding them in one hand as I watch in silence.

I don't know what to fucking say to her. I don't know if she even knows what she's looking at. I don't care, either. I'm not about to explain soccer to her.

If this goes well, it means that we have one date and she decides she never wants to see me again, and I can tell John and Charles I tried and figure out a different way to get back to Seattle and my family.

"That's all," I say once we're back inside. "You've seen the main offices and know the general layout now. Any questions?"

I don't really care if she has questions, and it's clear from my tone of voice.

She shakes her head, watching me carefully.

"What do you like to eat?" I finally ask, her silence in the past few minutes after her admission about always keeping ahead of the press making me feel . . . uncomfortable. Like she shouldn't have said that, like it's a peek behind her relentless good mood at something more real. "Where do you want to go tonight?"

"Why do you want to go out with me?" she asks.

My heart seems to stop, my stomach sinking.

"What do you mean?" My mouth somehow forms the words, completely detached from my brain.

"You haven't really been very nice to me. So, why?"

I grunt. She's not wrong. "You're trying to learn more about pro sports, right? I can help." There goes my promise to not explain soccer to her. I swore to myself that I wouldn't help her, but I'm starting to feel like that conviction flew out the window as soon as I saw her mismatched eyes sparkling with mischief.

She lifts an eyebrow. "You want to help . . . me?" Abigail's disbelief hangs heavy in the question.

I can't say I blame her.

"Fuck." I rake a hand through my hair. "No." Shit, shit. I need to fix this.

"Uh—"

"I think you're pretty," I rasp, interrupting her. "I'm not good with people." To my utter surprise, both of those statements are true. "You made me laugh."

I don't laugh easily, but this woman disarmed me nearly immediately.

Abigail tilts her head, studying me. "Why should I go with you? You haven't exactly been a peach to hang out with."

Why? How the hell do I tell her a why when my reasons are completely fucked?

All I have ever wanted was to play pro soccer. It's all I know how to do. I'm not ready to quit my dream. I can make this work, then get home to my mom.

I can't let Abigail Hunt and the deal with the owners slip through my fingers.

I should have been nicer to her. Too bad I'm not *nice*.

She's still watching me, a careful expression on her face.

"Because I know a really great Italian place, and I might be a stubborn ass, but I can help answer questions about soccer or the IFF." It's the best I can come up with. There. I'm selling it now, and when I tell the owners I tried, I'll mean it.

"And you think I'm pretty?" she presses, a faint pink coloring her cheeks, like this information is brand-new to her.

I grunt in affirmation, and when her eyebrows raise in clear skepticism, I grind my molars.

"I think you're out of my league, and too nice for me," I finally force out. "You don't need me to tell you you're stunning."

Her hands go to her hips, and my skin prickles in awareness at her careful perusal.

"Italian for dinner, then. Am I . . . meeting you there? Does this place have a name?"

"So you'll still go?" I ask. Hope tightens my throat. God. Maybe I *will* get to finish out the rest of my good soccer-playing years and be able to help my mom out while she's sick.

Maybe I *can* have it both ways.

A smile blooms on her face, and I blink. I wasn't lying. Abigail Hunt is stunningly pretty.

"Mm-hmm," she says softly, then wags a finger at me. "But you better be nicer to me."

Shame slides through me, ice-cold.

"I'll pick you up," I tell her.

I'm not agreeing to be nicer. I don't know if I can be.

"Here." I hold out my phone. "Put your number in, and your address."

"Or you could give me your number, and I can text it to you," she says, her phone already in her hand.

When did she pull that out?

I was too busy staring at her eyes to notice.

Great. Way to play it cool, Luke.

"That works, too," I make myself say once it's clear she's waiting for me to respond. Fuck, I've said more today than I normally do all week. I'm going to need a fucking cough drop at this rate.

"Then I'm going to need your number," she says, and that gorgeous grin returns, her eyes scrunching up at the corners.

"Of course," I say, mentally kicking myself as I rattle it off. "Pick you up at eight?"

She twists her lips to the side, her expressive face fascinating to watch. "Can we do earlier? I know it's weird, but I like to be in bed early."

I pause, caught off guard. And now I'm thinking about her in bed. Wondering what she wears to sleep . . . or if she doesn't wear anything at all. My brain short-circuits at the thought of all that smooth skin sliding between her sheets, sliding under me.

Fuck. I'm no better than goddamn Marino.

"Is that okay?" she asks, and I realize I've been staring at her, imagining her naked, and haven't answered her.

"Six work?" I finally rasp out.

"Six sounds great." That superstar grin lights up her face, and I can't help but bask in the glow, even though I know I shouldn't.

I shouldn't fucking enjoy this at all. I'm only asking her out because I want to get the hell out of LA. I'm only asking her out because the damned owners are pressuring me to.

But Abigail Hunt isn't like anyone I've ever met.

She doesn't deserve a jerk like me. Still, she keeps smiling at me, the silence thick between us.

"I just go back the way I came to find Michelle's office?" she finally asks.

She wasn't staring at me, thinking about me naked in bed like I was thinking about her. Nope, she was silent because I am a dick and forgot she doesn't know her way around here.

"Yeah." A beat passes, and I realize I'm an idiot. "Or I can show you how to get to her office."

"I can manage." She reaches out, her fingertips barely brushing over the top of my hand in reassurance. Surprise steals my breath at the minimal contact.

"Do you remember how to get there?" I ask, too aware of our hands hanging between us, too aware of her closeness.

She beams at me like I've just asked the most heartwarming, thoughtful thing in the world instead of the belated bare minimum.

A small part of me wants her to say no so I can walk her to Michelle's office.

The rest of me wants to wash my hands of this entire situation, including my skin's traitorous memory of her soft fingertips.

"I think I do. See you at six," she says, already in motion.

She disappears down the hall, and a muscle twitches in my temple. I shouldn't feel guilty. I'm the Wolf. I'm the biggest asshole in pro soccer, the villain known for picking fights and playing dirty, and the only reason anyone puts up with me is because I'm good at kicking a fucking ball. It's why the owners probably didn't think twice about putting me up to a stunt like this for ticket sales.

They knew I'd say yes—knew out of all the guys on the roster, I'm the one with nothing to lose.

My attitude on and off the field's what's had me traded more than any player on my team, and while my skills more than make up for it, most coaches don't want someone like me on their squad.

A lone wolf.

I scratch the five-o'clock shadow on my jawline, trying to push down the unusual guilt.

I'll wine and dine Abigail Hunt. Anything to get back to Seattle. It's not a real relationship or a real date—it'll be easy to forget her. Hell, she'll probably forget me by the time her IFF movie starts shooting.

Everyone already knows I'm a jackass, so what's one more person who thinks so?

CHAPTER THREE

Abigail

LUKE WOLFE IS not what I expected.

Not one bit.

Rough around the edges, yes, but also staggeringly handsome in person. Between his icy blue eyes and dark hair, he's unforgettable. His attitude put me off at first, but I must be a glutton for punishment, because I sense something . . . better under that hard shell surrounding him. Something soft and gooey.

Or maybe it's just that he said he thinks I'm pretty and I needed to hear something nice after sweating through my pits in the meeting with the owners.

I'll have to unpack that in therapy.

I'm so lost in thought I glide right past the door marked MICHELLE OXFORD: DIRECTOR OF OPERATIONS.

I pivot, turning back toward the office, voices growing louder as I reapproach.

"Not interested, Mr. Gold," a woman's voice says, every syllable hard and no-nonsense.

"Michelle—"

"It's Ms. Oxford to you," she says crisply. "Don't you have somewhere to be?"

My eyes go wide, my brain churning with scenarios. Should I beat a hasty retreat and leave her to whatever . . . is going on in there? Should I knock on the door and interrupt? Should I—

The door swings open, saving me from making a decision. Like a deer in the headlights, I freeze, my hand still outstretched toward the handle, and I come face-to-face with Tristan Gold, who's frown immediately smooths out as he recognizes me.

"Michelle, your new shadow is here," he booms.

Behind him, a woman stands, her arms crossed over her chest. A smattering of golden-brown freckles dust over her nose and cheeks, her shining dark brown hair tied up in a chic knot at the base of her neck. A smart pencil dress clings to her athletic shape, the asymmetric neckline setting off her bare collarbone.

"Hi, I didn't mean to interrupt," I say hesitantly, completely caught off guard.

"You're timing is perfect, actually. Mr. Gold was just leaving. He might be the team goalie, but there's no saving this conversation." To my surprise, the woman, Michelle, practically shoves him out the door, causing him to rumble with laughter as he makes his way past me.

"We're not done here, Michelle," the goalie tells her, a sly grin on his face.

"You don't get to decide that," she replies crisply. "Come in, Ms. Hunt."

"Abigail, please," I say, my gaze darting between Tristan and Michelle and the strange . . . energy between them.

"Call me Michelle," she says. "Have a seat."

"As the team captain, I think I do get to decide—" Tristan Gold starts.

Michelle closes the door on Tristan's face, cutting off whatever else he was about to say.

I blink, slightly shocked. For a split second, her smile cracks, and she closes her eyes, leaning against the door as she inhales deeply.

"That bad, huh?" I ask sympathetically, the question out of my mouth before I have time to think it over.

"What?" Her eyes fly open. "No, Tristan, er, Mr. Gold, just has one of those personalities that can't resist trying to befriend everyone in the building." She clicks her tongue. "Even when I've made it clear I'm not . . . interested. In being friends. With him."

I squint at her, but her professional mask slips seamlessly back into place, and then she's repositioning herself behind her desk, her hands clasped in front of her.

There's hardly a knickknack or picture in the whole office. Whereas I would've had my desk decked out in pink florals and pictures of all my favorite people, Michelle's desk is sterile. A large monthly calendar pad dominates the desk space, along with an engraved clock.

Other than her computer and one expensive-looking fountain pen, that's it.

Some of my hope for starting a friendship with Michelle shrivels up.

"So, they've assigned you to me," she says briskly. "I can't say I'm surprised."

I swallow my disappointment. She blinks at me, leaning back in her office chair.

"If you're too busy for me to shadow you, I get it," I tell her. "I do not want to get in your way at all, and I'm sure you've got a ton going—"

"Stop right there." She holds up a hand, and I snap my mouth shut. Michelle shakes her head, and not one strand of glossy dark brown hair dares escape from her bun. "I'm sorry—you misunderstood me. I could not be more *freaking relieved* to have you around, and I don't care how unprofessional that sounds."

For the first time all day, I'm rendered truly speechless.

"Listen, this place is . . ." She pauses, and I can practically hear the wheels turning in her head as she tries to figure out what to say next. "Sports franchises, especially these bigger ones, always come with a lot of history and baggage," she says carefully, then spreads her hands wide. "That's the whole point of the film you're doing, right? I mean, the IFF scandal should have created a sea change in the sport."

"Should have?" I ask, leaning my own arms against her desk, engrossed. "You mean there haven't been as many changes as there should have been?"

She sighs, pinching the bridge of her nose. "I'm not sure what I meant."

That doesn't seem to be the case at all, but, for once, I keep my mouth shut.

Good on me.

"Sorry. Tristan—Mr. Gold—frazzled me before you came in. I guess what I'm trying to say is this is an old boys' club. I can't speak for all the franchises, but this particular one . . ." She trails off. "You signed an NDA, right?"

"I will be," I tell her slowly. "You should know, though, that even if I hadn't, I wouldn't go blabbing to anyone. I know how hard it can be to have your life on display to the world." I take a deep breath to bolster myself and forge onward. "I'm here so I can get a sense of what it's like to be a woman in professional soccer, and that kind of background knowledge is exactly what I need." I'm speaking in a hushed, near reverent tone, as sincerely as I possibly can.

"I don't want to come off as ungrateful," she says, waving her perfectly manicured fingers at me. French-tipped, short almond, cute but professional. Everything about her appearance is definitely a carefully cultivated choice. "I *am* grateful. And I love my job."

Her mouth presses thin.

"I know exactly what you're saying," I say simply. And I do. We have to be grateful. We have to be the right mix of feminine without being too assertive. It's a high-wire act between friendly and bossy, and one misstep leads to getting called a bitch or a bimbo. "It's a lot. I get it."

She exhales, nodding slowly, and I don't have to say anything else.

We sit in silence, watching each other, and slowly, Michelle grins at me. "What do you know about soccer?"

I cringe, shooting her a pained expression. "Not as much as I should."

"Well, you'll learn fast." Her smile turns positively beatific. "I played through my sophomore year in college, until a knee injury sidelined my chances of finishing out the season or going pro. It gave me enough credibility to land a job with one of the smaller IFF teams, and, ah, now I'm here."

"I'm sorry about your knee. That sounds awful." I had my fair share of injuries on the physical set of *Blood Sirens*, but nothing at that level.

She sighs, steepling her hands on the paper calendar in front of her. "It was. I won't lie. My dreams evaporated after the third ACL surgery." One shoulder shrugs, the black collar moving with it. "And I'm lucky to be here. This is . . ." She gestures vaguely with one hand, a diamond-studded ring on her pointer finger catching the light. "I like being around soccer still."

"I'm glad," I manage, even though it sounds more like she's trying to convince herself than me. "You know, Luke Wolfe said something weird about the owners."

She stops, her brown eyes widening, then narrowing as she meets my gaze. I audibly swallow, realizing my misstep.

"Wolfe and the owners butt heads a lot," she says carefully. "I'd take whatever any of them say with a grain of salt where the other is concerned. I would also watch yourself around the owners. Mr. Treadwick and Mr. Pugilisi can be . . . unpredictable."

"Right," I say, feeling chastised.

"Why were you talking with Luke Wolfe?" She angles her head at me.

"Oh, they asked him to show me around the place." It's my turn to wave a hand.

A frown flickers across her face.

"They had Luke Wolfe give you a tour?" Disbelief colors her question.

"He's that bad, huh? Really earned his whole reputation?" It makes me feel a little bad for the guy.

"No, he's . . . he's fine." She coughs delicately. "He's a great player. Just surprised me. Especially when they had Tristan Gold *right* there," she says, pointing to the closed door.

"He seemed a bit busy," I say innocently. "Maybe Luke was the only one available."

I'm not sure why I'm defending Luke . . . but I can't help thinking of how he tried to protect me from the onslaught of other players and smile. And want to return the favor.

To my surprise, Michelle's cheeks flush slightly. "Luke wasn't rude to you, was he? I'd hate for you to have gotten off on the wrong foot with the Aces."

"No," I tell her, then laugh as I realize my unintentional lie. "Actually, you know what? He was extremely rude, but it was . . . refreshing. Funny, even? I don't know." I shrug. "It seemed like a defense mechanism more than anything sincere, and then when he asked me to dinner, I decided he's probably one of those secret cinnamon rolls." I wiggle my eyebrows at her.

Her mouth hangs open as she thrums her fingers on the desk. "He asked you out?"

"Yes?" My nose wrinkles. What's so wrong with that? Am I breaking some unspoken rule?

"On a date?" she clarifies.

"Yeah, I think so? He's really handsome," I say somewhat defensively.

"He is. But he's also an asshole. You just said he was rude to you."

"I think that's just his default . . . I don't know, awkwardness."

"Look, I know we just met, but you seem like a nice person. You deserve someone who isn't going to default to rudeness when they feel awkward," she says in a no-nonsense, extremely serious voice. "We all deserve someone who's already at their best, you know? Not some fixer-upper situation."

I blink at her, surprised by her vehemence.

"That's fairrr." I stretch the word out. "But I also believe in second chances."

Breath whooshes out of her, and she shakes her head, then smiles at me. A genuine smile. "You're right. I'm sorry. It's not my business. I just know these guys love to talk."

It's my turn to look confused. "Luke Wolfe seems like the last person to love to talk. About women. Or me. Or anything at all, really."

A startled laugh comes out of her, and she nods. "Accurate. He's rude, but he's not a gossip. He won't spread rumors about you, at least." Her smile turns slightly sour, like she's remembering something she'd rather forget. "Sorry. I have a younger sister—I know I shouldn't be, but I get protective." She rolls her eyes at herself, a small laugh coming out.

"No, don't worry. I don't mind. Honestly, if he were an asshole, I'd want to know."

"He is an asshole. Just not . . . like that."

"So I'll know where I stand with him," I say easily, and we both laugh.

"To be fair, that *is* a point in his favor," Michelle says, then visibly shakes herself. "God, I'm sorry. I should be talking about work, and here we are, as bad as guys in the locker room, talking about Luke Wolfe."

"No, honestly, I do appreciate it. I will never turn down someone looking out for me." It's true. I've been burned by a lot of assholes. Unfortunately, I think it was just a part of growing up as much as it was the Hollywood climbers.

"I tell you what," I say impulsively. "What if we get lunch after Luke and I have our date? I'll plan some soccer and IFF questions for you. Besides, I wouldn't mind coming out of this experience with a new friend."

It's a bold statement, and my pulse speeds up, because, god, making real friends as an adult is not easy, and for some reason, I'm just as nervous as I was when Luke asked me out.

Michelle's eyes crinkle at the corners, and she beams at me. "I'd love that. On one condition."

"What?"

"I want to hear about your date, too."

"Deal . . ." I pause, studying her. "But only if you tell me about what the hell is going on between you and Tristan Gold." I point between her and the door. "I picked up on that tension between you two."

She laughs uneasily, then blows out a breath. "You drive a hard bargain."

"I'm just kidding," I backtrack, not wanting to overstep. Ugh. Why is making new friends so hard?

"Oh please, no you weren't."

Her phone rings. She gives it a pained look.

"It's only fair." She scribbles something on a sticky note hiding in a gold box on her desk. "Here's my number. Text me where you want to meet, okay? I have to take this. The front office is right back through there." Michelle points. "I'm really looking forward to lunch and to working with you."

She's smiling so broadly at me that when she picks up the phone, her voice immediately dropping to a businesslike lower register, it low-key shocks me.

I jot down a mental note to make sure I do that same kind of code-switching on-screen.

I can't stop smiling as I walk back to the lobby, sending Jean a short update via text.

My time with the LA Aces is already yielding some great notes for the role.

And I have a date with a really hot soccer player who said I'm pretty.

Things are looking up.

CHAPTER FOUR

Abigail

I DON'T KNOW what to wear. Clothes litter the bed, the floor. I don't want to be overdressed. I don't want to look like . . . like I'm trying too hard. My hair's up in a ponytail, and besides putting a fresh layer of lip stain on, I haven't touched the makeup I put on for my meeting earlier today. Thank you, setting spray.

"Just shadowing Michelllle," I sing, pulling out my favorite pair of jeans and slipping into them. "Gonna get that Oscaaaaar."

"Beautiful singing," my best friend, Darren, says from where he's half paying attention on FaceTime, my phone propped up and plugged in on my nightstand.

"I'm manifesting through opera. Maybe I could pitch that method to a magazine or daytime TV show," I tell him.

"Oh, they will snap that up, for sure. I can see it now, just Lin-Manuel Miranda your way to your dreams."

I laugh and then return to the problem at hand.

"What the hell am I going to wear?" I ask him.

"Something cute," he says. "Something simple, because I'm not there to do your makeup."

"I didn't do too badly this morning," I sputter.

"Of course not, Abs, but you know I love a smoky moment on a date."

"Fair enough," I muse.

Sighing, I attempt the double-inhalation breathing that's supposed to calm me down when my heart's beating too fast. I'm counting chickens before they've hatched—we won't even start filming for another few weeks.

"I can do this!" I sing-yell.

"Yes," Darren agrees. "You can do this. We can do this."

"I'm proud of you," I tell him, grinning.

"I'm proud of you, Abs," he says instantly, and from the clinking noises going on over the phone, I bet he's reorganizing one of his makeup kits.

I blow out a breath, nodding to myself.

Shadowing Michelle is a good sign that Richard Grace believes in me. Maybe even the media will take me more seriously after working with the Aces. It's all good things.

"And I get some Italian food tonight," I sing in my very best dramatic falsetto.

"Italian fooood," Darren echoes in song.

"Nice. Call and response."

He laughs. "I am so ready to be on set with you. We are going to be a complete menace. The dream team. *Blood Sirens* wishes they'd had us!"

"Same." Darren being hired on as a makeup artist with the movie is just one of the many reasons I'm freaking excited to get started.

A cream-colored blouse calls my name from where it hangs in the closet. I pull it out, running my fingers over the silk. On it goes, and as soon as I finish throwing on some small gold earrings, I feel more settled.

"What do you think?" I ask, pivoting so Darren can approve my outfit.

It takes him a minute to look up. "Oh yes, trés chic, I love it."

"Oooh," I say approvingly. "Your French accent is so good."

"Thank the owl," he deadpans. "Duolingo, my lord and savior."

I laugh, then bite my lip again. "Going out with Luke Wolfe will be good, right? He can tell me more about soccer, what it's like to play pro, and I'll have even more knowledge. It's perfect."

"You don't have to convince me," Darren says.

"And even if he is an asshole, it will give me something else to think about," I continue.

At the very, *very* least.

But maybe . . . just maybe, he won't be the grumpy asshole I met this morning. Maybe he'll show me that soft, squishy side, the one I just know is hiding beneath that hard shell.

The doorbell rings.

"Shit," I breathe, my eyes wide. "He's here!" I yell at Darren.

"Calm down. Go answer the door. Have fun, and don't do anything I wouldn't," Darren says easily. "Bye, Abs."

The call ends.

Adrenaline surges through me. It's been a while since I went on a date with someone new. A long while.

I rush through the living room to answer the door, but that doesn't stop pride bursting through me as I give the space a once-over. I bought this small house a few years ago, nothing too fancy, when I got my first steady gig as the best friend on a now canceled sitcom. Built in the twenties, the small Spanish-style bungalow is full of charm, with white walls and dark wood beams crossing the space. It's in a gated community, too, something Jean insisted on when I was looking for a house, and I'm thankful now for her cynicism, even if it means I have to give the security there any visitor information . . . like Luke Wolfe's.

The security team was too happy to add him to my approved guest list, and I got the distinct feeling they might have been his fans—though they were too professional to say anything.

I make a mental note to send them some tickets to a game as I run my fingers across the cream-colored walls.

I love this place. I never felt like I had a real home before, and even the jitters of waiting for the latest tabloid rumor can't take that shine from me. They've relentlessly hounded me after the *Blood Sirens* red-carpet debacle, but maybe this will finally help them focus on something else.

Something positive for a change.

I worked hard for this, for my career, and now I'm going to dinner with a super handsome soccer star.

My feet pad against the wood floors, and I open the heavy wood door after a quick peek through the window.

Luke Wolfe stands on my front step, his back to me, his already broad shoulders looking even bigger in a dark blue suit jacket. His hair has a fresh-cut quality to it, and a little bubble of joy goes through me at the thought he might have freshened it up just for our date. For me.

Yum. I wouldn't mind seeing just how fresh he got for me. Everywhere.

I cough, as if clearing my throat will also punt away all my dirty thoughts.

Dare to dream!

"Nice view, isn't it?" My house is up in the hills, and I still can't quite believe I managed to buy it for myself. "That's one of my favorite things about this place."

He finally turns around, his expression much more relaxed than earlier.

"Beautiful," he agrees, but his gaze lingers on my face so long that my cheeks heat.

"Am I underdressed?" I ask, gesturing to my jeans and bare feet. "I can go throw on something fancier. I wasn't sure how swanky the place was—"

"Fuck them," he says. "If they have a problem with what you're wearing, they can take it up with me. They'll be lucky to have either one of us there." He pauses. "You look perfect."

The compliment comes out quieter, ringing with sincerity that makes my heart flutter.

"You might be one of the grumpiest people I've ever met, so I'm going to take your word for it." A slow smile turns the corners of my lips up, and he gives me a small grin of his own.

"Got these for you," he says, thrusting a bouquet of flowers at me. He shoves them so hard that a few petals rain down on the warm stones beneath our feet.

"Oh, wow, I didn't even notice them." I laugh. "I was too busy admiring the *whole* view." I wave a hand at him, and I swear to god, his eyes widen in surprise, like he's not used to people saying nice things to him.

Which makes my heart squeeze in sympathy for him. It makes me sad. Everyone deserves to be treated well.

No wonder he's a little rough around the edges.

Okay, a lot rough around the edges. Still, there's something I like about him. I like that he is who he is and he doesn't fake it.

"Come in for a minute? I just need to grab my purse, and I'll put these in water really quick." I motion for him to come in, and he does, staring around my little bungalow like he's never been in a house before.

"Kitchen's through here," I say, pointing past the tiny dining room. "You can come with me, or you can hang out here, next to the door. Up to you."

He grunts, and I can't help snorting at him.

"Tell me about the place we're going." I scrounge up a crystal vase and fill it, water pinging against the bottom. I set it on the counter before unwrapping the bouquet and arranging the flowers. Sunflowers and something purple, a striking combination.

"They're lovely," I say quietly, touched that he would bring them. "Sunflowers are so happy."

"They're just flowers," he says, tugging at his collar.

I raise an eyebrow at him. "Sunflowers that you brought me, that I like very much. So thank you."

He dips his chin in acknowledgment. "You're welcome," he says gruffly.

I put my hand on my hip, determined to crack him open like a walnut and see what's inside.

"For someone who asked me out, you sure are hard to talk to." I purse my lips.

Luke Wolfe stares at me, his icy gaze holding mine for a moment before it slips to my lips.

"The restaurant is good," he finally answers. "It's not fancy, not really. Homestyle Italian food. Small wine list. Intimate."

"Intimate," I repeat, wiggling my brows at him, wiping my hands on my jeans. "Is that right? And not fancy . . . but you're wearing a suit? You sure I shouldn't change?"

"Yeah," he mutters. "You know, maybe this was a bad idea—"

"Nope," I interrupt cheerily. "You asked me out, I said yes, we're going. I'm getting my purse before you take my flowers back."

He studies me, his lips a thin line, like he doesn't know what to make of me.

Well, that makes two of us. Odd couple, indeed.

"Maybe I should bring a nutcracker in case things get dicey," I mumble out loud.

"What?" he asks, taken aback.

"Nothing! Just need my purse," I say, holding up a finger and rushing out of the kitchen. Racing back to my room, it takes me a second to find it underneath a snug-fitting chocolate-brown dress I discarded on my pillows.

"There you are," I tell it.

"Holy shit."

I yelp, turning around to find Luke standing in my doorway, his eyes wide. "Does your room always look like a tornado came through?"

"Yep. I like to sleep in a pile of clothes. Makes me feel warm and cozy. Like a bird in a nest."

The look he gives me is so incredulous that I can't help laughing.

"I'm kidding. I couldn't figure out what to wear, and I wanted to look nice for you . . ." Oh god, stop me now.

Disbelief is etched on his face. "But you're already gorgeous."

"You're sweet." I grin like a fool at him.

"That's a fucking lie." He barks a laugh.

"Fine." A laugh bubbles out of me, too, and we stand there for a minute, grinning at each other. "That was sweet of you to say," I clarify.

He makes a low noise of assent.

I clear my throat, putting the thin purse strap over my shoulder and scooching past him out my bedroom door.

"Seems like we've both given tours today," I tell him, snagging my sandals from where I dropped them on the floor and carefully tugging them on.

"My tour wasn't very good."

"And my bedroom wasn't very clean," I counter.

He grins at me, and some of that glacial blue in his eyes melts away. "Fine. We're even."

"Even," I agree. "Should we go get some food now? I have an early day tomorrow."

"Food." He nods, and I follow him out of my house, locking the door behind me.

It's kind of amazing how he can make one word seem like an effort. I don't mind it, though. There are so many hyperverbal people in my life already, so many friends who need constant reassurance and constant conversation and constant approval, that his silence is . . . welcome.

It's not cold, not like I thought it would be. It's just . . . quiet. My brain is so noisy and loud all the time, it feels like there are thirteen hamsters running on rainbow-colored wheels while Queen croons a duet with Britney Spears. But he's calm, self-assured, and I start to wonder if some of that asshole behavior he's known for is just because he's introverted.

I mean, he is kind of an asshole, but . . . one who brings me flowers, one who holds the door to his sleek black car open for me. It's not flashy, like what I expected a star soccer player to drive, but it is nice. Understated. Elegant.

"Thanks," I say, sliding in as he grunts in acknowledgment.

I sigh. Maybe Jean is right and I'm too trusting. Maybe I should have taken my own car.

Except . . . I *hate* driving.

He gets in the driver seat, and another truth hits me. I hate first dates. I don't like small talk.

All of a sudden, my anxiety crashes into me like a tsunami, overpowering and threatening to tow me under.

"You all right?" he asks, carefully pulling the car onto the road.

I can't stop twisting the strap of my purse. The urge to pick my cuticles is strong, too, but I settle for bouncing my foot on the floorboard, knowing I can't afford to have fucked-up fingernails.

I can't afford to be anything less than pretty and pleasant and perfect if I want to get my career back on track. Especially in front of the paparazzi.

"Yes," I say on an exhale, and it's a lie. Double inhale, long exhale.

"You don't sound all right."

"I will be," I reassure him, but my usual smile falters and he shoots me a concerned look.

I don't think a total douche canoe would have noticed anything, which means that Luke Wolfe isn't quite the toolbag he seems to be.

I knew it.

"My sister gets panic attacks," he says, his voice low and reassuring as he pulls into traffic seamlessly, even though LA traffic makes me want to scream.

"I don't," I tell him too quickly. The last thing I need is for a rumor to get out about how I'm high-strung and anxious and prone to panic attacks. "I'm sorry about your sister, though. That must be hard."

He arches an eyebrow. "You don't."

It's a statement, not a question, and I relax. This isn't a test. This isn't an interview with some reporter trying to make a name for themselves by slandering mine. This is just . . . a first date.

Which is kind of a test and an interview all in one, but for fun. Right.

"I don't. What kind of music do you like?"

He goes quiet, and at first, I think he's just concentrating on navigating the sea of vehicles. Someone honks as he changes lanes, and I expect an outburst from the so-called Wolf of the Aces, a middle finger at the very least, but he just stays silent.

"I take it you don't listen to the sounds of LA traffic to relax?"

"You can't laugh at me," he says gruffly.

I blink. "Like, ever?" Now that's a bright crimson flag I can't ignore—

"No, at the kind of music I like."

"I won't," I promise, grinning. "Lemme guess, you only listen to Gregorian chanting. *Sesame Street* on repeat. A heavy metal band called Hell's Octopus."

He flicks a button on his steering wheel, and the next minute, the familiar strains of classical music fill the car. Cello.

"Listening to Yo-Yo Ma is hardly something I would make fun of you for." I pause, considering. "Now, if you could only *get off* while listening to Yo-Yo Ma, *that* would be weird, but—"

"Do you have a filter at all?" he asks, gaze skimming over me as he turns right onto a shaded side street.

"No?" I shrug one shoulder. "I mean, it would be easier if I did. My agent, Jean, probably wouldn't be giving herself an ulcer over trying to control my interview damage. But it's not like you have one, either," I say, and Luke grunts.

"Yeah, because it's too much fucking work to be nice." He cuts his gaze to me again. "Not because I bring up masturbation habits out of nowhere."

"Oh." I scrunch my nose. "Good point. It was just a joke. Sorry if I offended you." I give him a sly side-eye. "Especially if you do have to listen to Yo-Yo Ma to get off."

"I do not have to listen to Yo-Yo Ma to get off," he says, shaking his head. "I can't believe I am even saying that out loud. You're a trip."

"In a good way or a bad way?" I counter. "Like a trip to an island? Or a trip to *Rikers* Island? Or—"

"Neither," he says, shaking his head as he pulls the car into a spot in front of a little place with a red-and-white-striped awning.

There's no valet.

He's right, this place isn't fancy, or LA at all, and it makes this feel . . . real. Like he did want to get to know me, and he meant what he said about me being gorgeous, and he actually wants to help me learn more about soccer and the IFF.

I smile to myself, feeling pleased and warm all over.

He didn't have to dress up for this restaurant or the LA scene. He dressed up for me.

I like that. I like that a lot.

CHAPTER FIVE

Luke

ABIGAIL HUNT IS chaos in an adorable strawberry-blond package. The spray of freckles across her nose captivates me, and I don't know how I missed them this afternoon. She's barely stopped talking since I met her at her door, and her stream-of-consciousness chatter is both unexpected and hilarious.

I can't say I've ever had a first date accuse me of jerking off to the sounds of the cello.

Then again, I've never asked a woman out because the owners of my team wanted to sell more tickets.

I sneak a look at Abigail, though only the top of her head shows past the menu she's staring at. For a moment on the way here, I thought she was trying to tamp down an anxiety attack, and I was ready to step in just like I used to with my sister when we were younger.

But she pulled it together.

The table jostles rhythmically, and a surreptitious glance tells me she's still shaking her leg, ceaselessly.

For all that she radiates sunshine from her pores, Abigail Hunt is definitely anxious.

I don't like that.

I don't want her to be anxious around me.

Fuck.

I *should* want her to be anxious around me, I should want her to dislike me intensely, just like the rest of this stupid city, so I can throw in the towel on this farce with her.

But for all her weirdness, she's sweet. Genuine.

And I don't know the last time I could say that about anyone.

"I can't decide what to get." Her mismatched eyes are narrowed in concentration.

"Buonasera, Mr. Wolfe." The owner, Mateo, sweeps in front of our table, a delighted expression on his face. "And who is this bellissima signorina? You have never brought anyone here with you before."

"Hi." Abigail grins at him. "Does Luke come here a lot, then? By himself?"

"Oh, yes, he's here at least once a week. Never brought anyone, much less a woman like yourself."

He beams at her, and I loose a resigned sigh. Mateo loves to talk. Abigail loves to talk.

I might as well just leave and let the two of them yap at each other.

"Oh, is that right? Does he often listen to cello music while he dines?"

"Pervert," I tell her, an incredulous chuckle making its way out of my mouth.

Mateo shoots me a confused look, and Abigail lets out a little laugh.

"No, but if you would like me to put some on to set the mood, signorina, I will."

He stares at her for a long second, and I see the exact moment he recognizes her, delight flashing in his eyes.

"You're Abigail Hunt, the TV star!" He exhales noisily, clapping his hands together.

"*Star* might be a stretch," she says, laughing, and the table jangles more as she bounces her leg harder.

"Mateo, can you bring us tonight's specials? And a bottle of red.

Unless you like white?" Shit, maybe I shouldn't have ordered for her. Maybe I should have let her have more time. Fuck.

I tug at my collar, impossibly uncomfortable. I should have worn sweats, like I usually do.

"For Abigail Hunt and the LA Wolf? I will bring red and white. Whatever you want."

Abigail smiles, thanking him, a vein jumping in her temple. The candle on the table gutters, and she grabs the red mercury glass jar, turning it around and around.

I glare at Mateo. Can't he see he's making her uncomfortable? Jesus. I brought her here so she could just have a low-key night. So I could do the bare minimum required by Charles and fucking company and still get a good meal out of it.

"Thanks, Mateo. Go away, Mateo."

At that, he snorts, used to my shit, and finally saunters off, greeting a few other tables of diners, and I scowl as he points over to us, the other tables staring at us with pointed interest.

"I shouldn't have brought you here," I manage.

"Why?" She stares at me with luminous, mismatched eyes. "You must like this place if you come here so often."

"Mateo's nosy."

"I'm used to it. It's part of the whole . . . thing, right? Like, I have an incredible job. People recognizing me sometimes comes part and parcel with it." She shrugs one shoulder. "You know how it is."

"That's a rehearsed answer."

"I like people," Abigail says, playing with the white linen napkin in her lap. The table's stopped jumping, at least.

"Yeah, well, I fucking hate them," I say. "Fame is stupid."

A pot of mussels arrives, along with a bottle of white wine in a silver wine chiller. Thankfully, the waiter doesn't do more than blink at both of us before pouring the wine, leaving us with a loaf of crusty bread for the mussels.

"I love mussels and white wine," she says.

"Are you just saying that?" I peer at her.

"Yeah, I'm actually allergic to shellfish." She winks at me, ripping a piece of bread off and dipping it in the steaming pot. "But I'm going to pretend just so you like me."

"Then we're about to have a very interesting night," I tell her, putting a few mussels on a plate for her and a few on mine.

"Yeah, I can't wait to go to the ER. I'm going to pretend you're my secret husband, and then we'll leak the news of our wedding to the press." She says it all so smoothly that I'm entirely unsure if she's joking or not.

My throat gets tight at the thought of all that unnecessary drama.

"Secret husband?" I manage.

"Yeah, can you imagine the headlines?" She lets out a delicate snort, spearing the meat inside the black shell and taking a tiny bite.

"God," I say. It sounds like a nightmare. "You're not really allergic, are you?"

She winks at me, picking up her wineglass and swirling it around before taking a small sip. "Wouldn't you like to know?"

"Yeah, if I'm going to have to fucking take you to the ER and watch you tell everyone we're married, then I would absolutely like to know."

"Who doesn't love a good mystery?" she asks, taking another sip. "Have you read anything good lately?"

This woman's completely thrown off my equilibrium. "Read anything?"

"Yeah, you know, a book? Doesn't have to be a novel, though. Maybe you like to read poetry anthologies while you jerk it to Yo-Yo Ma."

I cough, and wine sprays slightly.

She just grins at me, laughter in her eyes.

She's making fun of me. I shouldn't like it, but I do.

I like it.

I like that she feels safe enough with me to make that joke, even though I can tell she's barely keeping a lid on her anxiety.

"You keep making jokes about me masturbating and I'll make you watch me come next time," I tell her darkly. I meant it as a joke, too, but I didn't say it like I should have. It didn't come out right, and I shouldn't have even fucking bothered to try.

This is why I don't say shit if I don't have to.

I chance a glance up at her, scowling, and what I see nearly takes my fucking breath away.

Her berry-red lips are parted slightly, her eyes wide as she stares at me, a slow grin spreading across her face.

"I can't tell if that was a joke or an invitation, but either way, I have to say I'm surprised to be included. I'll be sure to make a really killer classical playlist for the occasion."

Of all the things I expected her to say, that wasn't one of them.

I grunt, and the waiter magically reappears, this time with a white platter loaded with calamari.

"Oh, goodie, more things for me to have an allergic reaction to," Abigail tells me sunnily.

The waiter gives me a nervous look.

"She's joking!" I bark at him.

When she puts her delicate hand on my wrist, I go still, staring from it to her face in shock.

I can't remember the last time someone touched me like that. Gently. Her fingers grazed my hand today, but this feels . . . different. Not accidental.

It feels *important*.

"Don't yell at the poor man, Luke," she says, her green and hazel eyes dancing.

The waiter scurries off, but it's not him I'm worried about.

It's me.

I see exactly what it is that's made Abigail Hunt successful in a city that tosses people aside like yesterday's news as soon as the next best thing arrives.

She's magnetic. I don't want to look away from her. I like the way she says my name.

I shouldn't want to have anything to do with her at all.

I shouldn't want to keep watching her, the way the smooth column of her throat bobs as she swallows her wine.

I shouldn't want to keep hearing the small, delicious noises she makes when she eats something tasty.

I shouldn't wish that this was real, instead of something my asshole bosses put me up to.

CHAPTER SIX

Abigail

THE MOMENT THE paparazzi arrive is always marked the same way. People pointing at them, then craning to look at me, their target.

I hate this.

I hate that even though I crave privacy, I have to be nice. Have to be sweet. Hell, I want to give them good pictures, too. It will be good for this little Italian place, good for the paparazzi, good for my career.

"Fucking hell," Luke says. "We haven't even gotten to the pasta." He's spotted them, too, a look of pure fury on his masculine face.

"Don't worry about them," I tell him. "Just ignore them for now, and when we leave, we'll pose for a few pics and then they'll leave us alone."

"How can you be so fucking calm about it? They're roaches. Leeches."

My lips twist to the side, and I pop another piece of calamari in my mouth, chewing and swallowing before I answer. "Which is it? Roaches or leeches?"

"Rats," he says.

"A whole variety of vermin," I say casually.

He glares at the crowd outside the window.

Sighing, I push back from the table slightly, crossing my arms against my chest. "I'm calm because what else am I going to be? Mad?

So they can write awful headlines about what a bitch I am? Please. You know what it's like." Two heaping plates of what looks like gnocchi and some kind of seafood linguine arrive, and the waiter murmurs apologies for the paparazzi outside the window. Mateo's drawing heavy velvet curtains across the windows as a few other tables quietly applaud as the paparazzi disappear from view.

"Thank you," I say automatically.

Luke waits until the waiter leaves to speak again. "I do know what it's like, and I don't put up with that shit."

My appetite disappears. I don't like conflict or confrontation, and I sink back into the wooden chair. Teasing? Teasing and being silly I like. All-out arguments, absolutely not.

"Why do you put up with it?" he continues, arching his brows at me.

"Because if I don't, they win. And besides, they're just doing their jobs."

"It's a fucked-up job," he says.

"Look," I say slowly, picking my fork back up and pushing gnocchi around the plate. "I get it. If it's too much for you, just take me back home."

"Fine." He raises a hand and Mateo practically sprints over.

I gape at him. He's seriously going to call off our date now?

Disappointment sits heavy in my chest. I liked him. I like that he's not afraid to be his grumpy self. It's . . . funny. Refreshing and different and *real*.

I ruined our date.

I'm surprised at how upset that makes me.

"Can we get this to go? And some dessert. And a bottle of wine. Do you want anything else?" he asks me. "Since we're taking this to your house."

I glance back up at him, a smile kicking up the corners of my mouth. "We are?"

He stares at me like I've grown another head. "Yeah, I'm not fucking letting this food go to waste just because some assholes with cameras showed up outside. Or letting my time with you go to waste, either."

A small laugh trickles out of me, pure pleasure replacing the disappointment.

Luke Wolfe, my own personal dopamine. Who would've thought?

"Anything else, Signorina Abigail?" Mateo asks me, signaling to the waiters to wrap the food, which is whisked away nearly immediately.

I shake my head, and before I can decide on an answer, the food reappears in heavy white paper bags.

God. I have to face the paparazzi. Sweat begins to bead on my palms, Luke squinting at me like he can see the anxiety written all over my face.

I don't want to say the wrong thing or have them photograph me in the wrong moment. I don't want to see a headline tomorrow morning claiming I was drunk or something.

I cannot jeopardize my career with a misstep that will get me canceled or worse.

"We didn't even get a chance to talk about soccer." There's a thick lump in my throat that has nothing to do with anaphylaxis.

"We'll have plenty of time for that." His expression is fully focused on me. A prickling awareness of his proximity climbs across my skin.

My gaze dips to his lips, and I swallow hard. They're good lips. Kissable lips.

Suddenly, kissing him is all I can think about. He'd probably be a great kisser. *All that muscle* . . . I shake my head, like I can Etch A Sketch the idea from my mind, and finally register what he's said.

"What do you mean, plenty of time? Tonight? I need to be up early."

He shakes his head. "Tonight, tomorrow, the next time we go out. This is only the first date."

"Oh?" I raise my eyebrows, delighted. I am completely into that idea. For as rude as Luke can be . . . I'm actually enjoying myself with him. I suspect there's a squishy heart of gold under that hard facade he puts up for everyone else, and I'd like to see if I'm right.

I do love being right.

Also, there's no denying Luke is hot. He's fun to look at.

My attention slides to his mouth again, and I decide, once and for all, that he's definitely a good kisser. A little sigh catches me off guard.

"Unless you don't want to." He says it casually enough, but he's still watching me carefully. Like he wants me to say yes, like his feelings might be hurt if I don't say yes.

Heart of gold, I see you under there.

"Depends on how you play the game—" I start to tease him, curious just how far I can push.

"I'm a pro at playing the game," he interrupts, heat flaring in his eyes. "I always get what I want."

My thoughts have officially jumped the track, way past kissing. Yep. They're headed straight for the gutter. The deepest of gutters. The Mariana Trench of gutters.

The way Luke's looking at me? He knows it, too.

Why is that so hot?

I clear my throat, trying to refocus on our immediate situation, and not Luke's sincere innuendo.

Although . . . maybe . . . An idea strikes me, one foolproof way to test my theory about Luke being a good kisser.

I stifle an evil laugh.

"They're going to want us to pose when we walk outside. Maybe you could bring the car around back," I say. "You know, if you want this to be . . . private?"

Luke is clearly a private person. Very private.

"We could go out the kitchen. Or we could stagger when we leave, you know, I go first, you go second . . . or we could give them something to talk about." I bat my eyelashes, biting my lower lip.

"Give them something to talk about." He repeats the words slowly.

"You want to do that?" Glee ripples through me. I waggle my eyebrows.

"Might be fun." A devilish grin lights up his face.

"You think so?" A flutter of anticipation builds low in my stomach. "You think this is fun?" It *is* a hell of a lot more fun than letting someone else control the narrative. I can't stop grinning.

And I can't stop thinking about kissing him. Luke Wolfe.

Briefly, I wonder what Jean would say about it, me kissing him, then quickly decide she'd love me getting the attention.

"Do I think being stalked by the paparazzi is fun? Not really. Dating you? In public?" He shrugs. "Not terrible." He's smiling at me, though, and it's warm and makes me feel fuzzy.

"A ringing endorsement. Love being the 'not terrible' option." I laugh.

He glares at me, a hint of that terrifying Los Angeles Wolf persona in his expression. "You know what I mean."

"I do, but I would love even more hearing it spelled out." I give him an outrageous wink.

His grimace disappears, a slow, delicious grin replacing it. "You are the *best* option." There's an aching ring of truth to that, and it makes my breath catch in surprise.

Oh god, I want to kiss him, I want to know what all that intensity is like completely focused on me, completely focused on my body.

Oof. I've got a *serious* crush on him.

And it's kind of fun. When was the last time I let myself crush on someone? It's been a long time. A really long time.

"I agree," I say airily, pretending like everyone says shit like that to me. Like I'm used to it. "Going home and stuffing ourselves with pasta? That is definitely the best option."

I can't lie to myself about how it makes me feel, though. All kinds of warm and fuzzy.

I tilt my head, arching a brow at him. "You want to go out the front? Where they're all waiting?"

He grunts. "That depends."

"On what?" I cross my arms on top of the table, leaning in to hear him.

"On what you have in mind. I'm not about to be your secret husband while you have an allergic reaction to shellfish."

A laugh bursts out of me. "Fine. No secret husband, no EpiPen on the pavement. Boundaries are important. Anything else?" I arch one eyebrow, feeling slightly devilish as I consider an array of scenarios.

There's one in particular, though, that I'm dying to try.

For science.

"No," he says slowly, the word laced with a challenge. "If you're thinking what I'm thinking, then I'm in."

I let out an evil laugh. "Good. You ready?"

"Fuck." His lip is curled in disgust, but his blue eyes are full of laughter. "I guess so."

"This was your idea. You said you're game for *anything* else," I remind him sweetly.

"You're not making me feel great about this."

"Your safe word is *Yo-Yo Ma*," I tell him as I stand up, folding my napkin neatly on the table.

"Fuck no, it's not." He stands, too, surprising me by sliding an arm around my waist.

Heat curls through me, and I bite my lower lip. I look up at him through my lashes. "Was there a safe word you preferred, then? *EpiPen? Anaphylaxis?*"

"I can't think of three worse safe words." He shakes his head, but

I can tell he's amused as we walk through the restaurant. If anyone inside is snapping pictures of us, it's discreetly, and I don't even feel like glancing around for cell phones like I usually do.

Which surprises me.

I'm too entertained by Luke to even worry about that.

When we walk outside, though, it's chaos. My palms start sweating.

Even more paps had set up while we were waiting for the check, a whole flock of them squawking our names, flashes going off like lightning bolts, leaving me hot and overwhelmed.

Luke pulls me closer, a big hand curling around my ribs, as though he's going to personally shield me from all of them.

"You okay?" he asks, frowning down at me.

I tilt my head, and when I look up at him, I don't have to fake the smile for the cameras like I usually do.

Him like this, when he's being protective, sweet—it makes me happy. It makes me think I'm right about him, right about that secretly soft side. And a Luke Wolfe who's game for my shenanigans? *That* makes me positively giddy.

I lace my hands around his neck, my eyebrows arched in a silent question as I search his blue eyes, then I speak three syllables that I wouldn't have ever thought would be code for anything in my entire life.

"Yo-Yo Ma?" I flutter my eyelashes. My heart's beating so fast, it's a wonder he can't hear it.

I want to kiss him. I want to be right about him.

"Fucking hell, Abigail," he says, and I see the exact moment he realizes what I want.

"Is this what you were thinking of, too?" I rub my thumb on the back of his neck, drinking in the way he's looking at me, the way his gaze dips to my mouth, then back to my eyes in silent question.

I nod briefly, hoping he's thinking the same thing.

His kiss is the only answer I need.

The response from the paparazzi is immediate and utterly overwhelming. I have to close my eyes to keep from being blinded by the flashes popping off like crazy. The best part, though?

It's easy to lose myself in Luke Wolfe—to forget we have an audience. His body is warm against mine, his arms strong as he pulls me close, his hands wrapping around me as his lips brush against mine.

Sensory overload: from the way his warm palms span across my back, the feel of the hard plane of his chest against mine, the gentle pressure of his mouth.

I want more. I am greedy for this kiss, for him, somehow more satisfying than any of the delicious food we sampled.

I lose myself to it, to this moment, standing on my tiptoes and savoring it. The impression of pine-and-sandalwood cologne floats from his skin, and my tongue darts out.

Luke groans, a small, impossible noise that leaves me reeling as he finally pulls away.

He stares down at me, surprise and heat and a need I feel deep under my skin echoed in his own eyes.

It's easy to think that dating Luke Wolfe might feel very, very good.

"ABIGAIL!"

"LUKE!"

"KISS AGAIN!"

"KISS HER AGAIN, WOLF!"

"Fuck," Luke grinds out, finally pulling away as the noise of the paparazzi breaks the spell of our kiss. "Do you think that was enough?"

"Depends," I say, drawing out the word, nearly unable to answer, to think past how perfect that was. An evil grin spreads across my face, and I tilt my head. "Do you feel the need to listen to cello music?"

"You're fucking terrible," he says, laughing for real this time.

Between kissing Luke Wolfe (exactly as delectable as I imagined) and making him really laugh (even better), I don't even mind the paparazzi.

I can't remember the last time I was this relaxed around them.

Maybe I should try kissing him again.

He squeezes my waist, leading me to his car, as butterflies dance in my stomach, and I can't help hoping I get the chance to kiss him again.

CHAPTER SEVEN

Luke

THE SECOND ABIGAIL plugs her phone into the aux, I let out a groan. She laughs, the flashbulbs of the paparazzi still going off outside the car, and I can't do more than shake my head in amusement as the sound of a masterfully played cello sings through the car's speakers.

"I assume this is your guy Yo-Yo Ma?" I ask, pulling into the bumper-to-bumper traffic that helps make LA the hellhole it is.

"Uh-oh," she squeals. "Your safe word. Should I turn it off?"

I can't help the low laugh that ripples out of me. "No. I've never listened to him before."

"Don't lie. Your secret is safe with me."

"It's not a secret if you just made it up," I retort, weaving into the left lane.

She falls silent, and I sneak a peek at her face, worried I've offended her. No, she's smiling softly, her eyes closed. The white paper bag full of food sits on the back seat, the aroma of garlic and butter filling the car.

Her face is lovely in repose, relaxed, skin glowing in the dim light. Maybe I have a one-track mind, maybe I shouldn't have let her joke about masturbating to cello music all night, but fuck me if I can't stop wondering about what she looks like when she comes.

Or maybe it's the fact that I want to see it for myself.

The way she melted against me outside the restaurant, the taste of wine on her lips and tongue, the scent of her perfume and shampoo and all the other little things that overwhelmed my senses . . .

I'm intoxicated by her.

"You're quiet all of a sudden," I say.

She cracks an eye, the hazel one. "I'm enjoying the music. I'm surprised you've never listened to this."

"You were too invested in fantasizing about me to ask what I actually listen to."

"Fantasizing, huh?"

"I don't blame you," I tell her. "Everyone does." It's patently false, but I think it will make her laugh, and when she does, I feel like I've won a prize.

"Well, Mr. Wolfe, what do you listen to?" she asks.

"Vivaldi," I deadpan. It's the only classical composer I can think of, and as I hoped, her laughter fills the car.

"Which season is your favorite?"

"Soccer," I say easily, passing a black sedan with one headlight out.

She snorts. "I meant of the *Vivaldi* seasons. You know, more cello, violins, et cetera . . . not balls." She looks back down at the phone in her hands, scrolling until she finds what she's looking for. "Or is there another instrument you would want to finger?"

My jaw drops.

Abigail barks out a laugh, her eyebrows practically disappearing into her strawberry-blond hair in surprise. "I didn't mean it like that, oh my god, I don't know why I said it like that."

I'm silent.

Did she say that because she's thinking about . . . sex? With me?

I shake my head, frowning, because no. I'm not going to even entertain the thought of that. This is already . . . complicated enough with her.

It wouldn't be if I didn't like her—but I do.

Abigail Hunt is the stuff dreams are made of—she's beautiful, yes, but she's also funny and feisty and *real*.

Meanwhile, I'm the jackass taking her out to appease the LA Aces owners so they cut my contract short and allow me to be traded back home.

I'm using her already.

I don't get to even *think* about making it worse for us both.

"I'm sorry," she says, her voice small, barely audible through the sounds of classical music filling the space between us. "I didn't mean to make you uncomfortable. I really don't know why I said it like that."

I glance sidelong at her, and her face is so full of regret, her eyes wide and watery, that I'm reaching out to squeeze her hand before I've fully realized I'm doing it.

"I'm fine." Two words that barely convey what I'm thinking. Two words that if anyone else said it to me, I wouldn't believe the shit that came out of their mouth afterward. Ahead, red lights flash as a Suburban slams on the brakes and I slow down, glancing back at her.

Her nose is wrinkled, a faraway expression on her face. "Sometimes I get a kick out of being, well, ridiculous, but I honestly didn't mean to say something so sexual."

"Abigail, the only reason I'm uncomfortable is because now I'm thinking about touching you. Which is a problem because I'm trying to be a gentleman on our first date." The words come out rough, unpolished, and I look back at the traffic ahead of us nearly immediately.

The music ends on a long violin note, and then silence expands.

"Oh," she finally says. "I like that you are trying to be a gentleman." Her voice is soft, and again, I'm struck with how *real* she is, how vivid—like everyone else is in black and white and she's the Technicolor rainbow after a storm.

"I like . . . ," she starts, but she trails off.

Fuck. Now I'm thinking about whether she likes the idea of me touching her, too. If she's also thinking about me touching her.

I am not a fucking gentleman, or I wouldn't be so suddenly obsessed with the idea. A fucking gentleman wouldn't have agreed to trick her into dating him, either.

"Don't worry about it," I force out, just to say something to her.

I should tell her now. I should come clean, admit that the owners told me to date her.

"Thank you, by the way," she says. "For asking me out. I know it wasn't . . . a normal date." She purses her lips, her mismatched eyes so wide and full of hope that all notions of coming clean scatter like storm clouds before the sun. "I am still glad you asked me out, though." Her fingers unbuckle the metal clasp on her small purse, then refasten it, the metal clinking against itself as she unbuckles it again.

"I'm glad you said yes," I say, surprised into honesty.

When she smiles at me, wide, it hits me like a ton of bricks. I can't tell her. I can't come clean.

I won't ruin that look of hope in her eyes.

She doesn't need to know.

I'll finish out this date, then I'll let her down easy tomorrow. The owners won't be able to deny that I tried. Hell, the paparazzi showed up to our date. If that's not enough press for them, then they can get fucked.

I kissed her. She kissed me back, and there's photographic evidence to prove it.

And now I'm thinking about holding her tight little body against mine again, kissing her until she goes soft and pliant in my arms.

Until she moans my fucking name and begs for more.

"You don't look glad," she says, a teasing lilt to her voice, her pretty lips quirked in a half smile. "You look pissed off."

"That's just my face," I tell her. The GPS tells me to exit the highway, so I make my way through the sea of cars, grateful to have an excuse to stop thinking about the shitty situation I've put her in.

I just won't call her again after tonight. Problem solved.

She deserves someone better than me, anyway.

CHAPTER EIGHT

Abigail

LUKE PARKS IN the long driveway in front of my house, the rest of our ride home mostly silent.

It was nice—companionable silence.

Weirdly, I didn't feel the need to fill it with endless chatter. I wasn't even anxious about the awful LA traffic like I usually am. I felt safe with Luke at the wheel—he didn't try anything macho or stupid or risky.

He kept glancing over at me, too, like he wanted to make sure I was okay when I wouldn't stop messing with the clasp on my purse.

Now he's walking around the front of his car, and I start to open my door, feeling silly for sitting there and remembering the way he felt on my lips instead of moving.

I wonder if he's still thinking about our little public display of affection, too.

Luke beats me to the door, the scent of his spicy cologne lingering. "Let me get that for you."

His voice is like silken sandpaper on my overstimulated nerves, and goose bumps pebble across my arms.

I blink up at him, his big body filling the space . . . until my stomach growls.

"Oh, the food," I say, but he's already reaching over me, grabbing the large paper bag of food from the back seat.

His chest brushes against my shoulder, and I inhale deeply, surprised by how much his proximity affects me. He smells so *good*. Heat rises in my cheeks, and he carefully pulls the bag out, setting it on the ground next to the car.

When he looks back at me, a palm outstretched to help me out of the car, something's changed in his eyes, too.

All his intensity, the kind that's made him infamous on the soccer field, is focused on me now.

Oh. Oh wow.

For a split second, my brain skips ahead to a new possibility: of pulling his collar down to me again, of plastering my lips against his, until he carries me inside my house and ravages me all night.

Instead, I blow out the breath I've been holding since he leaned across me to grab the Italian food and take his hand. His eyes hold mine, pupils dilating, and all I can do is stare up at him, stunned.

It feels *electric*. Raw and powerful, like pure energy.

This. This is what people mean when they talk about chemistry.

I make myself step out of the car, overwhelmed by whatever just passed between us, and drop his hand.

Without a word, Luke turns and strides to the doorway, his long legs eating up the ground. Every bit of the man is like a piece of art, like some sculptor's soccer Michelangelo, every muscle and plane of his body in tune with each other.

I need to get a hold of myself.

I am really, really freaking attracted to him.

"Get a grip, Abigail," I mutter under my breath. We kissed, yes. It was a great kiss, yes.

It was for the paparazzi.

Luke Wolfe does not strike me as the kind of man to have a casual fling. I purse my lips, making my feet move toward the door of my house.

No, Luke Wolfe would be a force of nature, and there wouldn't be anything remotely flingy about it.

I need to keep my head in the game. I have to stay focused on the fact that I want this film to do well, I want that damned Oscar, and that getting entangled with a man like Luke Wolfe would only distract me from those goals.

"You going to let me in?" he asks.

I blink up at him.

Shit. I've been standing at the front door of my house, staring up at him while I think about exactly how I cannot pursue what is likely to be forest-fire-level hot sex with him.

"Yep, just wanted to make sure you knew the password before I let you in." What the hell did I just say?

The smallest of smiles turns the corners of his lips up. "Is that right?" he asks.

"Yep." In for a penny, in for a pound. Or whatever the saying is. "So what's it gonna be?" I bluff.

"May I come in?" he asks.

"Nailed it," I manage, rolling my eyes at my stupid self as I unlock the front door. "You're going to have to tell me who slipped up and let you have the password to my house, though. I'll have to interrogate my security team and find the mole."

"I'll make it easy for you. The mole is called manners, and I managed to remember some of mine."

"Aha! I'll be speaking to your mother, then," I quip, setting my purse down on the slender front entry table.

He doesn't answer, though, and when I glance over my shoulder at him, he's looking at me with an odd expression.

Great. "Did I put my foot in my mouth?" I ask, feeling shitty. "I'm sorry. I know family can be a sore subject. Probably not the best first-date topic." I'm blabbing, and I squeeze my eyes shut, forcing the words to stop.

"Food," he says gruffly, holding out the bag and stomping off to the kitchen area like he's intimately familiar with the layout of my house.

It's strange how good that feels. How normal. I mean, yes, I showed him around earlier, but . . . he feels *right* here.

That or I'm horny as heck and that one glass of wine and one single kiss short-circuited all my brain cells.

Great. Now I'm thinking about that kiss again.

I pull my phone from my back pocket, then hook a finger through the strap of my heels and sigh in relief at having bare feet.

"You coming, Abigail?" he calls.

"Just taking my clothes off!" I yell back. I smack my hand into my forehead, because what the fuck did I just say? "My SHOES!" I say even louder. "Taking my *shoes* off."

When I look up after nudging them into some semblance of organization, embarrassment beating through me, Luke's standing in the opening of the kitchen, watching me with that insanely intense expression.

"You didn't miss anything," I chirp at him, then clear my throat. "I misspoke."

He doesn't answer, just stares at me, a hungry look in his eyes.

"Food," I say, pointing limply behind him. "Let's eat." I wedge myself past him and the wall, my hip brushing against him.

"I hope you like dessert," he all but growls. "I'm starving."

His hand lands on the small of my back, and heat pulses through me at the light touch, at the possessiveness of it.

Dessert. Do I have dessert? My mind's racing, my body tight and wound up from the barest suggestion of his palm on my back.

"I think we have plenty of food," I squeak out. I am making an utter fool of myself. I need to get it the hell together. "But I might have something sweet in the freezer."

"They packed up dessert for us." His face is quizzical.

I bark out a harsh laugh. "Right, right, I forgot. Sorry. Someone scrambled my brain with their kiss."

My eyes go wide, and I purse my lips, trying to breathe through this embarrassing free fall.

"Why is it you have to be up early tomorrow?" he asks. His big hand leaves my back as he begins unpacking the bag full of food. Every movement is economical, not one shred of energy wasted.

I'm staring.

Whew. I went from being convinced Luke Wolfe was a total jerk to crushing hard on him in the span of just a few hours. Fickle, thy name is Abigail Hunt.

"Pilates," I finally blurt out. "It's a one-on-one, and if I'm late, my instructor will kick my ass even harder than usual."

He grunts.

"I know what that means," I tell him, tapping the side of my cheek.

He pushes a plastic tub of food toward me, along with a set of plasticware wrapped neatly in a thick paper napkin. I pop the lid off and grin at him, the food still steaming.

"What?" he asks.

"Your grunt." I nod to myself.

He raises an eyebrow, and I settle in on one of the counter stools at my kitchen island, forking some of the pasta into my mouth. Still delicious. It feels more casual to sit here than at the bigger table behind us, like this is some illicit, stolen moment, and I smile as I chew.

"What does it mean?"

I grin at him.

"That grunt meant you feel my pain." I lower my voice, doing my best Luke Wolfe impression. "Pilates instructors demanding five a.m.

workouts are clearly part of the devil's entourage in the fifth circle of hell. Dante himself wrote about it."

He bursts out laughing, disbelief wrinkling his brow. He perches next to me on the barstool, his elbow brushing mine as he studies me. "Is that what I sound like?"

I chew slowly, thinking it over before nodding serenely. "Absolutely. That was a spot-on impression. I am an actress, after all." I pretend flip my hair over one shoulder, then squeal as my stool rocks backward, threatening to spill me and my pasta all over the floor.

A strong hand wraps around my waist, and the chair rocks forward again before settling on all four legs.

"I've got you, Abigail." Luke's deep voice sends a shiver down my spine.

Oooh-wee, am I ever in trouble. I shove some more food in my mouth to keep from trying to shove him in my mouth.

"I might not be able to give my blessing to that impression of me, though."

I peer at him. "Was it the Pilates instructor slander?"

"No, I've been to Pilates. It was . . . much harder than it should have been." His thick brows furrow at the memory, and then he lets out a rough laugh. "It was my first pro season. They hired a few different fitness instructors to work on our mobility. That whole season was a fucking eye-opener." He shakes his head, taking a bite.

I laugh, because it's all too easy to imagine those guys from the LA Aces I met today crying during a Pilates session.

He grins at me, then motions for me to eat, and I'm only too happy to oblige.

The food is really good, true cheesy, creamy, carb-eriffic goodness, and we eat in that same companionable silence that settles over us.

That, more than my outsize physical attraction to him, is what has me on high alert.

Like the silence is some glimpse into a hazy crystal ball of my future, of what could be with him. Not just the potential for hot sex—which, yes, please—but the *ease* of this. The effortlessness.

I don't feel the need to pretend. To be Abigail Hunt, actress. To be onstage and entertain at a moment's notice.

We can just sit and eat, and he's not trying to play six degrees of Kevin Bacon with me, or preening and looking at his reflection in the cutlery, or any of the other weirdness I've experienced in the last few years of my woefully sad love life.

Easy.

Easy would be so *nice*.

I push the food away from me, suddenly too aware of my attraction to the man sitting next to me in my home on our first date.

My phone vibrates where I set it on the counter, and Luke grunts, reaching for what's left of my food with a raised eyebrow.

"Are you done with this?" I ask in my Luke Wolfe voice. "Can I eat the rest of your pasta?"

He presses a napkin to his lips, and I hear the laugh he doesn't quite let out. I grin at him, and he nods as he chews.

Ha!

I push it at him, and he swallows, muttering his thanks as I pick up my phone.

The text is from Michelle.

> **MICHELLE:** What the hell is going on with you and Luke?
>
> **MICHELLE:** There's a photo of you two on the gossip sites already. Kissing!
>
> **MICHELLE:** If he's being a jackass in any way shape or form, say the word and I'll send Aces security over there to extract him

I tilt my head, a curious rush of emotions flooding me. Michelle's worried about me? Or is she worried about Luke Wolfe? Or some mix of both? It feels nice that she's concerned about me—like maybe I did make a new friend in her today. Or at least we have the potential to be friends.

On the other hand, she might just be bracing for a PR firestorm.

My lips twist to the side as I contemplate it.

I hope she wants to be friends. Truly.

"Extract me?"

I clutch the phone to my chest. "Are you spying?"

"Yes." He frowns. "Do you want me to leave? I don't want Michelle Oxford sending an 'extraction' team for me." His fingers make air quotes around the word.

My heart rate picks up, because I know what I want to do. I know what I should do, too, and I settle on something in the middle.

Carefully, I lower my phone, holding it between us where he can see it. I'm about to lay all my cards on the table, and I feel just as nervous as I would if I were gambling with massive stakes.

The stakes at risk here are only my feelings, though, and I make up my mind to be brave.

I tap out a response to Michelle.

> **ABIGAIL:** Luke's been incredible. One of the best first dates I've ever been on! Thanks for asking, though def don't send an extraction team 😊
>
> **MICHELLE:** Sounds like we're going to have a lot to talk about at lunch
>
> **MICHELLE:** Have fun

"Best first date you've ever been on?" he asks, scowling furiously.

"Don't look so happy about it," I tell him with a surprised laugh. "I might get confused and think you like me, too."

There. All the cards in my hand, face up on the table.

His frown only deepens, though, his blue eyes nearly disappearing under his thick eyebrows.

My heart slows, heavy with regret, and I look down, running my fingers along the case of my phone.

"If this is the best first date you've ever had, then you've only dated real assholes."

"As opposed to the fake assholes?" I raise my eyebrow. I'd meant it as a joke, but his cheeks go ruddy, and I stare at him in surprise.

"Do you like to dance?" he asks, and I blink at the non sequitur.

"What?"

"You like music, so I wondered if you liked to dance."

"Don't you also like music?"

"Yeah." He scratches his neck, still looking at me like he's surprised I'm sitting next to him.

"What kind of music do you like?" I prod.

"Classic rock, mostly. Whatever's on the radio when I get in the car. Whatever the guys want to listen to in the gym." He shrugs a shoulder.

"We can't forget the cello when you're alone," I say, wiggling my eyebrows, unable to stop myself.

"Of course we can't," he says, and something like a smile plays across his lips.

"I do like to dance," I finally tell him. "I'm not the best at it, but I've had to fake my way through lessons for work."

"I bet you're good at it." He smiles at me now, his whole face transforming, and oh god, he's so nice to look at.

"Dancing? Or faking it?" I ask, screwing my lips up to one side.

"Both. But I meant dancing." He holds out a hand, and I stare at it for a long moment.

Realization dawns.

"Are you asking me to dance?"

"Yeah." He nods, standing up, still reaching out for me. "Do you know the kitchen dance?"

"The kitchen dance?" A laugh bubbles out of me. "Is that like the chicken dance?" I take his hand, tucking the other under my arm and flapping it like a chicken.

Embarrassment brings heat to my cheeks, and I cringe, closing my eyes. Did I seriously just do the chicken dance? In front of this guy I have a crush on? No wonder all my first dates were so crappy.

"Is Dante's fifth circle of hell for bad dates?"

"Wow. I really went from one of your best first dates to the fifth circle of hell. Incredible work," he says dryly.

My head tips back as I laugh, and I finally take his hand. Warm, strong fingers close around mine, and I let him pull me to my feet, avoiding another near spill off the stool.

Luke moves gracefully, pulling one arm over my head and spinning me around easily. I'm grinning like a fool, following his surprisingly smooth lead as we dance in the warm silence of my kitchen, our meal abandoned on the counter.

Easy.

Despite his tough demeanor, that crusty, grumpy exterior, being with Luke Wolfe is as natural as breathing.

Easy as dancing barefoot around the kitchen and laughing as he dips me, then has me up and spinning again. His hands are warm on my waist, on my fingers, his smile slight and intoxicating all the same.

"Let me guess," I say on a laugh, "you're thinking of Yo-Yo Ma right now."

That gruff laugh is the only answer he gives, and it feels like a reward.

When he finally stops, we're both breathing slightly hard, and I'm fairly sure it's not just from physical exertion.

His gaze pins me, our bodies pressed together. Every bit of him that's hard muscle stands in stark contrast to the curves of my body, and I swallow thickly, desire winding me tight. My skin prickles as his thumb makes slow, deliberate circles where it rests on the small of my back.

"See?" I say, trying to sound casual. "Best first date ever."

"Like I said," he answers, one dark eyebrow raised, his eyes dancing with humor, "the bar is in hell."

"Then why does this feel like heaven?" I try to keep the question light, casual, but it comes out breathy and low, and something changes in his eyes.

The air goes taut between us, and before I can talk myself out of it, I'm tilting my face up.

"How much of that kiss earlier was for show?" he murmurs, one hand coming up to cup my chin, his thumb still steadily stroking the dip in my lower back.

I'm a live wire, charged and dangerous, electric and ready to make things happen.

"All of it," I say. "But not for the paparazzi."

The blue eyes fastened on mine darken, and his hand splays across my back, pressing me closer to him.

For you, I want to say. *It was for you.*

His fingertips tighten on my chin, just enough to send a shiver of anticipation through me, and then his mouth meets mine. Soft, first, a featherlight brush against my lips, and it's like dipping a toe into a perfect pool on a hot summer's day.

It's not enough.

My hands tighten on his waist. He groans, his hand going from my chin to my neck, the possessiveness of the gesture taking me by surprise . . . but not in a bad way. I like it. A lot. I moan in response.

The kiss deepens, his tongue sweeping against my lower lip, and I open my mouth reflexively. I feel my way up the back of his shirt, the sheer power of his body at my fingertips, begging to be touched. He steps near, his hand tightening around my throat, his body looming over mine.

Need spirals through me, and I tug him closer, until I can feel the beat of his heart through his skin. His other hand brushes over my shoulder, whisper-soft over the curve of my breast in the silk shirt, my body instantly reacting to the barest hint of his touch.

My nails dig into the fabric of his shirt, and I slide my hands up his back, bracketing them against the delicious muscles of his shoulder blades. Goose bumps pebble along my skin as his hold shifts.

His palms run down my back, his hands finally landing on my ass.

Everything in me seems to fixate on each single sensation. The slide of his mouth against mine, the wine-soaked taste of him, the way his breathing turns ragged the longer he holds me in his arms.

When he pulls away, my eyes flutter open, the reality of the moment crashing over me. My body still searches for his, aching—and he's watching me carefully, that openness I thought I saw in his eyes only a minute ago gone, shuttering.

My mouth opens, a question on my tongue.

"I should go," he says roughly. He's looking past me, at the food on the counter, then the door to the entryway.

At anything but me.

"Oh." The world's shifted in half a second, the possibilities narrowing down to this reality, where Luke walks away, leaving me breathless and wanting.

"You have an early morning. I don't want your Pilates instructor upset."

"Right." I feel brittle, like the tension spun me too tight. If I move too fast, think too hard about this, I'll shatter.

His gaze finally skates back over me. Air whooshes from my lungs in relief. My equilibrium is a mess, and I am 99 percent sure it's not from being dipped.

"Can I see you again?" His mouth scrunches up, like he's tasted something sour, the expression so at odds with the question that it takes me a moment to realize what he's even asked.

"Only if you *want* to," I snort, putting both hands up between us. "Don't feel like you *have* to or anything."

"I do want to, damn it."

I squint at him. "You're sending mixed signals again, Wolfe. Bark and bite."

That loosens the tightness around his eyes a little, his whole face softening.

"I would very much like to see you again," he finally grits out.

"Good," I tell him. "Because I would like that, too. Now get out before you change your mind. Pilates waits for no man."

He grunts, but it's an amused sound, and delight bubbles in my chest at the way he reluctantly grins and shakes his head at me.

It takes no time at all to walk him to the door, and for a split second I think he might kiss me again—but he doesn't.

"Night," he says, looking back at me over his shoulder.

"Good night, Luke," I say.

He pauses with his hand on his car handle. "I like that."

"What?" I ask, leaning against my doorframe.

"When you say my name."

With that, he gets into his car, all athletic grace, and he's gone in the blink of an eye.

Leaving me alone with the taste of his mouth on my lips and the thought that I like the so-called bad boy of soccer much, *much* more than I thought I would.

CHAPTER NINE

Luke

WE'RE ON THE main practice fields today at the Aces complex, and from the way I'm performing, you'd think I'd never been on them before. I'm completely distracted all through the morning's drills and tactical skills training.

The guys don't care—they never expect conversation from me on the field. The golden LA sun pales in comparison to the radiant smile of a woman I can't get out of my mind.

Warm-up only succeeds in me pondering how flexible Abigail is, how good she must look in the tight little pants I know a lot of women like to wear to Pilates. It's not until Tristan says something I half hear that I realize the rest of the team is talking about me.

One of the coaches blows a whistle, the familiar screech halting drills and signaling a short water break.

Marino elbows Gold in the ribs and jerks his chin at me, causing some of the other guys to start laughing.

"What the fuck are you saying?" I finally bark out.

"I just said you looked good last night," Marino tells me with his typical cocky grin.

"Fuck you," I tell him. I grab a water, staring him down.

He clutches his hands to his chest. "Sticks and rocks, Wolfe."

"Stones." Gold laughs. "How was the date?" He raises his brows at me. I don't know how he manages it, but he looks like if California were a person.

"None of your fucking business," I growl, swigging from the water bottle. My calves ache, and I stretch one out while still giving Marino the death stare, daring him to say shit to me.

"You made it all of our business when you got the LA Aces back in the headlines, you dick," Marino tells me, but there's no heat in his words.

"You actually like her," Tristan Gold says. He frowns at me, tugging his fluorescent orange keeper gloves on his hands.

"It was one fucking kiss," I growl.

"Yeah, one kiss that the notoriously mean fucker named Luke Wolfe gave in front of an ass-bus of paparazzi," Marino says in his thick Italian accent, pinching his thumb against his fingers and shaking it.

"Ass-bus?" Tristan asks with a laugh. "What?"

"Ass-van," Marino corrects, then scrunches his forehead as Tristan wheezes. "Many asses."

I shake my head.

"Ass-load," Tristan finally manages, giving me a look of amusement.

That's the thing with Tristan, our golden-boy goalie. No matter how much he fucks with someone, they can't help but feel he means well.

Usually, he does mean well. He's not a bad guy.

Sun glints against the glass of the air-conditioned seating at the top of the field, and when I glance up reflexively, guilt slides through me all over again.

The damned owners might be up there now, congratulating themselves on orchestrating last night's tabloid feeding frenzy.

"Is she a good kisser?" Marino asks. "She looks like a good kisser—"

"Fuck *off*," I snarl at him. "I told you to shut up about her."

Marino blinks, a slightly confused and hurt expression playing across his face before he turns away, storming to the other side of the field.

"What crawled up your ass?" Gold asks me quietly. "I would have thought you'd be in a better mood. Is it your mom? Is she worse?"

"I never should have told you she was sick."

He flinches, actually flinches, at the words, and guilt oozes through me.

Gold recovers in a flash, though, cocking an eyebrow, his signature half smile on his face.

"Sometimes you're so full of shit I nearly believe what you say." He punches me on the shoulder, and even though it's harder than usual, I don't move. I just glare at him. "Dude, I know you're upset about your mom, but she wouldn't want you to take it out on me."

I blink, knowing he's right, and slightly hating him for it. And slightly grateful for it, too.

Gold might be more stubborn than I am. Fortunately for me, it's in the opposite direction. He's as stubbornly positive as I am stubbornly an asshole.

"We should do karaoke tonight."

"I'm not going to fucking karaoke tonight." I shake my head.

"It will make you feel better. We can cue up some classic Mariah Carey, let you sing out all those big feelings," he says with a grin.

"Singing Mariah fucking Carey isn't going to make me feel better," I growl at him, torn between amusement and annoyance, the way I usually am around Gold's brand of friendship. "What the fuck is your obsession with karaoke anyway?"

"I've told you this a million times." He pauses, easily catching a ball someone punts at him. He tosses it in front of him, beginning a series of showy-trick bullshit with it that's more likely to get him followers on social media than help in any way, shape, or form on game day.

I tilt my head as he continues to juggle the ball off his body, waiting with growing impatience.

Gold continues to showboat, the ball arcing overhead as he bounces it off his chest, where it lands on the back of his neck.

As soon as he pops upright, the ball sailing to his foot, I steal it, then kick it back down the field.

"Who peed in your cereal?" he asks, then sighs, pushing his hair out of his eyes. "I'm not obsessed with it. I just think it's a good way to blow off steam. You could say no, you know. I can work on the new car I just had delivered."

He gives me an evil grin, and I know he's goading me, but I take the bait, the way I always do with Gold.

"It's a not a new car if you have to—"

"Rebuild it," he finishes with me. He laughs, and a small smile finally kicks up the corners of my mouth. "Yeah, trust me, you've told me that a time or two before."

"I just don't understand why you'd spend all that time and money fixing something when you can just—"

"Buy a new one," he interrupts in a gruff growl.

"Is that supposed to be the way I sound?" I ask him, amusement finally winning all the way out.

"I can color my eyebrows in with marker if you want a more realistic impression," Gold tells me blandly. "Maybe find a pair of those black fuzzy caterpillars and superglue them to my face."

"Sorry we weren't all born as handsome as you are, ass," I tell him.

"You think I'm handsome." Batting his eyelashes, he pretends to flip his hair over a shoulder, and I snort in spite of my shitty attitude. "I mean it, though, man. I'm sorry about your mom. I know you don't like to talk about it, or anything, or even talk, but I'm here if you need someone to listen."

"Or to sing karaoke with," I grumble.

"Absolutely," he agrees, laughing. "So, you coming over tonight to help me with my new-old car, or we going out?"

My jaw clenches, and I'm saved from having to answer when the coach blows his whistle again. "Wolfe, you're up. Gold, get in goal. Set pieces."

He didn't have to tell us what he wants—it's the same thing every Friday after drills. Corners are my specialty, and I know that's what he wants to start with, because that's what he always wants to start with.

We'll break for lunch, and then it will be time for physical therapy and one last strategy film watch before our game tomorrow. My feet eat up the turf as I jog onto the field, dribbling a ball easily, an extension of myself.

I crave it: the schedule, the predictability, the rules, the physical exertion.

Game days are different, of course. There's no set plays like in American football—there's a fluidity to it, art and skill and technique all combining with heady adrenaline in an addictive biochemical elixir.

But my usual flow state's off today, and I pull right, the first ball arcing wide and pinging against the bar.

Gold jogs out of the goal and shoots me a look I don't need to be telepathic to understand.

It's pity, and he thinks my mom's the reason why I'm out of it today.

If only he knew the half of it.

He doesn't know it's because the woman I'm supposed to be romancing on the owners' orders could be the girl of my dreams, and if I don't do it, I can kiss spending more time with my family goodbye—and Abigail Hunt will likely hate me forever if she finds out.

Gold passes the ball to me, and I set back up for the piece, inhaling deeply.

I'm not the type of man to give up on either thing so easily. I want both: off the fucking LA Aces and a real shot at whatever I'm feeling with Abigail.

My breath slows, my pulse following where my mind tells it to.

I take a step back, and another, then speed up as I head back toward the ball.

This time, it sails into the net easily, Gold misreading my feint and heading the wrong way.

If I can still misdirect the goalie who knows me better than anyone, I can do this thing with Abigail Hunt. She won't find out the reason I asked her on a date was because two greedy motherfuckers in suits told me to. She can't.

Gold passes me the ball again, and I set up, this time using my left foot.

I'm Luke fucking Wolfe.

I've always managed to play both sides and score.

This time won't be any different.

CHAPTER TEN

Abigail

FRIDAY LUNCH WITH Michelle seemed like a great idea yesterday.

A splendid idea. The *best* idea.

Now, after Pilates was a torturous memory of leg circles and endless bicycle-crunch variations, the only thing I want is to lie under a heating pad and wish for the sweet release of death. The worst part is, I feel good mentally . . . but I know I'll be even sorer tomorrow.

Darren's sent me a flurry of messages and GIFs, along with doctored photos of me and Luke kissing from all different angles. I make the one where Darren's photoshopped himself into the image his new contact pic and settle on sending him as many heart emojis as my texts will allow.

My arm aches as I hold the phone, and I scowl. Absolutely despicable how something so torturous makes me feel better. Foul.

Ah, the conundrum of exercise.

I settle for soothing myself with a long shower at the hottest temperature my water heater can produce, bemoaning my choice of clearly sadistic Pilates instructors as I wince and try to soap up every sweat-covered bit of my body.

It proves harder than it should.

My phone rings on the counter while I'm in the shower, and I'm not foolhardy enough to think I can manage to reach it in time at the snail's pace I'm currently failing to muster.

It's got to be Jean, anyway. She's the only one who calls me regularly—even my mom and dad know my habits well enough to know I prefer either texting or having a set time to talk to them.

I don't have to wonder why she's calling me, either.

"Pa-pa, paparazzi," I sing into the shower mist, then regret using my diaphragm for my killer Gaga impression as my abs silently scream in distress.

The photos of Luke and I were all over the tabloid sites this morning. Not that I looked—nope, my Pilates instructor decided to tell me about it at length, and then I think she took it personally when I was too out of breath to comment more on whether the LA Wolf was any good at kissing.

Probably not, but it sure as shit felt personal to my abs.

When I finally manage to turn off the water, feeling slightly more human, I have two missed calls, both from Jean, and one voicemail.

I stare at the phone, then at my bedraggled expression in the mirror.

"It's gonna be a good day," I sing, wiping my palm across the glass. An action that reveals dark circles under my eyes and a rough-looking mouth.

Well, that simply will not do.

Sure, I barely got any sleep because I was tossing and turning all night.

But it wasn't from nightmares or stress, for once—it was because I was excited.

Not in my usual chaotic hyperactive ADHD way, either, but truly just *excited* for the future. I snagged the role I wanted, Michelle's going to give me a great sense of what, exactly, a woman in the International Football Federation deals with on the daily, and I can just feel all the things I've been working toward for so long start to come within my reach.

Heat blossoms on my cheeks as I dig through my stash of eye and lip patches, because that's not the only reason I couldn't sleep.

I couldn't stop thinking about Luke Wolfe, either.

The way he held my face, his hand around my throat, that gentle pressure . . . even now, it's like I can feel his fingers there. His mouth against mine, the intense focus of his gaze and attention.

I haven't felt that real, that alive, in a long time.

Which probably means it's time to set up an emergency therapy sesh, because being in the public eye is a desperately bizarre experience . . . or time to admit that I simply like Luke. Maybe he's the piece I've been missing for a long time.

Which is stupid.

"Stupid," I tell my reflection, shaking a finger at myself before peeling open the pricey collagen patches my studio-appointed derma-tologist gave me. Goopy, they slide out of the packaging, and I plop them under my eyes, where, thanks to some kind of snail mucin and collagen magic, they stick.

A medical marvel.

Snails. Who would've guessed?

I hiss out a breath, a memory punching me in the gut. Olivia, my former *Blood Sirens* costar, also swore by the snails. Back when we were friends, before I murdered my reputation and, according to her, our relationship, Olivia and I would trade beauty secrets.

I stare at the gold-tinted patches under my eyes and wish, for the millionth time, that I could take back everything I said on the red carpet.

"A season everyone will be talking about," I'd squealed at the in-terviewer, my eyebrows raised sky-high.

They said it made me look like I was being sarcastic. They said my response was an indicator I hated the writing, hated the show, hated my best friend for stealing the spotlight. So much extrapolated from that one expression, from the tone I'd said it in.

Then the coup de grâce, the final blow that had people talking about the show—and me—for weeks afterward, and the comment I regret the most.

If only I'd kept my mouth shut.

"My daughters love this show—they want more than anything to be blood-drinking mermaids when they grow up. So glamorous! What would you say to all the teen girls who are going wild for this show and looking for a boyfriend like Xavier?"

"A boyfriend like Xavier?" I'd barked out a surprised laugh. "I mean, he's beautiful, but he's also the worst. You're talking about the Xavier who cheats on Olivia's character with mine, right? I'd tell those girls to raise their standards." I'd laughed again, slightly outraged.

"What do you mean? He's so dreamy!" The interviewer had said awkwardly.

"Well, yeah, he is, but he's also a nine-hundred-year-old vampire mermaid. Anyone else would call him a predator! Our characters are in high school."

The interviewer had blinked, quickly asking me something about what I'm wearing.

And that was all it took. Those words were all I had to say for the producers to claim I was trying to tank the show, for fans to say I was ungrateful and spoiled and woke, for Olivia to stop trusting me, to tell me no friend would have said that about the show that made us both into mainstream actresses and block my number.

It took longer for my ex-boyfriend to realize I'd fumbled my career . . . at least until the episode where *Blood Sirens* killed me off.

No one wanted to hire me after that.

So I continue my beauty routine, because hopefully a year has been enough time for the press to bury that story, and the least I can do is control how I look.

Since it's clear controlling everything else, including my runaway mouth, will never happen.

A new lip patch follows, and so does a fresh wave of heat, because I know the reason my lips are chapped is because I made out with an athletic god of a man last night. Well, that and I'm probably dehydrated. I stare pointedly at the bottle of ice water I brought into the bathroom with excellent intentions.

Too late to drink it now. I sigh through my nose, seeing as how my mouth is currently unavailable for breathing, and press play on Jean's voicemail before I comb some conditioner through my hair.

Wouldn't it be nice if I could go out in public and not care if anyone saw me? Or took my picture?

That type of thinking is ungrateful, though. So many other actors would kill to be in my position.

Jean's voice finally starts, and I wrinkle my nose as I drag the brush through my damp locks.

"Abigail, I just saw the pictures of last night. Want to tell me what the plan is here? You know I'm not opposed to stunt dating—"

My skin prickles at the accusation, annoyance rippling through me so hard I miss the next part of her sentence.

"—should have run it by me first. You know I don't like being caught off guard by some sort of publicity stunt. We could have soft-launched this as a strategy instead of going whole hog right away. We don't want it to overshadow the film, right?" She sounds annoyed, and I can tell from the blender noise in the background she's making her usual morning matcha smoothie.

I scowl at myself, and the lip patch starts to slip sideways, a silent reproach at an action that will no doubt leave me with frown lines.

The blender stops, and Jean audibly sighs. "Don't do anything stupid. I don't think we're in crisis-management mode yet, but you can bet your ass every interview is going to focus on this stunt with this soccer guy now instead of your new film. Let's have a call this afternoon to discuss what's going on."

I don't want to discuss what's going on. I don't want to triage it in Jean's imaginary PR war room. I don't want to work with the idiotically named "tiger team" on how to best manipulate the relationship for the media.

I want this thing with Luke and me to be real. I might not have realized that in front of the paparazzi last night, but by the time he left my house, I sure as hell did.

* * *

THE PLACE MICHELLE chose for lunch is an adorable French bistro in Southeast LA, close to the Aces' home office and practice facility.

Despite the typical horrendous traffic, the driver I hired got me here only a few minutes late, and sure, I'm slightly shaky from his lane-changing choices, but I am mostly on time.

Michelle's seated in a small room on the side of the restaurant, and the lunchtime crowd doesn't bother clocking me as I walk past, too busy on their phones or working on their laptops.

I'm used to being recognized, but I still heave a sigh of relief when no one stops me as the hostess leads me to her table.

"Abigail," Michelle says, a wide smile spreading across her face. She's impeccably dressed, in a cream silk blouse with a little bow at the collar and sleek denim trousers.

"Hey, hi," I tell her breathlessly. I'm wearing my favorite underrated band T-shirt and denim cutoffs with sandals, and though I'm comfortable, I feel sloppy next to her. "I should have dressed up." I gesture at her and then myself.

"Please, you look great. I have to go work at an office where I can count the number of women on one hand. You don't. Trust me, I don't dress like this all the time." She shakes her head ruefully, and I file that factoid away for later. "So . . ."

"I know, I know." I hold up a hand as I sit, trying to stave off the inevitable torrent of questions I'm sure are coming about Luke and me. "As you know, I kissed Luke Wolfe. Yes, he's a good kisser. No, it wasn't a PR stunt. And, yes, I would like to see him again. Yes, I also like him."

She blinks at me, her glossy dark brown ponytail slipping over her shoulder as she leans forward. "What?!"

"You weren't going to . . ." I stare at her.

She stares at me.

"You weren't going to interrogate me?" I finally finish.

Guitar music fills her stunned silence, and a waiter rushes over with a pitcher of water and a fancy marble slab laden with bread and artistically sculpted butter that neither of us touch.

Yet. I have my eye on that sourdough.

"Well, I wanted to hear about it, but you don't have to tell me anything if you don't want to," she manages, finally coming out of what I can only assume is preemptive oversharing-induced shock.

"Oh. Well." I close one eye, but it doesn't help the situation any. Sighing, I grab the sourdough and destroy the rose-shaped butter sculpture as I glob it on the top. "My Pilates teacher wouldn't stop asking me about it. My agent wants to have a"—I put my fingers up in air quotes—"'war room' about how to handle it, and my parents sent me the pictures of us kissing, asking when they get to meet him." I wince at that.

I always seem to forget that my shenanigans get back to my parents' small town. LA can be a weird golden sunshiny bubble, and I don't know why I forget that bubbles are totally permeable and that if I kiss Luke Wolfe in front of a dozen paparazzi, my mom is going to see it.

I'm pretty sure my sister taught her how to set up a Google Alert for my name.

Traitor.

"Oof." Michelle takes a slice of pumpernickel, using one of the cute little rabbit-topped butter knives to spread a bit on it. She even bites into it elegantly, and if I didn't like her, I might be a bit intimidated by her. Everything about her just screams poise.

Everything about me seems to scream "hot mess," and I'm not sure that'll ever change.

I sigh, slumping into the low-backed wicker bistro chair. The floor tiles are tiny black-and-white octagons interspersed here and there with gold. It's adorable and, like Michelle, also more put together than I will ever manage.

"It was a good kiss?" she asks, more curious than anything.

"Huh?" I glance up from the floor to her. "Yes." I sigh again. "It was a great kiss, and then he kissed me again when we went back to my place—"

She holds up a French-manicured hand, her eyebrows skirting her hairline. "He went back to your place?" She leans forward.

My hand shakes slightly as I grab the sweating pitcher, and ice tinkles into the charming floral-patterned glass. "He did, but it wasn't like that, you know? We wanted to finish our meal without the paparazzi. My house was nearby, and . . ." I shrug, setting the pitcher back down. "It wasn't like that! We just chatted, and then we danced in my kitchen, and you know, then we kissed, and then he left." God, I'm blushing again. Damn my stupid fair skin.

"He left," she repeats, the question implicit.

The cup is cool against my palms, and I resist the urge to put it against my flushed cheeks.

"He left," I agree.

"You're bright red," Michelle comments. "What happened?" She narrows her eyes, her grip on the butter knife suddenly alarming.

"The thing that happened that I didn't want to happen was him leaving," I blurt out.

"Oh." She replaces the butter knife on the marble slab. "Okay, then."

Michelle pauses, tilting her head as she considers me. "We don't have to talk about this if it makes you uncomfortable. Even if you did bring it up. Very dramatically, I might add. But if you're going to get all weird, please, don't keep talking on my account."

I blow out a breath, my cheeks inflating from the ridiculousness of it all. A few wisps of hair tickle my temple, and I push them back, frustrated.

"This isn't why we set up this lunch. You didn't meet with me to hear all the dirty details of my personal life," I say, aiming for sweet but missing and landing somewhere around disgruntled.

"If these are dirty details, then you lead a very boring life," she says, sipping her water. "And, yes, we absolutely did meet up because I think we should be friends." It comes out crisply, all business efficiency, and part of me wonders if I met some criterion she has logged in a spreadsheet somewhere. "We can talk about soccer and work whenever. We're going to be spending lots of time together over the next few weeks."

She pauses, twisting the napkin in her hands, threading it through her fingers.

"Okay—"

"Besides," she blurts out, an earnest expression in her brown eyes, "I could use a new friend. Working in a male-dominated sport isn't always a walk in the park. Or the soccer field." She grimaces at her attempt at a joke, and I snort, feeling slightly mollified.

I drink the rest of my water just for something to do, trying to sort out my scattered thoughts and then refilling the cup.

"What is it that's bothering you, then, if you like him?" she prods gently.

"I'm mad at myself for kissing him in front of the paparazzi." It comes out in a rush of words, surprising both of us with the immediacy of the statement. "I knew I liked him, and I knew I wanted a second date, and then we kissed again, and I realized . . . I blew my chance at privacy with him. I put us on display for the whole world on an impulsive decision." I take a drink. *Thanks, ADHD.*

"Ah," she says, refilling my glass for me, then her own.

A waiter appears with a fresh pitcher, and we both manage to pick something off the barely touched menus in front of us.

When he leaves, she twines her fingers together and sets her chin on top of them, watching me. "Does this have to be a bad thing? Can't you make it private now?"

"I mean," I hedge, tracing my fingertip through the water puddling on the table beside the glass. "Yes. Of course I could be more private, but . . ."

"The cat's out of the bag." Her mouth twitches to the side as she considers it.

I nod. "Right. Now other people are invested. Now I'm going to have a microscope on me when I go to games, when we're out together. If he even wants to see me again."

"You don't know if he wants to see you again?"

"I think he does . . ." I tell her, then am immediately plagued with doubt. My fingers twist the napkin in my lap, a napkin I don't even remember putting there. "Maybe he kissed me a second time to make sure it was as bad as he remembered the first time, and then he decided to leave."

Michelle laughs, and even that sound is put together and musical. "That is not true. At all."

"We don't know!" I tell her, shoving sourdough in my mouth, beyond even attempting manners. Carb therapy. "Maybe I am a terrible kisser."

"How was his body language? Did he seem grossed out?"

I flush even redder. "He had his hand around my throat."

"He what?!" she squeals, and the people at the table next to us turn to look.

"I am going to make my agent send you an NDA," I mutter darkly, pressing my hand against my eyes.

She laughs, but this time, it's not musical, there's a inelegant snort in there, and she looks slightly startled afterward.

"I'm not going to tell anyone. Like I said, I need friends, and you're fun."

"I'm a mess," I groan, but I smile at her from under the shield of my hand.

"A hot mess, especially if he had his hand around"—her voice drops to a whisper—"your throat." Her own palm goes to her collar, and she fans her face with her other hand. "That's quite something."

"Right?" I nod enthusiastically, then steeple my hands together. "So why did he leave?"

"Maybeeee . . ." Michelle draws the word out long, clearly searching for answers. "Maybe he's a gentleman."

"You've known him longer than I have. Does he seem like a gentleman to you?"

"He's always seemed like a fucking asshole to me. Blunt, straightforward, and you know where you stand with him. He doesn't put up with bullshit or internal politics."

"So why don't I know where I stand with him?"

"He's also an athlete with a game tomorrow night, and these guys, all of them"—her mouth twists to the side, and her gaze skips to the ceiling—"well, almost all of them—they're single-minded. It's how they made it to this level. Give him a few days. I guarantee you'll know where you stand by then."

"Dating sucks," I say grumpily, shoving the rest of the sourdough into my mouth.

"Agreed. Now, what do you want to know about soccer and my

job? Anything I can answer for you before I have to get back to the office?" She sits back, crossing her arms over her chest. "Unless you don't want to talk about work. At this point, I don't, either."

I squint at her, wondering if it's too soon to dig into what she doesn't like about her job, trying to read the situation. I don't want to pester her, and considering I've just dumped all my immediate relationship stress in her lap, I probably should back the hell off and at least make an attempt at being professional.

I take out my phone and pull up my Notes app. "I actually had some questions I wanted to ask. Just a few things to get me on the right track before table reads next week."

"Table reads?" she echoes.

"Yeah, it's the first time the cast gets together to read the script as a group. It's a whole thing." I wave a hand dismissively, but I'm grinning like an idiot because I love table reads. They're fun, and this is going to be a big film. "I'm excited," I tack on, just in case she can't figure that out.

"Oh, that does sound fun."

"All right, first question. What *does* the director of football operations actually do?"

Michelle snort-laughs again before she starts to explain her job.

Our food arrives, and as we eat, I make my way through my list of questions, taking notes while she answers, thoroughly and thoughtfully.

I can't stop checking to see if I have any messages from a certain Wolfe.

When none appear, though, I try to take heart in Michelle's words.

He's an athlete, and he's in game-time mode or whatever.

I can be patient.

"Well, I'll see you tomorrow night," Michelle says as we pay the check.

"Hmm?" I ask, signing carefully.

"At the game. You're coming to the game, right?"

"Oh. I hadn't thought about it." I don't know why I hadn't, probably because I've hyperfixated on not knowing where I stand with Luke.

"I'm sure you have plans, I'm sorry. I didn't mean to put you on the spot."

"No, I don't, actually. I planned to reread the script and prep for next week's table read."

"Oh, that's more important—"

"No." I grin at her. "A night watching soccer sounds perfect. It's research, right?"

"Research," she agrees, returning the smile. "We'll have fun, and I can explain how the game works while you watch."

Neither one of us mention the fact I'll be watching Luke and totally preoccupied with more than just the rules of the game.

CHAPTER ELEVEN

Luke

I FINALLY LET myself text her when I'm sitting in what the guys like to call the torture tubs. Filled with ice water, the tubs are both the bane of my existence and one of the most effective ways to stop the persistent ache in my joints after practice.

Four of us at a time can sit alongside each other in the physical therapy room, and of course Gold chooses the tub next to me as soon as I pick up the damned phone.

"Who're you texting?" he asks.

I glare at him.

"Abigail Hunt?" he guesses, grinning at my scowl. "Have you called her since last night?"

"No," I answer, surprising us both by speaking at all. Fuck. Now I've given him an invitation to offer up advice on my love life or lack thereof, when all I want to do is figure out how to ask her to see me again.

"Is she coming to the game?" he continues.

I sink lower into the ice bath, the initial shock of cold beginning to turn to a sort of slow-burning fiery sensation. Pain prickles through my skin, and I grit my teeth, knowing it will turn to numbness soon enough.

And then the physical therapist will take out her frustrations on my calves while I bite my tongue and make myself hold still.

Marino still hasn't lived down the way he begged for mercy in Italian during his first session with her three years ago. I can't help snorting at the memory.

"Are you laughing about asking her to come watch?"

"Nah. I was thinking about Marino and the PT—"

"No," Marino says, glaring at me with his pretty-boy face. He gets on the other side of me, and I roll my eyes. "Do not think about me at all. Wipe it from your memory."

Gold lets out a laugh, and my fingers hover over the screen. Do I ask her to come watch? I haven't invited a woman to a game since . . . my last girlfriend, over three years ago. Haven't felt like dating since her, either.

Not that I would have even asked Abigail out were it not for the goddamned owners.

"He's deciding whether to ask the movie star to our match," Gold tells Marino.

"Shut the fuck up," I growl.

They both laugh, and then Marino curses in Italian as the ice starts working on him.

I should invite her. It would be one more way to convince the owners I'm trying things on their terms, that I want to be released from the roster of players they won't trade. I get to see Abigail, and I get another piece of ammunition for moving off the Aces and back to Seattle.

"He looks constipated," Marino says in a hushed voice to Gold. "Do you think she would date me instead?"

They *should* have asked Marino to date her instead of me. He's more outgoing, he's pretty, he's talented—even if he's not as talented as he believes he is—and he has just as much star-power potential as I do.

The thought turns my stomach, and I tap out a message.

> **LUKE:** I enjoyed dinner with you

I send it before I think about it too hard, then immediately regret it. I should have asked her to the damned game.

Abigail answers nearly immediately, and my chest tightens slightly. I flex my feet in the ice, the numbness beginning to creep through my body.

> **ABIGAIL:** Me too! I'm going to your game tomorrow.
> Michelle invited me. I hope that's not weird. I didn't
> want you to think it was too much

"She's already going to the game," I say gruffly.

Gold cracks his eyes open, his head tilted back on the lip of the tub. "Good. Now tell her you want her there."

"Unless you don't want her there," Marino pipes up. "Then I will date her."

I look at him. Casually. Hold his stare.

He drops his gaze and sinks into the ice.

That's what I fucking thought.

I shake my head at myself in disgust at the sheer annoyance building in me. I don't fucking own Abigail Hunt. I should just tell her I asked her out because I was blackmailed into it.

Problem is, I do like her. I like her a lot, and the thought of Marino taking her out makes me want to punch him in his smooth-talking mouth.

That wouldn't be good for the team, and I can't afford to get suspended. Again.

That's the whole reason I've been on thin ice with the owners, despite how good I am on the field. How many times have other teams traded me because I started shit with my teammates? How many times have I been called an asshole because I can't be bothered to do the touchy-feely team building some of the other clubs invest in? How many fights have I been in?

I breathe out.

I also actually like Marino, despite all our differences.

So I text Abigail again.

> **LUKE:** I am glad you're coming. Sorry I didn't get the chance to invite you myself.

> **LUKE:** I'll be looking for you in the stands.

"Fuck," I mutter, the last message turning blue as it delivers.

"What?" Gold asked.

"I sound like an asshole."

"You *are* an asshole," Marino tells me cheerfully.

"What did you say?" Gold squints at me from his tub.

"I told her I would look for her in the stands."

"You actually like this girl," Gold says slowly, surprise written all over his face.

Why the *fuck* is he surprised?

"I'm allowed to like people."

"No, you are not," Marino says in his thick accent. "You are the Wolf. A predator. You stalk the fields and terrorize our opponents with your ugly face. You do not like people."

I throw a handful of ice at him, and it hits his chest before sinking into the tub.

"See?" Marino says, looking outraged. "Terrorize. That is what Luke Wolfe does." He shakes his head slowly, frowning. "I feel sorry for the poor girl. Once she sees the wolf's teeth, that will be it."

"Fuck off," I growl.

It just makes Marino and Gold laugh harder.

I want to be more than the LA Wolf.

I have a feeling that might be partly due to a certain woman in my life.

Before I can think better of it, I'm on the team's fucking internal communication app, asking for a bunch of things I've never asked for before, and the secretaries are only too happy to arrange the delivery to Michelle's box seats tomorrow night and to Abigail's house tomorrow morning.

I can be *fucking* nice. I can hide my teeth.

I think of my mother, hooked up to an IV full of radioactive drugs, thinner and paler every time I video chat with her. My sister's pinched expression in the background as she tries to tell me everything is all right.

Abigail's face replaces it as I close my eyes, all sunshine and chaotic fun. I don't want to hurt any of them.

I can't break it off with Abigail, even if I wanted to. Which I don't. I change my mind, sending another message through the Aces chat, asking them to send the things to the locker room as soon as practice is over. There. That's better—that will help me control the situation with Abigail.

See? I can play *nice*.

Too much is on the line not to.

CHAPTER TWELVE

Abigail

WHAT DOES ONE wear to a soccer game? I stare into my closet, where I have several gorgeous designer dresses, zipped up in their respective hanging bags, and realize I have no idea how to dress for this.

The doorbell rings, and my phone starts vibrating on the charger on my nightstand.

"Shit," I say, checking my watch. Michelle said the club would send a car for me and that it would be here before the game, but this is . . . way before the game. Hours before.

Who the hell is at the door?

I tug a hoodie on over the tank top and ratty sweatpants I'm wearing and grab my phone, checking the doorbell camera. A box mostly blocks the view, but I can see a man's athletic form behind it.

A delivery? I wasn't expecting anything.

I press the talk button. "Hi," I say brightly. "Can you just leave the box on the step, or do I have to sign for it?"

"Shit," a familiar voice says, sending a shock of tingles through me. Luke's face fills the camera. "It's Luke. I thought I'd, uh, bring over some things for you for today. The guards at the gate let me through, but you don't have to wear it—"

I squeal in delighted surprise, and Luke blinks at the doorbell camera. Crap. I still had the talk button on.

"Sorry," I manage breathlessly. "I'll be right there."

I race to the front door, smiling at the bouquet of flowers on my entry table and fling the door open.

Sure enough, Luke is standing there with a slightly bewildered expression, holding a large box in front of him.

I pause, because I hadn't realized how dressed up he was.

"You look great," I tell him, meaning it. He's in head-to-toe black. "Why are you so dressed up?"

The word *sexy* doesn't do him justice. I force my mouth to snap shut.

He glances down at his own clothes, as if seeing them for the first time. "We get dressed up to get to the field on game days."

"Oh." I had no idea. "You look incredible."

"So do you," he says roughly, and I laugh at that, because, no, I absolutely don't. My sweats have blobs of paint on them, and I know I should throw them away, but they're my favorites and I love them.

"What are you doing here?" I ask curiously. "Aren't you supposed to be"—I gesture at him vaguely—"getting ready?"

"I don't have to be there for warm-up and pregame for another hour and a half." His finger runs around the collar of his shirt, and I realize his look of discomfort is because he is, in fact, uncomfortable.

He's *nervous*.

It's freaking adorable.

I beam at him. "Come inside." I usher him in, and he cradles the box like it holds something fragile.

He stands in my entryway, too big for my house, his black-on-black suit contrasting with all the light-color walls. He looks distinctly out of place here and even grumpier than usual.

I love it. I loop my arm around his, tugging him into the kitchen and easing the box out of his hands.

"Do I open it?" I ask when he remains taciturn.

Shy, I realize. He's not grumpy—okay, yes, he is—but . . . is it possible Luke Wolfe is nervous because he's *shy*?

I shouldn't like that. I shouldn't have a little thrill go through me at the idea that maybe I hold more cards here than I thought I did, that I can maybe . . . drive our situationship forward a bit instead of being the Wolf's passenger.

My smile turns slightly evil as he grunts.

"Yes, Abigail, light of my life, I have brought you a gift," I say in the ridiculously low voice I reserve for impressions of him.

"'Light of my life'?" he repeats, cocking an eyebrow.

"Your words, not mine," I say with a shrug. A knuckle pops as I make grabby hands. "What's it gots in its boxes, precious?" My voice comes out as a sibilant hiss, and Luke blanches slightly.

"What the hell was that? That's not supposed to be me, is it?"

I stare at him, truly flummoxed. "That's my award-winning Andy Serkis as Gollum impression." My lips purse. "Well, award-winning only in my mind, but I can tell from your reaction you're impressed." I wink at him.

He shakes his head, and the corner of his mouth twitches, like he might smile, but he doesn't want to encourage the Gollum-esque behavior.

Ha.

"It's not that exciting," he says slowly, and I realize his frown might be, yet again, from that self-consciousness that he wears like armor. "Just a few things I thought you might want since you're going to be at the games more often."

Affection curls up in my heart like a cat beside a fireplace.

"You brought me things to wear to your games?" My voice is soft, and, embarrassingly, I feel like I might cry.

"Don't get bent out of shape about it."

"Don't worry, precious, I won't," I say, taking a Gollum-size sledgehammer to what could have been a tender moment.

He side-eyes me, shaking his head with a snort.

Got him to laugh, at least.

The tucked-in edges of the box make a susurrus of sound as he lifts them open, pulling out a black-and-gold LA Aces jersey. I take the slick fabric from him, turning it around—and when the word WOLFE jumps out in gold, I practically melt.

"This is your jersey," I say quietly, all traces of a former-hobbit-turned-goblin vanishing. "Your name is on the back."

"You don't have to wear it," he says, all gruff and dark eyebrows, looking down his too-strong nose as he crosses his arms over his chest.

I tilt my head, studying him, weighing his completely unromantic reaction against the gesture.

Luke Wolfe, I think, is a man of few words, and the few words he chooses are not usually very kind. I'm getting the impression he uses them to protect the very soft, squishy, and warm person inside.

"I *want* to wear it," I say, squinting up at him. He's so damned cute. "But only if you're okay with me wearing it."

"Why would I bring it here if I didn't want you to wear it?" he growls, frowning.

He's a ray of sunshine wrapped up in a storm cloud. That's my Luke Wolfe.

My eyes widen. Not mine. He's not *mine*.

"So . . . you do want me to wear it." I aim for playful, but it comes out hushed and serious. I sigh.

So, basically, I missed that target completely. If it were darts, I would have just slammed the pointy end into some unsuspecting bystander. RIP. I mentally pour a drink out for them.

"I do," he finally answers, just as seriously.

"To your game," I add, still holding the jersey up between us.

"That's right." He nods, a muscle in his jaw twitching.

"I love it." Before I can think better of it, I'm vaulting onto him, wrapping my arms around him, the jersey crumpled in my hand.

He tenses as our bodies make contact, and for a split second, I worry I've misread him. Then his sigh grazes the top of my head, and he cautiously puts his arms around me, too.

I relax into him, inhaling the scent of his spicy cologne and wanting to live right here, inside this moment, as long as I can.

"I'm glad." The words are a whuff of air against the shell of my ear. "You didn't look through the rest."

"I already have everything I want," I tell his chest, and when he laughs in surprise, the vibration rolls through me.

"You'll want more than one jersey."

"I wasn't talking about the jersey." It pops out before I can think better of it, and I hardly breathe, terrified I've fucked it up, asked for too much, been too sincere too soon.

"I didn't mean it like that," I backtrack, trying to put the cat back in the bag. "I just meant you're more important than a box full of clothes, and I think you're funny and sweet, but I'm not putting any pressure on you. We've only been on one date. That was stupid of me—"

"Abigail." The caress of my name on his lips shocks me into silence.

"You aren't stupid." His fingers go to my cheeks, thumbs stroking along my jawline, brushing butterfly light over my lips. "I . . . haven't been able to stop thinking about you."

That's all it takes to ignite me, my body going deliciously tight and needy in one heady moment.

"I know." I blink up at him. "I mean, I feel the same."

"I know what you meant," he growls, and then he kisses me, and it's nothing like either kiss that's come before.

I moan, the jersey in my hand falling to the floor as I rake my hand up the nape of his neck, curling my fingers around his hair.

Teeth tug on my lower lip, and I gasp with the thrill of it.

Luke lifts me off the floor in one impossible movement—and damn, I was already a fan of his muscles, but now I'm ready to make a club and head it as president—and sets me on the kitchen table. The box goes sliding as my back hits it, and we break apart as I huff a surprised laugh.

He watches me for a moment through heavy hooded lids, so serious and intense that the laugh starts to die on my lips, then turns to a gasp as he surges forward. His thick thigh goes between my legs, spreading them, his mouth kissing down my jaw, my neck.

"I hate this fucking hoodie," he breathes into the dip between my collarbones.

"Take it off, take it off," I chant, practically squirming against his thigh. God, he feels so good, so right. I don't want to think about what this means. I don't want to think at all.

He doesn't hesitate, simply tugging up the ribbed hem as I raise my arms straight up.

"Fuck me," he breathes, leaving the sweatshirt where it is around my wrists. "Look at that, Abigail. Fuck. You're so beautiful."

I look down, and all I see is my normal-size boobs and my white tank top, and I flush as I realize I didn't even throw a bra on before I answered the door.

"I forgot a bra," I squeak, unable to keep one damned thought inside my head.

"I fucking love it," he says. His chest is heaving, his blue eyes darkening as his eyes dilate, gaze traveling back to mine. "Can you stand having the sweatshirt like that?"

"Huh?" I ask, not understanding. My sweatshirt catches around my arms, pushing my boobs out. My nipples harden, and he groans.

Oh.

Wow. Did it just get hotter in here? Because holy hell, I am incredibly turned on by this man.

"Can I touch you?" he asks, his blue eyes on mine. Waiting, despite the fact that he's clearly desperate for this, for my permission.

"Please," I say, and my voice cracks on the word.

He doesn't touch me, though, not at first. I arch invitingly, scooting forward on the table, and he makes an animalistic noise as he bends down, capturing my nipple in his mouth. Warm heat builds in my core as he sucks the stiff peak, and I want to bury my hands in his dark hair, but the sweatshirt effectively keeps me bound.

He pauses, swearing under his breath, and I rock against his thigh with a wordless sound. With his next breath, he blows a stream of cold air against the wet spot on my tank, and my whole body goes limp and loose.

"Luke," I gasp.

"So beautiful, Abigail, so sweet." He lowers his mouth to my other breast, repeating the treatment. I want him to touch me everywhere, put his mouth everywhere. I might explode if he doesn't, but I don't want to rush him, either.

It's too good to rush. He kisses his way up my neck, his rough fingers rolling my nipples under the fabric of my shirt, and when he kisses me again, it's softer, needier, than I've felt him before.

He pulls away, and I'm weighing the possibilities of running straight to my bedroom and stripping naked as he kisses the tip of my nose.

"I have to go," he says.

"What?" I explode, finally shedding the sweatshirt. "What do you mean?"

He gives me a pained look. "I can't do this right now."

Hurt is a slap in the face, and I blink rapidly, trying to come to terms with it. "You mean a relationship? Or sex? Or both? Is it me?"

Luke's smile is unexpected and slow, but it doesn't do much to staunch the flow of pain.

"No, it's not you. Believe me, I want you, Abigail. A relationship with you. Sex with you. Both. But not right now."

"Oh . . . did I move too fast?" The hurt lessens gradually as his words sink in.

"*No*. Fuck, no. You're . . . perfect." He shakes his head, and something dark passes over his expression as I watch him carefully. "I can't have sex before a game."

My nose wrinkles. "What?"

"Yeah," he blows out a breath. "I don't know, maybe it's superstitious."

I glance down at the bulge in the front of his black suit pants. "You're going to play the whole game with a massive hard-on?"

He winces. "It'll go away. Eventually."

I don't know what to say to that. "And if I wear your jersey to the game? Do I get to see you after?" If I hook one calf around his thigh, sue me. I am not about to let him forget what we could be doing.

"Fuck yes. After. All night."

"You're sure?" I ask, bravado dying away as quickly as it came. "I don't want to . . . rush you. Or make you feel uncomfortable. Or . . . I don't know, ruin things between us because I got impulsive."

"Abigail." He presses his big hand against my cheek, his fingertips gently scraping against my scalp. "I like how impulsive you are. I like how you say what's on your mind and do what you want in the moment. You aren't going to rush me. I will go at whatever speed you want, even if that means . . . I don't know, we cuddle on the couch and eat ice cream or some shit. If you change your mind after the game, that's your choice." He pauses, his blue eyes soothing something in my brain. "You don't owe me anything."

"I think that's the most words you've ever said at one time."

He raises an eyebrow, because we both know that's not a real response.

I know I'm dodging, because, damn it, this is scary and new. And exciting.

"I don't want to eat shit on the couch," I tack on. "Ice cream, maybe. Shit, no."

He laughs gently, touching his forehead against mine. "Got it. Tell me you understand this, though."

I wait for the other shoe to drop. He's going to tell me he's too busy for a relationship. That this is just about sex and fun. That he has to focus on the season. That I'm going to be a distraction if I want more.

"I am an . . . intense sort of person."

It's so quiet I have to strain to hear him.

"When I decide I want something, I go after it. But that doesn't mean I expect the same from my partner."

Well. That's a new one.

He's silent, his eyes closed, the impossibly thick fringe of his lashes the only thing I can focus on. That, and the delicious masculine smell of his cologne.

"Okay," I finally say when I realize he's waiting for a response. "I like that."

I do, too, and I like it even more when his hand skates down from my face, over the damp circles he left over my hard nipples, and between my thighs. He rests it proprietarily there for a minute, and I squirm, my breathing quickening as he runs his finger down the center of my sweatpants.

"If I don't leave now," he grits out, "I'm going to break my own rules, be very intense with you, and then play very badly because all I'll be able to think about is your soaked pussy."

"You better leave, then," I say wispily.

"I better leave." He strokes his fingers again, and I groan, raising my hips. "Fuck, Abigail."

"I'd like that," I tell him fervently. "Yes, please."

Luke doesn't move for a long moment.

"Fuck me," he says, and I moan as his thumbs hook into the waistband of my sweatpants, pulling them down over my thighs. "Tell me what you want."

"Everything," I breathe, hardly daring to blink, not believing my good luck. "But I don't want to force you if you have your game thingy."

"Game thingy," he huffs, shooting me a disbelieving look from behind those thick black lashes.

"Superstition." I am honestly beyond impressed that I've remembered a word that has more than one syllable. Go me.

"Oh," he says, a smile creasing the corners of his eyes. "That thingy."

"Can you blame me for forgetting the word?" I mean it to come out playful, but it doesn't. It's breathy and so, so needy.

He doesn't answer, just tugs my pants down completely, swearing inaudibly at the scrap of fabric left between us. I kick my legs a little, pointing my feet until the pants slide all the way off.

"Tell me what you want." The words are haggard, and when his eyes meet mine they're pleading.

"Tell me what *you* want," I say quietly, feeling fragile and afraid. Not of being naked in front of him, because he's looking at me like I'm a piece of art, like I'm some kind of wondrous creation he can't glance away from. "You're the one who has rules about this kind of thing."

"You don't have rules about sex?" There's an edge to his voice, and his thick hands clench around my ass as he pulls me closer to him. His mouth finds mine again, plundering, so needy and delicious I can hardly breathe.

"Not any that revolve around soccer," I finally squeak out. "Sex, though, sure. I suppose. Balls, sure, sometimes."

He tugs my shirt off, and it joins my sweatpants on the floor. "Balls?" he finally asks, a smile on his face. "What are your rules about balls?"

I squirm, completely incapable of thinking of anything clever at all. "They have to be clean. Clean balls." I cringe.

He laughs again, a throaty sound I could get very used to. "I'll try to remember that," he says. "Cleaning the balls before sex. I can do that."

My hands stroke up and down his arms, loving the feel of him, of his muscles and the way he's looking at me. Treasure. It hits me—that's how he's looking at me—like I'm some kind of treasure he's unearthed.

His gaze travels down my body, nearly naked for him, for us both, and I swear it leaves a hot trail behind on my skin. Seconds tick by, and I wonder how far I'd have to push him to get him to abandon his no-sex rule.

"Let me taste you." It's halfway between a demand and a request, and my throat goes dry.

"If you don't, I might die," I tell him seriously, flinging the back of my hand against my forehead.

He grins again, huffing a laugh that cascades across my bared skin, making me shiver.

Then his mouth is on mine again, so fucking right that if I do die, this is a damned good way to go. He pulls away only to kiss down the column of my neck, hot and needy and sending me spiraling tighter and faster.

"I might regret this," he says against my collarbone.

"I'm not going to talk you out of it, but I don't want you to regret eating me out."

Very sensible on my part. Very thoughtful.

He cuts his gaze back up to me, sliding his big hands down my thighs, pressing them apart. Bared to him, vulnerable, I press my palms against the table, arching my back and raising an eyebrow in challenge.

"It's not eating you out I'll regret. It's the fact I can't take my time making you come over and over again right now that I'll regret." He's so damn serious when he says it. I blink.

"Oh," I finally say.

"Oh," he repeats, grinning.

"Wellll," I stretch out the word, then wrap one leg around his hip. "Do you want your appetizer on the table, on the floor, or somewhere else?"

I can hardly believe the words coming out of my mouth, and we both stare at each other as if daring the other to make a move.

He breaks first, and he springs into action so fast that all I can do is make a surprised squeak as he pulls me against him, pulling me into his arms.

"Wheee," I say as he practically sprints for the living room. I laugh as he tosses me onto the couch. "Couch it is. TV dinner."

"No, Abigail, I'm the entertainment, and this is just a snack."

It makes me laugh a little, even though his eyes are serious, and then he's kissing down my chest, lavishing attention on each nipple again until I'm writhing with desire.

"You're so beautiful," he says against my chest. My breathing's ragged and rushed, and I can't even think of an answer, my mind blessedly quiet for once in my life.

My skin heats as he drags a finger down my stomach, gaze still watching my face, watching my reactions, I realize. It makes me smile, something warming deep in my chest that has little to do with the heat of desire racing through me.

There's an air of calculation to the way he's watching me, like he's cataloging every breath I take, every small noise or expression. Like he's mapping my body with every new touch, figuring out exactly what I want, reading me like an open book.

He moves lower, his breath teasing as he hovers over my underwear.

"Tell me yes."

"Please, please yes," I tell him, my fingertips scraping against his dark hair.

The faintest hint of pressure at my hips, and then his fingers tug my underwear from them. Ever patient, ever deliberate, he lifts one of my legs, pulling the black scrap of fabric over my foot, then repeats the process with my other leg.

Rough fingertips glide over my skin, and I shiver as his hands bracket my hips, pinning me to the couch. I'm afraid to breathe, afraid to say the wrong thing or think too hard for fear he'll change his mind.

My ex-boyfriend, who is the last person I want to think about right now, hated this. Didn't like oral sex at all, thought it was a waste of time.

I'm nervous, I realize. A second later, I realize I'm holding my breath.

I want him to like this. I want him to like me. "I don't want you to feel like you have to do this," I blurt out.

Well, shit.

"What?" His brow's furrowed with concentration, and it's a mix of the sweetest and sexiest thing I've ever seen. "Why would you think I feel like I have to?"

"I—" I don't have words. "I just wanted to say that," I tell him in a small voice.

He watches me for a moment before saying in a gruff voice, "If someone ever, ever made you feel like you had to say that, they can fuck right off." His thumbs gently sweep back and forth across my hip bones. "Being able to taste you, to give you this—that's a fucking gift."

Then his mouth is in between my legs, and my eyes roll back in my head.

"Luke," I murmur, desperate for more, for the coiling readiness tight inside me to find an outlet.

He licks my clit, working his tongue around it in delicious little circles, like a man on a mission. I groan his name again, my hips bucking against the press of his mouth right where I need it.

"That's right, Abigail, take what you want," he tells me. One hand moves from my hip to the curve of my ass. His fingers grip it so tight that I cry out in surprise, and he redoubles his efforts.

"So fucking perfect, aren't you?" he says.

"So close," I agree. My fingers tangle in his hair like it's the only thing anchoring me to reality.

"You're going to come for me, aren't you?" he says, looking up from hooded lids between my legs.

I nod, slightly frantic for him to stop talking and put his money where his mouth is. Or an orgasm where his mouth is. Either or.

Preferably orgasm.

His other hand slides between my legs as he continues to work me with slow, torturous circles. I suck in a breath as he slips a finger inside me.

"So wet." The observation is ragged, and I can't breathe, I can't answer.

"Feels so good," I practically wheeze.

"That's fucking right."

He adds a second finger, stretching me deliciously, his mouth picking up speed as I pant and writhe beneath him, holding on to his hair and the couch for dear life.

His two fingers pump in and out of me, and there are no thoughts. It feels *perfect*.

When he clamps down on my clit, sucking it hard, I cry out, seeing stars before I go limp, my stomach and leg muscles twitching.

He keeps licking, slowing down, pulling me slowly from that apex of pleasure, until I manage a tiny hiccup of a noise and push at his head, too sensitive for more.

When he finally pulls away from my body, he licks his lip, a smug smile firmly in place.

"That was . . ." I stare at him, a shiver wracking my limbs, totally satisfied and somehow still wanting more. "Awesome."

"Good," he says, kissing one knee as he pulls my underwear back on. "I'm glad."

I reach for him, until he finally laughs and clambers on top of me, kissing my forehead, the tip of my nose, and then my mouth.

It's soft, and yet there's still a hard edge of need to it.

I slide my hand down the incredibly hard stomach muscles, reaching for him. "I can return the favor—"

"Nope." He laughs, standing up and shaking a finger at me. "I might regret it, but I'm not going that far against my own superstitions."

"But—"

"Nope." He grins at me, his attention sliding down my spent and mostly naked body. "You are beautiful, Abigail. So beautiful. Thank you."

"Thank *you*," I say, still breathless with wonder and postorgasmic euphoria. "Are you sure I can't just maybe—"

"Wear the jersey," he interrupts, putting more space between us.

He takes a ragged breath, and I wriggle a little, giving him a tiny mischievous grin.

"Wear the jersey," he repeats, and I smile wider, wondering what he would do if I didn't. Wondering what he'd do if I did.

"What do I get for wearing the jersey?" I ask, batting my eyelashes.

"What do you want?" he says, his gaze darkening.

Ooh, I like that.

I drop my attention to his cock, which is bulging deliciously in his pants.

"A ballpark frank," I chirp at him. "With an encore performance."

He laughs, which I love, because I'm nothing if not absolutely needy when it comes to my terrible punch lines.

"That can be arranged." In one smooth motion, he bends, grabbing my hand from where it dangles off the side of the couch. Slowly, he drops his lips to it, brushing the barest of kisses across my knuckles.

"I'll see you tonight," he murmurs. "I'm sorry you don't have time to explain the finer points of your rules about balls right now."

It's my turn to laugh, and from the way slight surprise and gratitude flashes over his face, I get the feeling he's not used to it—to making other people happy, making them laugh.

It feels like a secret, and I turn it over in my head as he kisses my knuckles one last time before leaving.

The door closes quietly behind him, and I stare at it for a long time, still mostly naked on my couch, recovering from what has to be one of the top five best orgasms of my life.

I would say top three, but I don't want my expectations to peak early.

Although, Luke might just be the type to take that as a challenge.

CHAPTER THIRTEEN

Luke

I GET TO the field early. It helps that I went twenty over the speed limit the second traffic opened up on the way here.

I don't think that I've ever been this sexually frustrated in my life. I have certainly never let myself get so out of my mind over a woman before.

I can still taste her on my lips, and it's driving me fucking nuts.

Not only that, but Abigail Hunt's mismatched green and hazel gaze is seared into my brain.

Her sweet, silly mannerisms, the quick goofy comments, the way she laughs at herself and blurts out whatever she's thinking.

She couldn't be more my polar opposite.

I shouldn't have gone over there to deliver the fucking Aces swag. I should have let the front office deliver it. I definitely shouldn't have pulled off her sweatshirt and tasted her through her tantalizingly thin undershirt.

I should regret spreading her legs until she scratched my scalp and moaned my name as she came for me.

Considering I'm leaving LA as soon as I can and the only reason I asked her out in the first place is because my fucking bosses told me to, I might be the biggest asshole in the entire world.

Worst part is, now that I've had a taste, I can see making it a habit.

Kissing down her beautiful skin as she pants and unravels, watching her cheeks pink as I make her come with my tongue and my hands.

One taste of Abigail Hunt and I'm addicted.

Fuck me.

I pull into my parking spot in the player's garage and turn off the ignition, leaning my head against the steering wheel. What the fuck am I doing with her?

Moving way too fast, like I always do when I want something, single-minded to the point of stupidity.

What is sometimes the hallmark of a great athlete can also be the hallmark of an absolute asshole in a relationship.

I cannot bulldoze Abigail Hunt. I cannot satisfy whatever this craving is for her just to get my way off the Aces and back to Seattle.

I repeat the words to myself as I pull my duffel from the back seat and walk into the arena. I want to get home to my mother, to my family, help my sister and my stepdad with her.

I want to give back to the one parent who didn't leave me.

Unlike my father. My father, who taught me to play soccer. Who left when I was eleven. Who I just thought if I could be good enough for, he would come back.

The father who forgot so many birthdays the forgetting is almost all I remember of them. The father I left tickets for at will call every game of my first pro season, who promised to come.

He never did.

I was never good enough.

I haven't left a ticket for him again.

My knuckles are white where I clutch the handle of my bag. The sun beats down overhead, near blinding me when I emerge from the parking garage near the stadium.

I can't do this.

Using Abigail to get where I want, even if it's home to be with my sick mom, is something *he* would do. He made us all love him, made us think we were important, until it became clear that he was the only important thing in his world. A lesson I learned much too late.

There's a smattering of paparazzi here already, and I scowl at them, which they love, all the while telling myself I need to leave Abigail the hell alone and figure out another way off the Aces. Seattle isn't that far from LA, after all, and while commuting up there isn't the same as being down the street from my mom, I can make it work if the asshole owners don't trade me.

My jaw aches from grinding my teeth.

There is no reason to mix her up any more in this than I already have.

I should call it off with her tonight.

My phone's in my pocket, and once I'm safely in the locker room, I pull it out, fully intending to cancel our postgame date tonight.

There's a few texts from her.

My finger floats over the screen. I could delete them unread.

I tap on the messages.

> **ABIGAIL:** Thank you again—I can't wait to see you play later. I'm excited to cheer you on with your jersey on
>
> **ABIGAIL:** That was repetitive. Have a good game. Break a leg
>
> **ABIGAIL:** Shit. That's something actors say. It's probably not something soccer players say. I meant good luck.
>
> **ABIGAIL:** You probably knew that. Don't break your leg
>
> **ABIGAIL:** I have plans that involve all your legs and your ballpark frank. Do not break any of the above
>
> **ABIGAIL:** I'm embarrassed please pretend this conversation never happened

My cheeks hurt, and it startles me to realize I'm smiling wide enough for that to happen. *I'm not going to be able to break it off with her.* I am not sure I ever will.

Fuck.

> **LUKE:** I knew what you meant
>
> **LUKE:** I won't break a leg if I can help it
>
> **ABIGAIL:** You better not. You made some big promises today. I expect the full performance asap
>
> **ABIGAIL:** Maybe an encore or two

My dick immediately gets hard, and I grit my teeth.

> **LUKE:** I'll be ready

I make myself turn off my phone. If I keep texting her, I'll be playing with the worst case of blue balls in my life. Competing with a little excess testosterone is a good thing—unmitigated levels of sexual frustration, however, is not.

I want to win. I always want to win.

But today, I want Abigail to watch me win.

CHAPTER FOURTEEN

Abigail

AIR-CONDITIONING BLASTS IN the box, frigid cold battling with the balmy golden heat outside. My thighs are cold, the tip of my nose is cold, and my fingers are half frozen. I'm surprised the glass hasn't frosted over.

My calves and lower thighs are toasty, though, considering I shoved my legs into over-the-knee black boots, because I thought they'd look sexy with the Wolf's jersey. Underneath, I'm wearing teeny-tiny spandex shorts I usually reserve for Pilates.

Ridiculous double bubble braids complete the look, along with thick dark sunglasses that make me feel both glamorous and like no one can see the white-water torrent of thoughts in my head.

"Sorry, I'm late," Michelle calls out, and I turn away from the field, grinning at her.

"Okay, glam soccer queen," she adds, looking me up and down. "You look adorable."

"I feel stupid," I admit. "But thank you."

"No, you look so cute." She picks at her trousers. "I have to come to these things somewhat professionally. Your outfit is a breath of fresh air."

"I am getting a lot of air." I pluck at the short hem of the jersey.

"Did Wolfe give that to you?" Michelle asks, her brown eyes wide. "I heard a rumor he was having swag sent to your house."

"He brought it over this morning," I say, biting my lip and trying to ignore the fresh heat wave at the memory.

"He brought it over to your house?" she asks, her voice pitched higher. "Oh, that is so freaking cute. See? He does like you."

"He said he did," I agree, making myself look at her. I might have told her about our first kiss, but I'm not about to tell her about how he went down on me.

My glasses are a bit stupid facing away from the sunny field, so I push them up on my head.

"Oooh, glitter," Michelle says. "Shiny."

"I wanted to match the gold." I feel extra ridiculous now. Bubble braids and glitter eyeshadow. What am I, a kid?

"I love it. You really look supercute. Very WAG of you."

Michelle clocks my confused look and clarifies, "Wives and girl-friends."

She grabs a menu from one of the tables as I digest that.

"What do you want to eat?"

"Wives and girlfriends?" I repeat, still stuck on it.

"It's just what the player's, you know, wives and girlfriends are called." She doesn't look up from the menu, plopping down on one of the cushy couches and crossing her legs.

"Am I his girlfriend?" I mutter, glancing down at myself like the answer is written somewhere on the jersey he gave me.

"Maybe." She's looking up at me now, eyes crinkled in both amusement and something else I can't quite place. "If he's given you his jersey . . . I don't know. It's like a thing."

"A thing?"

"A thing," she agrees, as if that answers everything.

"A good thing?" I press.

"Yeah . . . if you want to be his girlfriend. It's kind of soon, if you ask me. But you seem into it, and he seems into it, so why not? It's not like you're getting married next week."

I'm silent, trying to process everything she's just said, when I realize she's staring at me.

"You're not getting married next week, are you?"

"What?! No." I laugh nervously.

"Good. Remember that football player that got married in Vegas to his team's cheerleader? That was something. Great for publicity, though."

"Oh. Yeah, I do remember hearing that."

"There are a lot more press here than usual," she continues, clearly in work mode. It makes me a little sad for her, that she's unable to relax even here, in her own box. The Michelle that had lunch with me yesterday is not quite the same woman sitting here scanning through the menu filled with cheese fries and tater tots and overlarge hot dogs.

"Hot dogs?" she asks just as I think it.

I have a craving for a different type of sausage, but I make myself nod at her before that thought can make it out of my mouth. Michelle might be friendly and I like her, but I don't think she wants to hear about *that*.

Look at me. I do have boundaries. Who knew?

"Sure," I say easily. "Cheese fries?"

"And beer?" she responds.

"Yes, definitely beer."

"Awesome."

She puts in the order, and I turn my attention back to the field. My Pilates instructor, Lauren, is going to kick my ass tomorrow, and beer won't help, but I'll deal with that when I sweat it out with her.

As soon as I turn back to the glass, I see them.

Not the players on the field, but the freaking paparazzi. They're in the stands below us, their cameras not on the green stretch of turf but swiveled on me, the lenses glittering in the late-afternoon sunlight.

I swallow hard and put my glasses back on the bridge of my nose, my palms immediately going sweaty despite the chill of the AC.

"What's wrong?" Michelle's standing next to me, shaking out her long dark brown hair from her severe bun. It settles in waves around her shoulders.

"Just saw the paparazzi."

"You don't like them."

"Nope."

Her cheeks puff as she blows out a breath. "Fuck 'em."

"I think that would be frowned upon."

"Shut up," she says with a laugh. "You know what I mean. Fuck 'em. Forget they're here. So they snap a few pictures of you having fun in the box. It's not like you're going to strip naked and jump down into the stands to crowd surf, right?"

That makes me laugh, and an evil little smile curls my lips. "No . . . unless?"

"No," Michelle says decisively. "Absolutely not."

"I was just kidding," I say on a laugh.

"Mmm-hmmm." She cocks an eyebrow, and I think we both know that I'm unpredictable enough that her worry was warranted.

A wave of disappointment in myself washes over me. Everyone thinks I'm an impulsive fuckup because I *am* one.

I just won't talk about this project. I'll keep my mouth shut about work. I'll stick to the script. I don't have to say anything.

Maybe getting involved with Luke was a mistake.

The mere thought makes my chest tighten up.

Michelle's still watching me carefully, so I give her a wan smile before I head out of the box and to the seats in front of it. Deliciously warm sun heats my cold skin immediately, and I sigh, tilting my face up to the cloud-dotted sky above.

In the distance, the LA hills live up to their icon status, the picturesque panoramic view easing some of my anxiety.

I am here not as Abigail Hunt, wannabe Oscar winner. I'm here as a fan to support a guy I'm dating.

I'm dating Luke Wolfe.

The simple thought makes me smile, and I scooch down to the middle seat and settle in, ignoring the calls of some of the more determined photographers below.

Tonight, I can just exist, hang out with Michelle, and try to forget all the Hollywood pressures as I cheer for Luke and the Aces.

I can just be me. The real me.

On the field below, the players are jogging around, warming up and chatting. Luke's easy to spot with his dark hair and huge stature, and he mostly keeps to himself as he stretches, which is no big surprise.

He looks good enough to eat.

"Foods here," Michelle says, and for a second, I think I've spoken aloud, until she makes her way to the seat next to me, handing me a cold beer in a plastic cup and a boat of fries swimming in cheese and topped with bacon and green onions.

"Thanks," I say.

"You sure you're okay?"

"I'm good," I reassure her. I like Michelle, I respect her, but at the end of the day, it's hard to know who to trust here, and I'm not about to unload my panicky thoughts to her and simply hope she won't sell them to the tabloids.

Instead, I paste on my biggest grin and swig from the cup before setting it next to me and digging into the gooey perfection that is the cheese fries.

"They're battered?" I say through a mouthful, my eyes rolling back in my head in bliss. "These are so good."

"Right? Not bad for stadium food. That was one of my major suggestions when I came on board."

"To batter the cheese fries? I didn't know your job required you to make those kinds of calls." I'm only half serious, and she laughs.

"No, just to upgrade the food in general. Have some more of the normal things like nachos and hot dogs, but offer a few stands that are more upscale and have the prices to match."

"You did good," I tell her, and I mean it. "These are delicious."

I shove a few more fries in my mouth, then remember I have an audience with cameras pointed at me, and decide I'd rather not be plastered all over the internet later with commenters picking apart my eating habits.

"There were a lot of little ways to make the organization more profitable, cut some of the unnecessary spend, you know." Michelle's scrolling through her emails, and I try not to read over her shoulder.

Nosy habits die hard.

"Are we the only two in the box tonight?" I ask. "I wasn't sure what to expect."

"Yeah, this box is one of the perks of the job, and I figured you might not want people listening in while we talked about the game and the business. Plus, it's a great place to talk without being overheard." She gestures vaguely at the fan section behind one of the goals, and sure enough, they're setting up what looks like an entire brass band and drum line, practically every seat filled with people in gold and black face paint and outrageous outfits.

"Wow." My eyebrows raise behind my thick black glasses. "They seem serious."

"That's one of the best parts of this team, in my opinion. The Aces' superfans are something else."

"How so?"

"You know," she says slowly, turning to look back at me, "Luke has his own little fan club over there. They're obsessed with him. They gave him his own chant and everything." She nudges me with her elbow, and I sip my beer, intrigued. "See?"

Sure enough, a fan dressed in a full wolf suit, like a mascot, is heading down the bleacher-style seating as people high-five them. There's a poster with glittering, fluorescent letters in their hands, and I strain to read it.

"'Hunt the Wolf,'" I finally manage.

Michelle lets out a surprised laugh.

Slight unease grips me. "I take it that's not the normal chant?"

"Nope. I think they did that for you," she says, her nose crinkling in sympathy. "Is that weird?"

"A little," I admit. "Part of the job."

It is part of the job, and I invited that kind of crap as soon as I kissed him outside the little Italian restaurant. It's my fault, and I shouldn't feel uncomfortable about it.

I should feel grateful that people care enough to make hand-lettered signs and bring them to Luke's game. Shouldn't I?

No sooner has the slimy feeling of discomfort and guilt hit me than I'm standing up, waving to the wolf-costumed fan holding the sign.

See? I can do this. I can be fine with constantly being on display and scrutinized. Just part of the gig.

Someone tugs on the wolf's arm, and they finally see me, then jump up and down, holding up their sign. I give an exaggerated laugh and blow a kiss at them before settling back down.

I'm fine with it.

Michelle's gaze pins me, though, and I get the very uncomfortable feeling that she sees right through my bullshit.

"Sometimes it's better to own the narrative," I tell her carefully.

The beer tastes better on the third sip, I decide, and it only shakes slightly as I put it back in the cupholder.

"Right," she says, and I know I haven't fooled her at all.

"Okay, tell me what to expect. For the game, I mean."

"How much do you know? About soccer?"

I give her a look. "Assume I know nothing."

She grins at me, then steals a fry from the boat on my lap. "You got it."

By the second half, I'm in love. The game is fluid, more graceful than I expected, and I'm constantly surprised by how engaged I am, especially considering the goals are few and far between.

The athletes themselves are stunningly graceful and fast, and none of them more so than Luke Wolfe, who I can't stop staring at.

He's magnetic all the time, but on the field? He's unbelievable.

It seems unlikely that a man of his size and bulk should be able to move as fast as he does, and the way his foot finds the ball like it's an extension of himself . . .

Makes me think what else he could find so easily.

I fan my face, despite the fact the sun's been replaced with stadium lighting and the air's turned slightly chilly.

When Luke breaks away, moving down the field like a huge wolfish predator, I jump to my feet, the rest of my now warm beer sloshing over the side of the cup.

"Go, Luke, go!" He's going to score, I just know it. There's no hesitation in him at all, that intense focus that I've become familiar with now set at the opposing team's goal.

The fans at the end zone are cheering like crazy already, like the ball sinking into the net is a foregone conclusion.

Sure enough, Luke feints left and shoots right, and the goalie or keeper or whatever they call it in soccer goes the wrong way. The ball glides past him, hanging in the air for an interminable length of time before slamming into the net.

I scream again, jumping up and down in my thigh-high boots, Michelle on her feet, clapping and laughing next to me.

"L-A WOLF, L-A WOLF, L-A, L-A, L-A WOLF!" The crowd chants as one, before breaking into a cacophony of howls. The noise from the drum line behind the Aces' goal is so loud I can feel it in my bones.

Down on the field, Luke jogs backward, scanning the crowd.

The moment he spots us is obvious. For one, he smiles so broadly that even the cameraman zooms in on it, his joyous expression displayed on the monitors all around the stadium.

Secondly, he points up at where I am, and though I can't hear him, it's clear what two words he's saying.

For you.

My nose scrunches up, my cheeks hurting from how hard I'm smiling.

"That was good," Michelle says when we can both hear again, still on our feet. She gives me a strange look. "That was like the old Luke Wolfe."

I don't know what that means, exactly, but it doesn't sound like a bad thing.

As for me, I feel like I'm shining from the inside, Luke's name emblazoned and glittering on my back.

It's good to be the one watching instead of being watched, for once.

CHAPTER FIFTEEN

Luke

I SIT FOR a long while in the locker room, after everyone's gone to the players' lounge to celebrate our win, listening to the voicemail from my mom over and over again.

"I just wanted you to know I'm so proud of you, honey. I don't think you hear that enough— Oh, stop it, Fred. No. Don't—" Her voice gets farther away from the speaker at whatever it is my stepdad is doing to make her laugh. "That was a great goal. What a foot! I wish we could have been in the stands today like we used to. I never get tired of watching you play. We miss you so much. Okay, bye-bye, Luke."

Gone numb from being curled around the phone for so long, my hand hardly registers the vibration of a text coming in.

I should be back in Seattle with my family. I should be there for my mom.

A lump forms in my throat, guilt flaying me, laying all my faults bare where anyone could see them.

A text comes through, and I finally make myself look down at the screen.

> **ABIGAIL:** Hey, I'm waiting for you
>
> **ABIGAIL:** You were amazing.

ABIGAIL: I can't believe I've been missing out on soccer my whole life

ABIGAIL: Ugh, sorry to send so many texts at once like a chaotic texting chipmunk—I'm in the players' lounge if you want to meet up here. If not, just let me know what you had in mind.

ABIGAIL: If you still want to get together, of course

The guilt intensifies, my stomach churning.

I do want to see her. I love that she was here. I hate that the only reason she's paying attention to me at all is because the goddamned owners wanted me to ask her out. The knowledge and guilt of it is a blister that only gets worse the longer it's there.

And I can't risk breaking it off with her, because my family needs me. I have to be released from my contract.

But I don't want to hurt Abigail, either. I like her.

I'm so fucking fucked.

"Fuck!" I yell, slamming my hand into the locker room bench. The sound echoes off the metal lockers, and the door slowly swings open.

"Dude," Tristan Gold says. "What the hell is wrong?"

"I fucked it all up. It's all fucked up," I mutter, shaking my head.

"Is it your mom?" Tristan closes the door behind him, leaning on it, and I'm grateful for that, because as much as I don't want to open up to him, I can't help but let it all out.

"She's still sick, but no. Yes. No and yes."

He peers at me, confusion clear on his face. "Right."

"They won't release me from the reserve players list. I won't get traded and can't sign until they do."

"Oh, shit," he says, realization dawning on his face. "I didn't even think about you going up there to play. What are you going to do?"

"Abigail," I tell him miserably, scrubbing a hand down my face.

"You're going to do . . . Abigail?" he repeats.

"I have to date her."

"I'm really not following here."

"The owners wanted me to ask her out. Get more fans here, increase sales, get people talking about the Aces again. They said if I did it, they'd take my name off the no-trade list."

I close my eyes, pressing my palms against them like that will make this go away.

"I thought you really liked her." The bench moves as Gold's bulk settles beside me on the bench. "You should just tell her the truth."

"That's the problem. I do like her. A lot. Too much." I shake my head, my voice hoarse.

"Oh. Shit. You don't want to break things off with her."

"I know I should," I snarl, standing up, pacing around the room, feeling wild. "I know that's the right thing to do."

"No, I get it," Tristan says, and his gaze goes far away. "When my mind's made up on the girl, I'm the same way. All in."

"All in," I echo, then shake my head. It's so fucking stupid. "You think I should tell her?"

"Yep," Gold says, nodding at me, refocused. "Come clean."

"You don't think it will hurt her feelings?"

"It might, but it's better than feeling like you do right now," Gold says.

I don't know if that's true.

It's never mattered what I've done, who I've tried to be. My own dad didn't care enough to ever check in on who I am.

My teammates only know me for the demanding asshole I am on the field.

My opponents know me as the guy who likes to fight, who plays dirty.

I'm the bad guy.

And I'll be the bad guy again with her.

"If you like her, you should try," Gold tells me earnestly, interrupting that nasty voice in my head.

"And if she breaks up with me and I still can't go up and play for Seattle FC?" I stop pacing, crossing my arms over my shoulders. "What then? My mom just gets sicker and sicker, and I have to fly up on the rare weekends we don't have games?"

"Shit." Gold rakes a hand through his blond hair, frowning. "I don't know, man."

I slam a hand into a locker, suddenly furious again.

"You could just take it slow with her," Gold suggests. "See what happens, let it run its course. If you really do like her, then what's the harm in that?"

I stop, staring at him. "That's . . . actually good advice."

Gold grins at me, all-American perfect straight white teeth. "Don't act so surprised."

I tap out a message to Abigail, feeling slightly more balanced.

> **LUKE:** Do you want to come over tonight? We can go back to my place
>
> **ABIGAIL:** Okay! If you don't mind dropping me off at Pilates tomorrow morning early. Just 8 a.m. though. Nothing too too early.
>
> **LUKE:** I can do that

I *can* do that, and I can take things slow with Abigail, and I will do what I need to do to take care of the ones I love.

I take a deep breath, shove my phone into my pocket, and head out the locker room door, Gold on my heels.

Just have to keep putting one foot in front of the other.

CHAPTER SIXTEEN

Abigail

I'M ONE BEER and a glass of wine in, but the warm and fuzzy feelings have less to do with alcohol and more to do with the fact that Luke Wolfe is sitting next to me. He drives the same way he does everything: with an intense focus that I never in my life would think was so hot.

He's slightly distant tonight, but I don't mind.

I'm talkative enough for both of us, especially now that we're out of view of prying eyes and the lenses of the paparazzi.

"It was amazing," I finally say, breaking the easy silence. "Watching you play, I mean."

He doesn't answer, not even a grunt, and for the first time, I wonder if the silence is as easy as I assumed.

The sharp angles of his face flash in stark relief as headlights of passing cars splash over him. A muscle twitches in his temple, and still, there's no response.

"I'm glad I had your jersey to wear," I offer up. Maybe he's just in a weird headspace after his game. I know sometimes it takes me a while to switch gears after a really intense scene or day of shooting.

Or maybe I should have him drop me off at my house.

I bite my lip, uncertain with him for the first time since we met only a few days ago.

His big hand moves from where it rests on the top of the steering wheel, and he folds it over mine, squeezing it gently.

A relieved exhalation leaves me all at once, and I scoot closer to the center console, leaning my head against his shoulder.

When he slams on the brakes, though, I gasp, the seat belt digging into my chest.

"Did you see that?" His eyes are wild, and I gape at him, shaking my head.

"See what? I didn't see anything. What was it?" My heart's beating a mile a minute, and I rub at where the seat belt hit me.

"I'm not sure." He glances over at me, then blinks at what he sees. "Are you hurt?"

"No, just surprised. Startled me," I say.

"I'm sorry, I didn't mean to scare you. Shit." He rubs a hand down his face, then looks back out the front window. "There it is."

My gaze swings to whatever it is he's looking at outside the window, but I don't see anything.

Before I can ask him, though, he's pressed the hazards and leaped out of the driver's side door. Thankfully, there aren't too many people on the road here, and I watch Luke run in front of the car.

He crouches down, the headlights drifting across his muscled back, his shadow long and stretched strangely in front of the car. His low voice is lost in the soft hum of the engine, but I hear him say something. Seconds tick by, turning to minutes, and eventually he jerks up, turning back toward the car.

There's a lump in his jacket, and he's holding it close to his chest as he walks back to the open driver's side door.

My phone's in my hand, because I'm not going to lie, I'm a little freaked out by his behavior and want to be ready in case he's absolutely lost his—

A tiny paw pokes out, an itty-bitty murder mitten tipped with filthy sharp claws.

"Is that a kitten?" I breathe, my eyes the size of saucers. He stopped on a dime for a kitten?

Be still, my heart.

The bad boy of soccer my left ass cheek. A villain does not stop the car on his way home, with a high probability of getting laid when he gets there, to rescue a teeny-tiny kitten.

He carefully, gingerly gets back in the car, murmuring sweet nothings to the hissing furball inside his canvas jacket.

"You stopped the car for a kitten?" If my voice goes up to an inaudible pitch at the last word, I can't be held responsible. It's just so damned *cute*.

"Got a problem with that?" he asks, thick eyebrows raised, a pointed challenge in the question.

My own eyebrows skyrocket, and I nearly ask him if he wants to have an eyebrow-raising contest until the kitten mews pitifully, and I'm making grabby hands at it.

"Of course I don't have a problem with it, you grumpy buffoon. Hand over the fluff."

"I don't want you to get hurt. Cat bites can be serious."

To my shock, he holds out his left hand, which has, I realize, a thick set of dotted scars on the meaty part between his wrist and thumb.

"Wrap the baby in your coat and give him to me," I insist. "You can't drive and hog the cat." A thought scampers across my awareness. "Were there more? Was there a mom?"

He gives me a long, searching look. "It was by itself," he says shortly. "I looked. Trust me, the mom is long gone."

"Oh," I say, crumpling slightly, getting his meaning. "God, that's awful. Poor baby," I croon to Luke's chest, the massive eyes of an angry kitten pinned on me. A low baby growl sounds, and I have to stop myself from positively screeching in delight.

"You like animals?" he asks.

"Are you joking? Who doesn't like animals? Now hand it over and let's get it home and take care of it."

"Right. Okay."

Luke moves so slowly as to not further distress the poor thing, and I swear, any solidity left of my heart completely and totally turns liquid.

There's just something so perfect and adorable about a huge muscled man taking care of a tiny animal—I could literally just bite him from the cute aggression.

"Do you ever think something's so cute you want to chomp it?"

He pauses, giving me a long look. "Do not bite the kitten. It probably has fleas."

"I wasn't going to actually bite it." I decide not to share that I wanted to bite *him*, not the cat.

"You're not worried about fleas?" he asks, somehow swaddling the precious bundle of needle teeth and bugs and soft baby fluff in his coat.

"We'll take care of the fleas. Should we stop by a pet store? Do you think he needs—what's it called?—formula? Kitten formula?" I have no idea how these things work.

"I have some at my place." He holds the angry ball of fur out to me, and I gently take it, grip as tight as I can manage to keep it secure without freaking the baby out.

"You have kitten formula." It takes me a moment to process what he's said. "Why do you have kitten formula?"

"I foster them sometimes."

"You do?" The question explodes out of me, and the kitten does his best Tasmanian devil impression in protest. Tiny fangs sink into Luke's jacket. "My, what a terrifying little kitty you are. So much teeth. Much claws," I coo at him.

"I'm not good with people. Cats are easy. You know where you stand with them." He checks his blind spot as he merges back onto the empty road. "We're only a few minutes from my house, so just keep a firm grip on him."

Sure enough, it takes less than ten minutes for Luke to navigate us through the rolling hills in one of the nicer parts of the city, thanks to the significant lack of traffic in this more upscale area.

I own my own house, which is, in my opinion, a pretty big deal, and I'm proud of it.

Still, my jaw practically unhinges when we roll up to a large steel and glass structure set way back on what must be a gorgeous property during the day. The exterior lights glint off the dark glass, everything about it sleek, modern, and gorgeous.

Definitely expensive.

I mean, rationally I knew some of the bigger-name soccer players make good money . . . but it's one thing to know it and another to see it in the form of what must be a multimillion-dollar mansion.

"And you rescue cats," I muse.

"Yeah," he agrees. "We'll get some formula in him, but there's not a whole lot we can do for the fleas with one this little other than give him a bath."

"A bath," I repeat. I squint at him in the bright light in the garage.

"Yep."

I consider it for a moment, the kitten in my arms quiet and seemingly resigned to its fate. "Cool. I'm happy to help, just tell me what to do."

"It will be nice not to be alone for once," he says gruffly, turning the keys in the ignition, the engine falling silent.

With that, he stalks around the car to open my door. I cuddle the kitten to my chest, wrapped up tight in Luke's jacket, a jacket I don't think Luke will be getting back anytime soon.

"I don't want to stop holding the baby, but can you grab my—" I don't even have to finish saying it, since my purse is already in Luke's hand. "Thanks."

Instead of his usual grunt, he gives me a slow, hesitant smile, his gaze traveling up and down my body in a way that makes me feel beautiful. Wanted.

Carefully, he puts it over my head, and I duck as he settles the thin strap so it lies across my body and away from the tiny ball of floof.

"Have I told you how stunning you look in that?" There's something warm and affectionate in his voice that makes my heart sit up and take notice.

"Oh, this old thing?" I bat my eyelashes, clutching the vibrating floof to my chest. "This guy I'm talking to got it for me."

"Talking to?" He tilts his head, gesturing for me to lead the way. "What does that mean?"

"Oh, you know." I want to wave my hand, but I can't do much in the way of gesticulation with the little ball of angry cat in my hands. "When you are maybe dating someone, maybe not, and no one wants to put a label on it. You're just talking." I can't put air quotes around it, and I cringe slightly, because it's coming off ruder than I meant.

"You don't want to put a label on this?" he asks carefully, unlocking his front door. More metal and glass, a sort of smoked-out finish that blocks the view of the interior. Not that any neighbors are around to see in.

"I didn't say that, I was just, uh, explaining." I narrow my eyes at his back, then stop and simply stare around when the lights turn on. "Your house is . . . wow."

"It's not as comfortable as yours," he says, brushing off my sad attempt at a compliment.

"I love it," I tell him, and I mean it. "It's open and warm and modern all at once." I might be gushing, but damn, I love a well-decorated space. Especially one slightly spare in conventions, probably a holdover from my mom's rooster-cluttered kitchen growing up.

How many roosters can you put in a kitchen? As many as possible.

"I bet you only have one cock in the kitchen." Oh god. Why did I say that out loud? I'm going to die.

"What does that mean?" he asks, looking over his shoulder.

"My mom collected roosters in the kitchen growing up," I blab. "Sorry. I'm being ridiculous. Shutting up."

"I like when you're ridiculous. I like to know what's going on in that mind of yours." He doesn't turn over his shoulder again, still headed for what looks to be a modern-style kitchen, done in light wood and a warm, soothing beige. I never would have picked it, but it's just so him.

"I love this house," I say simply. "It's so nice."

"Yeah, it will be hard to sell it," he agrees.

"Are you selling it?" I ask, incredulous. "Why?"

"No, not at the moment." He clears his throat as he ushers me into a smaller room, this one equipped with a stainless steel sink and all kinds of cupboards. "Athletes move a lot, is all."

It's a more utilitarian space than the gorgeous kitchen, with brick-paved floors covered in thick, vibrant rugs.

My head practically swivels as I look around. A mudroom?

He pulls out a large stock pot, and I watch in curious silence as he takes out item after item: a heating pad, Dawn dish soap, several fluffy towels, and an entire box of what looks like ice pops, but upon further inspection appear to be tubes of . . . meat.

"Treats?" I ask, jerking my head at one.

"Yeah. Not sure how old he is yet, but I thought I'd get them out." A can of kitten formula follows, along with a bottle and a warmer.

"You really do this a lot, huh?" I'm staggered by the level of preparation. Staggered, impressed, and slightly in love with him. "Do you have cats of your own?"

"Nah, I travel too much. When it's offseason I like to help the local rescues out with fostering, but it wouldn't be fair to have a pet and then be gone as often as I am for away games."

"That's . . . so freaking sweet," I finally say, unable to resist the adorableness quotient.

"Is it?" He seems genuinely surprised by my reaction, his dark eyebrows furrowing in confusion. "Might as well help if you can, you know?"

"It's just at odds with—" I sigh in exasperation. "I don't know. It's just not what I expected. Most . . . celebrities," I say the word delicately, "would want that plastered across the front pages, would be the go-to mouthpiece for the organizations they are trying to help, you know? I think it's cool you're hands-on."

"No one in their right fucking minds would want me as a mouthpiece," he says, the confusion turning to flat-out consternation. "It's not like it's Nobel Peace Prize–worthy, either. I'm literally wiping shit off cats' butts."

A surprised laugh erupts out of me, and the kitten growls in protest, suddenly all knives and spitting hisses again.

"He's definitely cussing us out right now," I tell Luke.

"They're all angry until they eat. Know what, though?" He frowns. "Let's go ahead and get him bathed." His gaze is stuck on my wrist, and I swallow, already knowing what I'm going to see there.

"There's fleas on me, huh?"

"I don't want you to be uncomfortable. We'll get him cleaned up and then feed him." The wrinkles around his mouth deepen as he frowns more. "Or she. Either way, the food usually works. Especially with one this young. You'll see."

With that, he turns to the sink, humming under his breath something that sounds suspiciously like a sea shanty until he gets the water temperature just right. When he's happy with the warmth of the water, he fills the stock pot up and adds soap. A light layer of bubbles forms on top.

I bite back a laugh at a peeling white-and-black label affixed to it that reads, KITTENS ONLY.

"We're ready for you, little cat." Luke's so sure of himself, his voice no longer the gruff rasp he usually affects but a low, gentle rumble. He glances down at me. "You ready?"

"Yep."

"Okay, I'm going to scruff him. It's going to look bad, but at his size, it's totally fine. He's going to react to your energy, so can you be calm?"

I'm nervous in spite of myself, but I nod fervently. "I can."

"Good. All right, hand him over to me, keep a firm hold, and I'll get him started."

"Got it. Just tell me how to help."

"I'm going to scruff him," he repeats in that same low, soothing voice that sends a shiver down my spine.

Bizarre reaction, considering I apparently have fleas crawling on me, but that's fine and normal and fine and great.

"Okay," I squeak, and he narrows his eyes at me.

"You don't have to stay if you're not an animal person. Or if bugs bother you," he adds after a moment.

"I'm good, it wasn't—um, it was nothing." Heat crawls up my chest and cheeks, and he gives me a strange look while I hold out the hissing lump of knives.

"You're doing great, princess, good job," he says in that same, delicious voice—sweet and smooth like salted caramel.

Princess. Whew. It's a good thing my hands are full of cat, because I might fan myself if they weren't, and that would be very embarrassing.

"That's right, princess," Luke continues, his huge hand disappearing into the folds of the canvas fabric around the cat.

"Princess," I repeat, my stomach flipping in delight. "It's a little early for pet names, isn't it?"

"Yeah," he says easily, "but she's not a boy, after all. Definitely a little girl. We'll call her Princess until the shelter or her new owner names her."

Oh. Fuck me. He's talking about the kitten.

I'm not princess—the cat is.

For some reason, this strikes me as hilarious, and a giggle bubbles out of my mouth before I can clamp down on it.

"There's a metal comb and a roll of paper towels there, isn't there, Princess?"

He's addressing the cat, and I'm so embarrassed about thinking he was calling me princess that I can't decide if I want to disappear or die laughing or some combination thereof.

"So if you could grab that and comb her out while I hold her, that would be great, Abigail."

I decide right then and there that the only name I need him to call me is my own.

It's never sounded as good on anyone else's tongue.

CHAPTER SEVENTEEN

Luke

ABIGAIL'S A NATURAL at this. She's gentle with the little kitten, who turns out to have one of the prettiest fluffy gray coats I've seen in a long time. Seal point with slight tabby markings and big blue eyes.

"She's covered in them, the poor thing." Abigail coos at the tiny creature, who's given up on fighting, limp and compliant in my hands.

"They'll die as the soap gets them," I tell her confidently, but secretly, I worry for the little creature. Fleas, especially on one so small, can make a kitten dangerously anemic.

"How old do you think she is?"

"I don't know." I shrug. "I think she's at least six to eight weeks, but she's malnourished." Skin and bones.

"Little princess," Abigail tells the cat, her tongue sticking out slightly in concentration as she runs the flea comb through the kitten's now soapy fur. She scrapes the bugs off on the paper towel, not wavering no matter how many times she's done this, as focused on the task at hand as I am. "We're going to get you all fixed up. Will she need formula?"

"Honestly, we can probably offer her both—wet kitten food and formula. Calories are calories, so whatever she'll eat. I think she must be older, or she would be in worse shape. Wouldn't you, Princess?"

Princess makes a plaintive mewling sound, and Abigail huffs a small laugh.

"It's okay, little girl, we'll get you feeling better."

We spend the next twenty minutes or so in relative quiet, each of us offering the beleaguered cat as much praise as possible and concentrating on the task at hand.

"I think we've gotten all of them," Abigail finally says, and I nod.

"Agreed."

"Wow, look how filthy the water is," she adds. "You poor baby, don't worry, you're in good hands now. We're going to take good care of you."

"Grab the towel?" I ask, but she's already moving, the towel I keep for my fosters in her hands. "Let's get you dried off and warm," I tell the kitten.

"I'll plug the heating pad in," she tells me, and I grin at her.

"That would be great."

I concentrate on drying off the long-haired kitten, who's stopped fighting and just stares at us both with wide, freaked-out eyes.

"Want me to try the treats?" Abigail's already tearing into one of the tubes of cat treat.

"Yep. Just hold it out—" I stop, because Abigail's already on it.

The cat hisses at the tube in its face.

We both laugh as she blinks, sniffing experimentally before licking once, then enthusiastically tearing into the food.

"That's a good sign, right?" Abigail says quietly, grinning up at me like she's won a prize.

God, this woman. "Your smile," I say slowly.

"What is it? Do I have something in my teeth? Please tell me it's not a flea."

"It's one of the best things I've seen all day." I make myself stop talking. I cannot fall for Abigail, I cannot make this any harder on either of us than it already is.

"You're the best thing I've seen all day," she says softly, nudging me with her knee. It's covered by a pair of the sexiest boots I've ever seen, and the only thing above it is the goddamn jersey I gave her.

"You look good, Abigail. In my number. And those boots." My voice is slightly hoarse, and the kitten stops licking the treat to give me a wary look.

"I bet you say that to all the girls," she says lightly, but her cheeks go pink beneath the light smattering of freckles.

We're covered in cat fur and flea dirt and dish soap, but none of that shit matters, because Abigail is so close and I fucking want her.

I like the person she is on the inside, and I like how it matches who she is on the outside, too. I like that I know what I'm getting with her.

But it's a bad idea.

Abigail clears her throat, and I realize I've been undressing her with my eyes while she feeds a fucking kitten in front of me.

I squeeze my eyes shut. What is fucking wrong with me? I need to make up my damn mind about her, about this fucked situation I've gotten myself into.

"What do we do once the cat is full? Do you let it roam around, or . . . ?" Her voice trails off, and her throat bobs as she swallows, her face pinker than ever.

I don't think I've ever been around someone who blushed so much.

"We could see what she does. Leave it up to her, let her lead the way."

"Litter box?" she asks, looking away from me as she tosses the empty treat tube in a trash can under the sink.

"Want to hold her? I can get that set up."

She nods, grinning at me, and the kitten lets out a half-hearted growl as Abigail picks her up, whispering nonsense at her. Eventually, the growl is replaced by a rumbling purr, and I dump fresh litter into one of the biodegradable boxes I keep on hand, smiling to myself.

"Look," Abigail says in a hushed voice, and I do, stuffing the litter back in one of the cabinets, just in time to catch the tiny gray kitten kneading the towel she's holding her in. "She's happy." Abigail's eyes fill with tears, and a muscle tightens in my chest.

"Set her down in the box."

"That's all it takes?"

I shrug a shoulder. "Some cats are harder than others, but for the most part, yeah. They get it right away."

"I've never had a cat," she says. "We had dogs growing up. My mom liked the little white fluffy ones. Pomeranians, you know?" Carefully, she puts the sleepy cat in the litter, and the kitten mewls in aggravation before sniffing around, then digging furiously, and finally doing her business.

I breathe a sigh of relief, because either kittens get it right away or they don't, and I'd much rather deal with the former.

Princess hops out of the litter box, still slightly damp, and Abigail scoops her back up. To my surprise, the feral baby gremlin is only too happy to let her, and that, more than my own feelings, seals what I'm going to do about Abigail Hunt.

I'm for damn sure not about to let her slip through my fingers.

I wash my hands in the sink as I mull it over, disinfecting the comb and other materials before putting everything back in its place. Nothing worse during a foster emergency than coming home to misplaced or missing supplies.

"Why don't you see if she'll settle on the couch with you and another treat?" I ask Abigail.

So I can figure out what to do about you.

The options are clear: I could tell her and ruin us before we've even started.

Or I keep the odd circumstances around the start of whatever the hell it is we have to myself.

Option two means I don't risk losing her before we've even seen where it could go between us.

Option one means I have to make sure no one else tells her.

Who the hell would I tell, anyway? Gold won't say shit, I trust him that much.

Besides, the odds that we make it work long enough to factor in me leaving LA are so low that it's not even worth thinking about. And if we did make it . . . we could figure it out.

I set the equipment back where it goes, my mind made up in the small matter of minutes it takes to get everything cleaned up and put away.

I'm going to choose trying with Abigail Hunt.

CHAPTER EIGHTEEN

Abigail

I DON'T EVEN bother turning on the TV. For one, I don't know where the remote is, and secondly, sometimes watching TV feels like work.

I can't turn off the part of my brain that wants to analyze other actors and their character development choices. Sure, I could watch the news or a nature documentary, but I can't be bothered when I have a sleepy kitten on my chest who needs to be socialized.

She deserves the attention, but frankly, cuddling up and petting a kitten while it eats treats from a tube sounds like an amazing night.

As for me, despite my extrovert self, I feel oversocialized, over-stimulated, and pretty much talked out. There's something wildly different about posting on social media or being on while acting compared to being on and aware of people out and about in real life, and the paparazzi made it all too clear that they were just as interested in me being there as they were in the game. Maybe even more so, which makes me feel uncomfortable.

A long sigh rips out of me, and the kitten startles, her sharp claws digging into the front of the jersey, where she sits licking the admittedly fragrant (and not in a good way) meat tube.

"Sorry, baby girl," I murmur, and she settles back in on my chest warily.

Carefully, I slide my phone out of my purse, and, sure enough, there's several new messages from Jean, who apparently has decided to enter the modern age and learn to text.

> **JEAN:** You did well at the game, the press is eating it up. -Jean

> **JEAN:** Paparazzi says you left with Luke Wolfe? -Jean

> **JEAN:** We discussed you keeping a respectful distance from gossip while the film production begins ramping up. -Jean

The last message is simply a devil emoji, and I puzzle over it for a moment before deciding Jean must have hit it on accident.

I bite back another sigh and decide to call her back in the morning. There wasn't anything in the contract Jean negotiated about my personal life, unless it was so egregiously rotten that it fell under their morals and ethics clause.

Going home with Luke Wolfe hardly counts as that.

Jean can wait until tomorrow.

A new text pings in, and my stomach sinks with anxiety, because I really don't want to deal with my agent and self-proclaimed PR specialist at the moment, until I see it's from Michelle.

> **MICHELLE:** Thanks for coming with me tonight! It was way more fun with you there. See you next week? We can go over some of the other questions you had about the IFF.

Funnily enough, as much as I like Michelle, I don't really feel like chatting with her right now, either. Problem is, if I don't respond right away, I'll probably forget to text her back for a few days . . . but right now? That doesn't sound so bad.

Just me and the newly cleaned and fluffy kitten, who wants absolutely nothing from me besides the treat in my hand and a warm place to hang out.

That? That I can do.

My eyes are getting heavy, and I'm about to give up and sleep when the couch dips slightly next to me.

"She likes you," Luke's voice makes me blink sleepily at him. As for the cat, she's out, though her little paws are still kneading as she snoozes.

"It's amazing how fast she went from angry to angel," I tell him quietly, then talk through a yawn that grips me. "I didn't think she'd ever warm up to me."

"I had a feeling she would," Luke tells me, his blue eyes holding mine firmly. "How could she not? I warmed up to you right away. That doesn't happen often."

I laugh at first, thinking he's joking, but he simply stares at me. Tiny crinkles form at the corners of his eyes as he smiles gently, and it hits me that he's being sincere.

And I laughed? Awkward.

"Thank you," I finally say, then purse my lips. "I have to say, I wasn't sure about you at all at first."

He sets his arm behind my shoulders, pulling me closer to his warm body, the smell of his bodywash and aftershave spicy and enticing. The kitten makes a soft noise, still asleep but aware enough to dislike the jostling.

"I wouldn't have trusted you if you'd been anything other than what you were."

Luke Wolfe makes it sound like him trusting me is the equivalent of passing the hardest lie detector test in the world.

"She's just so dang cute, I don't want to do anything but stare at her."

"I know the feeling," he says.

"Yeah, I bet you do. I can't imagine how hard it must be to give up these little cuties to their forever homes." I shake my head in disbelief, already totally besotted with the cat he dubbed Princess.

"I wasn't talking about the kitten," he says in a low, soft voice.

My head jerks as I look up at him. His cool blue gaze, the color of the sky on a clear spring day, holds me captive. Warm fingers stroke slowly down my arm, then back up, toying with the sleeve of the black-and-gold jersey.

His jersey.

"What if I don't want to have sex?" I ask him suddenly, surprising myself with the question.

I swallow, and it's alarmingly audible.

He pauses his ministrations for a moment before his gentle caresses start again. "With me? Ever? Then we could be friends," he says. "I like having you around."

A laugh huffs out of me, and I relax slightly. "No, I mean tonight. I thought I did, and then . . . honestly, and don't take this the wrong way"—I pause, licking my lips—"I'm freaking exhausted, and I feel bloated from cheese fries and beer."

He tilts back his head and laughs, the kitten opening one reproaching eye at the disturbance.

I shift, not sure how to feel. "My last boyfriend would be pissed. That's why I'm asking. He . . ." I stop myself, because talking shit about an ex is not the move. I may have been out of the dating pool for a while, but I'm still pretty sure that's the norm.

"He was a fucking asshole, then, Abigail," Luke says, no trace of humor left on his face. "It was that actor, right? The one who—"

"Yeah." I don't really want to talk about him. Shame curls through me, insidious and smoky. Whenever I've tried to grasp at why I feel ashamed about my ex, it slips through my fingers. "I shouldn't have brought it up. I'm sorry. Forget it." The cat treat tube is still in my hands, and I twist the empty half around, tying it in a neat little knot.

"You used to do that on the show you were on. Knots," he says easily.

"You watched *Blood Sirens*?" I ask, surprised, but I immediately know exactly what he's talking about.

That too-familiar mix of anxiety and gratitude that someone liked my work rears its head, a pendulum that swings farther toward gratitude as I remind myself that I'm with Luke.

Luke, who has chosen to date me, to like me, despite the utter fuckup I made of everything.

"A few times. That's the show that bas—your ex was on with you, right? You were the best part of it."

The pendulum deep inside me pauses its dizzying swing at his words, and I bask in that compliment for a second before picking the thread of the conversation back up.

"Yeah. That's the show." I brace the kitten with one hand—she's tiny enough she fits into my palm—as I sit up and put the treat tube on the coffee table.

I don't know what to say. I know I should explain, start to unravel this bundle of awfulness I keep shoving deep inside, but—

Easier said than done.

"You don't have to talk about him if it makes you uncomfortable. I didn't mean to pry." The words are gruff but kind.

I rub the kitten's fuzzy head, trying to sort out the tangled snarl of feelings I can't sort out about the way everything ended after that one fateful red carpet interview.

"Maybe I should talk about it." The therapist I went to a couple of times before giving up sure did want me to talk about it. Annoying to admit, but she probably had a point.

"We don't need—"

"No, it might make me feel better . . . and I want to tell you."

His fingers curl around my wrist, the touch tender.

I inhale, trying to sort out what I want to say. Where to begin.

"He . . . liked me as arm candy. He cared a lot about what people thought, and he used who I knew to make connections. He used *me*. Period. It made me feel—" I clear my throat. "It made me feel shitty. Then when it all blew up in my face after that horrible interview, and everyone on the internet decided I was ungrateful, and my friend Olivia—you know, the star of the show?—she didn't want to be friends anymore. I got written off *Blood Sirens*, an actual final final death, not one of the many ones where I came back to life the next episode . . . anyway, that's when my ex decided I wasn't a good look for him. That's what he said, too." I laugh, and there's no humor in the sound. It's bitter and jagged, and it scrapes against my throat. "That I wasn't a good look for him anymore. Said I'd committed career suicide and I'd drag him down, too. So yeah, when he said things like I was selfish for not . . . for not feeling well enough to—" my voice cracks. "It was just normal for us."

It wasn't normal. I know that now. The way he made me feel was not okay.

Knowing that doesn't make it better, though, not really.

It just makes me feel ashamed that I let it go on for so long.

I suck in a breath, staggered at everything that's just vaulted from my mouth into the air between us. "God, I'm dumping on you. Forget it. We don't have to talk about it."

He's quiet for a long minute, and I stare down at the kitten, glad to have something to look at besides the intense man still rubbing soft circles on my arm.

"You want to know what I would do if you were too . . . tired and feeling sick from beer and cheese fries? What anyone who wasn't a bastard would do?"

I glance back at him, then away again, because it's too much. He's so intense, and I think I might have fucked up by saying any of that, by assuming we were closer than we are—

"I would ask if I could get you a glass of water or a ginger ale, and tell you I had Tums if you wanted one. And then I would ask if you wanted me to take you home so you could sleep in your own bed."

"Oh." I bite my lower lip, feeling idiotic for all my internal catastrophizing. "That would be a better alternative."

"Than your ex-boyfriend?" He tilts his head, and I nod. My eyes prick with tears, and I'm not sure if it's because I'm just tired or if I'm feeling vulnerable for once or because Luke is being so damned . . . nice. Probably some mix of all of the above.

He's as gentle with me as he was with the scared kitten, and it makes me feel *safe*.

We've had straight-up chemistry since I first laid eyes on him. Of course, he acted like a total piece of shit in the LA Aces boardroom, but I chalked it up to him playing a part.

Now that I know him better?

"Were you nervous when you met me?" The question leaves my mouth before I have a chance to think it over, but he just curls a lip, peering at me through his heavy eyebrows.

"Very," he says, then scratches his jawline with his free hand, his right hand still featherlight stroking my arm. There's no pressure in the touch, nothing other than the small comfort of it, and that means so much more than the scorching chemistry and silliness that we've shared so far.

Luke Wolfe feels right.

"I was nervous, too," I say, leaning my cheek against his chest. He relaxes back, allowing me to get comfortable, and I loose a breath in contentment.

I don't remember the last time someone just cuddled me with no expectations. Or, at least, cuddled me and I didn't feel pressured to do anything else.

"Why were you nervous? You don't work for those assholes."

"No." I huff a laugh, then stifle another yawn. "No, I don't, but they're apparently friends with the person I do work for currently, and I wanted to make a good impression. That, unfortunately, is something I rarely do. I tend to annoy everyone at best or, at worst, confuse them by asking about Yo-Yo Ma and their masturbation habits."

A laugh booms out of him, and the kitten nearly jumps straight up in surprise, only to climb her way to his shoulder, curling up like a furry cinnamon bun in the crook of his neck.

"You look like a pirate."

"Pretty sure pirates have parrots."

"Pretty sure cats would make more sense, considering the vermin problem on those wooden ships."

"You are full of random information." He shakes his head, but there's no censure in the comment, and I snuggle against him more fully, draping one leg over his.

If I could curl up on his shoulder like Princess the cat, I would. It looks cozy up there.

"So do you need water? Or a ginger ale?"

"Honestly?" I smile up at him. "I think I just want to stay right here, like this. I think that's all I need."

CHAPTER NINETEEN

Abigail

PAIN ARCS DOWN my wrist, and I wake up in a panic, completely confused about where I am.

"Shit, shit, hi, shit," I tell the gray furball currently biting and rabbit-kicking the hell out of my arm. "Why are you doing that? Are you hungry? What is *wrong*?"

"Abigail?" A sleepy voice says, and it hits me all at once.

I'm at Luke's house. That's a fluffy street kitten attacking me, not a nightmare Furby.

I slept over, and all we did was cuddle, take care of the gremlin attached to my arm, and chat.

"Hey, I'm sorry, the kitten, Princess, I mean, she's—"

He pulls me tighter, and I melt into him, the cat leaping off me to chase something I can't see.

"Good morning," he says, his voice hoarse with sleep, even deeper than usual.

Fucking delicious, to be perfectly honest.

"Hi," I repeat, breathless and aware of him.

Not even a second later, my phone alarm goes off, and I bolt upright, nearly smashing his nose with my elbow.

"Whew, that was close, I nearly made you say your safe word."

"Anaphylactic shock?"

"Is that what it is?" I ask, my heart hammering from the immediate anxiety my phone alarm caused. Doesn't matter what ringtone I pick, doesn't matter if I set it to play goddamn Enya, it's going to start the day with a panic attack.

"You okay?" He sits all the way up from where we'd ended up crashing on the couch, and . . . he took his shirt off in the middle of the night.

Oh. Oh my god.

"Uh," I say, staring openly at his chest.

It's quite a chest.

Like, a fucking treasure of a chest made with me, personally, in mind. His abs are cut—like absurdly defined—which does make sense, considering he's a pro athlete and his whole job is being in superhuman physical condition. His pecs are delish, not too developed, but strong, lean muscle that all tapers to a set of scrumptious-looking hip bones.

There's a tattoo that winds across his side, and I want to lick it.

Start the day brushing teeth? Nope, straight to tattoo licking, like a normal human.

"What's wrong?" he asks, the muscles in his arm standing out as he rubs one hand behind his neck sleepily. "You have a weird look on your face."

"I was objectifying you," I say honestly. My palm smacks my face. *Too* honestly. A noise like *ergh* comes out of me, and then, to top it all off, my stomach growls.

"It turns out I like being objectified by you."

I peek at the LA Wolf from behind my fingers, embarrassed and starving and anxious about getting to Pilates on time so my instructor doesn't literally kick my ass with the reformer—and pleased.

No matter what part of my utterly nonsensical self I show Luke, he doesn't shy away or cringe.

It's a new experience. Brand-new.

I routinely embarrassed my ex-boyfriend, and I tried to shove all the strange, incongruous pieces of myself into a nice shiny dress and smile so hard no one noticed how much it hurt. He always told me that no one cared if I hurt, anyway. He certainly didn't.

The worst part was, I thought we at least were friends. That hurt the most—when I was forced to realize he hadn't ever been my friend. Not one bit.

My chest heaves as I take a deep breath, banishing the thoughts of him.

He doesn't deserve any space in my present. Or something like what my therapist told me to say to myself when I start spiraling.

"You just shut down," Luke says, rubbing the top of my thigh. "Talk to me."

At some point in the night, I must have pulled my boots off, because all I have on now are the fluffiest pair of socks I own to make the boots fit better.

And they're Halloween themed, covered in pumpkins and ghosties.

"Sorry." I manage a slight smile. "Just . . . in my head."

"I like what's in your head," he says, stretching both arms up.

Damn. He's like a work of art, and I am slightly mad at myself for my cheese fries indiscretions last night. I could have had all this man at my disposal. I could have had a repeat of what will go down in history as the best oral sex ever performed on a couch.

Ten out of ten, no notes.

I perk up, a sly smile turning the corners of my mouth up.

It's not last night anymore.

"So . . ."

The side of his mouth quirks up into a half smile.

"So," he repeats, his fingers making tiny circles, moving up at a snail's pace.

I don't want a snail's pace.

Now. What I need is him right now. I need him to know how much I appreciate him listening last night, validating me.

Fully decided, I walk my fingers up his chest, and he hisses in a breath, his thick eyebrows shooting up as goose bumps pebble across his skin.

"Hi," I say softly.

He groans as my fingers find one nipple, his eyes fluttering closed as I tweak it gently.

"What are you doing, Abigail?" One eye cracks open, the words guttural and low and delicious.

"Saying good morning." I continue walking my fingers up his skin, and he shivers. "Tell me if you want me to stop." The words come out with a smile, an echo of what he told me yesterday when he turned me into a limp bundle of blissed-out person.

"I do not want you to stop," he manages. The tendons on his neck stand out, and I trace my fingers over them, taking my time and mapping his skin, his gorgeous body.

"You know what you have under all this muscle?" I say lightly, dipping my head and flicking my tongue over his nipple.

His hand clamps around my waist, the jersey with his name on it riding up on my thighs. "What's that?"

"A squishy, lovely inside." I trace a heart around his left nipple, and he laughs softly.

"Is that what you think?" he asks.

I tilt my head, pretending to ponder the question. "Hmmm, let's see. Saved a kitten. Wined and dined me. Brought me a bunch of adorable gear with your name and number on it. I hear that means something." I kiss the inside of the invisible heart I've drawn, and his hand runs inside the jersey across my bare back.

"It means something, huh?" His voice is hoarse.

I like the way he sounds right now. I like having him right here, half-dressed, subject to my whims.

"Mm-hmm." I nod seriously. "But don't worry." I tap the side of my nose, and he groans as I swing one leg over his lap, straddling him.

Like this, I can feel the absolutely delicious hard bulge of his cock, and I lower myself slowly, relishing the heated way he's watching me.

"Don't worry about what?" he asks.

"I know you're hard where it counts." I let my hips fall all the way down, grinding against him.

He sucks in a breath, and I moan.

"Is that what you want?" he asks, his hand splayed across my back underneath the jersey. "You want this?"

His other hand brackets my hip, pushing me down harder onto his cock. Only two sets of thin fabric separate us, and it's too much. I want them gone *immediately*.

"You are so beautiful," he says. He bends down, his mouth seeking mine, and I laugh, pressing a finger against his lips.

"I have a condition."

He raises an eyebrow, his perplexed expression so adorable I melt.

"No kissing," I pronounce.

"What?"

"Morning breath." I nod sagely.

"I don't give a fuck what your breath is like, Abigail Hunt. I want to taste you all over."

I laugh again, tilting my head back, but the sound cuts off on a moan as he grinds against me. His fingers reach through the wide collar of the jersey, clamping on the back of my neck. His mouth is rough against mine, savage and claiming and totally devoid of the gentleness he's shown me so far.

I *love* it.

I respond in kind, scratching down his perfect chest, unleashing myself on him. The jersey comes over my head, and then he's abandoned my mouth for my breasts, sucking at my nipples through the lacy black bandeau.

He's right. I couldn't care less about my breath right now.

I'm gripped by a frenzy of need, nothing sweet or calm about it.

"You're so wet for me, I can feel you," he says hoarsely, his face buried between my breasts.

I moan in response, too impatient to talk, and scrabble at the waistband of his pants.

"Let me see you," he says, pulling away from me.

I blink, surprised at the shift.

Until his hands grip the bottom of the bra, pulling it over my head. My breasts swing free, and I bite my lip, nervous all over again.

He's so beautiful, so perfectly honed, and I'm just me. What if he changes his mind? What if I'm not enough? What if he—

"Fuck, Abigail," he breathes, and it's not because he's upset. "You are . . . wow."

Rough fingertips brush against my delicate skin, and I shiver, biting my lip.

"What's wrong?" he asks me, pausing, taking my chin in his hand and looking into my eyes.

"Just nervous."

"Nervous?" he repeats, clearly mystified. "About this? We don't have to do anything you don't want to—"

"Oh, I definitely want to," I say on a laugh.

"Then what?" he asks, his thumb rubbing back and forth on my jaw. I lean into it, then turn my head and kiss his hand.

"I just want you to like what you see," I finally admit quietly.

He stares at me. "Are you joking?"

I shake my head, unable to answer, feeling foolish.

"You are . . . stunning. Perfect. I haven't been able to stop thinking about you. All I wanted to do yesterday morning was turn my car around and fuck you until you couldn't walk straight."

"Oh."

"Oh," he agrees. His gaze darts between my eyes, and I narrow my eyes at him.

"So you wouldn't be mad if I . . . took your pants off?" I rise up on my knees, tugging at the waistband of his pants again. He groans as I finally pull them off, taking his boxers with them.

His cock springs free, and my mouth twists to the side, my eyebrows raised.

He barks a laugh. "What is that look?"

"It's really big," I tell him, now slightly uncertain that I have what it takes to handle that thang. "Don't worry, though, I'm not a quitter."

"Babe." He leans forward, his lips the barest of brushes against the column of my neck. "It would be my pleasure to get you ready to take it all."

Oooh, I do like the sound of that.

His fingers dip between our bodies, and I cry out as he quickly finds my clit again. "You are so wet and tight," he says, his voice thick with approval.

My toes curl.

"You can take me, I know you can." He pushes two fingers inside me, and I whimper with need.

Emboldened, I wrap my hand around his hard length, and his ab muscles flex enticingly.

"You're gorgeous," I tell him, and I mean every bit of it.

"Fuck, Abigail," he says, his mouth finding mine again. I cling to him, still working his cock in my hand as he manages to flip us.

His fingers pump in and out of me, his thumb making expert circles over my clit at the same time.

"That's it," he tells me, and I go limp against him.

My face nuzzles in the crook of his neck. I inhale the scent of him: a pine forest at night, grass clippings, and the salt and musk of his skin.

"Look how perfectly you're going to come. You're going to take me so well."

I moan, breathless, and his words put me over the edge. My body clenches around him, and he grunts as I cling to him, biting down on the muscled breadth of his shoulder.

I'm moaning his name, only half-aware as he picks me up easily. Long strides take us into his bedroom, and I kiss his shoulder, biting it, his fingers still deep inside me.

"Talk to me," he tells me, finally setting me on the edge of the bed, all of that magnetic attention focused solely on me. "What do you want?"

"More," I breathe. "More, Luke, please. I want you."

"Condom?" he asks, and I nod fervently.

"Whatever it takes to get you inside me."

That makes him laugh, and I grin up at him softly, limp and loose and yet so ready for what's to come.

Both of us, with any luck.

He doesn't stand on ceremony, reaching into the top drawer of his nightstand. Gold foil flashes, and he keeps gently working at my clit as he tears the packet with his teeth.

I raise an eyebrow as he manages to slick it over himself one-handed, slightly impressed and slightly intimidated.

"Are you ready for me?" he asks.

"I've never wanted anything this bad in my entire life. Except for when I cut cheese out for a show and—"

He throws back his head and laughs, then leans in and kisses me. Slowly.

Gently.

Like I'm something precious, and he wants this to be special.

I loop my arms back around his head, pulling him close. His room is dark in the early-morning light, and the plush bedspread behind me is cool against my bare skin.

I'm hot, though, burning up under his touch.

"Luke," I finally plead, and he relents, his fingers leaving my body with a wet noise that makes me blush.

The blush gets even deeper when he brings his fingers to his mouth, eyes on me, and laps at them.

Waiting is overrated, I decide, and wrap my legs around his waist, grabbing his cock and lining it up with my entrance.

"Now," I tell him, digging my hips into his perfectly muscled abs.

I cry out as he drives deep inside me in one rough thrust. My body accepts his, and we both pause, our chests heaving, acclimating to the unbelievable magic of how we fit together. The stretch is intense, but he's so patient, kissing me with gentle, sweet lips that have me moving against him in no time at all.

I'm lost. Lost for this, for him, for the blissful focus on where our bodies meet, where pleasure begins to spiral through me again.

"That's right. That's it, Abigail." His eyes find mine, and I'm staring up into them as the second orgasm hits me. Shallower than the first, but more satisfying with him inside me like this. Luke groans, lashes fluttering under those thick dark brows, a muscle twitching in his temple.

I reach up to smooth one brow out, captivated by his concentration— that and everything else about him.

"You feel so good," he grits out, his teeth scraping against my neck until I shiver.

His hand runs up my arm until he finds mine and laces his fingers through it.

"I'm not going to last long," he tells me, his teeth clenched, and I give him a slow, sleepy smile.

"Then fuck me hard and fast," I say, giving him my best mischievous grin.

That's all I have to say.

His hand grips mine tight, and I groan as he begins to slam into me as hard and fast as I told him to.

I can't deny that I'm slightly gratified by my effect on him as he holds me impossibly tight and finds his release, his cock twitching inside me.

He rolls us over so I'm on top of him, and I sprawl across his body like he's my own personal cuddle pillow person.

"Thank you," I finally say, needing to say *something* about what just happened.

Warm air huffs against the top of my head, his chest shaking, and when I glance up at him, bemused, he's laughing.

"That's the first time someone's told me thanks for a two-minute pump chump."

"A what?" I ask. "I've never heard that."

"That was hardly thank-you worthy," he says, rubbing his hand slowly up and down my back.

"I came twice," I tell him, caught between embarrassment and amusement. "Should we high-five? Would that make you feel better?"

He holds up a hand, grinning, and I slap my hand against it in the world's least exciting high five ever.

"I could slap your ass," I offer. "If that would make you feel more comfortable. Like one of your teammates. For encouragement."

"That would . . . that would definitely not make me feel more comfortable. And you are not one of my teammates, Abigail Hunt."

"So what am I, then?" I ask, aiming for teasing.

He blinks, though, his smile disappearing into an expression of sincere unease, and I force out the awkward laugh that always seems to be ready to go.

"I didn't mean to—"

"You're you," he interrupts. "And I like you. And I very, very much liked that. And I would like to do that again."

"From you, that's practically a marriage proposal."

He stares at me.

I stare at him.

Slowly, I close my eyes, horrified and wishing I could disappear. "That was supposed to be a joke," I squeak out.

Seconds go by slower than molasses, and I bury my face in his chest, refusing to look at him. Why do I always fucking do this? I am a moment ruiner.

A ruiner of moments, interviews, and relationships.

Move over Miley, there's a new wrecking ball in town.

"How about we take it one day at a time?" Luke finally says.

"It was a joke," I say, extricating myself from him, humiliated and absolutely livid with my dumb self. "I didn't mean that, I swear, I'm not—"

His hand grips my bicep, keeping me from moving farther away from him or rolling into a black hole on the floor and hoping to be swallowed up forevermore.

"I know it was a joke. I want to take it faster with you Abigail. But you deserve someone who . . ." His Adam's apple bobs. "You deserve someone who will take it slow."

He doesn't look uncomfortable.

His forehead is scrunched up, his mouth a puckered frown.

Luke Wolfe looks pissed off—furious, even. "You deserve someone better than me."

"Shut up," I tell him. "Only one of us gets to be the neurotic mess, and I called dibs today. You can be Debbie Downer tomorrow. Or even this afternoon, but right now—" My gaze lands on the alarm clock on his bedside table.

Realization sends adrenaline pumping through my body.

"Shit, shit, shit." I jump off the bed, evading his efforts to grab me and pull me back to him. I'm naked.

He's naked.

Well, he's wearing a used condom, but other than that, we are both naked.

"Abigail, please, don't freak out—"

"I'm actually not freaking out about this." I point between our very naked selves, who just got done doing the barnyard hoedown. "I'm running late."

"Late?" he echoes.

"I gotta get to Pilates. I don't think we're going to have time to stop by my house for my clothes, either."

He sits up, finally understanding. "I have sweats you can borrow."

"That's sweet of you," I tell him. Ugh. Why didn't I think to pack an overnight bag? I don't even want to guess at what I smell like. Sex and cheese fries. I cover my mouth, my eyes darting back to him.

"I have an extra toothbrush, too." He raises one dark eyebrow. "If that's why you're covering your mouth. Want it? It's brand-new. I bought a whole pack of them at Costco."

"Please," I say, not moving my hand from my mouth.

"Okay, beautiful. The bathroom is in there. I'll bring you some sweats. How does a mango protein smoothie sound? Fresh out of seafood, sorry to tell you."

I grin at him, and he leans in close, kissing my forehead before I can move away.

It's so sweet it makes me dizzy.

"I can't believe we fell asleep on the couch."

"I can. I'm sore as hell from the game."

"I can't believe we just did that." I gulp.

"Regrets, Abigail?" The question is surprisingly gentle.

"No." I shake my head. "No regrets. Just worried about how my instructor is going to murder my abs today."

"Murder your abs. Sounds rough." He rubs his hand down his own abs, and I stare at them for just long enough that he lets out a small huff of a laugh.

An idea dances in front of me, and I seize it before I make the choice to seize that strong, yummy hand and stay in bed all day. "You could do Pilates with me."

"I thought it was a private lesson."

"Lauren won't mind. She'll be thrilled to have someone else to torture—I mean teach." I bat my eyelashes at him, and they feel gummy. Yikes. I don't want to think about my mascara.

Luke crosses to where I stand, gently turning me toward a door.

"This is my bathroom. Take a shower, brush your teeth, do whatever. I'll leave some clothes on the hook." He points to one on the door, "and I'll make us some smoothies. Do you want anything else? English muffin? Coffee?"

"Do you have tea?" I ask him. I love coffee, but coffee and Pilates after a night of cheese fries sounds like a recipe for intestinal distress.

"Tea it is. Black?"

"Please," I say. "Any kind you have."

"You got it. Extra toothbrushes are under the sink." He gives me another kiss on the temple, sending a fresh flock of butterflies winging, and then gently closes the door, leaving me staring at it with a goofy grin on my face.

A man who lets me be me. Who lets me into his bathroom.

The urge to snoop hits me, and it hits me hard. Wrecking-ball strength. Hurricane-force winds strength.

I whistle a tune as I make a beeline for his cabinets, then immediately stop.

Not because it's suspicious to whistle the theme to James Bond as I spy on the dude I cuddled with all night, but because . . . his bathroom is impeccably neat.

"What the fuck?" I ask myself.

Sure enough, there's a package of toothbrushes, and I pop the pink one out for myself and get brushing ASAP. All while snooping, of course.

The towels are neatly rolled and folded.

Each drawer is organized, if spare.

There is a whole drawer full of Icy Hot and KT Tape. That tracks.

There are no beard hairs anywhere in the sink.

I raise an eyebrow at myself in the mirror, then grimace around the pink toothbrush. Mascara and eyeliner have decided to abandon their posts, trekking into the valleys under my eyes. It's not a good look, and my face scrunches up in response.

Shit. I didn't bring any makeup, either. Not that I normally wear makeup to Pilates, but Luke hasn't seen me without makeup.

I inhale slowly.

"You're being an idiot, Abigail," I tell myself in the mirror. "He kissed you with morning breath. He doesn't care about that shit."

Happiness bubbles to the surface, making me feel light and lovely. Maybe we could just skip the smoothie and have another quickie—

"Bad idea," I say to my reflection.

No time for more sex.

Only time for a quick rinse and Pilates.

No more sex.

For now.

CHAPTER TWENTY

Luke

ABIGAIL HUNT IS one of the cutest, most beautiful, and most refreshing people I have ever been around.

She's pulled down her giant glasses on her face, and they practically swallow her fine-boned features, making her look even more adorable.

"You're sure Princess will be okay?" It's the third time she's asked since we left the house thirty minutes ago, and I love how much she cares about the kitten already.

I also might be slightly obsessed with how much I like her in my clothes.

"I'm sure," I tell her. "She knows where the litter box is, she was eating well and keeping it down. I'll take her to the vet this afternoon and get her checked out, but she'll be fine while we're at your exercise class."

I sneak another peek at her, the long cutoff sleeves of one of my old Aces shirts showing off her toned stomach. I spent a good portion of the night fantasizing about pulling up the end of my jersey and finding out exactly what she had on underneath it.

And then I got to do exactly that this morning.

I am not sure anyone has ever woken up to something better than her tiny snores only to get to undress her and worship her body the way she deserves. Getting her to the class instead of holding her hostage in bed all day means I deserve an award, however.

Abigail hemmed and hawed about wearing a pair of old flip-flops my mom left here, but when I told her my mom wouldn't mind at all, she seemed to brighten up and put them right on. They're a little big on her, just like the shirt and the sunglasses.

My mom wouldn't mind, either. She would be thrilled.

She would love Abigail, and the thought hurts as much as it makes me feel warm.

"That's it right there," Abigail says, stabbing a finger at an upscale shopping center at the same time my GPS pipes up and tells me to turn right. She twists the hem of the Aces shirt in her hand. "You don't have to do it if you don't want to. I can call an Uber to get home."

"You are not calling an Uber."

"Okay, I could call a car service. I don't want to bother—"

"I *want* to spend time with you."

"Lauren is, uh, a little intense. I'm just warning you," she says, taking the sunglasses off and staring at me with her big green and hazel eyes. She looks even better without makeup, in my opinion—even more real, more beautiful, more Abigail.

Seeing her like this makes me feel closer to her, like I've been let in on a secret that no one else gets the privilege of knowing.

"You make me feel special," I say, then frown at my non sequitur. "I couldn't give a fuck about Lauren. Besides, I need the recovery workout after yesterday."

"The smoothie was delicious," she says.

"Abigail," I say slowly, taking her hand off where she's systematically destroying the hem of the shirt. "Why are you so nervous? Is it me? If it's too much, me coming with you, say the word. I will drive you home afterward, and you don't have to see me again. I don't want to push you away because I'm ready to spend the day with you and you aren't."

"Your bathroom was weirdly clean."

Okay, so we're taking turns with the non sequiturs. All right.

"Yeah. I like things neat, and I pay a service to keep my shit organized for me. They clean the house top to bottom once a week. I'm not a slob, but I can't be bothered." I shrug.

"Oh. That sounds . . . normal."

"Nah, I don't think it is, but I can afford it and I don't give a fuck." I watch her carefully, noting the way her hand twitches in mine, like it's too busy to stay still. "What's wrong?"

"I like you," she tells me, frowning, her eyes huge and dramatic even without the makeup I'm used to seeing her in. "I like you, and I am not used to liking someone so fast, and it's freaking me out. I don't know. I'm probably just being stupid."

I raise her hand, kissing her knuckles impulsively. Her breath hitches with a little moan, and my cock immediately gets hard.

"I like you, too. I don't know what this is . . . between us," I say, searching for words. "And I'm not good at, well, fuck, at all of this. At talking. But I can tell you I want to try. I think you're special. And if I move too fast, I want you to tell me. I want you to feel comfortable with me, because I like the way you smile and laugh. If that means I sit out here in my car and wonder what the hell it is Lauren is doing to you in there, then so be it. But you're not calling a fucking Uber."

"Okay," she says softly, a small smile playing around her lips. Then louder, more confidently: "Okay."

"So I'm going to sit out here," I say, unsure.

"Nope. Lauren is going to kick both our asses, and then we can talk shit about her on the way to whatever it is you have planned for the day."

All I had planned for the day was being with her, so I blink once, then twice, trying to scrounge up an activity that doesn't involve diabolical Pilates instructors.

"We'll take it little by little," I finally manage, but she's already opening her door.

I have no idea what I'm going to do with her this Sunday, but I do know we'll have a good time.

Because she likes me, and I like her, too.

•　•　•

PILATES WAS A fucking mistake.

Sweat drips down my brow, and Lauren is screaming at me.

She's every bit as tyrannical as Abigail said.

The rest of the team would be half-dead by now, and that's the only thought that's kept me from giving up.

"Scoop out your stomach, Wolfe!" she yells over the music, which isn't really loud enough to yell over, but I'm not about to risk earning more attention and more sets of whatever the fuck torture this is.

"Pull up through your anus, Hunt," she commands.

I startle in surprise at her directive, then roll onto my stomach, not caring one bit about anything other than stretching out my strained abdominals.

"I don't know what that means, Lauren," Abigail tells her, and there's a slight choked quality to it like she's going to start crying.

Startled, I glance over at her, and she's not crying—she's trying not to laugh.

I bite my cheeks, somewhat terrified of what Lauren will do.

"Don't make eye contact with me or I'm going to lose it," Abigail says on a pained exhalation. "Don't even *look* at me."

"Your anus, Abigail! Your pelvic floor! How do you not know what your anus is? Your butt! The butt hole! Pull it tight like you're cinching it up," Lauren chants at her like an ass-obsessed drill sergeant.

"I don't know what to do," Abigail moans, finally splaying out like a starfish.

Starfish was the wrong word to think, and I snort, pinching the bridge of my nose.

"Don't laugh, don't laugh," Abigail mutters, and that does it.

I collapse onto my side from the force of my amusement.

Abigail makes a sound like an angry hippopotamus, her cheeks blowing out as she tries to hold her glee in.

"Your anus, Abigail. Holding your pelvic floor correctly is no laughing matter." Lauren's tone is crisp and unamused, and I see the exact moment Abigail loses it.

She rolls over to her side, and we face each other, laughing hysterically. "I'm gonna pee my pants," Abigail wheezes.

"And that is why proper form is so important," Lauren snaps. "Now get back in position and focus on your anus while you pull your core in."

"Please stop saying that," Abigail finally manages, wheezing.

"FOCUS ON YOUR ANUS," Lauren bellows, and Abigail forces herself onto her hands and knees, shaking with laughter as she crawls to the door of the room, then practically sprints from it.

"You should probably stop saying *anus*," I tell Lauren, forcing myself to flatten my expression.

"That's the proper name for it." The Pilates instructor frowns.

"We can't concentrate on our form while we're laughing."

"No one made you laugh." She sniffs. "It isn't my fault you both came here with the maturity level of preteens."

I sigh, stifling the urge to roll my eyes. "Right. Why don't we leave, then?"

"You two are my only clients right now," she says, her eyes going round in surprise. Her ponytail swishes as she shakes her head. "No. You can't leave."

"Then stop saying *anus* like that," I grumble, "and we'll stay."

"Okay." Abigail breezes back into the room, her cheeks red from laughing. "Okay. I'm ready to focus on my anus," she says seriously.

I snort.

"We're done with your anus," Lauren says primly.

"Don't put words in my mouth," I counter mildly.

Abigail crumples to the floor, laughing hysterically.

"Class is dismissed," the brigadier general of Pilates says tartly, and with that, she flounces from the room.

"I can't," Abigail moans, tears streaming from her eyes, her entire body shaking. "I can't with you."

"You can, and you will," I tell her, unable to keep the smile from my face. "Is she always like this?"

"Yes. Yes, she is, and I usually hurt so much I just concentrate on getting through the class, but then, I looked at you when she said it, and—" She bursts into a fresh bout of laughter, holding her stomach. "Oh my god, this is about as intense as the hundred."

"Fucking hundred." I shake my head. "Why is that such a god-awful exercise? The team would probably sweat bullets trying this out."

"Probably because of the position of the moons around Uranus."

"Shut up," I tell her, laughing roughly as I shake my head. "Come on. I'm hungry."

She hesitates, watching me carefully.

"What?" I ask her. "What's wrong?"

"Is it okay if we don't eat out?" Her nose wrinkles. "I am not in the mood for peopling."

"Do you want me to drop you off at your house?" Disappointment tightens my chest, and it's absurd to think how much I'm already invested in her. I don't want to leave her side. I want to know her, soak her up like sunshine.

"Oh—you don't want to hang out?"

"You just said you were tired of peopling."

"You're not *people*. You're my person."

I blink at her, pleasant warmth spreading through me, loosening the knot in my chest. "Your person, huh?"

"Too much?" Her strawberry-blond ponytail tickles the side of her arm as she tilts her head.

"No," I say hoarsely. "I would very much like to be your person." There it is: the truth of the thing simmering between us.

CHAPTER TWENTY-ONE

Abigail

WE DECIDE TO pick up a few things from my house—namely, clean clothes—before heading back to Luke's. I wanted to see Princess the Gray Floof again, but when Luke said we could swim and hang out by his pool, I was immediately game.

I sigh in contentment as he carries the tote bag I stuffed full of clothes and a bathing suit into his bathroom. He might be gruff on the outside, but the conversation between us flowed easily the whole drive, and I love the hints of his dry humor.

Making him laugh isn't easy, but hell, I've always loved a challenge.

Laughter sounds good on him, too.

It doesn't take me long to rinse the Pilates sweat off and tie on my favorite royal-blue bikini, and I search through my tote to find the gauzy cover-up I thought I brought with me.

"You done?" Luke says through the door, knocking lightly.

"Yeah, sorry, come on in. Didn't mean to hold your bathroom hostage," I say, still bent over and digging for my cover-up. Wearing one is something my mom drilled into me when I was a teenager, and even all these years later I can still hear her admonishing me to put one on. "How's Princess? She okay?"

"Fuck me," Luke says, and I jerk up, concerned at the statement.

"What's wrong with her?"

"She's fine," he grits out.

The intense expression on his face shuts me up immediately.

Lust roars through me at his heated gaze, and I stare up at him like a deer in headlights. Sexy, sexy headlights.

"That's not why I was saying fuck me." He clears his throat. "You are . . . stunning."

"I mean," I say awkwardly, "I wouldn't be opposed to it. Just remember your safe word is *cello*."

One corner of his mouth kicks up in recognition of the joke, and that's all I need to step closer to him.

The chemistry between us has been undeniable nearly from the moment we met, a sort of molten heat that's threatened to combust since the first fake kiss we shared turned real the moment our lips touched.

All it takes is a thought and a few steps until I'm standing in front of him, every cell in my body begging to be touched.

He lifts a hand, then hesitates before tucking a strand of hair behind my ear, his gaze fixed on my face.

A second ticks by. Another.

It doesn't matter that we had sex this morning. In fact, I think it's made how much I want him even worse, like his touch is the cure to everything that's ever ailed me.

"What do you want, Abigail?" he finally asks, and there's no humor left in his face, burnt out by the intensity of the same desire I feel blazing through me.

My gaze darts between his blue eyes, and I weigh the question.

Impulsivity wins the day, though, and I stand up on my tiptoes, wrapping my hands around his neck.

A groan slips out of him at the contact, his eyes half closing as I trail my fingernails down the nape of his neck.

"Everything," I finally say. "I want you."

"Fuck" is all he says before his mouth slants against mine, his hands immediately going to my hips, to the scrap of fabric covering my ass. "I want that, too. You can stop me anytime, okay? I meant what I said about moving slow, and what you deserve this morning. Sex is not the only reason—"

"If you don't shut up and kiss me . . . ," I tell him, practically frantic with need.

He huffs a laugh, his warm breath ghosting across my mouth before his lips make contact again.

It's like the wheels come off my inhibitions entirely as soon as his mouth meets mine. He squeezes my butt, gentle and firm. A moan escapes my mouth in response, and he takes advantage of the opening, his tongue sliding against mine possessively, deliciously.

I hook a leg around his thigh, pressing my body into his, losing track of everything but how good he's making me feel already, of how much I want more.

He breaks off the kiss, and I whimper, only for him to nibble at the lobe of my ear. His hands run up and down my bare back, tripping over the small bow where the flimsy material of the bikini top ties together.

"Tell me if you need to stop or slow down."

"If you don't go faster, I'm going to scream," I tell him, and I mean it.

"Oh, you're going to scream all right," he murmurs. "I already know what you like, Abigail."

I shiver, tugging at the hem of his shirt, wanting to feel all that lean muscle under my hands, wanting so bad to touch him that I think I might explode with the ferocity of my need.

"Please." My voice is a low whine.

"If you think I'm not going to take my time with you, Abigail Hunt, if you think for a minute I'm not going to enjoy watching you beg for me to make you come this time around—"

I take my hand and wrap it around his cock, an absolutely evil smile on my face. "Who's doing the begging? Should I put on your favorite classical get-down in the bedroom playlist?"

"Fuck, Abigail," he groans, and I grind my hips on the thick length of him, shameless and absolutely beyond caring.

"That's the idea," I say with a laugh.

When he bows his head, clamping his mouth around the small triangle covering my breast, the laugh dies in my throat, and I moan instead.

"Want you so fucking bad," he mutters, then pulls aside the fabric on my chest, ravishing the tips of my nipples with his tongue.

My fingers rake across his back, all that delicious muscle mine, all mine. I am positively greedy with lust.

"You wet for me yet?" No sooner is the question out of his mouth than his fingers are trailing carefully, sensuously, down my abdomen, teasing the top of my bikini bottom.

Waiting. For me to tell him to slow down or speed up—in spite of his rough words, he's all sweetness and patience.

"Maaaybe," I say slowly, grinning like a fiend. I feel like someone just offered me a candy store and let me have free run of the place. Or an adult playground. Or both.

"Am I allowed to find out?" he asks, arching one of those thick eyebrows.

I shimmy my bare breasts at him, my brain making the decision for me that if he's going to have me, he's going to have the real me. Not the fake sex goddess some of the other men I was with wanted, but the real Abigail, silly and over the top.

Me. *Just me.*

"Why are you shaking your tits like that?" he asks, clearly confused.

"It's my mating dance," I tell him very seriously. "This is part of it." I shimmy again, this time doing a head pop thing I learned in a tap class for actors. "I didn't get to do it this morning, so I have to do it now."

He barks a laugh, and I grin at him.

"You are fucking absurd, and I love it." With that, his finger edges under my string bottoms, and I grin up at him, pulling at the string on the side until they simply untie and slide down my leg.

"Whee," I squeal, kicking them all the way off with a little jazz-hand razzle-dazzle.

He's not laughing though, nope. Luke Wolfe is staring at me like he wants to devour me whole.

Nervousness floods me, and I let out a little laugh. "Was that not the kind of striptease you're used to?"

"You are the most stunning woman I've ever seen in my life." There's a feral growl to his voice, and in the next moment, he's lifting me up, his hands palming my naked ass. His mouth meets mine, and my nervousness disappears, the jittery feeling that gripped me replaced by molten heat running through my veins.

I wrap my legs around his waist, and this time, when I tug my hands at the hem of his shirt, he obliges, pulling it off.

As soon as I've got him naked, I pull away, breathing hard, my bare pussy slick with moisture and pressed against the bulge in his pants.

"You are a work of art," I tell him, breathless and needy. I run my hands down his delicious abs, loving the light fluff of curly black hair scattered across his chest, tracing the tattoo on his side.

When he does an approximation of a shimmy, I let out a delighted laugh.

"Did that do the trick?" he asks with a lopsided grin. "Do you accept my mating dance? Second time around is for the mating dance, right?"

"Yes," I say sincerely, nodding. "Very much yes."

"Good to know," he says, growling against my ear. He nibbles down my neck, and I squirm against him, needing more, needing it now.

Suddenly, there's nothing funny about this at all, and all I can think about is how much I want his hands on me.

"Bed. Now," I say, arching against him as he kisses the sensitive spot under my ear.

"Fuck," he groans, and the next thing I know, he's carrying me out of the bathroom. He tosses me onto his bed, and I sink into the soft duvet, my bikini top hanging on by a literal string.

"I could stare at you like that forever."

"Take your pants off," I tell him. "I want more than staring."

"Because of the mating dance." His blue eyes sparkle with humor as he nods wisely.

"Because of the mating dance," I agree, laughing a bit.

It's different now, the hot need of this morning replaced by this easy back-and-forth, like we broke through any nerves we might have and now we can just be us, completely ourselves.

My heart's so full it hurts.

He grabs one ankle, kissing it, then my calf, then the ticklish underside of my knee. I squeal a little, giggling at the sensation. "I'd like to show you the rest of the mating dance," he says. "I hear it has a really excellent finishing scene."

"I'd love to finish," I manage, still laughing a little.

"That's what I fucking wanted to hear," he says, his mouth on my inner thigh. One blunt finger strokes across the edge of my pussy, and I arch off the bed. "Just how I fucking knew you'd be. So wet and perfect."

His fingertip slides through my slickness, and he hisses in pleasure at it.

I buck my hips, a wordless whine on my lips, my body ratcheting tight and loose all at once as he finds my clit, making gentle, delicious light circles around it.

This morning wasn't a fluke. Nope. This is a man who knows what he's doing. This is a man who knows exactly what he's doing.

"Luke," I moan.

"You want more, Abigail?"

I nod.

"Say it."

"More," I manage, my breath hitching in anticipation.

His smile turns devilish, and he doesn't move, still making slow, tantalizing, and incredibly frustrating circles around the part of me that needs him most.

My eyes widen. "Please?" I breathe. "Please give me more."

Blue eyes turn triumphant, and then his face disappears between my legs. The first lick of his tongue against my sex nearly undoes me.

The world narrows to this moment, to him and me, to how safe I feel with him right there, despite how vulnerable this has always made me feel before.

"Luke." It's a plea and a curse all wrapped up in one syllable.

"Perfect," he says, and my hands wrap around his dark hair.

I lose track of everything but sensation, and when I shatter under his touch, I wonder if this is what it feels like to truly *be*.

Panting, I glance down at him, and when he moves up to roll my nipple between his thumb and forefinger before lowering his mouth to suck on it, my toes curl and the galaxy seems to expand and retract all at once.

"Fuck," Luke says with a groan, then, "Abigail."

Without a second thought, I grab his shoulders, pulling him up to me and kissing him.

His blue eyes are still dark with need. "You are so incredible." He shakes his head, and I grunt at him.

"What was that?" he asks, grinning at me.

"That was me saying, we're just getting started, cowboy."

"Cowboy?" he chuckles, but I reach between our bodies, to where he's still wearing his stupid shorts, and run my hand over his cock. "Why cowboy?"

"If you want," I say, propping myself up on an elbow and winking at him, "I can call you my pony and take you for a ride, instead."

"That should not be so hot," he says in a low voice. "Please don't call me pony," he adds.

I pull the elastic band of his shorts down, laughing quietly. "You got it," I say, pushing his hips gently, until he rolls over with a typical Luke grunt. "It's my turn."

I take my time, running my hands over him. Luke Wolfe is hung.

"What do you like?" I ask him. "You've spent all this attention on me, and I've hardly returned the favor."

"There is literally nothing you could do that would be bad," he says, his voice strained. His gaze leaves trails of heat in its wake, and goose bumps rise all across my bared skin.

"What if I bite it?" I tilt my head, pursing my lips to keep from laughing.

"That would be bad," he says easily. "Why are you nervous?"

Shit. "I'm not nervous."

"You get silly when you're nervous," he counters.

I blink at him, flummoxed. I'm naked in his bed, his cock in my hand, and he's gotten to the heart of the matter, of *me*, with that very statement.

"We can stop. If you aren't comfortable with anything else, we can stop right now."

"Luke." A sigh erupts from me. "I don't want to stop."

"Then what's wrong?"

My eyes squeeze shut, and that pesky, awful feeling of being on display, of vulnerability, rears its ugly head. Much uglier than the one I have my fingers on.

"It was that fuckhole you dated before, wasn't it?"

I open one eye, amused in spite of myself. "Fuckhole?"

"What did he say to you?"

"I don't want it to be bad for you," I whisper.

"Abigail." He sits up, his big hand cupping my face. "You are literally a fucking wet dream come to life. Every time you touch me, I—" He goes quiet, looking away from my face, then back, utterly sincere. "I knew I wouldn't last five seconds inside you earlier. That's how attracted to you I am." He gently strokes his thumb across my bottom lip. "There is literally nothing you could do wrong."

"Unless I bite it."

"Please don't bite it. That's a cause for anaphylactic shock, or whatever." He doesn't look away from me, and I loose a relieved laugh.

"So *anaphylactic shock* is the safe word, then?"

"Are you using it?"

"No, definitely not."

"I think safe words are typically for, uh, slightly more wild encounters in the bedroom, by the way."

I open my eyes wide. "Like with tigers?"

His laugh erupts out of him, and it makes my chest clench with affection so sharp that I pull his face to mine, kissing him as hard as I can, trying to show him how much he means to me already. I'm afraid of it.

Scared.

Nervous.

But ready. So ready, needing this, needing *him*—and desperately wanting another non-vibrator orgasm.

I push him to the bed gently. His teeth graze my lower lip, and I start to move down his body again, worshipping every inch of fabulous muscle. I pay special attention to his tattoo, and when he grunts at me, I laugh softly into it.

"Want you," he manages. "Abigail, let me make you come again."

"Who am I to pass up that offer?" I ask sweetly. "You don't want a blow job?"

I squeal in surprise as he pulls at my hips, shocked at how strong and gentle he is all at once.

"I want both," he rasps out. "Sit on my face."

I start to object, until his mouth meets the apex of my thighs once more, and I go loose and tight and needy all over again. I work him with my hand, then as best I can with my mouth, considering our height difference—loving the feeling of control I have in this position, loving the way I can feel how close he's getting.

When he slides two fingers inside me, still working me with his tongue, I rear back.

"Fuck," I cry out.

He speeds up, working me hard, and I climb toward my peak, sweat breaking out all over me until I break again, coming harder than before.

"Luke." I go limp, and he rolls over me.

"Can I?" he rasps. His lips are glistening from my sex, and I reach up to his face, nodding, still out of breath.

"Please," I tell him. "I want to feel you come inside me."

"Fuck, Abigail," he says, fumbling at his bedside. "Condom," he mutters, and I reach down to his cock, loving how it jerks at my touch, at the way his muscles contract.

Finally, he pulls the condom on, and a needy noise erupts from me.

He slips a hand under my head, the other on my hip, and just like that, I know.

I know I have nothing to be nervous about.

I'm in good hands with Luke Wolfe.

I trust him.

CHAPTER TWENTY-TWO

Luke

I SLIDE INTO her slowly, and she's so wet and ready and tight that I almost fucking come right away. Heaven. Abigail Hunt is heaven on earth, and I never want this moment to end.

Her mouth is pink and swollen, and I can't take my eyes off her. The way her eyes half close in pleasure as I surge into her, her perfect cunt squeezing my cock as I start to work my hips faster.

"Luke," she moans, and I grit my teeth together, stilling my hips, trying to drag it out, trying to make her come again.

"What do you need?" I manage, exerting some self-control. I've wanted her from the moment I walked into that boardroom, from the moment she laughed and made me feel lighter.

I want to give her whatever she wants. I want to give her the goddamn world, and I want to feel her come around my cock so bad I could fucking die.

My fingers curl into her damp hair, and I repeat the question, barely keeping myself from driving into her.

"More, harder, please, please," she whines, her mismatched eyes meeting mine.

I slam into her, and she urges me on in a desperate whisper that's going to be seared into my memory forever.

"Come for me," I demand, my voice rough.

"Uh-huh," she says, and when she starts to reach for her clit, I growl and catch her hand.

"That's mine now," I tell her fiercely.

"Touch me," she says breathlessly.

"Yes," I say, my balls drawing up as I get close.

The minute I touch her clit again, her eyes go wide, and she sucks in a harsh breath, her fingernails digging into my shoulders.

"Right there, right there," she pants.

I touch her gently, slowing down, so fucking close to coming.

The next second, her cunt clamps around me, and then she sighs, going limp, a dreamy smile on her face. I pump in and out of her, wild with my need, wild for this woman, my rhythm forgotten.

The smile on her face sends me over the edge, and I bow over her, holding her close as I find my release.

"Abigail," I whisper, and for a long time, I just hold her.

I don't want to let her go.

* * *

ABIGAIL'S CURLED UP naked in my arms. She's half asleep and snoring lightly, a catlike sound that makes me smile.

"I ordered Mexican food," I tell her, unsure if she'll answer or not.

Unsure if I should have woken her before I ordered food.

I'd order whatever the hell she wants, so if she doesn't want Mexican, I'll order something else.

"Mmm, Mexican."

Relief spikes through me. I trace a circle on her hip, and she grins sleepily up at me.

"I'm starving."

"I should have made sure I got what you wanted," I say awkwardly.

"I'll eat just about anything, honestly." She stretches her arms up, yawning, and then hooks them around my neck. "Except dick. I've been told I'm not allowed to bite it."

She bats her eyelashes at me, and I burst out laughing, then grimace at the image she's painted.

"You are definitely not allowed to bite it."

"I'm just kidding, you know." She walks her fingers along my chest, then pinches one of my nipples with a mischievous smile. "I wouldn't bite it. It just makes me laugh."

I pull her tight to my chest, kissing the top of her head. "I know."

"Good," she says, her voice muffled into my chest. "Just making sure."

She's quiet for a minute. "I wish I could peel your skull back and peek inside it."

"What?" I ask, slightly alarmed.

"I was just wondering what you're thinking about . . . what just happened."

"Sex? With you?" My dick starts to get hard again, and I push my hips into her thigh, making her laugh. "I liked it."

She pulls back slightly, pressing her palms against my shoulders. "You didn't think I was weird? I'm sorry if I was weird."

There it is, lurking just behind her enchanting mismatched eyes, that spark of hurt and fear I've seen a few times now.

"Abigail. I liked it. I like *you*," I say, serious as I can be. "I don't want to have sex with someone who's . . . pretending to be something they're not. I like that you . . ." I'm struggling with words. Words are not my thing. "I like that you are who you are."

It's inadequate. It's not enough. I don't know how to tell her that I'm afraid I'm going to become obsessed with her, that her realness and quirkiness is going to absolutely be all I want. I don't have the words to tell her my last girlfriends thought it was strange how hard and fast I fell for them, that they accused me of being jealous when I wasn't—I trusted them.

I just wanted to spend as much time as possible with them.

I don't know how to tell her that without scaring her off, too, and that's the last thing I want.

Guilt and shame slam into me, because my next thought is that the stakes with Abigail are higher than ever—I want her, and I'm going to keep wanting her, because that's how I'm wired—but I also need her.

I need her to stay with me if I have any chance of getting back up to Seattle to help my mom.

CHAPTER TWENTY-THREE

Abigail

I'M ON CLOUD nine, feeling delicious in triple postorgasmic bliss, feeling comfortable with Luke, if not a little anxious about . . . well, my weirdness. What else is new?

Then his face shuts down, going blank, and my heart beats a bit faster.

"Don't make me peel back your skull," I tell him.

He winces.

"Too much?" I ask lightly.

He grabs my wrist, pinning me against him as he flips us onto his back.

"I like that," I tell him decisively. "Big strong man."

"I need to tell you something," he says slowly, and fear leaves a bitter taste on my tongue.

"You're married. You have a girlfriend," I blurt out. "You are pregnant with the president's baby. It's a litter of puppies."

He tilts his head, giving me an incredulous look. "Where do you come up with this stuff?"

"I'd let you peel back my skull, but I don't know if you'd get what you were looking for."

He pulls me tighter, and a little squeak comes out of me. "I don't want to hurt you."

"Luke, you're kind of freaking me out," I whisper. "We called the marriage off this morning, remember?"

His grip loosens. "I don't have any of those things, especially not the puppy pregnancy. What I do have . . . is—"

He lets out a huge breath, and some of my now-dried hair flies up from the force of it.

I'm going to be sick from anxiety over whatever he's working up to telling me.

"My mom."

"I have a mom, too," I say breathlessly. "See? We have so much in common."

A hint of a smile quirks one corner of his mouth before disappearing into a frown.

"My mom is sick. With cancer. Stage three."

"Oh, Luke," I say, my eyes immediately welling with tears. "I'm so sorry. What can I do? Do you need to go visit?"

He closes his eyes, his throat bobbing. "I can't visit as often as I like during the season."

"I can't imagine how hard that must be for you both." I frown. "Is there anything I can do to help?"

"She's in Seattle—"

"I could fly us up there. I have work up there—"

"It's just hard," he says slowly, cutting me off, then rubbing a thumb across my cheekbone. "That's all."

I get the feeling there's more there, under the surface, but he doesn't say anything else, and I shouldn't poke at a clearly open wound.

"Okay, well, if you want to talk about it, if you need to talk about it, I can be serious." I draw out the word. "I am sure that's shocking to hear, but I can be a great listener if you need me to be."

He stares at my face for a minute with the same intensity I've come to expect from him, but with a hint of softness underneath.

"Luke," I say, taking a deep breath. "Last night . . . when I told you that stuff about . . . well, basically my most embarrassing moment and career suicide all at once, it was hard." I blow out the rest of the breath, trying to figure out what I'm saying. "But I feel better. I feel better having told you. Whatever it is, you can tell me. I'm happy to return the favor and listen."

"What if I told you I wanted to move back to Seattle?" The question is so low it's barely audible. His blue eyes are full of emotion.

"I would say that makes perfect sense." I squint at him. "Is that what has you all torn up?" Butterflies take flight in my stomach, because gosh darn it he's cute. "You're worried about . . . me? Being in LA?"

He shrugs.

My mouth twitches to one side. "So no. All right, spill. Whatever it is, I can handle it. I'm a big girl."

"My mom is part of it," he says slowly, the words clearly unwilling to come out. "What if I told you that you're going to find out that I'm an asshole? That I'm not worth your time, or your care, or your beautiful smile?"

I frown at him, confused, a million questions on the tip of my tongue that I somehow manage to quash. I told him I'd listen.

I'm going to listen, dammit. This is not the Abigail Fills the Awkward Silence Show.

"Why would you say that?" I ask him, trying to lead him to wherever it is he's heading. Patiently.

"Because I *am* an asshole, Abigail. People get tired of me, they leave me, and I'm not worth the trouble because I'm rude, I pick fights, and maybe I should just . . ." He gives me a bewildered, pain-filled look, and it takes my breath away. "You don't want me. You shouldn't want me."

"Well, I think I get a say in that," I tell him. So much for shutting up, I guess. "Where is this coming from?"

That's what I get for thinking things were going so well.

"It's who I am, Abigail. This is who I am. Everyone knows it on the field, that's how I've been able to play as long as I have—because they're afraid to start shit with me."

Oh. I see. "Luke," I hold out my hands, the universal sign of surrender, and he blows out a breath, some of that hard-fought tension leaving his shoulders. "Luke, I see you. I see the *real* you. Not the soccer-star bad-boy image that you have. I see Luke, who did a mating dance to make me laugh. Luke, who suffered with me through Pilates, which I'm pretty sure is banned in many countries thanks to the Geneva Conventions."

That wins me a small smile.

"You pulled up through your anus," I tell him softly, putting my hands on his hips, unable to keep from touching him. "Like a champion."

"I don't see what that has to do with—"

"Ah-ah!" I bark, interrupting him. "You aren't this person that you pretend to be on the field. That's part of you, sure, but it isn't all of you. Trust me. I'm a different person for every job. My whole line of work is putting on someone else's life and taking it off like clothes at the end of the day. Some days are harder than others. But I'm not the characters I play. You are also not just Luke Wolfe, bad boy of soccer. You are Luke Wolfe, kitten rescuer. Luke Wolfe, Pilates survivor. Luke Wolfe, giver of multiple orgasms and Mexican food orderer extraordinaire. The press? They don't control who we are. They might control the narrative, but they don't control this." I poke his chest, then lay my palm over where his heart thuds under his skin. "No one controls this but you."

His arms circle around me, and it feels like relief.

"I just need you to be you," he finally says gently. "I need you, and I need you to remember what you just said. For me."

Then he swats my bare ass, and I yelp in surprise.

"Want to swim?" His expression's turned mischievous, and I'm glad to see whatever darkness he's struggling with has receded for the moment.

"Mmm, definitely." I waggle my eyebrows. "Suits optional?"

"We won't be swimming if you don't wear something."

That makes me laugh, and I wrap myself tighter around him, nuzzling against the crook of his shoulder. My eyes close as I inhale the masculine musk of his skin, sweatier now but still tinged with the spicy scent of his bodywash.

"I like how you smell," I mutter.

"You wouldn't say that to me after a game," he says, and the rumble of his laugh tickles my skin.

"Maybe I'm into that. Maybe stinky men are my kink."

"That can definitely be arranged," he says, caressing my butt playfully. But when he grasps it firmly, then pins me underneath him and ravages me with a kiss, it's anything but playful.

We don't make it to the pool.

CHAPTER TWENTY-FOUR

Abigail

THE FIRST PART of the week blurs by in a mix of reading revised scripts, strength training and cardio, and random (but fun) meetings with Michelle, who's intent on cramming everything she knows about soccer and the IFF into my already too-busy brain. Darren's MIA, busy on the sets of multiple projects, but we still manage to send each other the most unhinged content we can find on the internet.

And then there's Luke.

Grumpy Luke, who's harboring one of the sweetest souls I've ever seen. Every afternoon when I get home, there's a new bouquet of flowers waiting.

Daisies on Monday.

Sunflowers and roses on Tuesday, followed by bird-of-paradise and giant glossy green-leafed ferns on Wednesday.

It's too much, and I make sure to tell him that, but each evening when I arrive home to another unexpected floral arrangement, I'm giddy as hell.

Luke Wolfe, the romantic. Who would've guessed?

I smile at the assortment of flowers on the counter as I shovel some eggs in my mouth. Jean's not mad about the PR we're getting, our pictures at Saturday's game splashed across tabloid websites.

It's always weird to have strangers root for a relationship in my personal life, and according to Jean, our new celebrity couple name is Wolfhunt, which, honestly, is pretty cute.

Lukibail doesn't have the same ring to it.

My phone buzzes, and I scoot it closer to me, sipping on my English breakfast tea, light brown with milk but still hot and steaming. Perfect. Everything feels that way lately, like Luke's brought me to life, like the stars are finally aligning in my professional life, too.

I must be the luckiest woman in the world.

> **LUKE:** Wolfhunt, huh?
>
> **ABIGAIL:** It's good, right

I'd sent him the article after Jean forwarded it to me, and it makes me laugh to imagine him waking up to the news of our celebrity couple name.

All we've done is two dates in the public eye, and already people are shipping us and naming our potential offspring.

That part's a bit weird, I must admit.

> **LUKE:** Good morning, sunshine
>
> **ABIGAIL:** Hi ♥
>
> **LUKE:** Are you ready for your desk read?
>
> **ABIGAIL:** Table read lol and yes
>
> **ABIGAIL:** I think so
>
> **LUKE:** You're going to kill it
>
> **ABIGAIL:** You ready for practice today? Game night tomorrow!

LUKE: I'm glad it's only in Vegas. Traveling gets old. At least it's not too far

ABIGAIL: How's your mom?

LUKE: She's hanging in there. Has a treatment today.

My heart sinks for him—it's become clear over the course of the week that the intensely private Luke Wolfe is also intensely protective of his family.

Which is freaking cute as hell.

Luke Wolfe is a cutie, too.

Pleased with myself, I decide to video call Luke and forgo the texts, and when he picks up on the first ring, shirtless, I congratulate myself on a job well done.

"Hiiiii," I say.

"You look gorgeous," he says in his gravelly morning voice. "I'm coming to see you as soon as I get back."

"Oh, really?" I raise an eyebrow. "You're just going to invite yourself over?"

"Yeah. I'll cook for you, too."

"The nutritionist put me on a high-protein diet," I tell him, wrinkling my nose.

"Good. That's what I'm on, too," he says, patting his abs.

"You know what else has high protein?" I smirk at him. "Besides meat?"

"Abigail," he says.

"You can drink it. Supposed to be very good for you," I continue, fluttering my eyelashes and sipping my tea.

He groans, and now I'm sure I've hooked him. Heh.

"Protein powder," I finally say, and am rewarded by a snort of a laugh. "Why? What did you think I was going to say?"

"That you were planning on giving me the best blow job of my life."

His bluntness makes me burst out laughing, and I'm glad I had swallowed my tea or it would have sprayed all over my phone.

"Well, I suppose that could be arranged if you play your cards right."

"I like the sound of that."

"Yeah, I'll make sure to cue up the classical playlist you prefer to jerk it to so you can feel right at home."

He lets out a rough laugh, and we grin at each other for a long while.

Easy. That's how it is with Luke Wolfe. Easy and so, so fun.

I don't think I've ever felt as much like myself with a man as I do with him. There's no pressure to be anyone but my normal, ridiculous self.

"I'm going to be thinking about you all day now," he says roughly, and I bite my bottom lip.

"An all-day boner might make practice awkward."

"It might." He rubs his jawline, where there's just a bit of stubble shadowing it. Yum.

"I'm not wearing underwear," I announce, just to be a dick.

He groans, covering his eyes. "You're going to your script reading without underwear?"

"No, that would be risky, even for me. I just haven't put any on *yet*." I wink at him.

"Fuck."

"Later," I tell him in a singsong voice.

His expression goes serious, and I tilt my head.

"What's wrong?"

"I should tell you something . . ." He rubs a big hand over his face, suddenly so serious that a pit opens up in my stomach.

It was too good to be true, I should have known it was too good to be true. One week in and I'm already entertaining fan-generated baby names. Stupid.

I should *probably* talk to my therapist about my codependent tendencies.

"What?" I ask. "Is this where you tell me you have a girlfriend in Vegas? In every city?" I try to keep my tone light and joking, but I feel like I might cry.

Ahhhhh, the joys of being a sensitive weirdo.

"No, Jesus, nothing like that." He frowns at me, and I wish I could reach through the screen and touch him. "I don't cheat. Don't tell me that last douche you dated did."

"Maybe," I say. "He hurt me enough in other ways. Tell me your thing."

"I just . . . really care about you already." It's so quiet that it takes me a minute to register. "I'm afraid of hurting you."

Pressure spikes in my chest, a sort of bubble of happiness that expands the longer I process what he's said.

"I care about you too," I tell him. "And you won't." I pause, trying to be careful with my words for once, trying not to . . . freak him out. "You make me feel safe," I finally manage.

He doesn't look better, though, no, instead, he looks . . . angry. Thick brows furrowed, blue eyes icing over as his mouth forms a thin, pinched line.

"I better go," he says curtly.

"Okay. Have a good day," I manage, totally thrown.

He hangs up without another word, and I stare at my own face on the phone for a long while, trying to make sense of what the hell just happened.

Who goes from announcing their affection to being angry about it?

I sigh and shake my head, cupping my tea in my hands, letting the warmth leach into my palms before I drink the rest.

Luke Wolfe, the grumpy soccer star, would get annoyed with him-self about showing any sign of vulnerability.

That must be all it is.

Still, the incongruity of it dogs my thoughts all through the car ride to the table read at the studio. I'm distracted as the assistants offer me a variety of beverages, and I take more hot tea and water.

I slip into the leather office chair at the large wooden table where a mic and my name written on a place card denote my spot.

There's a leather folder embossed with the title of the film on the cover, and I run my fingertips on it, excitement and a fresh bout of nerves starting to drown out my concerns over Luke's strange behavior this morning.

I did this. I landed this role, and now I get to finally sit with the rest of the cast and read the part I've been prepping for with Michelle and over long nights with the script.

A faint smile wipes away my frown, and I open up the thick folder to find a newly revised script, a pen with the studio's logo on it. A creamy envelope juts out of one of the pockets, and I lift it out care-fully, my smile broadening at the pretty script my name's written in.

People are streaming through the door, the rest of the cast getting settled around, and part of me knows I should be greeting everyone and making small talk, but this expensive stationery has my full at-tention.

I pull out the card inside, printed on some kind of cloth-paper compound, the fibers soft and boasting rainbow flecks against the eggshell.

Dear Miss Hunt,

I am beyond pleased to have you join our production of
THE ADVANTAGE GAME. Your audition was truly
a standout for me, and I have full confidence you are

ready to step into the limelight on your own terms. You
bring the sort of earnest innocence edged with
toughness and steel this role requires, and I know that
nuance will be evident in your every moment on-
screen.

Yours,
Richard Grace

My hand goes to my heart, and I stare down at the card, my eyes filling with tears at the sincerity of the sentiment.

I can do this. I will do this.

I have a whole team of people supporting me, cheering me on, and I'm finding my way with their help more every day.

My phone vibrates—probably Jean wishing me luck—and I shove the card back in the pretty envelope before tucking it into my purse.

The text isn't from Jean, though—it's from Luke, and I laugh out loud when I read it.

LUKE: Don't forget to focus on your anus today

I send him back a stream of peach emojis, and set my phone to airplane mode, feeling light and confident.

And if I do a couple Kegels in Lauren's honor for good luck? I think she'd be proud.

CHAPTER TWENTY-FIVE

Luke

I HATE VEGAS.

It's too loud, too many people, and too many fucking things everywhere.

Even though we don't stay on the strip because the stadium is on the outskirts of the city, there's no getting away from the constant cacophony of slot machines that seem to be in every fucking business.

"You look like more of an asshole than usual," Marino tells me cheerfully, clapping a hand on my shoulder.

"Fuck off," I mutter.

"You should be in a good mood," Marino continues, ignoring the death stare I'm leveling at him. "You are living the dream. You have a beautiful woman. You get to play with your balls for a living."

"That's not—" Tristan starts, shooting me an amused look from the other side of Marino as we walk through the overloud lobby. "That's not the right word."

"I know." Marino smirks at me. "I said it on purpose."

I pinch the bridge of my nose just as Gold breaks into a laugh. Marino, pleased his joke finally landed, takes off for the elevator before it closes, leaving me with Gold and the annoying chime of all the gambling machines.

"How are you holding up?" Gold asks, and there's a world of meaning in the question.

"Fine."

"Still crazy about the Hollywood girl?" he asks.

I glare at him.

"Right." Gold purses his lips, narrowing his eyes at me. "Still feeling shitty about it?"

"Fuck off," I tell him, an equal opportunity champion of the directive.

"That's a yes," he says, but he doesn't laugh or make fun of me. "So you haven't told her," he continues.

"Shut the fuck up," I hiss. The last thing I need is anyone to overhear anything about me and Abigail. I like most of the guys I play with, but do I trust them not to tell someone who would turn right around and sell it to the paparazzi?

Abso-fucking-lutely not.

"Listen, man, I don't care if you tell her or not. I do care if you let your personal shit affect the way you play tomorrow. You've been off at practice, and more people than just me have noticed it. You think another team is going to want you if you fall apart? You think we will? Some of us do give a fuck about things other than ourselves." Gold, for the first time I can remember, looks genuinely angry with me. "I'll take the stairs."

With that, he slings his Aces duffel over his shoulder, jogging for the double doors that will take him up to his room.

"Fuck you, too," I mutter, and a moment later, the elevator door dings, and I lug my bag into it.

Problem is, Gold is right. I need to stop obsessing about Abigail and how guilty I feel.

One of the Aces owners, Charles, walks into the elevator a half second later, giving me a broad fake smile.

I resist the urge to tell him to fuck off.

It's a close call, though.

Another player, one of our talented newer guys, tries to walk in, but Charles puts a hand up. "Take the next one. Thanks."

My teammate gives me a confused and concerned look, but shrugs and turns back.

Charles presses the door close button, and no sooner have they shut than he smirks at me.

"Ticket sales are up," he says, and I swear to god if he pats himself on the back, I'm going to fucking punch his smug face. "I had a feeling your little ruse with Ms. Abigail Hunt would help, but I had no idea how much. We've sold out the next two home games. You keep this up, and we'll be sure to let you off the reserve list."

My hands itch with the need to wrap around his neck and strangle him so he can never say her name again.

"How's your mother, by the way?" Charles continues jovially, like we're old friends and I'm not currently imagining throwing him off the top of the hotel.

My lip curls in a snarl. "None of your goddamned business."

"That's no way to talk to your boss," he says with all the sincerity of a fox in a henhouse.

"I'll talk to the asshole who's blackmailing me however I want," I say, seeing red. I take a step closer to him, making clear just who is the bigger man in this situation.

"Please, spare me. Like you aren't enjoying being between her legs." The elevator dings, and he winks at me as the doors open. "I know I would."

I'm gonna fucking kill him.

"Fuck you," I spit.

"Nah, I think Ms. Hunt's got her hands full with that," he calls down the hall, jamming his hands in his pockets.

The elevator door closes, my own furious face reflected in the mirrorlike doors.

What the hell have I done?

CHAPTER TWENTY-SIX

Abigail

MICHELLE'S TUCKED IN on the end of my couch under one of my fleece blankets. Another blanket follows it, then another, this one in a hot-pink-and-cream-checkered pattern, and I keep digging, looking for my favorite in the hall closet.

Princess makes a figure eight around my ankles, not sure what we're doing but happy to be included.

"How many of these blankets do you have?" Michelle asks, cuddled up to her chin.

"I got a deal when I bought them in bulk."

"You know we live in a place where it hardly ever gets cold."

"I like to be prepared," I trill, finally landing on the navy-and-baby-pink supersoft blanket I like the most. Princess mews as I collapse onto the couch and immediately climbs into my lap.

"Sure. Okay." Michelle laughs, and then she reaches for a piece of cheese from the last-minute charcuterie I threw together for our Aces viewing party.

"There he is!" I squeal as the camera pans to Luke's scowling face.

"As happy as a clam," Michelle says around a cracker. "Never seen someone who always seems like he's in a good mood."

I snort. "That's his game face."

"That's his resting bitch face," Michelle corrects, but she smiles at me.

"Wine?" I ask, then fill up her glass with some of the white wine I grabbed from the store without waiting for her response.

"Are you trying to get me drunk?"

"Nope. Just trying to get rid of this."

She peers at me. "Are you not drinking anymore?"

"It just makes me feel gross lately. Besides, the studio has me on this workout program, and if I have more than one drink, I'll sincerely regret it later."

"Less than ideal," Michelle says. "Do you mind if we switch to water after this?"

"Dude, that's totally fine."

"Thanks, dude," she says, and holds up her glass. "To hydration."

"To hydration," I repeat. I clink mine against hers, and I snort before wrapping myself up in the fleece like a burrito.

The camera on the TV is going down the line of the starters, and last up is Tristan Gold, the keeper. Luke's talked about him a little, and it seems like out of all the guys on the team, the goalie is the one he's closest to.

"Tristan seems nice."

Michelle makes an ugly sound of derision. "*Seems* is doing a lot of heavy lifting there."

I turn to her slowly, which ends up being incredibly dramatic, and Michelle rolls her eyes at me. "Don't even ask me about it."

Princess, clearly sick of how much we're talking, jumps off me and prances away.

"Nope, you're not getting off that easy." I narrow my eyes at her, then nudge her with my socked foot. "Tell me."

"You'd have to pour that bottle of wine down my throat," she says.

"That can be arranged," I tell her sweetly.

She rakes her hand through her dark glossy hair, which tumbles over her shoulders in supermodel waves today. "I really don't want to talk about it."

There's no hint of humor in the statement, and for once, I decide to shut up.

I like Michelle, and we've developed an easy friendship over the last week. Which either speaks to how friendly we are, how lonely we are, or some combination therein.

"Do you have a lot of friends?" I ask her.

"Are we friends?" She sips her wine.

"You're under a fleece blanket on my couch. I'm gonna say yes."

"Then I have a couple," she says, her lips stretching in a smile that seems anything but super happy.

"Mood," I tell her. And the mood is: depresso.

She drains half the glass of wine, then sets it back on the coffee table, grabbing a piece of jalapeño-dotted smoked cheddar.

"Why do you think it's so hard to make friends as an adult?" She breaks off a tiny piece of cracker, and I try to pretend like I didn't hear her voice crack.

"I don't know." I want to shrug, but the question lies too heavy on my shoulders. Or maybe it's the blanket burrito I've tucked myself into. Blanket burrito with a side of existential-adult-relationship-question guacamole.

"Do you think it's LA?" she asks, then pops the cheese in her mouth.

On TV, a little girl in braids is singing the national anthem, her eyes shimmering with emotion that could very possibly be patriotism or just as possibly be straight-up nervousness.

I wouldn't blame her for either.

"I don't think it's the city."

"You don't sound convinced."

"I don't know. I really don't. I think . . . people are different here, yeah, but that doesn't mean they're bad." I roll my head back, staring up at the wood beams crossing the ceiling. "I think that by the time we get . . . to being old enough to have less time for friends, that we're also less prone to falling for bullshit."

"That's . . . deep."

"Deep and full of shit," I tell her. "That's my brain."

"Don't talk about yourself like that." She chucks a grape at me. "That's my new friend you're bad-mouthing."

I curl my feet under my butt, feeling warm and fuzzy. Also a possible side effect of the fleece tortilla, but more likely from Michelle.

"We clicked, huh?"

"Yep. Clicked like a pair of high heels on tile."

"Okay, simile, go off."

"I might already be tipsy."

"You had a glass and a half." I laugh, tossing the now-scorching-hot blankets off. "I'll get us some water."

"Was it like that with the Wolf?" she asks, her expression serious and her brown eyes a little sad. "Did you click right away?"

I stand up, stretching my arms out, sore as hell from the weight lifting regimen the studio has me on, and consider the question. "No. No we didn't. I thought he was a jerk."

"But you said yes to a date with him." It's not a question.

"I did. He complimented me, and I'm a sucker for that. Also, I just . . . it seemed like there was more to him than just the Wolf image, you know? I wanted to give him a chance." I turn my attention back to Michelle and smile. "I'm glad I did now, though. He's just as sweet as I hoped he'd be."

"That's so cute it makes me sick. Gonna throw up rainbows," she says, but she's smiling at me.

"Water," I say in a singsong voice. "We need water before we start crying and telling each other how beautiful we think the other is."

"Oh, that's my favorite part of the night!" Michelle says, then drains the rest of her wineglass.

"Slow down, Captain Ahab, that's white wine, not the white whale."

"A-plus *Moby Dick* reference," Michelle says, tilting her empty glass at me. "A scholar *and* a lady."

"Oh yeah, you like a *Moby Dick*, huh?" I yell over my shoulder.

I hear her laughing as I fill up a glass pitcher I'm not sure I've ever actually used before with ice and filtered water, thanking the gods of dihydrogen monoxide.

A moment later, I'm filling up our glasses with fresh ice water, and the Aces are gamboling across the green Vegas turf, chasing a black-and-white ball.

"Oh, go Luke!" I yell, jumping up from the couch, my wide-leg pajama pants flaring out with my enthusiasm.

"Go, go," I chant. The next second, though, my mouth drops in horror as he goes flying over a red-and-yellow-clad player, hitting the ground hard.

The camera zooms in on his face, and I cover my face with my hands.

"He's hurt, oh god, he's hurt." I sink onto the couch, still watching through my fingers. "Why didn't they call a foul? How was that not a foul?" I ask.

"They didn't call it because the foul was to the Aces' advantage."

I can't even figure out what that means.

Michelle laughs. "Don't worry, this is confusing to almost everyone, almost as much as offsides."

I groan because, god, offsides literally is the most confusing thing. And apparently one team can trap the other into being offsides? And that's just part of soccer?

Talk about goalposts moving.

Or offsides moving. I frown, even more confused. Poor Michelle has explained offsides to me at least a dozen times now. We even went and got a whiteboard so she could draw it out for me.

I'm not sure it took.

"Basically them being fouled didn't hurt the team who was fouled, and it actually helped move the ball down the field for the Aces."

"Oh god, that's right, duh, that's the advantage rule, right?"

She beams at me. "Yes!"

"That's what the film is called. The film I'm starring in." I pinch the bridge of my nose. "That's the least I could remember, huh?"

Michelle laughs. "You're doing great, Ms. Perfectionist, okay? You've learned a ton, and you're going to nail the role."

I glance back up at the game, still worried about Luke. The camera has already panned away from where he writhed on the ground, and I swear, my whole heart is in my throat as the other players pass the ball down the field, moving so quick I can hardly keep track of it.

"Is he okay? Do you think he's okay?" I ask Michelle, suddenly frantic with worry.

"Probably. They would have stopped play if he were really hurt. Besides, soccer players are some of the biggest drama queens in the world." She looks up at me, cringing. "Sorry."

"I've made a career out of drama queening," I manage, but I can't quite get over how awful Luke looked in that last shot, holding his shin like he'd broken it completely. "You really think he was . . . faking it?"

Michelle blows out a breath, her lips buzzing slightly. "The Wolf? Yeah. If he thought it would give him an advantage in the game, I think he would fake a literal brain injury. I think he would fake anything to win."

"Luke Wolfe, the guy I'm dating, would not do that." It's emphatic. Almost aggressively so, but I can't help thinking back to the mini breakdown he had in his kitchen.

Her expression turns incredulous, and then the announcers are celebrating, the shot panning wide to the crowd, then back to the celebrating players.

The Aces just scored the first goal of the game, and within the first five minutes of play, no less.

As for Luke, he's up and running to his hugging teammates, without even a hint of a limp, his face as happy as I've seen it.

I'm stunned into silence for a beat. "I guess he didn't get a chance to do that at the last game."

"It's not a big deal. All of them do it sooner or later. It's just a tactic to turn the tide in their favor." She frowns at my expression. "It's why soccer players get so much crap from American football fans. Don't read too much into it."

"Luke Wolfe isn't just soccer. That's his job, you know? Faking it like that, that's not all he is." It's odd, how my first instinct is to defend him. How I don't want to see anything but that version of him—the version of him with a heart of gold. I so badly want that to be true that it makes me wonder if I've deluded myself completely.

The herbed goat cheese sits on the board I put together, and I smear it on top of a cracker before hefting it into my mouth.

It's my favorite, but I hardly taste it.

I can't help but feel like maybe I don't know Luke Wolfe as well as I thought I did.

CHAPTER TWENTY-SEVEN

MY KNEE'S A little fucked up from the tackle I took earlier in the game, but other than a few wobbles, my adrenaline's kicked in and I'm hardly feeling it.

We're tied with Vegas, 1–1, with six minutes of stoppage time on the clock. Sweat drips from my brows, the familiar sting of it in my eyes.

I want to fucking win this game.

I always do, because I'd be a shit player if I didn't have that drive. I want it more than usual, though, because I know, back in LA, my girl is watching.

I want her to be proud of me.

It's her I'm thinking of as a hole opens up in the defenders' line, Marino effectively distracting the hell out of them with some fancy fucking footwork. Guy might be over the top, but he is a damn fine player.

He calls my name, and I run up the field as he passes it. The ball connects with my foot, and any exhaustion leaves my body as the play materializes in my head. One of our outside midfielders, Logan Steel, manages to get right where I need him just as the defenders catch up to me, and I pass him the ball.

It sails across the turf, going exactly where I wanted it to, and Logan runs it farther up the field. My quads burn with fatigue, but I push down the pain, push it all away until there's nothing of me left besides the need to win and the sound of my blood roaring in my ears.

The defenders are shouting at each other, trying to catch up to us, but they've played like shit all game and now they're fucking scrambling.

My cleats pound against the ground, and a Vegas defender charges at me, but I manage to get past him in a burst of lung-stinging speed.

"Wolfe!" Logan shouts. "Time, *time*!"

He's right. We have time. He's still taking the ball farther up, I just need to get there. I need to get there—so I do.

I make it to the top of the box just as Logan hits the outside of it, and somehow, thanks to the hundreds of excruciating days of drills and sprints and running plays—I'm in the perfect position for Logan's near-perfect cross.

It's a bit high and too forward. My heart hammers against my ribs and I fucking run for it. My feet leave the ground for the header right as the defender on my right does, too. Fuck him.

I nail it, then fall back, my teeth clanging together as I slam into the turf.

The ball sails past the keeper and into the back of the net.

Beautiful.

Fucking beautiful.

I hope Abigail saw it.

*   *   *

THE WHOLE HOTEL bar is singing, and I wince at the sound of too many drunk men being too loud. Even so, I can't help the small smile on my lips as the header that won us the game against Vegas replays on TV.

Gold's standing on a table as fan after fan buys him shots, and from the way one of his eyes is half-closed, I'm going to have to make sure someone gets him back to his room safely tonight.

I attempt to politely wedge my way through the crowd, most of whom slap me on the shoulder or scream "L-A WOLF" in my face, as if I might have forgotten my name at some point between when I walked in the bar and now.

A beer splashes against my shoes, the smell of yeast and hops nearly overbearing.

Finally, I make it to where one of the team trainers is drinking a Coke from a bottle.

"You hurting after all?" she asks. "That one foul looked bad."

"As if I'd tell the likes of you, Lexi," I growl at her. "You'd just find where it hurts and shove your elbow into it."

The two other trainers laugh, and I jerk my head toward where Gold's now singing, a fresh beer in his hand sloshing all over.

"I pledge allegiance to thee, Texas—" He pauses dramatically to take a massive swig from his pint.

"Someone needs to get him up to his room, and the sooner the better."

Lexi sighs, her nose wrinkling in annoyance. "Between the three of us, we should be able to get him upstairs."

Gold chooses that moment to leap off the table, then slowly crumples to the floor. After a long moment, he tips back his head and laughs.

"Well, shit. I take that back—we might need a little help."

Marino materializes out of nowhere, grinning from ear to ear. "Amore, did you say you needed help?"

Lexi rolls her eyes at him. "Yeah. You wanna get your drunk captain upstairs? I'd appreciate the assist."

Times like these, I forget Gold is the team captain. Better him than me, though—I can't think of anything I'd like to do less.

The other two trainers share a look.

"I will help." Marino puts his hand over his heart. "It would be my honor."

"I don't fucking care who does it," I bark. "Just get him out of here before he pukes."

"Why aren't you helping, then, if you're so worried?"

"Because my fucking knee hurts, and I want to go ice it," I admit, surly about it. My head's aching, too, but nothing out of the usual after a tough game.

"Okay. We'll get Gold to bed, then I'll come work on you." Lexi's grin is pure evil.

"Fuck that," I tell her. "If I want to make it hurt worse I'll hit it on the doorknob."

"Rude."

"We'll bring you some ice and ibuprofen," the other trainer says with a laugh. "No massage necessary."

"Yeah, fucking take notes, Lexi," I say, scowling, but she just laughs.

She's probably the best out of all three of them, but I'll never tell her that.

She'll just take it out on my glutes if I do.

"He is in good hands," Marino calls out as I start to wind my way out of the bar. "We will take care of Gold."

"Thanks, Marino," I throw over my shoulder. "You played good today."

Surprise turns to a wide smile on his face, and I frown at him.

Why the fuck is he acting like I never say anything nice?

Probably because I don't.

CHAPTER TWENTY-EIGHT

Abigail

"THIS IS THE best part," I whisper to Michelle. On-screen, the cars whip around a city block, towing a bank vault.

"You've said that after every car chase scene," she says, grabbing a handful of popcorn and stuffing it in her mouth.

I harrumph. She's right.

"That's the whole point of these. They're ridiculous. Over the top. Absurd."

"I see why they appeal to you so much," she says, then smiles at me.

"Burn." It doesn't bother me, though. It's true. All of those things could apply to me.

"Too soon in our friendship for bullying?"

"It's not bullying if I like it," I tell her.

"Kinky," she says, and we both start laughing.

On the table, Michelle's phone lights up, vibrating across the surface like it wants to be a part of the car chase on-screen.

I stare at the name on it for a second. "Is Tristan Gold calling you?"

"Ugh." She throws a piece of popcorn at the device. Finally, it turns silent again.

One of the cars smashes through a huge window, going flying, and I snort.

Her phone begins to vibrate again.

"Answer it," I say. "What if it's an emergency?"

"Then someone who is working at the game with them can deal with it."

"What if he just wants to talk to you?" I ask, as sweet as pie.

She glares at me.

"Answer iiiiiit," I say in a singsong voice.

"No," she says primly.

"Fiiiiiiine," I sing in my best soprano impression, then fling my arm out, grabbing the phone. "I will."

Michelle's eyes and mouth both go round at once, and before I can stop myself and the manifestations of my intrusive thoughts, the phone is in my hand and I'm answering the call.

"Michelle, hi." Tristan's voice comes through on speakerphone.

She looks at me.

I look at her.

We look at the phone, and I point at it, mouthing for her to say hi.

She shakes her head, and I throw the phone at her.

The phone smashes into her hand, and she drops it like it's a live snake, staring at it on the floor.

"Say *hi*," I hiss.

"Is that you, Michelle? Why are you whispering? Is this a game?" Tristan's voice is slurred, and Michelle and I both look at each other in horror as it hits us at the same time that he's drunk-dialed her.

Fuck.

"Michelle, I just wanted to talk to you." He hiccups, and Michelle covers her mouth in clear mortification. "I love you. I just wanted to tell you that. I know you don't think we can be together, and I mean, we haven't been, but I think you're great. I mean, I don't *love you* love you, but I think I could."

Oh. Oh shit.

Bad choices. I am made of them.

"It's not Michelle," I finally say. "Hi, Tristan. Uh, Michelle's in the bathroom. It's Abigail. Abigail Hunt?"

Michelle falls back against the couch and smashes a throw pillow into her face.

Argh.

"Ooooh, you're having a girls' night? That's so great. I'm so happy for you. Michelle is so great." Another hiccup, his words so slurred that I'm having a hard time understanding him.

"She is great. I'll tell you what, I can have her call—"

"I think Luke really likes you, too, you know?"

I pick at the corner of the fleece blanket that I'm now too nervously hot for, shoving it off my lap. "Uh-huh. That makes two of us—"

"Yeah, like he *really* likes you, I think, because you know, he's kind of hard to read. Anyway, it's great, because now everyone gets what they want."

Michelle slowly moves the pillow from her face, a combination confused and curious look contorting her expression.

"What?" I don't understand. "What do you mean, everyone? Me and Luke—"

"And the owners. Because they put him up to asking you out. Forced him to. He was so fucking pissed about it. He did not want to date you, not at all. But it's all working out now."

My stomach drops, and the phone falls out of my hands with it.

I can't breathe.

Michelle grabs the phone, horror bleeding into her face.

"I—I don't understand?" I ask.

"The Aces owners, they're kind of dicks, right? But they're good at business. They thought you two dating would kick up ticket sales— raise ticket sales? Rise ticket sales? Make people buy the tickets. So they asked your director for you."

"They asked my director . . . for me?" I am literally going to throw up. Cheese was, for once in my life, a very bad choice.

"Yeah. It was, like, a scheme. A scheme. Scheme. What a weird word. That's a weird word, right? So yeah. They forced Luke to ask you out. For what's it called? Marketing. Public marketing. Personal relations. Relationships are hard."

My chest hurts. I rub at it, like that will make the pain lessen, but it doesn't.

"They are hard," I say softly. "We've gotta go. I'll tell Michelle you called. Drink lots of water, okay?"

"Okay. Love you, bye," Tristan says, and the line goes dead.

Michelle stares at me.

I take a deep breath and then burst into tears.

CHAPTER TWENTY-NINE

Abigail

"HEY, HEY, IT'S okay to be upset, it's okay," Michelle tells me soothingly, rubbing between my shoulders. "It's okay to be sad. But let's think. Do we believe Tristan?"

"I'm not sad," I say, wiping my tears away.

A lie.

"Oh?" Michelle asks, her voice gentle and her eyes disbelieving.

I am devastated. Completely, utterly devastated. Luke . . . I thought Luke was it for me. I thought he might be my person. I thought he meant all those things he said about liking who I was: the chaos, the silliness, my absurdity, and the constant too-muchness.

He made me like who I was. Luke Wolfe made me think I was just right for him.

I confided in him. I showed him the real me. And he told me my ex was an asshole for using me.

Then I took him to bed.

"I can't breathe," I say, sucking in great ragged breaths.

It was a lie. Everything he said, all the wonderful ways he made me feel.

All of it. One huge fucking lie . . .

All to sell tickets.

The world spins in front of me, like a top thrown off its axis. I feel so, so stupid. Stupid and hurt and used and sick and dizzy with it all.

When am I ever going to learn? When will I learn that I should be careful with my heart, with myself? I'm always saying the wrong thing, always trusting the wrong person. It hurts. Everyone told me to be careful with him. *Luke* even told me he was an asshole, and I was the idiot who wouldn't listen.

I am a fool. Again.

This time, though, he made me one.

Luke Wolfe used me, just like my ex, just like my so-called best friend, Olivia, and he'll drop me the moment this is no longer a convenient ploy.

Maybe I should be the one to make it inconvenient for him this time.

Just like that, the sadness turns to something hard and hot inside me, something bitter and jagged.

Fury.

"It's okay, just cry it out. It's okay," Michelle says, and my eyes flutter open, the world suddenly righted, no longer spinning.

"I'm not sad," I repeat, glaring at her phone where it lies on the floor. "I'm *angry*."

"*Oh*," she repeats, and there's a world of meaning in that one syllable.

"Call Tristan back," I say, my fingers scrabbling over the hard case of the phone. "We need details."

"What? Why?" Michelle asks.

"Because Luke played me," I grit out. "And I'm going to get even."

"Oh!" she says on an exhale as I push the phone into her hand. "I mean, you could just break up with him, right?" Her tone is full of trepidation, and for some reason, it pushes me completely over the edge.

I'm no longer dog-paddling in an ocean full of hurt.

Nope.

Now I'm diving straight to the bottom of the Mariana Trench, ignoring the way the pressure squeezes my lungs.

I'm headed for vengeance.

"Call Tristan," I repeat, jumping to my feet, my brain skipping along like a pissed-off hamster on a wheel. "This is the last time someone tries to use me."

I sniffle, wiping my nose. Why can't I stop crying? We barely dated. A week. It's been a week.

It's the fucking principle of the thing. I thought he liked me for me, all my weirdness, all my quirks.

"Hello?" Tristan's voice slurs across the room on speakerphone, and I give Michelle an enthusiastic thumbs-up.

"Hey, Tristan, great game. You were amazing," she gushes, twirling a lock of her brown hair around a finger.

"You really think so? Did you see the save I made at the end of the first half?"

"Yeah, I did! It was brilliant. You were brilliant."

I narrow my eyes at her. She doesn't sound like she's lying. She doesn't even sound like she dislikes Tristan, which is what I assumed.

My feet sink into the thick rug on my living room floor as I pace, leaving a trail of footsteps in my wake.

"Thanks. I wish you were here," Tristan manages to say, sounding half asleep.

I make a circle with my finger when she glances up at me. "Get him talking," I hiss.

"So, about the thing you told Abigail—"

"I talked to Abigail?" he asks.

I groan, then in a complete give-in to all my intrusive thoughts, I pluck the phone out of Michelle's hands.

"Hi, Tristan, it's Abigail. I need to know what happens to Luke if I break up with him. Does he get what he wants still?"

"Oh. How did you know about that?" Tristan's voice is thick with sleep and confusion, and I want to grab his shoulders and shake him back awake through the phone.

"That doesn't matter!" I growl. "I need to know what happens if I break up with him."

Michelle blinks at me. She's never seen my truly manic side before.

She recovers quickly, though, pouring some more wine into her glass and then shoving it at me.

I hesitate, but a shrug later, I chug it.

Fuck hydration.

"Uh," Tristan finally says. "Nothing. He's supposed to date you the rest of the season, I think. That's the condition."

"Condition?" I say, my voice so sweet I'm pretty sure my molars just rotted straight out of my mouth.

"Yeah. Condition."

"And if he breaks up with me?"

"Oh. Then he doesn't get off the protected-player roster."

It's on the tip of my tongue, asking what that means.

I decide I don't give a fuck what he wants and swallow the question down with wine as I take another swig from the bottle.

"Thank you, Tristan," I coo at him. "Be sure to hydrate."

"Is Michelle there?" he slurs at me.

I end the call.

Michelle's knuckles are white on the stem of her wineglass, her brown eyes huge.

"You heard him," I tell her, with all the intensity of a general rallying their troops.

Or troop, a single troop, in this case.

"I did," Michelle says tentatively. "Are you sure you don't want to just break up with him? I think that might be the healthier—"

"Do you know what my last boyfriend did?" I interrupt her. She needs to know.

I need her on my side.

She shakes her head, her lips pursing.

"He used me, too. He made me feel this big," I tell her, barely spreading my fingers apart. "I was so desperate for him to like me, to approve of me, that I set up dozens of meetings and dinners and parties so he could meet people. Network. Make connections. And still, he made me feel like nothing I did was good enough. That *I* wasn't good enough."

The wine's made my stomach hurt, and I blink back tears as I gently set the bottle back on the coffee table.

"As soon as I was written off *Blood Sirens*, he broke up with me. Even said I didn't look good next to him on the red carpet. That I wasn't useful for his career anymore."

"Abigail."

"He used me. He used me, and as soon as I was strong enough to climb out of a depressive hell and dust myself off, I promised I would never let another man use me like that again."

This is worse. This is so much worse.

I cradle my stomach, holding myself carefully as if I'll break apart like fragile glass if I don't.

I inhale shakily. "Luke made me feel like he liked me the minute he met me, and that made me feel safe. He made me feel like even the weirdest parts of me were fun. He made me feel seen." Furious tears spill over my cheeks. "He made me feel like it was real."

I choke a little, and Michelle's lips are thin in anger.

"He was lying the whole time."

Michelle nods once, perfunctorily, her eyes drifting from my face to some faraway spot on the wall.

"We make his life hell," she finally says, and I hiccup a laugh, brushing the heel of my hand against my cheekbone. "You make his life hell, until he breaks up with you, and that will keep him from getting anything out of this."

"That's the spirit," I say weakly.

"Where do you want to start?"

I wanted her help. Now I have it.

"I have some ideas," I answer slowly, thinking fast. A slow grin curls my mouth, wicked enough to rival the Grinch's. "I definitely have some ideas."

We open another bottle of wine and plot together late into the night.

Once I go to bed, I lie awake for a long time, trying to piece together my shattered feelings. Princess curls up in a little fluffy cinnamon bun shape in the crook of my neck, but even her sleepy purrs fail to soothe me.

With Michelle's help, I have no doubt we can make Luke Wolfe break up with me. Spectacularly.

Which is *exactly* what I need.

It was only a week of a fake relationship with him, after all.

Yet, no matter what I tell myself, I still feel the empty hole in my heart.

CHAPTER THIRTY

Abigail

I PICK AT the hem of my long balloon sleeves, knowing all too well they're going to be completely ruined in a matter of a few hours.

Worth it.

I'm sitting in Michelle's office in the perfect dress, a bundle of completely evil nerves. After spending most of the day doing makeup and costume tests at the studio, I ended up here both to ask for some clarification and get Michelle's take on a few IFF-related points in the script that have been throwing me . . .

And to enact part one of Operation Wolfe Shock.

I begged off seeing him yesterday, knowing I was too furious and hurt to be able to pretend with him.

A pang goes through me, but I shrug it off, schooling my expression into . . . nothingness.

I'm fine.

"So, we're on for the session with the whole team?" I ask as soon as Michelle hangs up the phone, returning her attention to me.

"Yep," she says. "And you're sure it won't make me look like an idiot?"

"No, she's the real deal. Just be sure to do what we talked about."

Michelle moves her mouse around, clicking here and there. "I can do that."

I hold up a finger. "Tonight is step one: dinner out."

"If he breaks up with you, you still want to go ahead with the whole team session?"

"Yes," I say glibly. "I'm sure they could all use the mobility training."

"Right."

"Come on, Michelle, I thought you were all in on this."

"I want to support you," she says slowly, still focused on whatever she's working on at her computer. "I just think it might be better if you broke it off with him."

"Kind of like how it might be better if you told Tristan to stop drunk-dialing you?" I regret the question as soon as it's left my mouth.

To my relief, she simply makes a low humming sound, as if considering my suggestion at face value, instead of in the mean-spirited way I'd said it.

A knock sounds at her office door, and she shoots me a meaningful look.

I nod once. Smoothing my dress with my hands, I school my expression into innocence with a dollop of delight.

Good thing I'm a trained actress, because as soon as Luke Wolfe appears in the doorway, the only thing I can think of is how much I want to throw up or start crying.

Instead, I smile.

"Michelle, you said you wanted to see me?" He falters when he finds me sitting there, and I throw both hands up.

"Surprise!" I exclaim, the corners of my mouth stretching uncomfortably with the wide grin I'm forcing it into. "I'm taking you to dinner."

His blue eyes light up, as if he's genuinely excited by the prospect, and a wave of anger and hurt goes through me.

How dare he act like he's not doing anything wrong!

"I thought you might be in the mood for seafood, since that's *our* favorite." I bat my eyelashes after the special emphasis on *our*.

Michelle and I brainstormed a million and one ways to make him run for the hills—using the royal relationship *we* was one of them.

"I do like seafood," he says, scratching his jaw and looking at me oddly.

"Of course you do, silly. It's our favorite."

Michelle presses her hand against her mouth as her eyes dance with laughter.

"Our favorite," Luke agrees. "We can listen to Yo-Yo Ma on the way."

I want to punch him in his handsome lying face for mentioning Yo-Yo Ma. How dare he speak about Yo-Yo Ma in front of me so glibly!

I inhale deeply, centering myself. Focusing.

He might be a better actor than my ex. I'll have to keep him away from any industry pros, the asshole.

"I've been on a heavy metal kick lately," I lie. I don't think I'll ever be able to hear the cello again without crying.

Luke's forehead creases in confusion, and a little mean part of myself relishes in it.

"She has. It's been driving me crazy." Michelle entwines her fingers and stretches them in front of her. "You two have fun."

"Am I driving?" Luke asks me as I stand up and make my way to the door.

"I rented a car," I tell him.

This is the part of the plan I hate the most, but I want him to go down in a big way. If I can soften him up enough to break up with me in public, it's worth it.

"Did you?" He grins at me, and I flinch when he grabs my hand as we leave Michelle's office.

I tuck it into my chest.

"I, uh, burnt my fingers this morning." I am an awful actress at the moment—not winning a fucking thing for this performance, that's for damn sure.

"Oh, shit, I'm sorry, babe."

"Don't call me babe," I blurt. Then I smile. "Please. I like it when you say my name."

Now that, that's the truth, and I hate him for it.

I hate us both a little bit.

"Okay, Abigail." Hurt and confusion flit through his expression, and guilt makes my breath hitch. "Sorry. Can't seem to get it right today."

"No worries. I know you're under a lot of pressure to make this work."

Fuck me. Why did I say that?

He blinks rapidly. "What?"

Smooth as a crunchy peanut butter sandwich, Abigail.

"With me," I forge ahead, practically running to the lobby and the car I rented parked outside. "I know you want this to work with me, because I'm just the freaking best."

Yeah, play up the weirdness and fake confidence. That will do the trick.

"That's true," he says, but his gaze lingers on me for a bit too long.

I clear my throat and fish the keys to the rental out of my bag. "I hope you're ready." The car alarm beeps as I hit the button on the fob, and I hold back a laugh worthy of a supervillain as he stops dead in his tracks at the car.

"Holy shit, Abigail. You rented a fucking Maserati?"

"Yeah, I did," I say with a snort and a flip of my hair. One of my rings gets stuck, and I curse under my breath.

Luke stares at me. "Can you drive a stick?"

"Can't everyone?" I dodge the question, frowning as I try to extricate my hand and my ring from the curls the studio did for the last screen test.

"What are you doing?"

"Ring is stuck," I say.

He reaches a hand toward me, and I start to flinch away, my heart hammering in my chest as his fingers brush across mine.

The bare, gentle touch of his fingers sends a traitorous shiver through me.

I'm holding my breath; I don't dare breathe.

I don't dare acknowledge the fact that even when I know he's faking this, faking all his feelings for me, it still feels real.

I should know better.

Finally, he manages to extricate the ring from my tangle of hair, giving me that grin that makes me weak in the knees.

Or used to, at least.

I cough to give myself an excuse to step back from the way he's leaning in, like he wants to kiss me, and stare at the ring instead.

It's heavy as hell, a huge cocktail ring I got as a wrap gift for another show, and one I only picked to wear tonight because it's truly obnoxious.

Obnoxious is my new best friend.

I'm wearing the worst of myself on the outside today. I continue making my way toward the yellow sports car.

Luke is going to dump me for sure after this, and the more publicly, the better.

"I had the rental company drop it off here as a surprise," I tell him. "I didn't want anyone to spoil it for you."

Also because, as Luke's about to find out, I have no freaking clue how to drive a Maserati.

CHAPTER THIRTY-ONE

Luke

THIS IS HOW I die.

The gears grind as Abigail attempts to shift into fourth from first, and I say a silent prayer as she stalls out for the third time. On the fucking highway.

The fiftieth person to drive by honking also shoves a middle finger out the window at us, and Abigail just smiles.

"Oops," she says, also for the fiftieth or so time.

My hands cramp from where I've wrapped them around any goddamn surface I can find.

"Start the car again," I mutter, trying my best to keep my cool. I am afraid for our lives, yes, but I do not want to yell at Abigail.

Well, I do want to yell at her, because what the actual fuck was she thinking? She doesn't even like driving.

The truth hits me like a ton of bricks.

I turn toward her, my mouth wide open.

She happily turns the key over in the ignition, and the Maserati roars back to life, then dies again, because she's still in third gear.

I smash the emergency hazards button, an eighteen-wheeler driving by so fast that the whole car shakes.

"I know what you're doing," I rasp.

Her hand stills on the ignition. "What?" Her cheeks go pale, then bright red.

Gotcha.

"You wanted to prove to me that you're not afraid of driving. That you're not anxious."

A choked laugh comes out of her, relief blooming on her pretty, albeit red, face.

"My sister used to do the same thing, you know. She has panic attacks, remember? She'd decide that today was the day she was going to conquer whatever her fear was . . . and then she'd get in over her head and . . ."

She's staring at me, her forehead drawn up and wrinkled.

"Let me drive."

"I am not getting out of the car in this traffic," she says, her voice thin and constricted.

"I know you're afraid—"

"I am not afraid," she snaps. "I am furious."

My eyes narrow at the strange change in her. She closes her eyes, taking a deep breath.

"Don't be mad at yourself," I say gently. "I'm proud of you. Trying to overcome your anxiety is hard."

I also want to get us the fuck off the highway before the yellow Maserati gets hit and turns into a tin of something like cat food in which humans are the main ingredient.

Abigail gives me a strange look, then sighs, staring at the headliner. "Fine."

"Good girl," I tell her.

Her cheeks turn pink. "I still don't want to get out of the car."

"Slide over the center console," I tell her. "Crawl onto my lap, and then I'll get behind the wheel."

Her white teeth flash as she bites her lip, considering it.

Another truck rushes by, honking, and that seems to make up her mind. Her heeled foot stretches over the console as she unbuckles her seat belt, whimpering slightly as another huge truck shakes the Maserati as it drives by.

My molars grind together, because all it takes for my dick to get hard is Abigail's toned leg sliding across mine.

"Shit, shit, shit," she pants, clearly panicking.

"It's okay, Abigail. It's okay," I tell her, then grab her hips. "I've got you."

Desire rushes through me, so fucking heady that my eyes nearly roll back into my head. God, she's so soft here, where my fingertips dig into her delicious body. The scent of vanilla and something spicy floods my nostrils, and I graze my nose along the arch of her neck.

"Luke," she says, gasping a little. "Please stop."

"Right," I grit out, placing her between me and the car door as I manage to climb into the driver's seat, much less gracefully than she did. "Sorry. I missed you."

She covers her face with her hands, and I strap her seat belt over her, then mine, before getting the car back to neutral and starting it back up.

The cacophony of honking finally relents as I turn off the hazards, pulling the purring Maserati forward and back on our way to whatever restaurant Abigail wanted to go to.

I love that she said seafood was our favorite.

Like she and I are one person, inseparable.

Seafood can be my favorite if that's what it takes to keep her thinking like that.

My palms stop sweating against the wheel as traffic thins slightly, though Monday LA afternoon traffic is ever anything but light. Abigail's phone dings, the GPS spitting out directions to get off the highway.

She's silent in the seat next to me, so quiet that it sparks concern. The GPS is useful, but it's not great company.

Finally, I can't take it anymore. "What's wrong?"

"Nothing, I'm just hungry," she says, but the corners of her mouth are turned down, and she crosses her arms over her chest. "I could eat a horse."

"I don't advise it," I tell her dryly.

A soft smile shimmers across her face, and when her gaze darts to me, there's a glint of humor in her eyes.

I exhale slowly, relief unwinding the knot in my chest.

The restaurant is all LA charm—meaning it's completely over the top and consciously hip. A valet practically exudes glee as I hand him the keys to her rented Maserati, and a bevy of photographers blind me as I help Abigail out of the low car.

"I thought you didn't like this kind of thing."

"Well, I'm sure you of all people understand that sometimes we have to do lots of things we don't like for work," she says primly. With that, she sashays away, the skirts of her dress floating delicately around her shapely legs.

I can't drag my gaze away from her. She works the crowd of photographers and now, curious onlookers, waving and signing photos.

When she blows a kiss to a starstruck fan, I wince.

Something is wrong.

I might not know her as well as I'd like to, but I would like to think I know her well enough to tell if something is really bothering her.

I wish she trusted me enough to let me know what it is.

When the crowd of people on the sidewalk starts overflowing, I finally wrap my arm around her waist and squeeze. A tight smile on my face, I direct her inside the restaurant, and she pouts prettily at me.

As soon as we're inside the cool and dimly lit interior, discomfort hits me in the chest. The normal post-training clothes I'm wearing stand out like a sore thumb, and I tug at the hem of the Aces shirt I threw on.

A refined-looking man immediately greets us, giving Abigail air-kisses that further set my teeth on edge.

"Bonjour, Ms. Hunt, I am Gerard LeFou. Merci beaucoup, thank you so much for choosing Salt of the Sea for your dining experience tonight," he gushes.

An annoyed grunt slips out of me.

"We've prepared a private dining experience for you, exactly as you asked." The manager finally turns to me, eyeballing me from head to toe. "Sir? Would you like a dinner jacket?"

Abigail bats her eyelashes at me, and I clamp my hand more firmly on her waist. "No."

"Yes, he would," she trills at the same time.

"Very good, very good," Gerard says, his French accent suddenly thickening, all congealed butter. He nods to someone behind me.

I hardly have time to react as a jacket slips over my shoulders. My molars grind together.

"Don't you look so handsome." Abigail bats her eyelashes at me, smoothing out the sleeve with a small coo of happiness.

Fuck.

If she wants me to wear the stupid jacket, I'll wear the stupid jacket.

"Thank you," I say gruffly.

"You will both be happy to know that we do not allow this riffraff into our dining establishment." He waves a hand at where the paparazzi stand. "Nor do we allow phones of any kind."

Ah, that's why the name of this place was familiar. They were all over the headlines when they opened a couple of years ago for their very controversial no-phone policy.

"If you could put your devices in here," Gerard continues, pulling out a clear acrylic container with a combination lock on the outside. "Ici, ici," he orders, and Abigail immediately drops her phone into the bin.

Reluctantly, I pull mine from my pocket and carefully place it next to hers.

Not that I'm opposed to a dinner without screens.

I am, however, opposed to being told what to do, and I've already put on their scratchy borrowed sport coat.

"The food here is delicious," Abigail says, and when I meet her eyes, her lower lip is trembling slightly as if she's going to cry.

"I trust you," I tell her, and I do. I do trust her.

Except around stick shifts and Italian sports cars, but now isn't the right time to bring that up. There might never be the right time for that, in fact.

"If monsieur could take his shoes off?" Gerard asks lightly.

"What?" I blink. No way I heard him right.

"Oui. Pas de chaussures. No shoes allowed."

"You've got to be joking," I say slowly.

He breaks into a laugh, and Abigail joins him while I stare at them both, finally shaking my head at him. "You almost got me—"

"Take them off," he demands, and another man flits into our circle, holding another acrylic case, though this one doesn't have a combination lock on it.

I guess they're less worried about people stealing someone else's used shoes.

"It's part of the experience," Abigail whispers, her eyebrows cinched together. "You don't mind, do you?"

"No phone, no shoes, and a sport coat." I sigh as I bend down to do as I was instructed.

When I stand back up, Abigail and Gerard are sharing a strange look, one that quickly smooths out into smiles as I narrow my eyes.

"Why do I get the feeling that I'm being pranked?" I mutter.

Gerard's nostrils flare, then he inhales for so long and loudly through his nose I start to wonder if he's having some kind of fit.

"Mon Dieu, l'homme est trop grossier, je suis dégoûté. Dégoûté."

He keeps muttering to himself in French, then sharply turns around, beckoning us to follow. "We have private paths to all the rooms here to ensure the celebrities who frequent our establishment are allowed as little contact with le paysans comme toi as possible."

The carpet sinks under my socked feet, and I shake my head, completely bemused by the entire evening so far.

I wish Abigail and I were at my house eating Mexican takeout and sunning by the pool.

This is not my thing.

A sidelong glance at Abigail brings me up short, though—if this is what she wants, if this is *her* thing, then I'll go along with it.

"You upset him," Abigail tells me, looking for all the world like she's about to burst into tears.

"I'm pretty sure he just called me something rude," I whisper in her ear. "My French is rusty, but I'm ninety-nine percent sure *comme toi* means 'like you.'"

My gaze cuts into Gerard's back.

A sniffle interrupts my murderous thoughts, and I glance back at Abigail, horrified.

"I've ruined our night," she wails as soon as my attention lands fully on her.

"No, no, sweetheart. You haven't."

She stops walking, sinking to her knees on the carpet that god only knows how many bare feet have trod over. I swallow hard.

"Yes, I did! I ruined it. I ruined our date. First with the car . . . how was I supposed to know how to drive a stick shift?"

I bite my tongue as a tear rolls down her cheek.

She covers her face with her hands, and I take her momentary lapse as an excuse to scoop her up into my arms and continue following Gerard down the dim lush-carpeted hallway.

Abigail simply stares up at me like I've shocked her out of her tears.

"Sorry," I grunt. "I have a feeling you're hungry and need to eat. Let's get some food in you." At least, I hope to any god that's listening that she's just hungry and not having a full meltdown.

"What is this?" Gerard asks, giving Abigail an odd searching look. "VAT EEZ THEES?!"

Yeah, his French accent is definitely stronger now.

"You are not allowed to carry the Abigail Hunt around like a sack of pommes de terre."

"Pommes de what?" I repeat, nonplussed.

"Potato!" he yells at me.

I did not have "small angry Frenchman shouts *potato* at me" on today's bingo card, but here we are.

"I demand you put her down."

I sigh. "No."

"No?"

I have at least a foot on the man, and though, contrary to popular belief, I don't like intimidating people, I step closer, forcing him to look up at me.

"I am not putting her down so she can lie on the carpet. I am going to put her in a chair, and then you will bring us food. Do you understand?"

He swallows audibly, his Adam's apple bobbing. "Yes. Oui."

Gerard finds somewhere else to be nearly immediately, and I set Abigail's tense body in one of the strangely shaped chairs.

Still seething silently, I pull out my own chair, a clear acrylic thing that looks like it's more likely to break than hold my weight. Moving at the speed of a drugged sloth, I gingerly sit down, relieved when there's no catastrophic cracking sound.

A long sigh heaves from my chest, and I steeple my hands in front of me, finally taking in the room we're in. Dark patterned wallpaper covers the space, black sconces providing enough light to see but not enough to feel harsh.

It doesn't feel like we're in LA.

I'm not sure where we're supposed to feel like we are, but other than the fact I'm wearing someone else's sports coat, socks with no shoes, and have a budding movie starlet sitting across from me, I could be anywhere.

"This is very nice," I say quietly, trying to prod Abigail out of her strange state.

She blinks at me, her green eye glowing in the soft light, contrasting even more than usual with her hazel one. Dark lashes flutter as she glances down at her hands, and there's a strange nervousness to her movements that's completely out of character.

I reach across the table—also clear acrylic—and cup my hands over hers.

Her shoulders stiffen slightly, the movement so quick and near imperceptible that I wonder if I've imagined it completely as she looses a long breath, a quick flash of a smile across her face.

"Are you okay? Was it the drive?"

"I'm wonderful," she answers.

It tastes like a lie.

My fingers go to the collar of the sport coat, and I grunt in annoyance at it before shedding it completely. If Gerard wants me to wear a sport coat, then he's going to be sorely disappointed.

I squeeze her hands, and a muscle twitches in her jaw, something like hurt sliding across her face.

"I'm proud of you for trying to drive. You want me to teach you to drive a stick? It would be easier in the traffic here with an automatic, but if you want to learn, I can show you."

"No," she says with a strange smile. "I don't want to learn."

I frown. "But you rented a car with a stick shift."

"Bread," Gerard says in a singsong voice, practically sprinting through the door.

I rub my eyebrows, annoyed at the interruption and slightly

disturbed at the idea of the answer behind why Abigail would have rented a car she had no intention of driving. She's clearly stressed, upset about something she doesn't want to tell me about.

"Rosemary sourdough ici," Gerard continues, practically getting on my lap as he leans over me. "Et ici," he points, "a cranberry-and-walnut-studded pumpernickel." He takes a breath and leans back, finally out of my personal sphere.

I open my mouth to ask Abigail more about the car—

"Et ici, a proper baguette, oui?" He's leaning over me again, pointing to another piece of bread on the slate serving tray.

"Thank you," I tell him icily. "We can figure it out from here."

Abigail pouts at me.

"Monsieur does not want to hear about the butter?" Gerard asks.

"Mademoiselle does," Abigail tells him brightly.

My arms cross over my chest as my annoyance solidifies into frustration.

"Parfait, parfait. This butter is a house specialty."

I raise an eyebrow. "Butter is the house specialty?"

"Mais oui, bien sûr." Gerard slaps a hand over his heart, as though my questioning him is beyond the pale.

"Right," I mutter.

"Tell us more about the butter, please." Abigail gives him that megawatt smile, and I sigh in defeat. I don't know that I could deny that smile anything.

"There is a secret to it," Gerard says pompously, leaning nearly completely over me, his hip nudging my elbow. I can't even see Abigail now, completely blocked by the butter aficionado who's clearly trying to piss me off.

"Ooooh, we love a secret, don't we, Luke?" She claps her hands together.

At least, I assume that's what the sound is, considering I still can't see her.

I lean back in my chair as far as it will go.

"We have a cow," Gerard tells her. "It says moo."

"It does say moo." Abigail gasps. "Luke, did you hear that? They have a cow that moos!"

"Is this some kind of joke?" I ask, completely flummoxed.

Gerard finally backs up off me, and I tilt my head, popping my neck as I stare up at him, frustration now reaching a boiling point.

Breathe in, breathe out. Focus on the only thing I can control: myself.

The Aces sports psychologist's mantras echo in my head, and they're maybe the only thing keeping me from reaching up and pushing Gerard as far from me and Abigail as I can.

I smile at him, and he flinches slightly.

I should probably work on that.

"It is not a joke," Gerard says, pulling out a pocket handkerchief and dabbing it against his head. "We have a cow. We milk the cow. The cow says moo. We make the butter. That is not a joke."

I glare up at him, and before I realize what's happening, Gerard begins dabbing his handkerchief around my mouth.

"What the fuck," I grit out, standing up so quickly that my chair falls over behind me. "Don't fucking touch me."

Abigail gasps in horror, her mismatched eyes huge in her elfin face. "Luke," she admonishes. "That's just the excellent service here."

"He put his fucking sweat on my mouth," I argue. "What the fuck?"

"Monsieur is not used to the finer things in life." Gerard's tone is stiff, and I stare down at him until he backs up several steps.

I keep staring until he nears the door.

"Is there a hidden camera in here? What the fuck is going on?" I demand.

"This is why people come here, Luke. For the experience." Her whisper is low and furious. Truly furious.

I've never heard her like that.

I hate that I'm the one who made her sound like that. I glance back at Gerard, who's somehow looking down his nose at me despite being a foot shorter, then pivot my attention back to the strawberry blonde who looks like she might cry.

I would *hate* to make her cry.

"I'm sorry," I tell her after a beat. "I shouldn't have . . . lost my temper."

My apology doesn't seem to make a difference. In fact, she looks more disappointed than ever.

"Perhaps monsieur and mademoiselle should kiss and make up," Gerard suggests.

To my surprise, it's Abigail who skewers him with a look. "No." Her tone is completely flat. "Perhaps you should take our order."

"We haven't looked at the menu—"

"I want the lobster and so does Luke. We both want lobster. Steak, too. Surf and turf. And mashed potatoes and some salad. Right, Luke? You want a salad?"

I shrug, giving up. "Sure. That sounds good."

"Excellent." Gerard, however, winces. "If you will both follow me to the kitchen to select your lobster—"

"That won't be necessary." I shake my head. I don't want to walk to the fucking kitchen and pick out a crustacean.

"Luke," Abigail says, and now, tears shine in her eyes.

"Fuck me." I roll my own. "You want to pick out your lobster? Let's go."

"It is worth it," Gerard assures me.

I assure my fist that it wouldn't be worth it and fake a smile instead. "Do we get to pick out our own cow, too?"

Abigail sucks in a breath, and at first, I think she's laughing at my joke, until I catch a glimpse of the horror on her face.

"No," Gerard tells me. "No, you do not get to slaughter a cow. Barbaric." He shudders.

"Lead the way to the lobsters," Abigail says in a choked voice.

I shake my head. What the fuck ever.

If going along with Abigail tonight puts a smile on her face, then I'll put up with it. Whatever she wants, it will be worth it.

With that, the zen I was searching for settles over me, and I follow the pair of them to where our unsuspecting dinner awaits.

CHAPTER THIRTY-TWO

Abigail

I'M FUMING.

Luke, on the other hand, seems confused but willing enough to go along with all the nonsense of the night.

The nonsense that took me several days of cajoling Darren's partner into playing along at the restaurant he owns, and while I paid in advance for the private room, I know he's still not thrilled with everything I have planned for tonight. Darren, on the other hand, was only too happy to play the part, because he's always ready to participate in my brand of chicanery. Usually.

Luke, however, wasn't supposed to be fine with all-out shenanigans.

How dare he be so patient and accommodating! It's infuriating. He must really want whatever the stupid Aces owners promised him, and that thought makes me even more determined to make sure he doesn't get it.

Asshole.

Big fake fucking asshole.

By the time we get to the part of the dining experience that Salt of the Sea is most famous for, I'm steaming. Absolutely livid with Luke Wolfe, who's somehow kept his cool, for the most part, completely.

Well, I guess I'll just have to up the stakes.

Gerard, a.k.a. Darren, pauses dramatically before throwing open the door to the room that houses the tanks. The aquariums.

I made sure that we would have privacy for this, because as much as I want to, eh, tank our relationship, I don't want to drown my career in the process.

Just make Luke squirm like a worm on a hook.

Make him squirm until he's forced to call it off between us out of sheer desperation to get away from my petty ass.

Emboldened, I toss my hair over my shoulder and saunter into the room. Massive aquariums provide the only light, and I don't have to fake my delight at it. Delicate air bubbles make the water reflections dance along the ceiling, and colorful fish swim in schools.

"Have you heard anything about this?" I ask Luke, sure of his answer.

He grunts, and I hate that I know him well enough that I know it's a no in Luke-shaped form. The light from the tanks paints him in deep blues and gray shadows, and he's even more beautiful here.

"You're in for a treat," I trill.

"You're all the treat I need," he tells me.

Asshole.

Incredibly sweet fucking asshole.

Fuck!

"Gerard," I say as sweetly as I can manage while I'm imagining wrapping my hands around Luke's stupid neck, "I think I see the one I want for dinner."

"Hold on," Luke says, frowning at me. "This is where we pick the lobsters?"

I laugh, slapping him slightly harder than necessary on his shoulder. "Luke Wolfe, you are *such* a joker."

He returns the slap with a gentle nudge and a confused look. "This is where we're supposed to pick our dinner?"

Darren/Gerard steps in between us with a nervous throat clearing. "Bien sûr, where else would we pick them?"

"From a normal lobster tank," Luke growls at him. His hands twitch at his sides.

Ha! He's not as calm as he's pretending.

"Why have normal when you can have this?" I ask him.

I've been psyching myself up all day for what I'm about to do.

"Depends what you mean by *this*," he mutters.

I clap my hands twice, and Darren bites his cheeks in a familiar expression that I know means he's trying not to laugh.

"I'm ready," I declare.

"Oui, mademoiselle." Darren nods, and then he scurries off, clearly relishing his role.

Luke stares after him, then swings the weight of his gaze to me.

"How the fuck are they going to get it out of that?"

"Oh," I coo. "I don't want to spoil the surprise for you."

If he doesn't break up with me after this particular display of weirdness, I'll have to truly up the ante.

I don't think that will be a problem, though.

Satisfaction makes me smile, and I roll my shoulders back.

Darren returns a moment later with a ladder on casters, one they reserve for the divers who clean the huge tanks.

When he hands me the swim cap, I tuck it over my head expertly, thanks to all the time I spent in pools filming *Blood Sirens*.

I see the exact moment Luke realizes what I'm about to do.

"No, Abigail."

"Prepare to feast on lobster," I say grandly, unhooking the wrap dress and revealing the swimsuit I have on underneath it.

"Abigail, what the fuck are you doing?"

"I have a plan," I tell him, and I say it with a sharp enough bite that he blinks in surprise, stepping back. "Don't you like me enough to trust me?"

He shouldn't, but I know now that liking me never had anything to do with it.

I force a gentle smile on my face and nod at Gerard.

He hands me a net bag, and then winks at me.

With a flutter, my silky wrap dress falls to the floor in a pile of cream floral fabric. I ascend the ladder like an Olympic diver, and the urge to laugh hysterically hits me so hard that my foot slips a little as I hold it in.

"If she hurts herself, I will hold this place and *you* personally responsible," Luke growls. "Not an inch of her gets hurt. Or else."

"Mon dieu," Darren manages, then breaks out into a coughing fit. He's also trying not to laugh.

There's an opportunity here. An evil, awful one, and the Grinch would be proud.

I twist on the top step of the ladder, looking down at Luke, who's glowering at everything, and Darren, who's holding up really well, considering Luke is pretty fucking intimidating right now.

It would be hot if he were serious.

Maybe Luke Wolfe should win an Oscar.

"Don't you trust me?" My voice breaks. "You don't think I can do this? You don't think I can swim in the tank and get my lobster? *Our* lobsters?"

Wordless, he considers me. Triumph surges through me.

This is it. This is the moment he breaks up with me. Just one more push.

"Why don't you believe in me?" I ask shrilly.

Maybe laid it on a little thick.

Darren raises one eyebrow at me. "I cannot believe that he would not believe in you, mademoiselle."

"Goggles," I tell him, and he pulls a set out of his inside jacket pocket.

It's so absurd I nearly break character. But I am an actress, dammit, and I am going to do this.

"I think you can do whatever you want," Luke finally says, sweeping a hand over his wavy black hair, clearly distressed. "I just don't want you to get hurt."

"It would be hard to go to your games if I were hurt," I say blithely.

He blinks. "Well, that's true, but I don't care about that. It would be hard for you period if you got hurt—"

"If you don't believe in me, just tell me," I interrupt him, nearly throwing a hand across my forehead in true dramatic fashion.

"Abigail, if you really want to do this, then do it," he says. "Gerard, you'd better have a towel. I don't want her to be cold."

"Why are you always worried about my temperature regulation," I cry out. "My body is perfectly capable of regulating!"

"Of course it is," Luke says slowly.

I cringe, turning back to the tank. That was a little far. I pop the goggles on, pressing them into my eyes and making sure they're sealed.

Maybe improvisation isn't my strong suit.

Swimming, however, is. I grin at my wavering reflection on the top of the tank, and then I step in. Fish scatter all around me, the water colder than I expected.

It's always a shock when you first jump in, but this takes my breath away.

Shit. Maybe I spoke too soon about temperature regulation.

Something red and armored scurries across the bottom of the tank, and I grin at it, bubbles coming from my mouth as I laugh.

If Luke isn't running for the door already at all the red flags I'm throwing at his face, the third act of our date is about to be the coup de grâce. My legs scissor kick, and I break the surface of the tank, taking a deep breath, then surge down as fast as I can, the mesh bag still in hand.

The lobster stops right where I wanted it to, and I narrowly avoid sucking in a lungful of water as I swallow my laugh.

From inside the tank, it's clear how fake it is, but I doubt Luke can tell, especially at the angle the robot lobster stopped.

Good job, Darren/Gerard.

I kick a few times, reaching the lobster easily and tucking it inside the mesh bag. I give a thumbs-up to the wavering shapes of Luke and Darren, then swim quickly back up to the surface, my prize secured.

Triumphant, I emerge, dripping water as I plop the mesh bag and lobster toy on the top stair of the ladder, then pull myself out.

"That was amazing," Luke says.

Just like that, my self-congratulatory high withers.

"I forgot for a minute how well you swim," he continues. "You must have spent hours training for that show, huh?"

I scowl at him, then glance at Darren.

To my surprise, Darren's face is one of extreme trepidation. "That's not the right lobster," he whispers.

"What are you talking about? That's going to be great." Luke frowns at him, then hands me a fluffy towel.

I give him a real smile, preening at his praise, until I remember I hate him.

"Put the lobster back," Darren says, his dark eyes narrowed. He jerks his chin meaningfully to the bag at my side.

"This lobster?" I ask, laughing at him. I reach for the bag, and pain slices through the soft skin between my thumb and forefinger. "What the fuck?"

"Abigail," Luke says, his voice anguished.

The pain in my hand and that tone from him only makes me madder. "What the *fuck*?" I repeat.

The lobster isn't a fake. It's not the pool toy Darren sent me a picture of. How the hell did I manage to grab the real lobster in the tank?

"Shit, ouch, shit," I chant. "Let go, you mean little fucker." The ladder I'm perched on shakes, and the next second, Luke is there, crowding me in, cradling my hurt hand against his chest, his blue eyes livid.

"I warned you what would happen if she got hurt," he snarls at Darren.

"It's not Dar–Gerard's fault," I tell him, my voice sharp with pain. "Here," I say, and it sounds a little like a whine, even to my ears. "I'll fix it."

I dangle my hand, and thereby the lobster, into the salt water, choking on a curse as the salt hits the open wound. The lobster grips hard, and I suck in a breath.

"Do something," Luke growls at Darren.

"Leave him alone," I mutter, somewhere between wanting him to really be this upset about me being hurt and wanting to kick him in the shins for pretending so well. "He's not the one pinching me—"

No sooner have the words left my mouth than the lobster decides he'd rather be nowhere near me and scuttles off.

Red blooms around where my hand's still in the water, and I hiss as a fresh wave of hurt hits me.

"Right," Luke says efficiently, hauling me up and into his chest so quickly that it makes me slightly nauseous. "We're going to the hospital."

"I don't need to go to the—"

"You don't know what you need," he says to me so coldly that it burns away any lingering feelings.

I can't stand Luke Wolfe.

Of all the overbearing, mean, hypocritical assholes.

I glance down at my hand and immediately wish I hadn't.

"You're right," I say wispily. "I think I do need to go to the hospital."

And then, embarrassingly, I faint.

CHAPTER THIRTY-THREE

Abigail

"DOES SHE FAINT often?" a voice trickles through the dark curtain of my bizarre dreams, and I open my eyes, blinking at the brightness of the lights.

"No, she doesn't," I croak. "I don't like blood."

Something tugs at my hand, not painful so much as strange, and I glance down at where a nurse is stitching me back together—and, groaning, immediately pass out again.

. . .

"—VASOVAGAL RESPONSE. HAVEN'T seen one that lasts this long in a while."

"Stop talking about her like she's some research project," a familiar voice rasps angrily.

Warmth fills me at it, and I open my eyes again, very carefully not looking at my hand, and smile up at him.

Luke.

Wait. No. Luke is not good.

I frown, shaking my head. Luke is an asshole, who drove me to the—

"You're awake," he says, rushing from where he was talking to the doctor and pressing a hand against my forehead.

Irritable, I brush his hand away with mine, or try to, only to manage a hiss in pain as the IV line they put in catches on the side of the bed.

"Gross," I whine.

"Is it needles in general, then?" the doctor asks, peering at me from above his spectacles. "Or blood? Both?"

Luke's right. He does sound much too excited about the prospect of what makes me pass out.

"It's overly enthusiastic doctors," I snap.

"Your husband said you got the wound from a lobster?" he asks, raising his eyebrows in disbelief.

"Yeah, it was a lobst—" I stop.

Slowly, so slowly, I turn my head to look at Luke, who is staunchly avoiding my gaze.

"Do I want to know why you were handling a lobster?"

"No," Luke and I say at the same time.

"Dinner," I finally say, and it's at least a partial truth. "We were going to have lobster for dinner, and it pinched me."

"I thought they had bands around their claws," the doctor muses.

"Well, this one didn't," I say rudely. "Can I go home now?"

He gives me a long look. "Blood, then? Or needles? Which is it?"

"Get us the paperwork and leave her alone," Luke says.

Finally, the doctor relents, leaving the two of us alone in the aqua-and-purple hospital room.

"My husband?" I ask archly.

"They wouldn't let me in with you unless I was family. Said it was protocol. I said we didn't go public with the marriage so the paparazzi wouldn't have a field day with it."

It shouldn't hurt so much. The fact he didn't want me to be alone, even though this would be an easy out for him.

"You didn't have to do that," I say, blinking back tears. My head thumps against the lump of a pillow behind it, and I count the squares on the ceiling.

"You gave me the idea," he says, holding my good hand, his thumb making tiny circles.

"How in the world did I give you the idea?" I snort, unable to keep from looking at his face.

He raises one of those gloriously thick eyebrows at me. "The first time we had seafood together, you threatened anaphylactic shock and a hospital visit as a married couple. I thought I'd make your dreams come true."

I laugh in spite of myself, and then it abruptly stops.

He leans close, some of the worry relaxing from the corner of his eyes, his lips ghosting over my ear. "I think maybe our safe word should be *lobster*, though."

Bossy, grunting Luke is already hard for me to resist. Teasing Luke is practically impossible to.

This man would be a lot easier to hate if I didn't like him so damned much.

It would hurt a lot less, too.

"I want to go home," I say, then turn on my side away from him, watching the IV drip down the line.

CHAPTER THIRTY-FOUR

Luke

"A LOBSTER *PINCHED* her?" Gold asks incredulously.

A ball sails past him into the net, and he doesn't even blink.

"Yeah. Eight stitches. Could have been worse. But when she fainted . . ." I shake my head. "It scared the shit out of me."

"How the hell did a lobster do that? Why was she even *around* a lobster?" He tilts his head, frowning. "Is this some kind of a kink thing?"

I snort, grinning as I remember the way Abigail's eyes lit up in humor when I suggested *lobster* as a safe word at the hospital. "No. We were— you know what? I don't think you'd believe me if I told you."

Gold gives me a long look, tossing his longish hair over a shoulder before tying it up on top of his head.

"I drunk-dialed Michelle in Vegas," he says slowly.

I grunt, stretching out my quad. "And?"

"And she called me back." He clears his throat. "The same night."

"Was it good? A good talk?" I clarify. Goddammit, when did I get invested in Gold's love life?

It's like being with Abigail has helped me remember how to be a friend, how to hold a conversation with someone.

She reminded me how to care.

My chest seems to expand, and I catch myself smiling at absolutely nothing, just the mere thought of her.

"I don't remember." He stretches his arms long overhead, then jogs in place. "I think I'm done drinking."

"I don't blame you," I tell him.

"What if I said something embarrassing?" he cringes at the thought.

"You probably did," I say.

"Fuck you, Wolfe," he says, but he laughs.

A whistle blows, and we blink at each other in confusion. It's not like them to change up our routine. Coach Garrett likes things the same, day in and day out.

"Listen up!" Coach shouts, scowling at all of us. That's nothing new, though—Coach always looks like he just bit into a lemon.

I bend over, adjusting my shin guard. Probably time to retire this pair of practice cleats, too. Unlike a lot of the guys, I don't like wearing the latest brand-name shit.

"We have a guest instructor here at the request of none other than the LA Wolf."

I jerk up straight, glancing around in confusion.

"Nice, Wolfe," Gold slaps a hand on my shoulder. "Coulda warned us, you jerk."

"I don't know—"

"It's my pleasure to introduce Lauren Reacher, of Reacher Pilates. Let's give her a warm Aces greeting."

"You've got to be fucking kidding me."

Coach Garrett pins me with a glare, and a moment later, Lauren appears, decked out in what appears to be a gold-and-rhinestone bodysuit.

"Dude," Gold says, shooting me an incredulous look. "What the hell?"

Applause breaks out, the guys whooping, and when Lauren waves at them, her ponytail bouncing, I think it's for her.

Until I catch sight of Abigail, waving her bandaged hand.

And just like that, it all makes sense.

Abigail did this.

Affection spreads through me, a sweet addiction. I'd barely heard from her all week, since what will forever go down in history as the absolute worst date of my entire life.

The urge to run to her, to hold her and ask if she's all right, crashes over me, so strong it's like a punch to the gut.

It's been only four days since I last saw her, when I took her home from the hospital and tried to tuck her in bed. She wouldn't let me.

She barely looked at me, and when I asked her what was wrong, she said she was fine.

I'm by no means an expert at women, but I have no doubt that was a lie. Abigail was anything but fine.

The messages I'd sent her were perfunctorily answered, and I assumed it was because it hurt her hand to type, or because she was embarrassed about how the date went.

Now she's here, though, a smug look on her face that makes me want to kiss her until it turns into the sunrise of a smile I'm fully addicted to.

Feedback crackles from the practice fields' speakers, and then Lauren's voice blares out, filling the space.

"Thank you so much for having me, LA Aces." She waves a hand, her gold bodysuit practically blinding in the morning light. "Now, who's ready to work?"

A few of the guys cheer, and I shake my head, bemused at how Abigail always knows just what to do. I mentioned in passing how Lauren would have kicked our asses, and here she is, trying to make us all better, stronger.

The time it took for her to set something up like this so quickly with the team and Lauren speaks volumes about her thoughtfulness, and the fact that she did it at all nearly brings a smile to my face.

It's tugging up the corners of my mouth as soon as Lauren says,

"Now, I've heard a special man here, Mr. Luke Wolfe, has asked me to spend plenty of time working your pelvic floors today. We are going to be concentrating on allllll the teeny-tiny muscles that are so important for bladder control and erectile function. Thanks to my client Abigail for pointing out how much you all need it!"

The entire team turns to me at once.

My smile disappears, and I stare at her in shock.

"Erectile function?" Gold manages through a laugh.

The rest of the team is laughing, too, several pointing at me and holding their stomachs. My shock turns into a scowl.

Marino launches himself into a sprint, running for where Lauren stands, clearly at a loss. My own embarrassment pales at how rude the rest of the team is being to her. And, by extension, to Abigail.

"Fucking hell," I mutter. My gaze shifts to where Abigail stands, her bandaged hand over her mouth as she watches Lauren flounder.

"This is no laughing matter!" Marino yells, standing next to Lauren and her miked-up headset. He gestures wildly. "It could happen to any of us. We should be thanking our good friend and teammate Wolfe for bringing this attention to us. To our attention, I mean." Marino looks sincere and angry, and that, more than anything, surprises me the most this morning. "Lauren, bellissima, continue, per favore. Forgive my idiot teammates. They will understand soon how little we pay attention to the muscoli there."

Even from this far away, I see Lauren's chest rise and fall as she inhales deeply, then nods.

"Right, Thank you . . ."

"Enzo. Enzo Marino," he says easily, then, to none of our surprise, he takes Lauren's hand and presses a kiss to her knuckles. "Bellissima."

With that, he turns around, giving us all a death stare.

"If everyone could move up and take a spot closer, that way I'll be able to correct your form."

No one moves except for Marino, who sits on the grass before the glinting Lauren.

I glance at Abigail, who continues standing stock-still.

"Fuck," I repeat, and then I jog over to Lauren and Marino.

After I stare at him for a moment, Gold joins us, grinning at all of us in that easy way of his.

"Get your asses up here!" I yell at the rest of the team, frowning ferociously.

I will not let them ruin Abigail's day because they're a bunch of immature pricks.

"If taking care of everyone's lower bodies—"

"Pelvic floors," Lauren's voice booms out over the crackling speakers again, and I hold in a wince.

"Right." I take a breath, pinching my nose and gathering myself again. "If Coach and Lauren think this is important and will improve our gameplay and protect our bodies as we get older, then we should fucking do it. Now get your asses up here so you can focus on your anus."

A couple of the guys laugh, but when I give them a glare, they glance at each other uneasily and finally form ranks around us.

"Luke Wolfe took the words right out of my mouth." Lauren claps her hands together, clearly heartened by my impromptu speech.

"From his anus to your lips," someone says, and a couple of the guys crack up.

That's fucking *it*.

"The next person who tries to say something funny about any of this can run wind sprints for the rest of the day, and I don't give a fuck how many of you throw up. You will respect Lauren and her time, or you will be hurting."

I glance at Coach Garrett, and he shrugs one shoulder in approval.

"Right. Now be respectful and focus on your anuses," I bellow.

CHAPTER THIRTY-FIVE

Abigail

TO SAY THE team exercise session did not go the way I planned is a gross understatement. I blow out a breath, sending my hair flying.

"Thank you for the great session," another player tells Lauren, who beams at the praise.

"You're the best for finding this gem of a trainer," one of the guys tells me, grinning widely before wincing as he gingerly steps past where Lauren and I stand. "I am going to be sore in places I didn't even know I could be."

I make myself smile at him, but inside, I want to scream. I want to tear my hair out.

As for the real target of my ire, Luke Wolfe watches me carefully, and I wonder if he's finally guessed what I'm playing at. *Call me on my bluff, bitch*, I think at him, giving him a razor-sharp smile.

I'm coming unraveled with every step he takes toward me, torn between wanting to smack that smile off his face and kiss it off his face.

Which, truly, is a sign of how unfair life is.

Why does he have to be so handsome? Why does he have to put up with all this shit and act like I'm doing him a favor?

I need to raise the stakes.

He's in front of me before I can sidestep him, picking me up and spinning me in a circle while my legs dangle.

It would be so easy to accidentally let my knee slip straight into his balls. Watch him crumple into the turf like the giant shit he is.

I savor the idea for a minute, then he sets me down on my feet, and I blink back into reality.

"Violence is not the answer," I mutter.

"What?" Luke tilts his head, then laughs. "What did you say?"

"I said violets are the answer," I hedge. "Violets. As in my favorite flower. Uh, because I'm sure you're thinking, *What can I send Abigail to thank her for organizing this?* And violets are the answer."

He quirks an eyebrow, a slow smile transforming his face into something even more delicious than usual. "Good to know."

"Yep, good to know."

He tightens his grip on my hips, and I go hot all over, which just makes me even madder. How dare my body still be attracted to this man! I mean, yes, he's gorgeous.

But he's also a *liar*.

Luke Wolfe is just like every other person who thought they could charm their way into my life and use me up for all I was worth.

Hurt races through me.

"Can I see you tonight?" he asks, raising an eyebrow. I hate how much those overly bushy eyebrows affect me.

I would rather never see him ever again, especially not when I can't seem to control myself around him.

"I'm having my annual *Lord of the Rings* rewatch," I lie blithely. "Then I have to wash my hair."

"Can I come watch it? The movie . . . and maybe the hair?"

"Yes," I say slowly, an idea taking form in the ether. "But I have to warn you, I take my rewatch very seriously."

"I can handle whatever you throw at me, love," he says, brushing a kiss against my forehead. "See you tonight."

He tosses me a grin as he jogs off to rejoin his teammates, and I want to sink to my knees and fucking cry.

No, not cry. That can't be it. I'm not sad about this.

I'm not sad, not at all. I'm mad. My throat tightens, tears beginning to sting my eyes.

I must be confusing the need to cry with the actual need to scream in frustration.

Love? Love?!

Who the hell does he think he is?

I'm fuming. It's one thing to lie about liking me, to use me to get ahead, and to get me in bed all while making me think he genuinely cares—but calling me *love*?

Oh, he's about to get a live fucking theater experience of *Lord of the Rings*.

Yeah!

It'll be the cock-blockbuster showing of his lifetime.

An evil laugh burbles out of me, and Lauren breaks off whatever conversation she's struck up with the Aces coach to turn a concerned eye on me.

"I gotta go," I say to her jovially, my spirits buoyed by the pure chaos burning through my veins. "Things to do, costumes to secure."

"Okay, bye," she says, looking slightly terrified. "Uh, thanks again for inviting me here."

"You were perfect," I tell her, and even though it didn't go how I wanted, with stupid Luke defending me to his whole stupid team, I'm grateful she made time for me. And said *anus* an inappropriate number of times.

Can't fault the woman there.

* * *

THE TIP OF Darren's tongue sticks out as he concentrates, misting setting spray over my face.

"There," he says, sitting back to take in the effects of several hours of hard work.

"How do I look?" I ask, attempting to bat my lashes. Unfortunately, my face doesn't allow that to happen.

"Horrendous. God-awful. Disgusting." Darren's lip curls.

"Perfect." I clap my hands together in glee. "Let me see." I half stand, and the vision that meets me in the mirror is truly something spectacular.

A few wisps of greasy gray hair hang lank across my otherwise bald head. My nose is flatter, thanks to the power of contour, and he's somehow managed to make my nostrils seem larger. I turn my head, admiring the overlarge ears.

"I mean, I'm happy to have the chance to try out some of my special effects prosthetics, but it's also kind of like ruining my favorite canvas," Darren laments with a sigh. "Here, let me take some pictures for my portfolio."

"You are legitimately the best. A king among kings. The emperor of makeup. The demigod of contour." I tighten the back of my throat and drop into my admittedly immaculate Gollum impression. "My preciousss," I lisp at him.

"I fucking hate it," Darren says with a laugh, shaking his head as he pulls out the fancy camera he reserves for before and afters. "Can I put it on my socials?"

"It?" I sniff. "We are not an it, precious."

"Seriously, stop. You are freaking me out."

"Of course you can. But maybe wait until after tonight. I don't want anyone giving him a heads-up."

"Fair enough," Darren agrees, raising the camera and clicking away. "God. It's even worse in high-def."

"Proud of you," I trill, beyond pleased. "You think this will work?"

"Do I think you role-playing Gollum while Luke Wolfe thinks you're going to Netflix and chill will scare him off?" He laughs again. "Honestly? I don't know. It would scare me off, that's for damn sure. But I also . . ."

I bristle. "You also what?"

"I also think he's motivated to stay with you."

"Right," I say. Because someone is making him stay with me. Fucking asshole. "Teeth," I demand, doing *Gimme* hands.

"No. We aren't doing teeth."

"But—"

"No. I have to meet Jason for drinks, and I am not sitting here and making you any uglier than I already have." He sniffs, and I sigh.

"Fine. How is Jason?"

"He's good. He's going to get a kick out of the latest installment of 'my movie-star best friend might actually be coming unglued,'" he says with a snort. Makeup tubes and containers clack against each other as he carefully repacks everything.

"I am not coming unglued." Then, in the same breath, "I'm also not a movie star."

He cuts me a brief look as he continues to pack his bag. "Yet. This film is going to put you on the map, Abs."

I bite my cheeks, uncomfortable with his sincerity. "I hope so."

"You're already successful as hell." He flicks his hand, gesturing to the bathroom I've just had renovated. "Look at this place. Look at what you've accomplished." His brow furrows, and he places his hands on my shoulders, forcing me to look up at him.

"Honey, what's wrong? What is it about this one man that has gotten under your skin so badly?"

I shrug him off, annoyed at his questions. "I'm tired of people using me to get ahead," I tell him. "Isn't that enough?"

"Abs, this is unhinged behavior." He points at my reflection in the bathroom mirror. "I know you have a big, hilarious, chaotic personality, and I love that about you. But even for you, this is a bit much. I'm a little worried about you."

I frown at him, and it's a testament to how great he is at makeup that nothing cracks or feels loose on my face.

"Ew," he says with a laugh. "That right there. That will run him off." He sighs, rolling his eyes. "All I'm saying is, maybe you should think hard about why you're so determined to make him pay instead of making a clean break. If you're so upset about the idea of him using you, then maybe you're in the wrong industry, Abs."

I scoff, picking at my cuticles.

"I think . . . maybe you should dig a little deeper about why you're so upset. That's all I'm gonna say about it."

I glance back up at him. "Liar."

"You're right," he says cheerfully. "I will absolutely keep scolding you about this as long as you keep this up."

He looks around the room for any misplaced makeup, then nods once. "Right. I'm off." I lean in and he air-kisses both my cheeks. "Please don't go out in public like that," he says with a rueful glance. "You'll be the death of poor Jean."

"I won't," I promise him. I trail after him as he wheels his makeup kit out the front door, and we blow each other one last kiss before he gets into his car and drives off.

Of course, now that he's told me not to go out in public like this, all I want to do is . . . go out in public like this.

I sigh, leaning against the doorframe only to realize my neighbor's stopped dead in the street, staring at me.

I wave at her, then hustle inside and close the door behind me.

Maybe Darren has a point.

About staying home tonight, at least.

As for whatever he was trying to say about Luke and me—I'm not sure I want to think too hard about any of that.

I rub my hands together and sink into a hunched half crouch.

"He's not ready for thisssss, is he, precious?"

CHAPTER THIRTY-SIX

Luke

I PULL UP to Abigail's house, anticipation at seeing her making it hard to keep from grinning. My knuckles rap against her front door.

"Just a minute," she calls from inside the house, and my fingers tighten on the bottle of wine and bag full of food.

It's only been a few hours, and I already can't wait to see her.

When she opens the door, though, I nearly drop everything in my hands.

"What the *fuck*?"

The thing in front of me grins wide, and I stare.

"You likes it, preciousss?" The freakish creature claps its hands, then cocks its head at me. "Did the nasty hobbitses bring us food?"

"Abigail?" My voice comes out strangled. "What the fuck are you wearing?"

She—because I'm fairly certain it is Abigail under that . . . mask, or makeup, or god knows—plucks the bag from my fingers.

"This is my kink." She turns around, leaving me to gawp at her retreating back.

"What?" It seems to be the only word I'm capable of forming right now.

"Yeah. You're into masturbating to Yo-Yo Ma and anaphylactic shock, and I'm into role-playing Gollum."

"What? Why?" I ask, my voice high-pitched, and I'm not sure if I'm asking her, or me, or god himself. "None of those things are true in the slightest."

"Is this going to be a problem?" Abigail turns slowly on her heel, pure sugar in each syllable. "This is who I am, Luke. Take it or leave it." She blinks slowly, the effect exponentially creepier in that makeup.

I suppress a shudder.

"If you do decide to leave it"—she takes a crouched step closer to me, animalistic—"I get to keep the food you brought."

The unexpected comment startles a laugh out of me, and for a second, I see the real Abigail under the special effects makeup, her smile shining through. It's gone before I can truly appreciate it, though, but I hug her to me regardless, the paper sack full of food crunching in between our bodies.

She's stiff, holding herself apart from me—and that, more than her bizarre appearance, worries me.

"Hey, what's wrong?" My brow cinches together as I study her.

Or, at least, attempt to study her, considering her true features are nearly completely obscured from view.

"Oh, ah, I just didn't want to get my makeup on you," she says. "It would be sad to ruin it before we even get started."

"That's ominous." My snort surprises us both.

For a half second, I swear I see her eyes light up, but then she's scurrying off to the kitchen. My feet follow her almost of their own accord, as if they can't stand the idea of being away from her any longer.

An electric thrum of excitement goes through me as I enter her kitchen. Not because I'm hungry.

This place, the heart of her home, will forever hold the memory of the night I kissed her for the first time.

Even if she's dressed up like some kind of freaky goblin.

"What, exactly, are you supposed to be?" I ask.

Her jaw drops, and I grimace at the effect.

"What do you mean, what am I supposed to be? I'm supposed to be Gollum, played by the ineffable and brilliant Andy Serkis." Abigail hands me a plate, then starts pulling containers out of the bag.

"Right." My lips scrunch to the side.

"Wait," she says slowly. "What do you mean, *right*?"

"I meant, yes, that's right."

"Oh my god. You haven't ever watched the movies?"

"I have not," I admit, helping myself to a huge portion of the butter chicken and grabbing a piece or three of naan.

I nearly drop the plate at her melodramatic gasp.

"You actually haven't seen them?!"

"It's hard to take you seriously with that on," I tell her, tearing into the naan while standing at her island.

"Good," she says with a sniff. "Thank you for reminding me." She pushes around her food, but she has yet to eat a bite.

"Reminding you of what?" I'm totally lost.

"Nothing," the creature that once was Abigail says, waving a hand. "Don't you worry your pretty little head about it."

We're quiet for a long moment, both of us apparently hungry past the point of politeness.

Despite her hideous costume, Abigail is still Abigail.

Amusement makes me smile as she struggles to eat without ruining her makeup.

"That is makeup, right?" I ask.

"No. I had cosmetic surgery to look like this forever," she says, stretching her mouth in a disgusting grin. "Are you turned on yet?"

"Absolutely," I say nonchalantly. "I look forward to the reality show Bravo will want to do on you."

"You know Bravo, but you don't know the *Lord of the Rings*?"

I shift my weight, chasing rice around with my fork and the naan. "I like a little *Housewives* every now and then."

"Shut up." Her eyes look even bigger than ever.

I glance sidelong at her, chewing the naan and butter chicken slowly.

Her expression changes suddenly, from faint hilarity (I think) to sadness, her shoulders drooping.

That's not normal. That's not my Abigail. Fear courses through me, worry for Abigail spiking my adrenaline.

"What's going on?"

"Nothing," she says.

"Bullshit," I tell her. "You look like someone just killed your dog."

"I don't have a dog," she says carefully, and when she glances up at me, that despair I thought I saw looks more like . . . anger.

I knew something was wrong with her. "Talk to me," I say softly. "Whatever it is, I want to know. Let me help. Did the press say something? Is it your ex?"

"I'm fine. Why? Do you have something you need to tell me? Is this"—she gestures slowly between us—"projection I sense?"

My lips twist to the side in confusion. "No? I'm good."

"Then me, too. I'm good, we're good. We are so good." Her voice is high and chipper and brittle.

Right. I clear my throat, deciding to take a different tack.

"Did you put that on yourself? It's really impressive. Gross, I mean, but it's, uh, something else."

Chasing away the forlorn, miserable look in her mismatched eyes is the only thing I want to do right now.

"No, Darren did it." She shoves her plate away from her, her biryani barely touched.

"Darren?" I ask. Jealousy stirs in me, and I grit my teeth to keep from saying something pigheaded.

"My makeup artist. You met him the other night—" Her jaw drops, then shuts.

"I did?" I ask, flummoxed.

"Never mind us, preciousss," she hisses, back in character. "Give us a kiss, my beauty."

My lip curls in disgust, because the last thing I want to do is kiss whatever the hell this thing is—but it's also Abigail.

My Abigail.

"All right," I say easily, carefully placing my fork on the edge of the plate. "I'd love a kiss."

To my surprise, she makes a noise of pure distaste.

"Sorry." Abigail coughs. "I'm not really hungry." She coughs again.

"It's impossible to read you under that makeup," I tell her.

"Well, then don't try to. Let's go watch the movie." Without so much as a backward glance, Abigail practically sprints from the room.

I stare at the uneaten food on her plate while I shovel the rest of mine in my mouth. After emptying her biryani back into the take-out container and setting the rest of the leftovers in her fridge, I splay my palms on the cool stone surface of her kitchen counters.

What the hell is going on with her?

Maybe it's the pressure of her new role, and this little playacting thing is part of how she's blowing off steam.

Still.

I can't get her deep, defeated look of sadness off my mind. The defensiveness when I asked about it, the anger right there along with it—I know something is wrong.

I would do anything to help her through whatever it is. If that means putting up with her . . . odd impression tonight, then that's what it means.

Anything to help her smile again.

CHAPTER THIRTY-SEVEN

Abigail

PRINCESS WON'T STOP growling at me. Her little back is arched, her tail completely fluffed up.

It makes me feel *awful*.

Not that I felt great to begin with, some of my malicious glee evaporating as Luke continues to be his usual self. I also just kind of feel . . . off. Not hungry, which is strange. A little out of it.

Maybe I just need to amp up the weirdness.

He sits with his arm around me, watching the film with interest.

On the same couch where I found out all of his lies only a week ago. I'm so tired and I'm starting to feel like shit.

I want him to admit what he did wrong.

Sweat breaks out on my forehead, and I decide I need to up the ante.

"What's it got in its pocketses, precious?" I say, jumping onto the balls of my feet. My fingers flutter against his upper thighs.

One eyebrow raises, and instead of shoving me off, which I hoped for, his hands raise to steady me, grabbing my hips.

He pulls me close, our noses nearly touching. Well, his nose and my Darren-made nose.

My chest hurts, and my eyes go wide as I pull back from him.

"What is it?" His grip on me changes, gentling, and my stomach cramps, my heart hammering against my chest.

But not in a good way.

"Oh no," I pant. "I can't breathe."

"Tell me what's wrong," he demands, eyes wild, pressing a hand to my forehead.

His touch hurts. I can't bear it.

My heart hurts. It hurts like it's cracked irreparably, sending splinters into my lungs. I am going to throw up or have a heart attack or die. I don't want to die dressed as Gollum.

My fingers scrabble at the prosthetics on my makeup. "I can't breathe," I repeat.

"You're sweating," he tells me, eyes narrowed.

"Can't breathe," I hiccup. Tears squeeze out of my eyes, my anxiety escalating. "I need this off of me, I need it off."

"Oh, shit, Abigail." Luke leaps to his feet, hugging me tight to his chest as he literally carries me to the bathroom.

"No, no. I don't want you to see this," I say. I'm sweating profusely now. "I don't want to throw up."

"Love, you can't help it. If it's gonna happen, just let it happen."

I groan, tucking my knees in tight to my chest, like that's a good idea.

It is not, in fact, a good idea. It doesn't help at all.

"Bathroom, bathroom, bathroom," I chant. It's like all the air in my body is trying to leave at once. I'm positively slick with sweat.

"I'm gonna die," I tell him, my chest impossibly tight.

"It's okay, I've got you. I've got you, Abigail." His head whips around. "Where do you want to be? In front of the toilet or—"

"I don't know, I don't know what I want. Take the mask off, please, take it off," I chant, hardly holding onto consciousness. "Can't breathe."

A cool washcloth lands against the back of my neck, and I whimper as another wave of pain pummels me.

"What else can I do?" Luke's voice is gentle and worried. "I think you're having a panic attack."

"I don't have panic attacks," I tell him, sobbing, peeling back the makeup as best I can. The nose piece is the worst, and I tug at it, Luke also helping pull the prosthesis from my ears and neck. "I am so stupid, I'm sorry."

"You are not stupid, and don't you dare apologize." He sounds thunderous and looks terrified all at once.

He's right. Why am I apologizing? He's the liar here.

I try to suck in a breath, and I can't, I can't do it, I can't think straight. My chest hurts. I clutch at it, still sweating so much. How is it possible to sweat this much?

"Call Darren. Please."

"Darren?" Luke asks, his tone shifting slightly.

"I need the rest of this stuff off my face. Now," I moan. "Call him, please." I manage to tell him the password to my phone. "He'll know how to take care of me."

"I can take care of you, Abigail, if you let me."

"No," I say, my voice cracking on the word. "You can't, and you won't."

I can't look at him. I don't want to. Eventually, the door closes quietly behind him, and I wish for death. I wish for death for a long, long time.

* * *

THERE'S A KNOCK on the bathroom door, and for an extended depressive moment, I hope the grim reaper will walk into my bathroom and put me out of my anxious spiral.

Death does not come.

Darren, however, is here.

"Help," I whisper, crying. How there is still any moisture left in my body is beyond me.

"Goddammit, Abigail." He shakes his head. There's a mask over his face, and he has on latex gloves, too. Smart.

"I'm dying," I tell him.

"You're an idiot, but you're not dying. You're having a panic attack." He takes his mask off but leaves the gloves on as he winces, getting to work on the rest of the makeup he's done.

I whimper, because that's mean as hell. It also might be true, but we don't have time to unpack all that.

"Luke's gone to get you electrolytes, though why he's bothering with you still, I can't tell."

I blink at him mournfully from where I've curled up on the cold tile floor. Cold tile is my new best friend.

"You've sweated half this off already. But I have to say, the whole deathly ill and piteous sobbing thing is really selling the Gollum look."

"What do you mean? About Luke?" I ask hoarsely. My stomach aches, my chest, too, and it's not all from the physical torment of whatever virus is plowing through me.

"You fucked up, Abigail," Darren tells me, pulling at the edges of the silicone cap that's covering up my hair.

I heave a sigh of relief—much better than the alternative—as he tugs it all the way off.

"By having a panic attack?" I ask. It's nasally, because now he's forcefully cleaning up my skin.

"Please tell me you're not going to be sick. You smell like a sweaty locker room, and I swore I'd never be in one again after my freshman year." He gives me a long look. "And, no. Not because you are having a panic attack."

Dread settles all around me, sitting on my chest. "Why?" I wheeze.

"Because he recognized me."

"He follows you on socials?" I ask, confused.

"You must be really out of it." This time, he sounds slightly gentler. "No, he recognized me as Gerard, Abigail."

"Who—" Oh. Ohhhh. "I feel sick."

I clutch at my heart.

He lurches back, eyes wide. "You mean—"

"No, you're safe. I'm not throwing up. For now, I think," I amend, lest the porcelain gods decide to curse me for my hubris. "He knows?"

"He isn't stupid. He's also . . . well, you idiot, he's nice. Not charming. But he's good, and you. Fucked. It. Up."

"He lied to me." My cheek presses against the cold tile, and sweat drips off the tip of my nose.

"And what you're doing is better?" He rolls his eyes. "You liked him, Abigail. Really, truly liked him. I know you did. And he liked you—hell, why else would he be getting you Gatorade and chicken soup and crackers or whatever the fuck else he's getting? He's not faking it with you, you moron."

Tears dribble down my cheeks.

I'm shocked there's enough liquid inside me to make them. Fascinating.

Darren sighs, his eyes softening somewhat. "Abigail. Talk to the man. Don't self-sabotage this time."

I sniffle, and Darren continues wiping the makeup off my face with gentle strokes.

"I'm still mad," I tell him.

"So you're going to keep acting like this until you're not mad anymore? Until you push him away completely?"

"Darren, stop," I say, sitting upright so suddenly I almost smack him in the forehead.

"No, Abs, you need to hear this. I can tell the worst of this is over, thank god, but I'll wait around to see if you need a pill or something. Do you want me to call your doctor? Or Jean?"

"I don't want to hear anything and, no, don't. Please don't." I almost stick my fingers in my ears but decide that'll probably just convince Darren to call my doctor and Jean and maybe even my mother.

"I'm calling your doctor," Darren tells me. "She's all yours."

And that? That is not directed at me at all.

A grunt sounds at the door to the bathroom. Luke.

CHAPTER THIRTY-EIGHT

Abigail

I WAKE UP under one of my many fleece blankets, tucked in tight on the couch. A moment passes, and I wait for the inevitable surge of nausea that will accompany consciousness.

"I'm alive," I whisper, my mouth as parched as a freaking desert, and then louder, "I'm alive."

I didn't have a heart attack, after all.

Which means I did, in fact, have a panic attack.

Shame goes through me, which rationally, I know is stupid. I could control a panic attack about as much as I could control a bout of food poisoning. But the shame is there, all the same.

There's a huge cup with a straw in it, and I moan, my hand shaking as I reach for it. Ice clinks against the side, and the moment the lemon-lime-flavored sugary drink hits my tongue, I let out a sigh of pure relief.

It's fresh . . . which can only mean one thing.

"Abigail?" A hoarse voice says.

I jerk my head up and immediately regret it.

Shock ripples through me.

Luke Wolfe's curled up on the floor, one of my couch cushions under his head. "You okay?"

"Yeah. I feel . . . rough. Really tired. But I'm gonna make it."

"Right. You had me really worried. That was a bad one."

His expression shutters, and the sharp blade of reality cuts through my lightheaded haze.

"I'm sorry," I say softly. There's a brown paper bag on the table, a prescription for antianxiety meds. I vaguely remember taking one last night. "Darren called my doctor?"

"He got Jean to do it."

"Jean knows?" I want to cry. I don't want Jean to think I'm more of a fuckup than I already am. I need Jean on my side.

"Abigail, you can't just pretend like the anxiety is nothing. It won't help."

There it is again, that shame, because deep down, I know he's right. I don't want him to be right.

"Why are you here?" I ask him softly. There's an undercurrent of anger running through me, but after last night, I just feel tired.

Tired and so confused.

"Why do you think I'm here, Abigail?" he counters, and I see that same anger in his eyes.

It hurts so much more than it should.

My eyes squeeze shut, and I take a long, deep breath. I'm too tired to keep it up anymore. In a moment of clarity, I make up my mind and open my eyes.

"About Darren—" I start.

"Gerard?" he interrupts, a mean set to his mouth. He's never looked at me like that before.

"You don't get to be mad," I tell him, gathering the little strength I have left. "I know all about how you didn't want to date me, how you've been faking it with me just to get something out of your stupid fucking bosses."

My chest shakes, and I suck in a shaky breath, sure I'm about to cry hot, angry tears.

But nothing happens. Well, that's probably thanks to the antianxiety meds. Or the fact I might have actually managed to sweat out all my extra liquid last night.

I suck down some more electrolytes, my head pounding.

All the tendons stand out on his neck, his pulse throbbing in his temple. He's paled, his blue eyes dark with some emotion I'm too tired to figure out.

"Who told you?" he asks. His voice is so low I hardly catch the question.

"Gold. He called Michelle when he was drunk. In Vegas."

"Fucking hell." He rakes a hand through that deliciously silky black hair.

The urge to comfort him, to wipe that dejected expression off his face, rides me hard, catching me by complete surprise.

I never thought I was a people pleaser, but the wave of unease that creeps over my skin has less to do with how physically awful I feel and more to do with the sudden realization that Darren is right: I completely fucked up.

And yet, I'm still mad. So mad. And hurt.

"This is why you've been so off these past few days, huh?" His mouth's a tight line, and if we weren't talking about all the ways we've fucked each other over, I might think he wasn't trying to smile.

As it is, he might be holding back screaming at me.

I wouldn't blame him. I want to scream at him. I want to explode.

I don't, though. I just wait, my heart in painful pieces.

"You've been trying to . . ." He trails off, shaking his head.

He laces his fingers together, then looks back up at me with a dejected expression.

"This entire thing was a lie. So yeah." I wet my lips, then pause, drinking more. "Yeah. I did some things to make you call it off. To call your bluff."

"The fucking Maserati." A look of astonishment transforms his face. His hand goes to his jawline, where a dark five-o'clock shadow has grown, making him look even more rugged.

A humorless chuckle drifts out of me, and I lean the back of my head against the couch for support.

"The lobster? How did you plan on it pinching you?"

I inspect the bandage that's covering my stitches and sigh. "I didn't plan on that."

Princess prances into the room, ignoring Luke's legs, sprawled over the floor. A condescending sniff of my socked feet ensues, and we lapse into silence, watching her.

"Why, Luke?" I finally ask. "Why would you make me think—" My throat tightens, and I can't force the words out. *Why did he make me think he loved me?*

I thought this is what I wanted. To get even.

To show him how much it hurt when someone used you, when they pretended.

It feels like shit.

"You should have asked me that a week ago. I would have told you. Now? Now I'm not sure I want you to know." His voice is tight, guttural, his knuckles white where he's fisted his hands.

It's a verbal slap in the face, and I recoil.

"What kind of person doesn't just ask? You did . . . all of this, and you could have just *fucking* asked." He spits the words out, more venom in each syllable than I've ever heard from him before.

My anger rises immediately.

"No. *No.* You don't get to blame this on me." My stomach lurches, and I put a hand over my mouth. "What kind of person doesn't admit it if they really like the other person?"

"The kind of person who's *falling in love with you*, Abigail!" he roars. "The kind of person who's afraid to fuck it all up! But I guess I already have. We both have."

I clamp my lips together, refusing to apologize. I don't want to look at him.

I can't bring myself to look away.

"It was supposed to be one fucking date, Abigail, and you were supposed to realize right away that I'm an asshole and ghost me. I'd do the bare minimum—tell the owners I tried and get off the damned protected roster." He laughs, and it's abrasive. It hurts. "But I liked you. You, Abigail Hunt. I wanted to, god, I wanted to tell you why I asked you out, why it started like that—but then you told me about your ex. And I couldn't. I was a coward. I couldn't tell you. I didn't want to fucking hurt you." He glances up at me, and those blue eyes knife through my chest.

I want to tell him it's okay, to tell him we can work it out.

The words won't come.

"Joke's on me," he mutters. "We're both hurt now."

With that, he scoops up Princess, who lets out a little mewl before looking at him adoringly.

"What are you doing with her?" I ask, my throat thick.

"She's my foster," he says bitterly. "You're not on the paperwork. I'm responsible for her, I have to take Princess."

"Luke," I say on a sob, then swallow it.

We stare at each other in silence for a long, horrible moment, where all the might-have-beens for us disappear into the ether.

He is taking my cat, and for that, I might hate him the most.

"Please leave," I whisper. "Now."

He does, slamming my front door behind him.

I spend the rest of the day crying and dozing on the couch, and no matter how many times I check my phone, no apology appears.

I can't bring myself to apologize, either, can't bring myself to think that this could have been anything but fake the whole time.

I got exactly what I wanted.

Luke Wolfe finally broke up with me.

So why does it feel like he broke my heart, too?

CHAPTER THIRTY-NINE

Luke

THE SOMBER STRAINS of Bach's Cello Suite No. 1 in G Major blare through my headphones.

A song I put on my playlist for *her*. Like it would help me figure her out.

"Fuck," I say out loud, then increase the pace and resistance on my bike, trying to blot out the emotional pain with the fatigued burn of my muscles. It's been two weeks since Abigail and I last spoke, since I took Princess home.

Gold, sweating his ass off on a bike a few spaces over, shoots me a meaningful look.

"Fuck off!" I yell at him, and he rolls his eyes, standing up in the saddle and refocusing on the day's cardio set.

It's not enough.

Every day for the past two weeks, I've worked myself to the bone with the faint hope of exhausting myself into sleep.

And every night for the past two weeks, I've stared at the ceiling and regretted everything, every single one of my choices.

Except Abigail.

I don't regret spending time with her, getting to know her. Even the over-the-top absurd ridiculous version of her she was once Gold told her—

Fucking Gold.

He had the drunk courage to do what I couldn't, and he told her the truth when I should have.

It's stupid. All of it is so stupid, and I am so fucking angry.

My knuckles turn white on the handlebars, my bike flashing a warning on the screen about my RPMs being too high. I couldn't care less.

I turn up the resistance more, the lactic acid buildup in my quads the punishment I deserve.

When I finally get off the bike, my legs are on fire. I cringe as I try to stretch out my aching muscles.

They hurt, but not as much as my foolish heart does.

How is it that Abigail managed to burrow into the deepest, darkest parts of me?

Now that she's not around, with her quick wit and ready smiles, the truth comes crashing down all around me.

I'm lonely and sad. I think I have been for a long time.

And that's all my fault, too.

I take out an earbud.

"Gold," I call, already shaking my head at myself.

He turns around, and his half-pleased, half-surprised expression tells me all I need to know: Even Gold, my closest friend on the team, doesn't expect anything from me.

"I'm having people over," I tell him.

"What?"

I grunt, annoyed already. "I'm having people over. Do you want to come?"

"Um, yeah, man. Sure. Who else is coming? When?"

"I haven't asked anyone yet." I pause, squinting at him. "Except you. And . . . I don't know. When do you think?"

He stops walking, wiping his forehead with the white towel on his shoulder.

"Do you want me to tell some of the guys? We could do it Sunday. You can order some food in and I'll do a beer run." He winces. "Scratch that last part. I'm not touching alcohol again for a while."

I glare at him, and he sighs.

"Look, man, I'm sorry. I don't remember it, but I didn't . . . I didn't mean to tell her everything."

"It's fine."

He tilts his head at me.

I grunt. "Don't fucking make me say it."

"It's not fine," Gold says, rubbing the back of his neck.

"I fucking forgive you, okay? Fuck."

A huge grin stretches across his face, and disgust wars with annoyance as I realize Tristan Gold has fucking dimples. Asshole.

"You make that one word mean so many different things." He shakes his head at me, laughing, then sobers. "And thank you. It means a lot, man." His big hand claps me on the shoulder, and my tired legs nearly give out under his weight.

"Yeah." I consider him for a moment. "I think I should apologize, too," I say slowly.

He looks taken aback. "For what?"

"For being an asshole. I . . ." Shit. I'm not good at this. "I should have tried harder with the team, and with you. You're a good guy."

"Aw, c'mere," Gold crows, pulling me into a bear hug.

"Get the fuck off me," I growl.

When he doesn't, I reluctantly pat his back.

"You smell like shit." I can hear the grin in his voice.

"Then we have something in common," I fire back at him.

He laughs, and it makes me smile, soothing some of that bone-deep hurt.

But not the place that cradles Abigail's laugh like a lifeline.

I'm not sure anything will soothe that.

CHAPTER FORTY

Abigail

THE ATLANTA AIRPORT is, bar none, one of the worst places I have ever been. There are so many freaking people, and I'm grateful for the anonymity afforded by my oversize sweatshirt (thank you, midnight insomnia purchase) and my oldest pair of Levis.

No one is looking twice at me.

I text Jean quickly.

> **ABIGAIL:** I'm here
>
> **ABIGAIL:** No problems at all, other than Atlanta's humidity which might actually kill me
>
> **JEAN:** Enjoy it
>
> **JEAN:** This is probably one of the last times you'll be able to travel commercial without people bothering you

I swallow around the anxious lump in my throat at that. My hands shake, and I cross one over my chest to hold steady as I keep an eye out for my luggage.

> **JEAN:** You're going to do great, hon. I'm proud of you

I blink back surprise at that.

> **ABIGAIL:** Thanks, Jean. I wouldn't be here without you

> **JEAN:** You would. But I'm glad you chose me to be a part of it with you

> **ABIGAIL:** Do not make me start crying in the airport

> **ABIGAIL:** Wait, am I sure this is Jean? You didn't sign your texts. Is this an imposter?

Jean sends a string of wind emojis.

> **ABIGAIL:** I literally have no idea what that means

> **JEAN:** I'm blowing you

> **JEAN:** Kisses

I decide not to touch that one with a ten-foot pole.

Luckily for me, my bag is finally making it around on the luggage conveyor belt. The bag's overpacked, and I grit my teeth as I lug it off, trying my best not to hit the people reaching for their bags next to me.

My phone buzzes in my back pocket, and my first thought—the way it has been for weeks now—is of Luke.

Is it him? Finally reaching out and apologizing?

The disappointment hasn't gotten easier, and it's not this time, either, though I'm happy to see Michelle's name on my screen.

> **MICHELLE:** Did you make it okay? Miss you already! My office is so boring without you

> **ABIGAIL:** Just landed, about to find my driver

MICHELLE: Love this for you SO. MUCH

ABIGAIL: I'm excited to impress everyone with how much you taught me

ABIGAIL: And I'm glad I can count you as a friend

It's a little squishy, a little too earnest, even for me . . . but I mean it. Sure, Luke and I didn't work out, but at least I'm lucky enough to have walked away from the Aces with a new friend.

The wheels of my bag clack against the floor as I tug it behind me. People crowd around the doors past the security cordons, holding signs and balloons for their loved ones. A smile spreads across my face at one little girl, holding a bear that dwarfs her, waving a still-chubby hand at someone returning home.

A couple embraces near me, one woman wiping away the other's tears before they kiss, leaning their foreheads together.

This. This is real—this crowded, too-busy airport, teeming with people reuniting.

What would it be like to have someone look at me like I was their person? That I created a hole in their life while I was gone?

What would it be like to be worthy of a love like that?

My throat closes up.

One of the women glances in my direction, and I offer a small smile before looking away from their hug.

"Abigail?" A familiar voice calls my name, and surprise drops my jaw.

"Oh my god, Darren," I cry out, jogging awkwardly, my luggage trailing behind me like a clumsy puppy. "You did not have to pick me up. I thought the studio was sending someone," I tell him, wrapping my arms around him. He smells like sandalwood and vanilla, and I breathe it in.

"I figured you might need a friend," he says. Then he jerks his head toward the black-suited man behind him. "It's not like I drove. I just decided to come along."

"I'm glad you did." I squeeze him again, in desperate need of touch.

He gives me a long look, and I swallow hard under his perusal. "You okay?"

"Yeah," I say slowly, pushing my hair back behind my ear.

"For such a good actress, you really are a terrible liar."

I finally let him go and give him a watery smile.

Darren tucks me under his arm, and we follow the driver to the waiting car. "It's okay if you're not okay."

"It's stupid," I argue. "We had, what, one good week together?"

"You liked him. He hurt you, and you made . . . a few choice choices."

"I did like him," I whisper.

"Have you . . . talked to him? He was frantic when you were sick, Abs. I don't think . . ." He pauses, shaking his head as we both get in the car.

"You don't think what?" I prod, clicking my seat belt into place.

The car bounces slightly when the driver sets my luggage in the trunk and slams it closed.

He sighs, stretching his legs out, then fixing me with a serious look. "It might have started as something they put him up to for a publicity stunt. I'm not saying he was right for that."

Silence unspools between us. Darren's jaw twitches, and he twists his mouth to the side, considering me.

"But?"

"But I think he cares about you."

"Cared, maybe," I correct. "Past tense. If he cared about me, he would have apologized by now." It comes out bitter, and the words leave a foul taste on my tongue.

"Oh?" Darren cocks an eyebrow at me, crossing his arms over his chest. "And how did he take it when you apologized for trying to make his life hell?"

"Something you were a willing partner in," I grouse.

"Don't deflect."

I scowl at him.

"That's what I thought."

"Why should I?"

"Because you're still a wreck over this guy. Your under eyes look like they've never seen a collagen eye patch, and it's going to make my life harder on set. Rude of you."

I snort, because while he's not wrong about the bags under my eyes, I know he's not saying it to be mean.

The car navigates slowly through the airport traffic, and Darren and I lapse into silence as the landscape transforms as we get closer to the hotel the studio's putting us up in while we film here before going back to the set in LA.

"I can't understand why it hurts so much." It comes out so softly I half hope he hasn't heard me at all.

He does, though, cutting me a look that's equal parts exasperation and fondness. "Because he's a good guy, Abs, and you haven't dated one of those before. Plus, he put up with your shit."

"My shit?" I repeat, playfully shoving his arm.

"Don't fucking even," he says with a laugh. "You know exactly what I'm talking about. All your glorious weirdness, you quirky little freak."

"Well, that's much nicer than *my shit*," I say primly.

He laughs, reaching out to squeeze my hand. "Call him."

"I have to focus on work this week," I immediately say.

We share a look, the unspoken communication clear as day.

"I don't know how to tell him I'm sorry and that I'm still upset with him for lying to me."

"Oh, Abs." Darren squeezes my hand. "That *is* all you have to say. Do you think . . ."

He purses his lips together, squinting at me in the Atlanta sunlight.

"What?" I urge. "Do I think what?"

"Do you think he would have even asked you out if they hadn't put him up to it?"

"Isn't that the problem?" I retort, but there's no bite in it, not at all.

"Noooo." He draws the word out. "I mean, he doesn't strike me as the type to just . . . date around. You never hear about him in the tabloids like that."

"Until I got a hold of him." I sigh, resting my head against the car window and watching the green landscape rush by the highway.

"Right. But what I'm saying is . . . I know it hurt your feelings, but maybe, uh, if you two can end up working it out—maybe it would be fortuitous."

"We don't even know that that's going to happen." This time, it is snappish. "I do need to focus this week, and I can't focus if I'm busy thinking about Luke Wolfe."

My voice breaks on his last name.

"Right. So we'll just film this soccer movie, and we won't think about him. Got it. Zero thoughts."

I glare at him.

"You look especially awful when you do that with those eye bags."

"Why are we friends again?" I grump at him.

"Because no one else would one"—he holds up his forefinger—"orchestrate the most chaotic date of your life at a fancy restaurant, and two"—he adds a second finger—"love you completely no matter how harebrained your schemes."

"Thank you," I tell him. My forehead's left a greasy spot on the window, and Darren chuckles when I frown at it.

"Now come here and let me fix your face before we get back to the hotel," he says.

I acquiesce, closing my eyes and tilting my head back against the seat as Darren digs through his bag.

It's easier not to talk, especially when he starts slapping on under-eye patches and dabbing various creams on my skin.

Darren is right about our friendship, of course.

But I thought I'd found someone else who might love me no matter how harebrained my schemes got, and it's still too raw and painful to think fully about what I might have lost.

CHAPTER FORTY-ONE

WHEN I SEE the name on my phone, I pick it up immediately.

"Mom, hi? How are you?"

"Hi, honey." My mom's voice is tired, and it makes my whole chest hurt. "I'm okay. But I'm worried about you."

"You're worried about me?" I say on a small, disbelieving laugh. "You're the one who's doing chemo right now."

She sighs, the long-suffering sound coming through loud and clear on the phone. "Will you stop?"

"Stopping," I agree. The caterer's busy setting up all the food for the team, the smell of pork carnitas, carne asada, and fresh tortillas permeating the entire house.

"And, yes, of course I'm worried about you. I'm your mother."

I snort at that.

"It doesn't matter how old you get. You will always be my baby."

"I hear you, Mom," I tell her, shaking my head and grinning into the phone at the scolding in her voice.

"This girl, Abigail Hunt, why did you two break up?"

I sigh, pinching the bridge of my nose. The tabloids got wind of the fact Abigail and I hadn't been seen together after our very public whirlwind of dates, and they've been relentless about following both of us.

"I don't want to talk about it," I finally answer.

My mother sighs, and I don't have to see her face to know the exact expression of disappointment that's on it.

I hate disappointing her. "I'm . . . I'm ashamed of how it ended," I admit.

She lets out a long breath, and a chair creaks as she sits down.

"Are you in the kitchen?" I ask, certain I know exactly where she is—in the antique rocker my stepdad and I found for her when I was sixteen. We were out of town for a tournament, and he pulled over when he saw the antiques depot.

My mom's face when we pulled up with the old rocker late that Sunday was worth the hassle of strapping it down, and now it lives in the wallpapered kitchen with a flock of ceramic geese and my mom's fresh-baked sourdough bread.

"Yep, just fed the starter."

"I miss your bread," I tell her, and it's inadequate for the well of emotion.

One of the caterers jeers at another, and the entire crew starts laughing.

"What's that?" my mom asks, her tone changing to one of pure interest. "Are you out somewhere?"

"I'm having the team over for dinner and to hang out."

The phone is silent for a long moment. Then the chair squeaks again.

"*You?*" She's breathless. "My son, Luke Wolfe, is having people over?"

I turn away from the noise in the kitchen, walking to the backyard and the clear blue waters of the pool glistening in the California sun. "Yeah."

"My goodness. Well, that's just lovely." She sniffs.

"Don't cry," I tell her gruffly.

"I'm not," she says, but her voice is watery. "I worry about you. My oldest child. You always thought you had to be so tough for us all when your dad left. I worried you'd . . . I worried you'd shut yourself down so hard that you wouldn't trust anyone again. You were always so solemn."

"Mom—"

"No, now you listen here. I called to tell you something: that I'm concerned about you after this Abigail person but also that I'm so very proud of you. So proud. And to hear you're having people over, well, it gives me hope."

I grunt, and then I think of Abigail and how she'd make fun of me for grunting, and I clear my throat and try to form the words engraved on my heart.

"I love you, Mom. Thank you for calling to check on me. It means a lot."

"Oh, Luke." She sniffs again. "Now you're going to make me cry."

My eyes squeeze shut. "No, Mom, don't cry."

"Well, whatever happened between you and this Abigail they keep taking photos of, I think she must have been a good influence on you."

A pain lances through my chest, and I rub absentmindedly at it.

"Yeah," I agree softly. "She was."

"Are things really over with her?"

I grunt again, and my mom lets out a laugh.

"Well, I'll take that as a maybe."

"You would have liked her." The words come out so fast, I didn't even realize I'd bottled them up until they hang between us.

"I would like just about anyone who made you smile like she did, Luke. Now, go have fun at your party."

"It's not a party," I say gruffly.

"Fine, go have fun at your not-party. I'll talk to you later."

I chuckle at that, and my mom starts scolding my stepdad about something before the line goes dead.

I would like just about anyone who made you smile like she did.

The guys start filtering into the front door just as the catering company's leaving, and still, my mom's words ring loud in my ears above their good-natured ribbing.

Abigail would like my mom, too.

Gold takes one look at my face over a plate piled high with tacos and guacamole and cringes. "Do you need Tums or something?"

I glance sidelong at him as I fill my own plate. "What?"

"You look like you have heartburn. You're having a party at your own house, and you look like you need to pound a bottle of Pepto."

I force a smile, and Gold grimaces.

"That's just worse."

From the floor, a pitiful mewl sounds, and Princess stares up at me with her huge blue eyes, one paw raised in the air.

"Little beggar," I tell her.

"Since when do you have a cat?" Gold asks, astounded. "I figured you were more of a big-dog type. Rottweiler. Doberman. I don't know, an Irish wolfhound."

Bending over, I feed Princess a tiny piece of chicken off my plate. "Don't need a dog."

"She's a very cute cat—" He frowns at me. "Wait. Michelle told me you rescued a cat with Abigail . . . and then adopted the cat out."

I grunt. "So?"

"So . . . Michelle also said that Abigail was beyond heartbroken—but even angrier about the cat." He eyes where Princess is gobbling down the bite of chicken like it's the best thing she's ever had in the world. "That . . . wouldn't happen to be the cat, would it?"

I grunt again.

"You kept her fucking cat," Gold whispers. "Oh, this is good."

"What's good?" Marino wanders over, then makes a wordless noise of excitement when he spies Princess. "Oh, mi amore, look at you."

He scoops her up, and Princess looks at him with those blue eyes, hopeful for another bite of chicken.

"This is your woman's cat?" Marino asks, scratching under her chin.

"Abigail isn't my woman."

"But you have her cat?" Marino presses. "I was there when Michelle was talking about it." His dark brown hair flops over.

Princess's purrs are absurdly loud, and I sigh in resignation.

"Yeah. That's the cat."

"Dude," one of our midfielders, Logan Steel, says from where he's spooning queso over a plate of chips. "That's the actress's cat, right?"

"How many people heard Michelle talk about the cat?" I ask, slightly irritated.

Marino raises a hand, and Gold . . . and then the rest of the team follow.

Logan laughs. "That was ice-cold, brother. And man, you fumbled the bag with her. Can I have her number?"

My hackles go up immediately. Gold's hand weighs heavy on my arm.

"Kidding, Wolfe, kidding." Logan, who's the youngest on the team, at twenty, backs off, looking slightly terrified.

It's petty, but that's probably what calms me the most—the memory that Logan is barely an adult and that he's clearly scared of me.

He clears his throat, and all our teammates, who are doing a horrible job of pretending not to watch, are suddenly incredibly interested in their plates.

Guilt washes over me, and I heave a sigh, staring at the wooden beams crossing my ceiling as I regain control over myself.

"I'm just saying, I think Abigail, er, Ms. Hunt—she seems really nice. And, I don't know, it seemed like she really liked you. And she's pretty."

A couple of the guys laugh, and Logan has never seemed as young as he does now.

Heartened by the fact I'm still staring at him and haven't tried to physically assault him, he clears his throat again, glancing around nervously. "That's all I was saying. We were rooting for you."

Gold shoots me a warning look, as if he's unsure of what I'll do.

I make myself smile.

Logan takes another step back, belated self-preservation kicking in at the sight.

"Thanks," I say roughly. "I wish I hadn't fucked it up between us."

The entire team starts talking at once, my house suddenly filled with voices I've heard every day for the past several years, but never once in my own home.

Voices giving me advice for how to win Abigail back. Offering different ways to apologize.

My teammates are trying to help, and I don't know what to do with that information.

Gold puts two fingers in his mouth, letting out an earsplitting whistle.

I wince.

"Enough," he bellows before turning to me. "Wolfe, do you want to get this woman back?"

I pause. I've never been public about anything, not like this. I've shut everyone out for far too long.

But I think about Abigail, her laugh, her smile. The way she made me feel.

What would Abigail, my Abigail, want me to do?

She made me feel . . . whole again. I think she'd want me to tell my team exactly what I want, to push out of my own admittedly microscopic comfort zone.

"Yeah," I rasp, scratching the scruff along my jawline. "I think I do."

A cheer goes up from all the men around me, and Marino dives toward me, catching me up in a way too enthusiastic hug.

"Get the fuck off me," I tell him.

"No," he says, then plops a kiss on my cheek before finally moving away.

"Are you fucking crying?" I ask, incredulous.

"I am just so happy you are finally coming out of your skin."

Everyone gets quiet.

"What?"

"Shell," Gold supplies. "Your shell."

"Shell, skin." Marino shrugs. "You blossom like a flower, fratello mio."

"What does that mean?"

Marino grins at me. "It means 'my brother.' My bro, but more, ah, meaningful. Bruh."

I grunt, overcome with emotions I don't want to put a name to, and the room erupts into easy laughter.

"All right!" Gold yells, his voice nearly deafening me. "Let's make a fucking plan."

For once, I'm only too happy to listen to their advice.

And I'm surprised, and grateful, that they even care enough to offer it.

No matter what happens between Abigail and me, if she forgives me or not, at least she helped me have this realization: I might have been lonely the past few years . . .

But I'm not alone.

I've never been alone.

CHAPTER FORTY-TWO

Abigail

TEARS FLOW FREELY, my character's rage and frustration upon learning the truth about the IFF's corruption coming to a boiling point.

My scene partner stares at me, and I deliver my line with as much sincere emotion as I can muster.

"And that's why I . . ." My voice falters. I shake my head, forging onward. "That's why—"

My voice breaks completely, and my shoulders begin to shake.

Turns out, it's a bit too much sincere emotion.

"Cut." Richard Grace's command slices through the set, and I blink furiously, trying to pull myself out of this character.

Now that I'm crying, though, I can't seem to turn it off. Can't seem to stop the tears from turning into ugly sobs.

I'm not sure how long I stand there trying to force myself under control, but it's the cool hand on my shoulder that brings me back to the present moment.

"Abigail." Richard's voice is soft, and I glance up at his kindly face, his longish white hair waving around his temples. "Let's take a walk, okay?"

I nod, hiccupping, and wipe my hand across my cheeks.

"I'll fix your makeup when you're back." Darren shakes his head at me from where he's poised to touch up my face.

Great. I've ruined his work.

I've ruined this entire fucking take.

Forlorn, I follow Richard from the set. I wring my hands as we walk, twisting the diamond engagement ring my character wears around my finger.

Finally he stops under the relative cool shade of a towering oak tree. Sweat begins to bead between my breasts, and I fan my face. Shooting outside is why we're here, after all, where we can use different locations and the studio gets a massive tax break from Georgia.

It's humid as hell, though, and I miss LA's softer sun.

"Are you all right?" Richard asks, the wrinkles on his forehead deepening as he frowns at me. Not an angry frown, though—it's a look of true concern, and a fresh wave of tears threatens at his kindness.

"Ye-es." I blink up at him, grimacing as a tear slides out against my will.

To my surprise, the director gives a gentle chuckle, smiling at me kindly.

"Now, you are a fine actress, Abigail Hunt, but you make a terrible liar." There's a faint Southern twang to the words, and it reminds me of sunshine and summer and my grandfather.

I sniffle, feeling overcome once again.

He clucks his tongue, then sighs as he crosses his arms over his chest. Richard Grace is tall and thin, the lean muscle of the endurance runner he once was still keeping him looking fit even well into his seventies.

"Listen." He purses his lips, and I'm ready for him to fire me, to tell me that he made the wrong choice. "I cast you because I believe you are the right actor for this role. The only actor I wanted for it, in fact. I sent you to study with Michelle for a reason."

"Michelle . . ." I falter, and there's a question in my voice. "Not the LA Aces. Just Michelle?"

"Michelle," he agrees. "She was one of the whistleblowers for the IFF. Didn't she tell you?"

My jaw drops, my unbidden and unwanted tears finally drying up with the shock of it.

He sighs. "How do you think Michelle would have reacted in this situation?"

I consider it, the way Michelle snaps into business-bitch mode when she needs to, wearing her makeup and suits like armor and wielding her perfect manners and intellect like a weapon.

"She would be . . . angry. Cold. She would aim to hurt and to win."

"I like the emotion you were channeling there," Richard blinks at me, his lashes nearly invisible in the bright daylight. "But I can't help but think something else is going on with you that isn't related to your work here." He pauses, studying me with a tilted head. Every inch an artist. "Well, not directly related, at least."

"What do you mean?" I ask cautiously. I'm worried, though, that I know exactly what he means.

Who he means.

"The funny thing about me, my dear, is that I follow tabloids quite relentlessly."

My eyebrows rocket up as I cringe.

"You see," he continues, "I'm a bit of a romantic, too. So . . . when I saw all the press you and your Wolf were generating, I have to say, I was both amused and enchanted."

"He's not my Wolf," I mutter, pacing a little. "He never belonged to me."

"Of course not," Richard says, eyes keen and knowing. "But you did seem to tame him, all the same."

I stare at him, my mouth working but no words coming out.

"Forgive me if I am overstepping." His face is so genial, and it makes me want to trust him. "But I know how . . . *deeply* artists feel. I can't help but thinking, perhaps your emotions today are not on behalf of your character but are your own."

My throat constricts as I swallow. I nod once, unable to find the right words.

"Well. I can't say I am upset to hear this. In fact, since it is Friday afternoon, I hoped you would say that."

"What does it being Friday have anything to do with it?" I ask him.

"Because I scheduled your flight back to LA to leave tonight. You're taking the studio's private plane, and if you can hurry, you should make it in time to see the Wolf play with the Aces."

Shock and gratitude war inside me, and all I manage to do is gape up at my boss, who is possibly one of the kindest people I've ever met.

"Why?" I ask, completely stumped.

He spreads his hands wide, sighing slightly. "Because I am, partially at least, a pragmatist. I believe you have some unfinished business with this Wolf of yours. Unfinished business that's keeping you from being fully present in your craft."

Embarrassment washes through me. I open my mouth to apologize, but Richard holds up a hand to stop me.

"Mostly, however, I am a hopeless romantic. To the point of no return, I'm afraid. So, while the rational part of me wants you to come back here refreshed and ready to focus, the romantic part of me wants you to fix this thing between you and Luke Wolfe."

He nods once and starts to walk away, then turns back to where I'm staring after him.

"If I were you, I'd hurry to the airport. My assistant will send the details of the flight to your email. Oh, and I'd call Michelle, too. I have a feeling she'd be happy to plan anything you'd like regarding your return." He winks, and on him it's somehow sweet and charming.

"How? Why?" The questions explode out of me. I clap a hand

over my mouth. Oh no, here we go again. "I'm not trying to look a gift director in the mouth or anything. I just, you know, I uh—" Floundering, I cross my arms over my chest, like that's going to keep me from sticking my foot in my mouth.

Maybe I should sit cross-legged to keep that from happening.

Richard Grace simply beams at me, though. "Why are we here?"

My mouth twists to the side, because *what*? "In Georgia? To make a movie? Because they have the best tax breaks for film productions?" I venture.

"Why are we here," he continues gently, "on this Earth, if not to love one another? I have made art my life, and it took me too long to realize that love is the backbone of all art. Love gives us purpose." He watches me closely. "It gives our art purpose, yes?"

Am I supposed to respond to that? I have no idea. Is it a rhetorical question?

"Do you know why I picked you for this role, Ms. Hunt?" he asks, and I let out a relieved breath before I realize he's asking me another question I don't know if I want to know the answer to.

"You liked my audition?" My brow furrows and I try not to cringe at myself. Try and fail.

He lets out a laugh. "Of course I did." Richard Grace leans closer, and he smells, of all the things, like the kind of hard caramel candy my grandfather always had in his pockets. Well, caramel and expensive cologne, but it's familiar all the same.

His voice drops to a whisper. "I picked you not only because of your audition but also because of who you were with the press. You lead your life with your heart. You say what you mean, what you think, and that is all too rare a quality these days. Your character also believes in what she says, and I saw that same spark in you."

Richard steps back, his hands braced on my elbows as I gape at him.

He sighs. "You didn't let it destroy you, either. The press, after the whole *Blood Sirens* scandal, I mean. You kept trying. You kept being yourself." A shrug lifts his shoulders, and I can only blink at him in surprise. "So to answer your question, Ms. Hunt, I am a hopeless romantic, and I think you might be, too, deep down. Just remember that I was nice today when I inevitably drive you bonkers on set in the coming months."

With that, he lets out a hearty laugh, turning away as one of the producers steps in, an iPad in hand and a pinched expression on his face.

I'm in a black sedan before I know it, my phone pressed to my ear as the blessedly cold air-conditioning blasts across my overheated skin. The ringer trills against my cheek.

"Pick up, pick up, pick up," I chant, willing Michelle to drop everything and come to my rescue.

The beat of my heart is a snare drum in my chest, hope a hummingbird that dares to spread its wings.

"Hey, babe." Michelle's voice is crisp and clipped, like she's busy but still pleased to hear from me. "It's like you read my mind. I was just thinking about you. I need to tell you something—I know you might not want to hear it, but I found out from the guys what the damned owners were holding over Luke's head."

"What?" I breathe, completely forgetting to tell her I'm on my way back to LA. All I want to know is *why*.

"His mom is sick, you know?"

"Yeah," I say, worrying the hem of the Ninja Turtles T-shirt I threw on in my trailer. "I know—" My eyes widen in horror.

"He wanted to be traded so he could be closer to home. To help with her care and, you know, spend time with her. They refused to take him off the protected-player lists—which means he wouldn't be eligible to be traded—unless he dated you. That's why he did it, Abigail. So he could be with his family."

"Fuck," I say on a sigh, my stomach knotting. "*Fuck*. Why didn't he tell me?"

"Probably because he thought you hated him."

"Fuck." I am such an asshole. I just couldn't be bothered to act like a normal adult. No, I had to get all worked up and then dress like Gollum to try to get even.

That is the opposite of normal.

"You okay? Hey, why are you even calling? Aren't you supposed to be working, too?"

"Uh, see, that's the thing." My mouth is suddenly full of anxious spit, and I swallow it down, then clear my throat. Gross. "Richard sent me to the airport. To fly to LA."

"Holy shit, Abigail. He fired you?"

All of this is too much.

"Why didn't he tell me that?" I moan, covering my eyes. "I am an idiot."

Michelle's silent. "Richard Grace?"

"No, Luke." I flap a hand in front of me, waving away her question even though she can't see me. The driver cuts me a look in the rearview, and I tuck my hand under my jittery thigh. "Grace wants me to try and either fix things with Luke or get closure. He said he is a romantic. He also seemed to think that me being hung up on Luke was . . . not helping my performance. Which, by the way, we also need to discuss, Ms. IFF Whistleblower."

"Oh. He told you about that, huh?"

It stings a bit that *she* didn't.

Then again, I don't think I've been a very good friend lately.

I heave a sigh. "I'm sorry you didn't trust me enough to tell me that. I am going to try to be a better friend, okay? I want to hear about it if you want to talk to me about it."

"Oh," she says again. "Okay. Yeah, I think I'd like that."

"Good. That makes me really happy, Michelle."

"Just don't make me go to that Pilates class with you."

We both laugh, and then Michelle goes quiet.

"What do you want to do? How do you need me to help?" she asks, her voice serious. "I'm assuming you want to do something at the playoff game, and that's why you called me."

"Do you think Luke even wants to see me again?" My voice cracks on his name.

Just asking the question hurts, the thought that maybe this is totally one-sided and unrealistic a thorny vine around my tender heart.

"Uh, yeah. I lied before. Luke's actually the one who told me why he agreed to the owners' terms. This morning, in fact. Apparently the team's been getting on his ass about getting you back, too. He was asking me for advice on how to apologize."

"Michelle! You couldn't have led with that?!" I shriek. "Shit, now we have to go big. I can't let him have a better apology!"

The driver eyes me, then discreetly raises the privacy screen between the front and back seats.

Michelle's laughing at me. "Well, in my defense, I thought you were being fired and that you were still furious with him."

"I'm not," I say, shaking my head. A sob chokes out of me. "I'm not at all. I thought I was still mad, but I was an asshole. I've been selfish and petty."

"How're your stitches?" Michelle asks slyly.

I ignore her. "I need to fix it. I want to try to make it right." Jutting my chin out and rolling my shoulders back, I attempt to gather myself. "And my stitches came out a couple of days ago."

"Good. I would hate to hear they'd left you in a pinch."

I huff a laugh, but my brain's too busy to do more than that. "That was a terrible joke."

"Just a little lobster humor," she deadpans.

"I want to do something big." My mind's racing a mile a minute, picking through a bevy of ideas and discarding them just as quickly.

"What do you have in mind?" Michelle asks. "I'm game."

It's not until we're pulling up to the airport that we settle on a plan. It's going to be a metric shit ton of work.

"Are you sure?" I ask her for the umpteenth time. "I don't want to . . . jeopardize anything for you. Or be a shit friend. I want to be a better friend, too."

She lets out a dark laugh. "Oh, no. I'm going to enjoy this. Trust me on that." Her voice softens a little. "I'm glad to help, and I'm glad you want to be my friend."

We both go quiet.

"I promise not to dress as Gollum with you," I tell her, breaking the moment.

Michelle snorts. "Please. That was going to be my number one condition. That you do the Gollum voice . . . to all my exes."

We both laugh, and then something crosses my mind.

"I have one more favor to ask," I say slowly, fresh fury rolling through me at the callous treatment Luke's received from the owners. "Can I be there when you, er, ask them? Both for my own personal enjoyment and for . . . research purposes."

"Absolutely," Michelle agrees, and there's a vicious edge to it. "What are friends for, if not for taking down the man, right?"

"Yeah!" I agree, fist-pumping.

The driver shakes his head, and though I can't hear him, I'm pretty sure he's sighing.

"Okay, let me start getting shit together. Do you need a ride from the airport?" Michelle asks.

I do not deserve her. But I'm gonna try to.

"Believe it or not, Richard Grace has a town car on standby for me."

"Perfect. Meet me at the club office this evening, say, around six p.m.?"

"Got it." It baffles me how organized Michelle must be if she's ready to do this at a moment's notice. "You're a little scary sometimes," I tell her.

"Good. That's what I like to hear."

"See you soon," I tell her, and we hang up.

Not a half second later, a meeting request pops up on my phone, and I swallow hard when I see the owners' names on it, too.

The plan is in motion.

If it goes well, it might be enough to show him I'm sorry.

If it doesn't go well, then the whole world will know Luke and I are over for good, but at least I will have closure—and so will everyone else who was invested in our relationship.

And the owners of the LA Aces will get what's coming to them, too.

Maybe I can fix this thing with Luke. Sure, we weren't together for very long . . . but when we were, it was good. I like Luke.

I care about Luke. Even when I was furious with him, I cared.

Things with Luke were better than they had ever been with anyone I'd dated before.

If I'm being honest with myself, I think I was falling in love with him.

I'm going to, at the very least, try to repair the damage we both did.

I owe it to both of us to try.

CHAPTER FORTY-THREE

Abigail

I'VE THROWN ONE of my mom's permanently borrowed cashmere sweaters over my stupid ratty Ninja Turtles T-shirt and done the best I can to slap some makeup on my face and braid my hair into submission.

I look a mess, but honestly, I think I like that even better than how hard I tried to be polished and professional and not me the last time I saw these assholes.

Michelle meets me in the parking lot, and she emanates confidence.

"Holy shit," I say, dragging my gaze over her. "You look like you're ready to go to war."

"Because I am," she says, and flips her glossy hair over one shoulder.

I pluck at the hem of my T-shirt, then tuck it inside the hem of my jeans.

"You look like you're ready to raise hell," she says with a quirk of her lips.

My chin raises at that. "Because I am," I tell her. "And then I'm going to take you to dinner, and you're going to give me all the dirty details on the IFF and exactly how it went down. If you want, I mean," I tack on.

"You're on," she says, her eyes glimmering with humor. "But first, let's show these assholes they fucked with the wrong people."

"Yeah," I cheer, fist-pumping. If there was ever an occasion for too much fist-pumping, this was it. "Oh, by the way, I got the printers you recommended—I was able to rush the order through. It should be ready to pick up first thing tomorrow. Your people can make it happen, right? That's enough time?"

She grins at me, then nods once. "It's going to be fucking perfect."

"Fuck yeah."

.   .   .

WE WALK INTO the boardroom of the Aces club office, and John Pugilisi and Charles Treadwick glance up at us momentarily before resuming their boisterous conversation.

Michelle gives me a meaningful look as we sit across from the men.

Lacing my fingers through each other on the shiny top of the conference table, I clear my throat and wait.

One laughs at something the other has said before they finally turn to us.

"Ladies. Now, Michelle, why did you feel the need to call us in here on a Friday afternoon? I'm sure we all have better places to be. Ms. Abigail is probably busy charming the pants off everyone in Atlanta now that she's a free agent." Charles leers at me.

I grimace as his breath hits me. He reeks of bourbon.

I would very much like to vomit.

"Ew," I say, giving him the nastiest look I can muster.

Judging from the way his cheeks turn ruddy, I'm positive it hit home.

I smile prettily at him. "Now that you're done making suggestive and inappropriate comments, we have a few items to discuss."

"Come on, girls," Charles slurs slightly. "Why don't we all go out and discuss this over dinner? Maybe somewhere private, with a nice bottle of wine."

My nose wrinkles, and Michelle glares at them.

Oh shit. Michelle is about to rip them to shreds.

I lean back in the office chair, narrowly avoiding tipping the thing backward, and cross my arms over my chest. Yeah. Falling out of my chair would not have been my chosen way to begin the meaningful part of this meeting.

"While acting as director of operations with the Aces—"

"And we are so lucky to have a smart girl like you with us," Charles interrupts.

Michelle gives him a look so full of distaste that he rears back.

Call her girl one more time, I dare you. I shouldn't be so gleeful.

Oh well!

"Are you finished?" Michelle asks crisply.

There's no answer, though Charles appears slightly apoplectic.

"Are you on blood pressure medication?" I ask him out of true concern. "You might want to take it."

He makes a garbled sound of outrage, and I smile at him again, batting my eyelashes.

"As I was saying before I was so rudely interrupted," Michelle continues, "I've noticed various taxation discrepancies when it comes to certain write-offs for the business. I have also been made aware of a situation regarding Luke Wolfe, one that IT was only too happy to provide records of once I alerted them to possible legal and financial ramifications for the entire team."

She opens up a black leather folio, producing several copies of printouts of emails she forwarded to me while I was in flight.

Emails between the two of them, outlining their plan to blackmail Luke, as well as discussing the increase in ticket sales after we were dating.

"You're bluffing," John says, though he's gone stark white.

Truly, the number of color changes in their faces in such a short span of time is alarming.

"Seriously, do either of you have any heart conditions?" I certainly don't want to have to perform mouth-to-mouth if one of them keels over. Gross.

They swivel toward me like a pack of mean old dogs.

"What's she doing here?" Charles snarls.

"Abigail Hunt is here as my shadow. She is currently starring in a film, as you may remember, about the corruption within the IFF and a certain whistleblower intern." Her eyebrows arch, and she studies them with a sort of casual indifference that I make a mental note to emulate on-screen. "What you don't know, gentlemen, is that I was the whistleblower and that I have enough evidence of this organization's corruption and incompetence with which to bury you. Right now, all of that evidence is with my attorney, who is prepared to release it should I give the word."

"Are you blackmailing us?" They're outraged, sputtering, and utterly feckless.

I bite my cheeks, trying not to laugh. "Doesn't feel good, does it?"

"Fuck you, you slut." Charles leans in, radiating menace.

"Right. Did I mention I'm recording this?" I tap the phone in my sweater pocket, which is camera out. "I'm recording this, and it's streaming to my agent's phone, as well. Anything else you'd like to add to *slut* while you're at it?"

He's practically rabid, foaming at the mouth, but John sighs and sits back.

"What do you want, Michelle? Are you trying to ruin the Aces?"

"That's the thing, Mr. Pugilisi. I love soccer, I love LA, and I love the Aces. What I don't love is working for men who have as much moral backbone as a worm. Here's how this can go." She sets another sheaf of papers in front of each of them, her smile absolutely caustic.

It's a contract, and she slides one in front of me, too.

"Option one: You agree to sell the club and see your way out with your dignity intact. Option two"—she puts another contract in front of them—"Abigail and my lawyer and I go to the press and you will be forced to still sell the club, but you will also be dragged through the mud."

She grins, and I've never seen a human look more like a shark in my entire life.

I wonder if she knows where the Mariana Trench is.

The men make more outraged noises, but they know they've been outmaneuvered, and I've never been prouder to be someone's friend. My fist trembles with the need to throw it in the air like I just don't care, but I settle on giving them my best Michelle boss-bitch impression instead.

Until she glances over at me, and it's clear she's stifling a laugh.

Then I want to laugh.

Mostly because I know I shouldn't.

I definitely should not laugh.

Oh no. This is not funny, nothing about this is funny.

"Are you trying not to laugh at us?" Charles seethes.

"Nope." My voice is pitched ridiculously high, and it's disturbingly clear I'm lying.

"You fucking slut," he starts again.

"You really need to work on your vocabulary." I sniff.

Michelle holds up a hand. "You should know that I am part of a regulatory oversight board for the IFF and all the football leagues that are a part of it. Would you like to continue your speech and let Abigail release it onto her social media, which, last I checked, had over four million followers across different platforms, or . . ." She glances at the contracts in front of them.

"You bitch," he says, this time directing his very unoriginal ire at Michelle.

John hands him a pen. "Jesus Christ. Sign the papers, Charles. Trust me."

He shoots me an apologetic look.

The urge to laugh dies as quick as it came on, and some of the reckless glee I felt turns into guilt. Until I remember what they did to Luke.

Then the guilt magically disappears.

"What's this part of the contract?" John asks, pointing to a clause on the third page.

"That allows for Luke Wolfe's immediate release from the roster of protected players."

"You'll drive this club right into the ground," Charles says with a smirk. "Enjoy it while you can, girls, because it won't last long without us."

"Oh," I simper. "Thank you. I'll be sure to remember that."

Michelle snorts.

The men manage to skim through and sign the papers quickly. I don't know what all evidence Michelle has on their own corruption, but they seem very willing to leave the club in her hands rather than risk the IFF oversight board nosing around it.

They finally leave, each of them staring daggers at us, dropping the contracts in front of her.

"My attorney has already sent copies to your counsel," she says cheerfully. "Pleasure doing business with you. Your personal belongings will be packed and mailed to you."

The door closes, and there's no shortage of curses from the hallway.

Michelle blows out a long breath, folding her hands behind her head.

"That was incredible. I'm in awe." My phone begins vibrating against my chest, and I pull it out.

"Hey, Jean," I answer.

"Why are you sending me a huge video file?"

"For insurance against the former LA Aces owners."

Jean sighs so noisily the phone practically exhales into my ear. "Christ, Abigail. Do I want to know?"

"No, I don't think you do."

"Thank fuck."

"Wait," I tell her. "Actuallllly, you might want to hear about what I'm doing Saturday." I clear my throat. "At the LA Aces game."

"Please tell me you're getting back with that soccer player."

I pout. "Yes. That's what I was going to tell you. How did you know?"

"Abigail, I've known you since you moved to LA as a teenager. That man made you happier than I've ever seen you. Also, Richard Grace's assistant called to tell me already."

"Awwww—oh." I let out a surprised laugh. "Okay, then, glad that's cleared up."

"Bye, hon. Talk to you later. Don't make me bail you out of jail."

"What?" I screech, but she's already hung up.

"What did she say?" Michelle asks.

"She told me to stay out of jail."

"Good advice," Michelle says noncommittally. "We did it." Her grin is pure mischievous happiness.

"I have a question . . ." I narrow my eyes at her. "How are you going to make sure the club ends up in good hands?"

"I already shopped the club . . . and I sent the information packet I had on the former owners to them." She tosses her hair over her shoulder. "I wanted them to know who they would be working with and what they could expect if they decided to behave badly."

"Nice," I say in approval. "You little shark. I love it. Let's go get dinner and talk about how you got to be so smart."

"Food," Michelle agrees.

I squeak as she stands, making a V with her arms.

"VICTORY!" she screams.

I blink.

"Too much?" she asks after a moment.

"Nope. I loved it." I jump to my feet and do the same, until we're both laughing tears.

And it feels fucking good.

CHAPTER FORTY-FOUR

Luke

THERE'S A WEIRD excitement in the locker room before our match. The Miami Krakens are a good team, and the game will likely be a tough one, especially as it's the first game of the National Cup Playoffs.

That's not the energy, though—it's not the usual nerves coming out as macho bravado. No, there's a little of that, sure, but it's happier, expectant maybe.

I catch more than a few of the guys talking in low whispers to each other, only to stop once I lock eyes with them.

I don't have time for any bullshit, though, or energy to spare wondering what the hell they're up to. I need to be on my fucking game today.

If I have any chance of a team even being interested in taking me, I've got to play the very best I'm capable of.

The pressure is on, and as one of the team physical therapists tapes up a few sore spots on my glutes, I hardly hear their chatter.

Anticipation and adrenaline race through my veins. My blood's roaring in my ears, and I'm ready to leave it all on the fucking field.

Coach Garrett comes into the locker room as I finish tying up my cleats. The hot pink laces remind me of my mom, and it makes me smile as I tie them in her honor.

"Warm up!" he shouts at us, which is his equivalent of a pep talk.

"It's early, Coach," Logan says. "We still have twenty minutes until warm-up starts."

The rest of us move as a unit, swiveling our attention to the clock on the painted cinder block wall.

"He's right," someone says.

"I said warm up," he roars again, then stalks from the room.

"What the hell," Logan mutters, looking mutinous.

"Fuck," I murmur to myself, then louder: "You heard him. Get your boots on and get out there."

Half the team straightens, doing as they're told immediately. The other half share incredulous looks but reluctantly fall into line.

I bring up the rear, scowling at the few stragglers as I follow them all out. We jog out of the tunnel, and I close my eyes for a long moment, savoring this feeling of being on the field, my cleats digging into the turf, the sunshine on my skin.

This has to be the best job in the world.

"Wolfe," the chant begins in the stands, and I'm so focused on loosening up the tight muscles in my glutes and quads as I jog, that it takes me a moment to realize it's not the normal cheer.

"Luke," Gold's voice jerks me out of my concentration, and I glance up at where he's abruptly stopped jogging in place beside me.

He's not looking at me, though—his gaze is fixed on the sideline.

"Look," he urges.

I follow where his attention's landed, and what I see there nearly undoes me completely.

My feet stop moving.

That can't be real. That can't be what it looks like.

"Wolf . . . Hunt . . . Wolf . . . Hunt," the crowd chants, and Gold curses under his breath next to me. They're holding thousands upon thousands of colored cards above their heads, and all put together, they spell out WOLFHUNT in black and gold.

I'm speechless, and my gaze dips to the woman standing under a balloon arch of black and gold, holding a sign that simply reads: HI.

The jumbotron in the middle of the field zooms in on her, and she raises one hand in greeting, her beautiful face perfect even magnified on the screen.

The crowd holding the signs flips them over, nearly at once, and I'm in awe at the amount of planning this must have taken.

Now flipped, the signs read: I'M SORRY.

I shake my head, and my feet begin moving again.

Not to warm up, not to the goal, but to Abigail, who's standing there, trembling and as nervous as I've ever seen her, under the gold-and-black balloon arch.

Her sign floats to the ground as I approach, her lower lip trembling.

"Hi," she says as I approach her. "I'm so sorry, Luke. I was selfish and stupid and I'm so, so sorry."

I don't hesitate. I wrap my arms tight around her.

"You aren't the one who needs to apologize," I tell her. "I am. And I'm so sorry, Abigail. I never wanted to hurt you."

"Can we start over?" she asks, her pretty green and hazel eyes full of tears as she stares up at me, her elegant hand cupping my cheek.

I consider it, really consider it, turning over the request before shaking my head.

"No," I grunt.

Her face falls.

"I don't want to start over," I tell her. "I want to keep going. There's nothing about you I don't like. I want the Abigail who isn't afraid to be herself, the one I already know."

"Even Gollum?" she asks, crying, though she's smiling through her tears.

I catch one on the tip of my finger, lit up with happiness, like a fire's burning through me just to have her in my arms again.

"Even Gollum," I manage, grinning like an idiot.

She presses herself into me, and I groan.

"I need to admit something. I don't really have a Gollum kink," she whispers.

"I know," I tell her, laughing. The laugh dies. "I need to admit something, too."

The breeze whips a lock of her reddish-gold hair across her face, and I smooth it back, my gaze darting between her stunning eyes.

"What?" She licks her lips, and it takes all my self-control not to kiss her.

"I still have Princess." I grimace at the admission, sure she'll be furious.

"Oh my god," she whispers, then she squeals loudly. "Seriously?"

I grunt, grinning at her pleasure at my admission.

"Yes, oh, light of my life, queen in the west, lobster hunter extraordinaire, Gollum of my heart, I have had Princess the whole time. I never put her up for adoption . . . because I always planned on finding my way back to you," she says in her ridiculous rasping imitation of me.

"Yep," I agree, skimming my thumbs over her cheekbones. "In fact, I bought two concert tickets to see Yo-Yo Ma when he's here next month. I hoped I could get you to forgive me by then."

"Shut up," she says, tipping her head back with laughter. She's so wildly beautiful my heart might explode from it.

"No," I tell her with a shrug, which only makes her laugh harder.

"I'll bring a pair of extra socks and lube for you," she says, a smirk on her delicious lips.

"Good." I can't seem to stop smiling. I don't want to.

When she goes to her tiptoes, pulling my face toward her, I decide I don't mind kissing her in front of the entire stadium.

And when our lips meet, the crowd goes wild.

CHAPTER FORTY-FIVE

Abigail

"I STILL THINK I should have worn the Gollum outfit," I tell Luke.

He doesn't take his gaze off the bumper-to-bumper traffic, which is par for the course for LA, but he lifts an eyebrow, a hint of a smile on his face.

"I mean," I continue, trying to keep a straight face, "it's our first public outing since we got back together. I think the people would want to see Gollum."

"Babe," he says in that deep, delicious voice of his, "you already know what Yo-Yo Ma does to me. Add Gollum to the mix, and I'd probably be arrested for public indecency."

I bark a surprised laugh, and Luke reaches over to squeeze my hand.

It's been a month since I crashed his game, mostly long distance, which it would have been anyway, considering Luke's travel schedule.

Being back in LA with him this weekend is like a dream.

"Fuck off!" he shouts, flipping the bird and honking at a Corvette that cuts us off at the last minute. "You had that entire time to merge, fucking hell."

I snort. "A dream come true."

"What's that?" he asks, still focused on the scarlet sports car revving its way in front of us.

"Just talking about making you come," I tell him innocently.

"You first," he says, and I grin.

"Duh," I tell him, tossing my hair.

"Did you bring your meds?" he asks, narrowing his eyes at me.

I scoff, rolling my eyes. The magnetic clasp on my purse clicks open, and I tug out the prescription my new therapist and psychiatrist approved to help manage my panic attacks.

"Got them right here," I tell him, shaking the bottle.

Luke glances over at me. "I'm proud of you, Abigail."

"For shaking pills at you?" I flutter my eyelashes, tucking the pill bottle back in my purse.

"For everything you're doing for your mental health."

"I could say the same to you." I nudge him with my elbow. "Look at us. Therapy! Who would have thought."

"I think everyone would have thought," he says in his gruff voice.

I laugh again, just so damned happy to be next to him, to be happy, to be giving us another shot. A real shot.

"That's fair," I finally agree, lacing my fingers through where his hand rests on my thigh.

He glances over at me, a huge smile on his face, before shaking his head and returning his attention to the awful traffic.

"What?" I ask, laughing at his expression.

"It's just so fucking good to have you next to me. Seeing you in real life, you know? You're so goddamn beautiful."

"Better watch that dirty mouth or I'll just have to kiss it," I say, amused and so totally beyond happy.

"Not sure that's the threat you want it to be," he says.

"What if I told you I hadn't brushed my teeth in three days because I know that morning breath is your kink, along with a certain cellist?"

"That's fucking gross," he tells me finally, blessedly exiting the highway . . . only for us to get stuck in traffic again nearly immediately.

"You're gross," I tell him. "I'm just trying to match your dirty mouth, Mr. Yellow Card."

"I knew you were going to bring that up. Listen, that ref was being an asshole, and he deserved someone to tell him that."

"Mm-hmm," I agree. "Definitely."

"If you don't stop making fun of me, you're going to wish Lauren's Pilates classes had done more work on pulling up your anus."

"Are you . . . threatening me with butt stuff?" I'm slightly shocked, and that doesn't happen a lot.

"It's not a punishment if you keep asking for it," he says, a wicked grin on his face.

I flip my hair over one shoulder, rolling my eyes. "I was simply exploring our options."

"You want me to explore Uranus."

My jaw drops, and I poke him in the ribs, making him laugh. "How long have you been waiting to say that?" I finally ask.

He just grins, turning onto the road that will take us to the Staples Center, ahem, I mean, the good ole Crypto venue.

"You practiced it in the mirror, didn't you?" I insist. "Did you workshop it with Gold?"

"Maybe," he admits.

I burst out laughing. "I knew it."

"When Gold laughed so hard that Marino thought he was having an asthma attack, I decided I had a winner."

"Bunch of man-children," I mutter, but I'm holding back a laugh, a fizzy feeling of delight in my chest.

"It made you laugh, too," he says seriously.

"That's because I'm just as bad as you are."

"Know why I . . . what did you call it? Why I workshopped it?"

"Hmm? Why's that?"

"Because your laugh is the best sound I've ever heard."

I beam at him. My cheeks get hot, and I fan myself. "Careful, or you're going to make Yo-Yo Ma jealous."

"That would be a real shame, considering we've got backstage passes to meet him."

"Yeah, we certainly can't let him know how you're falling so hard for me. It will make him sad."

He swallows audibly, and I cringe.

"I didn't mean to put words in your mouth—"

"Abigail, there's no falling. None at all."

"I am so sorry, I know we're taking it slower this time—"

"There's no falling because I'm already there. Fallen. Hard. The minute you joked about anaphylactic shock, I should have known I was a goner."

"Luke," I whisper, and tears sting behind my eyes. "If you make me cry and mess up my makeup I'm going to be so mad."

"We can't have you being mad. I won't get to see Uranus if you're upset." His voice is low and steady, so bland that if I didn't know him better, I'd think he were completely serious.

"I love you," I tell him, the words rushing out of me. "I know we said we'd take it slow, and my therapist is probably going to do a sigh so heavy that the floor collapses under her when I tell her, but I love you, Luke Wolfe."

"Good," he says, flashing that delicious grin at me. "I'm glad we've got that settled."

I awkwardly scooch closer to him, planting a kiss on his cheek. "You are so getting lucky tonight," I say.

"Okay, but *cello* is my safe word."

I cackle. "You got it. *Cello* it is."

He pulls into the valet parking area of the Staples Center, and I rub my hand over the rhinestone clutch I bought just for the occasion.

It's a bit weird, a bit quirky, but it looks cute with my cream-colored dress.

Nothing says fashion like a purse shaped like a shrimp, after all.

Nothing says happiness like the ache in my cheeks from smiling, either.

Abigail

MY ENTIRE LIFE seems to revolve around packing and unpacking at the moment, everything I need condensed to a suitcase that's never empty for long.

Well, everything I need that can be packed, that is.

After the Aces made it to the last game of the finals, only to lose during an overtime shoot-out when Gold made an ill-timed mistake, Luke had his pick of teams.

Of course he picked Seattle.

Good thing I've always loved the Pacific Northwest. The seemingly endless emerald forests shrouded in morning mist, the rocky coastline and quaint small towns and quirkier larger cities.

I unpack my bag, and Luke's hands reach around my stomach, his mouth trailing kisses along the nape of my neck.

"Missed you so much." His low voice against the sensitive skin under my ear makes me shiver. "So glad you're here."

I turn around, wrapping my arms around his neck.

"This place looks good on you," I tell him. It does, too. He fits here like it was a missing puzzle piece.

Floor-to-ceiling windows stretch across an entire wall behind him, the A-frame-style living room giving a view of a dark stretch of beach and teal waters beyond a gorgeous tree line. It might be A-frame in style, but the so-called cabin is anything but small.

Large beams cross the ceiling, a cream patterned rug softening the heavy wood, a plush couch set off by warmly glowing lamps. There's a huge stone fireplace on one wall, a cool blue abstract painting hung over it.

It's stunning and so very Luke.

I inhale, taking in his yummy pine scent that just makes him feel even more a part of this place, like it's an extension of him.

The stressed lines of his neck and shoulders have relaxed, his smile easier, his laugh less surprised. "It makes me happy to see you like this."

"Like what?" he murmurs, his nose nuzzling my neck.

"Relaxed. At home. You seem so much happier here."

"I do love it here," he says, his hands running up and down my back. I sigh, melting into him as his strong fingers work out the knots there. "But I think, Abigail, that home might be wherever you are."

"Then it's a good thing I'm here." I smile into his chest. If I could melt into his skin, I would. "I love you."

It doesn't matter how often I say it to him, how often he says it back. It always feels like the first time, exciting and bubbly and perfect.

"I love you, too, my precioussss," he says with a hiss.

I tilt back my head and laugh. "You know, I really shouldn't love that as much as I do."

"Mm-hmm. It's a bit weird. But that's why it works." He kisses the side of my neck, and those warm, fuzzy feelings start to heat into something needier, something much hotter.

"We are a bit weird," I agree, tilting my head to allow him better access.

"How much longer are you going to be filming?" he asks, his lips brushing against my ear, making me shiver.

A laugh bubbles out, because he's only asked me this about one million times. I love it, though. I love that he wants me with him so badly that he can't help himself.

"The soccer reshoots should be over in about a month." I bite my bottom lip, because I have been putting off telling him my latest news until we're together. "I have to tell you something."

"You will be on set too much?" The kisses stop, and there's resignation in the question.

I squeeze him closer, and he makes a soft oomph at the increase in pressure. "Most of the long filming days are done."

"So I get to see you more?" he asks, his fingers skating between the fine fabric of my blouse and my skin. "Right?"

"Right," I say, kissing him.

"So what's the news, then?" He takes a step back, his eyes nearly the same color as the blue-gray sky outside.

"I got the part in the rom-com." I beam at him, and he whoops, picking me up and spinning me around. "The lead. The romantic lead," I squeal.

"Of course you fucking did!" he yells, then slaps my ass for good measure. "I told you you would."

"You're supposed to tell me things like that," I protest, laughing.

"Yeah, but that doesn't mean it's not true," he says, peppering my mouth with delighted kisses.

"So most of the filming will be on set in LA," I tell him. "And the other half will be . . . about an hour from here."

"Oh my fuck, love, this is the best news. I'm so damned proud of you."

Princess, who is now roughly the size of a house tiger, meows loudly, demanding treats.

It's been six months of a long-distance relationship, and while it hasn't been easy all the time, it's been good. Really good.

"I've never been happier than I am right now," I tell him, then bite my lip. "Sorry."

He huffs a laugh. "Why are you apologizing?"

"Because I didn't exactly mean to get all sappy on you," I say.

Luke's hands go to my hips, possessive and sweet all at once. "I like when you're sappy. In fact"—he tilts his head, kissing one corner of my mouth, then the other—"you might say I love it. I love everything about you."

"Even my Gollum impression in bed," I say seriously.

He cringes slightly, and I laugh, because he absolutely hates it.

Which makes it ten times funnier.

Luke gives my hips an affectionate squeeze, and suddenly it's not enough just to be in his arms.

I moan, kissing him again. His tongue slides against my lips, and I part them for him, desire roaring to life as his strong body presses against mine.

Then Luke Wolfe proves to me just how much he loves it when I get sappy over him.

He proves it several times.

ACKNOWLEDGMENTS

It is a truth universally acknowledged that a writer in pursuit of a traditionally published book must be in want of an amazing team. First and foremost, thank you to my incredible agent, Jessica Watterson, for believing in me and championing my work over all these years. Thank you to the brilliant Sareer Khader for taking a chance on my writing, for being an incredible partner, and for sharing my need to rewrite that relationship arc. IYKYK. To Lauren Cox, the best personal assistant and friend a person could ask for.

A huge thank-you to the consummate professionals at Berkley: Yazmine Hassan, Katie Ferraro, Anika Bates, Lindsey Tulloch, Sarah Oberrender, and Christine Legon. Thank you also to Chloe Quinn for the beautiful cover—you brought these two to life!

Thank you to all the many author friends who have cheered for me, laughed at the unhinged snippets in group chats, cautioned me to not make those jokes and then let it go when I ignored you: First, the lovelies, Tiffany White and Ashley Reisinger, you are everything. Hattie Jacks, you are my ride or die across the pond forever, sorry not sorry. Kelly Dowling, Lauren Accardo, Caitlin Bailey-Garafola— thank you for giggling with me along the way. To the Rat Chat: Bruce, Ronnie, Trisha, Stephanie, Anisa, Olivia, Penn, and Gia—you are such a wonderful and hilarious safe space for all things writing related. Thank you also to Kaylin for your insight and help on the initial first rough pages.

And most importantly, to my husband, who put up with endless questions and tirades, and offered university-level lectures about offsides, Beckham, Messi, and the advantage rule: You are my hero. To my three little boys for helping me experience life through fresh eyes, you are my entire world.

Last but not least, to you, readers, for taking the time to read to this point, and especially to those of you who've been with me since book one—I couldn't do this without you, and you have my eternal gratitude.

Photo by Alison Palma Photography

BRITTANY KELLEY writes hilariously hot romance . . . of all kinds. When she's not writing, she's usually playing with her kids, keeping them from jumping off things they have no business jumping off, and laughing with her husband. Brittany lives in the northern US with her family, pack of dogs, trio of cats, and flock of ducks.

VISIT BRITTANY KELLEY ONLINE

BrittanyKelleyWrites.com

BrittanyKelleyWrites

WriteBrittany

Ready to find
your next great read?

Let us help.

Visit prh.com/nextread

Penguin
Random
House